Jokers

By Vern Hammill & Edward Kral

D063215B

ISBN-13: 978-1502594464
ISBN-10: 1502594463

In February of 1971 famed newscaster Harry Reasoner was covering the Vietnam War for ABC Television. On the February 16, 1971 broadcast he posted this commentary from South Vietnam.

You can't help but have the feeling that there will come a future generation of men – if there are any future generations of men – who will look at old pictures of helicopters and say, "You've got to be kidding."

The thing is, helicopters are different from planes. An airplane by its nature wants to fly, and if not interfered with too strongly by unusual events, or by a deliberately incompetent pilot, it will fly. A helicopter does not want to fly. It is maintained in the air by a variety of forces and controls working in opposition to each other. And if there is any disturbance in this delicate balance, the helicopter stops flying, immediately and disastrously.

This is why being a helicopter pilot is so different from being an airplane pilot, and why, in generality, airplane pilots are open, clear-eyed buoyant extroverts and helicopter pilots are brooders, introspective anticipators of trouble. They know if something bad has not happened it is about to.

All of this, of course, is greatly complicated by being shot at and American helicopter pilots are being shot at more often and more accurately these days from Khe Sanh to Tchepone than at almost any other time in this whole war. It has been a helicopter war all along – and the strange, ungainly, unlovable craft have reached the peak of being needed and the peak of being vulnerable at the same moment.

This is a war we could not have considered without our helicopters and the pilots are beginning to feel like Mark Twain's man who was tarred and feathered: If it weren't for the honor of the thing, they would just as soon have missed it.

Acknowledgments

Although this is a work of fiction, much of it is based on real characters and true stories that took place in the 48th Assault Helicopter Company based at Ninh Hoa, South Vietnam, during the years 1969 and 70. The names of those in the book have been changed to protect their privacy and prevent any embarrassment or glory.

They were called the Blue Stars, which was the call sign of the Slick pilots in the company. The gunship pilots went by the call sign Jokers. Most of the pilots were warrant officers, a rank below commissioned officers and above the sergeants and enlisted men. A large number of them had attended college, but few had degrees. A few of the participants planned to continue their flying careers after the war. The others were just a bunch of guys fulfilling their military commitments by flying helicopters in the jungles of South Vietnam. After the war they went back to their previous lives and never flew again, but while they were in the 48th they did fly, and they flew a lot. This is their story and the book is dedicated to them.

We would like to thank Joe Kline for the aviation art used on the front cover of our book. If you would like to view other prints by Joe, go to joeklineart.com.

Secondly, we want to thank our editor, Dennis Held, for his tireless work at making our manuscript what it is today.

We are also indebted to Clay Morgan our mentor, Jane Freund our book coach and to Thom Hollis who designed our book cover.

Lastly, we would like to express our appreciating to the friends who read our story and provided encouragement to keep it going.

Innsbruck, Austria – April 2, 1970

Snow fell heavily as Eric Bader and Paul Eason waited for Dr. Gottfried Muller in a wine bar on Garden Street. It was early afternoon, so the cozy room they were in was nearly empty. They sat near one of two large windows that faced the street. The waitress approached with a bottle of white wine, and said that Dr. Muller called and said he was delayed and he hoped they would enjoy a bottle of Mosel while they waited.

As they sipped the wine the two friends plotted their strategy with Dr. Muller. Eric reminded Paul that it wasn't uncommon in Austria and Germany for the president of a bank or company to be called "doctor" and that he was probably looking for a corporate pilot.

Their first impression of Dr. Muller led them to think otherwise. One of their ski buddies in St. Anton, named Klaus Muller, had said his uncle would be in Innsbruck on vacation. They'd imagined a typical Austrian skier: ruddy cheeked, muscular and dressed in ski clothes.

The man who walked toward their table didn't look anything like that. He was older than they expected. He wore a black overcoat with a white scarf, carried a black homburg, and walked with the assistance of a silver and black cane. Klaus's uncle didn't appear to be in Innsbruck to ski.

Eric introduced Paul and himself, worrying that his German would not be sufficient for the conversation to follow. Dr. Muller continued speaking in German, introducing himself and begging their forgiveness for being late. He was an amiable man and Eric liked him immediately. After a few other pleasantries, the doctor asked if they could switch to English as he needed the practice. Eric couldn't tell if the doctor really meant it, or it was a polite way of saying he didn't want to listen to his halting German. In any case, Eric was happy to speak English and not have to translate for Paul.

The doctor and Paul had turned to look out the window and were talking about how good the skiing would be the next day. Eric was amazed at how well the doctor spoke English. Although it wasn't unusual for professionals in Germany and Switzerland to be fluent in English, it wasn't that common in Austria and definitely not with the proficiency of the man who sat next to him.

Dr. Muller explained that the *Wine Stube* they were in was owned by Swiss friends of his. He said they made an excellent fondue. The doctor ordered some of the melted cheese and Eric complimented him on his English. "Doctor, I was a student of languages in college and I'm wondering where you learned to speak English with such a perfect American accent."

The doctor laughed and said, "I have your fathers to thank for that."

"Our fathers?" Eric asked.

"Yes, during the war I was a fighter pilot in the Luftwaffe. I had to bail out of an ME-109 over Holland and as luck would have it, I came down on the American side. Consequently, I was obliged to spend a year as the guest of your American Army."

Eric didn't respond, wondering if the doctor harbored animosity toward Americans. Dr. Muller read his thoughts, and said, "Don't worry. I have no grudge against your country. I was treated well."

He paused while turning the stem of his glass in his fingers. When he began speaking again, his voice had become serious. "It could have been worse. I could have come down on the Eastern Front." He looked into his glass and said, "You know, what we tried to accomplish in that war wasn't entirely wrong."

Eric glanced at his friend and saw that Paul looked as perplexed as he felt. Images of the Holocaust filled his thoughts: lines of naked people walking to the gas chambers. Surely the doctor wasn't defending Nazi Germany. Eric decided to break the silence with a guess. "By that you mean Germany's attempt to crush the Bolsheviks."

"*Ja, naturlich,*" the doctor blurted. "Look how they have divided my country. I can no longer visit my mother and the city of my birth, Dresden, which is in East Germany. After the war I moved to Switzerland where I studied medicine. Then I moved to Vienna where I have lived ever since. I tried to talk my mother and sister into moving to Austria, but my sister was engaged and my mother didn't want to leave her house. Unfortunately, when the Iron Curtain went up, they were caught on the wrong side."

Dr. Muller poured more wine and said, "That brings us to the reason why I wanted to meet with you two." He had returned to the amiable doctor they had first met.

Eric looked around the room filling with couples dressed in ski garb. The women were attractive, their faces radiant with the exhilaration of a day's skiing. Bankers and businessmen were seated amongst them.

The doctor took a sip of wine and continued. "My nephew Klaus has spoken very highly of both of you. He says you are a couple of sharp guys that he knows he can trust."

Eric smiled. "We value his friendship."

"Klaus also tells me you both spent a year and half flying helicopters in Vietnam. Is that true?"

"Yes it is."

"With that much experience you must be pretty good pilots."

"We're comfortable in a helicopter," Eric answered.

"With that many months in combat you also must have become used to being shot at."

Eric shrugged and said, "As much as anyone can get used to it I suppose, but we don't need to tell you that."

The doctor nodded. "Did Klaus tell you I'm looking for such a helicopter pilot?"

"He told us you were looking for a good helicopter pilot. Not necessarily one who was used to being shot at."

Eric glanced at Paul as the doctor continued. "There *is* an element of danger in this job, but I plan to keep that probability as low as possible."

"So it could involve being shot at."

"Yes."

"And that's why you are interested in the two of us instead of an Austrian or German pilot."

The doctor lowered his voice and said, "Precisely. What I propose to do is get my family out of East Germany."

Eric leaned toward the doctor and said, "You want somebody to fly into East Germany?"

"Not East Germany, Czechoslovakia--the border is not as secure between there and Austria."

Eric leaned back in his chair. He had suspected something like this all along. Paul had been uncharacteristically silent and it was time to get his best friend involved. Eric turned toward Paul and asked, "What do you think?"

In a confident voice, Paul said, "I think we need to hear more details. If it's well planned and everything goes right, it should be a simple mission, but if things go south after we cross the border we could be spending the rest of our lives in a Gulag prison camp."

Dr. Muller interrupted. "We have plenty of time for details. Right now it is time for dinner. Come with me. There is an excellent restaurant in the hotel where I'm staying."

They walked outside and found that the snow had turned to a drizzle. Paul pointed up and said, "What happened to the snow? I hope it's not raining on the hill."

The trio walked down a narrow, cobbled street among a sea of people carrying multi-colored umbrellas. The rain had made the street slippery and Dr. Muller was having a hard time negotiating the cobblestones.

Eric took his arm and said, "Allow me."

"Thank you Eric. You don't mind me calling you Eric do you?"

"Of course not, doctor. You know us Americans."

"Yes I do and I think we should adopt your American custom and use our first names. You may call me Gottfried, but I would appreciate when we get to Vienna we don't use first names around my wife and friends. They wouldn't understand."

"Of course," Eric said. He noticed the doctor was talking as if they had accepted his proposal and asked, "Can we call you Doc? That's what we called our medics and doctors in the Army."

"That will be fine," the doctor answered, stopping in front of the *Hotel Schwarzer Adler*. "Here we are."

6

The restaurant was warm and steamy, smelling of roast pork and noodles. Dr. Muller led them to a table in a far corner of the room. Most of the other patrons appeared to be locals.

When they were seated, the doctor asked if they would like another bottle of wine, or something else. Eric said that he preferred a dark beer. Paul said the same, and the doctor agreed that a beer sounded good. He signaled a waitress and said, *"Fraulein, bringen Sie uns drei dunkle Bier, Bitte."*

The waitress nodded, and Dr. Muller turned back to the table. "And now Eric, I would like to know where you learned to speak German. You don't have an American accent, which leads me to believe you learned it as a child. Am I correct?"

"That's right," Eric answered. "How did you know?"

"It's believed if children learn a second language before adolescence, they will often speak that language as a native. Your parents are German?"

Eric shook his head. "My grandparents and father emigrated from the Arlberg."

"Ah, they're Austrians, and now you have come back to visit the country of your roots."

Eric nodded, and thanked the waitress in German when she returned with their beers.

The doctor continued, "I trust it has been a pleasurable experience."

"Yes, very pleasurable, but with the end of ski season approaching it is time to move on to other things. That brings us back to the business at hand."

"Yes it does," The doctor said, before taking a generous sip of beer.

"Have you given any thought to what kind of helicopter you want to use?" Paul asked.

"No, I thought I would rely upon your expertise."

"How many people do you want to get out of Czechoslovakia?" Paul asked.

"My mother, my sister and her two young sons."

Paul turned to Eric and said, "We should use an Alouette III. A European helicopter will attract less attention when we cross the border."

Eric was about to agree, when Dr. Muller said, "I will pay to have both of you qualified in the aircraft. Hopefully it won't take much to get your American licenses transferred into Austrian licenses."

The two pilots exchanged glances before Eric confessed, "We don't have American licenses."

The doctor looked confused. "I'm afraid I don't understand."

Eric frowned and continued. "We were only certified to fly in the Army. A pilot has to have that certification transferred into a civilian license if he wants to fly civil aircraft."

"Didn't you plan on continuing your flying careers?"

"Sure we did," Paul interjected. "We didn't have the time. We were only home for a little more than a week before we left for Europe."

"I see," the doctor said, rubbing his chin. "If I understand you correctly, you both endured the deprivation of a foreign war for eighteen months and when you got home you only stayed for a week before you left the country again. Isn't that a little unusual?"

"It may be," Eric said. "There were reasons why we left. Maybe we can talk about them later. Are you a doctor of psychiatry?"

"No, I'm a plastic surgeon," the doctor answered. "However, that does involve some psychology doesn't it? As you said, we can talk about that another time."

The waitress returned to their table. After they ordered, Paul asked, "Where will your family be when we go in to get them?"

"In the town of Vaseli. My mother is originally from Prague and still has relatives living in Vaseli. The pickup area will be about fifty-eight kilometers from the Austrian border and that will be as close as they can get without raising suspicions. My sister has applied for visas to visit our relatives in Czechoslovakia. She was told they would be ready in a month."

Paul said. "Apparently you are able to correspond with her without fear of being detected."

"We have our means. Of course they will have to remain secret."

"Of course. After they arrive in Vaseli, where will they be when we actually pick them up?"

"They will be on a hill southwest of town at an observation point where people go to picnic. They will have a blue and white checkered quilt to identify them."

Paul took a sip of beer and said, "Okay Doc, if I understand you correctly, you will pay to have us both certified to fly in Austria. Is that correct?"

"Yes, I will pay all of the expenses for whatever qualifications you need."

"Then how much are you prepared to pay for the actual mission?"

"That I thought we could negotiate. I have a figure. You boys give me one and we'll see how close we are."

Paul locked eyes with the doctor and said, "You realize it will take some time. We weren't aware of the nature of your proposal until now."

"I know," the doctor said rising from the table. "I have to use the men's room. Do you think you can reach a figure in ten minutes?"

Paul looked toward Eric and said, "We can try."

"Good," the doctor said as he left the table.

When he was out of earshot, Paul asked, "How much do you think he's prepared to pay?"

"I'd guess five, maybe ten thousand dollars."

Paul looked around the restaurant before continuing. "That's what I was thinking, but it's not enough. If everything goes right, this shouldn't be any harder than the ash and trash missions we flew in Nam, but if it doesn't go as planned we aren't going to have friendlies on the ground to help us."

"That's true," Eric said.

"I'm not so sure Dr. Muller thinks this is going to be that easy and he's probably already asked the Austrian and German pilots you mentioned and they've turned him down. We've implied we'll do it, we just have to agree on a price. He also has to know if he doesn't get us, he probably won't find anyone else."

9

"How much do you think we should ask?"

"We started this trip with twenty grand and now we're down to about two. I say we go for another twenty."

Eric frowned and said, "Twenty thousand dollars sounds too high."

Paul lowered his voice. "It may be, but how much do you think the doctor charges to rearrange somebody's face, especially one that's seeking a new identity? I've read that Vienna is considered the spy capital of the world."

Eric shrugged. "I'd say at least ten thousand."

Paul nodded and said, "That's what I was thinking. I say it's twenty or nothing. The way we go through money, we'll need at least half that to get to Indonesia. Besides, have you ever seen me lose a negotiation?"

"Can't say that I have," Eric said, enjoying this side of his friend.

Paul leaned back and said, "Then don't worry. Just let me do the talking. Here comes the doctor now."

Eric watched the doctor approach and said, "Okay, have at it. You're the one with the silver tongue."

As he pulled out his chair, Dr. Muller asked, "Well gentlemen, have you come up with a figure?"

"Yes we have," Paul answered. "We'll do it for twenty thousand dollars."

The doctor looked surprised as he took his seat. "That's quite a bit more than I had in mind."

Paul raised his hand. "It may be Doc, but let me explain a few things. Earlier, when Eric said we were comfortable in a helicopter, he was being modest. We are a lot more than comfortable. We are two of the best pilots to come out of the conflict in Southeast Asia. Between us, we have over three thousand combat hours. You may be able to find someone to do it for less, but you're not going to find anyone with more experience. That's what will count if something goes wrong on the other side of that border."

"I don't doubt that," Dr. Muller countered. "It's just that twenty thousand dollars sounds like a lot of money for one hour's work."

"You bet it is, but is it that much different from paying for a surgeon? If you were going to have heart surgery, wouldn't you want the best specialist you could find and not worry about the price? You're not just paying for one hour's work. You're paying for years of training and experience. With your family's lives at stake, don't you think you need to hire the best? If you do, that's us."

The doctor leaned back in his chair and studied the faces of the two young men before him. He finally said, "Okay, I'll pay you ten thousand dollars before we go and the other ten after we get back. How soon can you come to Vienna?"

Paul deferred to Eric, who said, "Our rent is paid through the end of this month. We can be there the first of May."

"Excellent," Dr. Muller answered. He raised his beer glass and said, "Cheers. Now let's enjoy our dinner."

Eric joined in the toast and then looked out the window. The rain had turned back to snow. He smiled and thought, this is going to be interesting.

Ninh Hoa, South Vietnam – July 7, 1969

Chief Warrant Officer Eric Bader peered through the rain on the windshield of his helicopter as the two ships ahead slowed for their descent into the LZ. Usually, the landing zones were large enough to accommodate five or more helicopters, but this small clearing had just enough room for one.

A company of friendly soldiers had been separated from the rest of their platoon and had engaged a superior force of North Vietnamese regulars. They needed reinforcements, and the six helicopters in Eric's formation were trying to insert as many men as possible.

Their first trip in had been uneventful, but when they returned the lead ship called they were taking fire. Eric listened as a soldier on the ground yelled into his radio they would be putting dead and wounded onto the ships as they returned. The sound of small-arms fire crackled in the background.

Eric needed a break and told his co-pilot to take the controls. Tom Paris was a new man who had been with the company two weeks. Although he had only flown with Paris three times, Eric could tell he was going to be a good addition to their unit. He was a confident pilot who got along well with the other men in the company.

Eric took a gloved hand and wiped away the sweat that streamed down his face as he watched the whirling black rotors of the ship ahead. After thirteen months in Vietnam he had taken on a gaunt look. The sweltering heat and Army chow had reduced his six-foot frame to nothing but muscle and bone. At twenty-three he was one of the most experienced pilots in his company.

The lead helicopter climbed out of the clearing and the second one began its descent. As it did, Paris maneuvered their ship into the next position. That gave Eric time to look at the eight soldiers in the back who were staring out of the open doors, oblivious to what awaited them below.

He glanced at his crew chief, seated in his door gunner's position and said, "You gunners get ready to go hot. They're taking fire this trip."

The battle had intensified when he looked toward the front. More tracers streamed out of the trees toward the landing zone. As the helicopter ahead of them approached the ground, the Aircraft Commander radioed to the lead gunship pilot, "Joker Six-Six, we're taking fire from our right. Do you see those tracers at our two?"

The gunship quickly called back, "Yeah I've got them, but there are so many of our own guys on that side we can't use rockets. I'll see what I can do with my mini-gun."

"Good, just do something," the Slick pilot radioed back.

Eric and his co-pilot watched the scene ahead as the infantrymen began leaping out and scurried for cover. Other men dragged rain ponchos filled with bodies toward the helicopter. When it was loaded, the ship lifted off and the pilot screamed into the radio, "Taking fire. We're hit."

It was their turn to descend, so Eric adjusted his armored chest protector and signaled for his co-pilot to release the controls. Paris let go and asked, "Are we still going down there? Look at all those tracers."

Eric nodded solemnly and said, "This is what we do."

As they approached the ground, their ship was filled with the sound of bullets hitting metal. The right door gunner pointed his machine gun toward the tracers and returned fire. The crew chief yelled from the other side of the ship, "I've got fire coming from my side at ten o'clock. Wait--now there's more at our nine."

The two machine guns chattered behind Eric, with an ear shattering staccato, as he yelled into the radio, "Joker Six-Six, Chalk Two is taking fire from both sides. We've got new fire coming from our left. Do you see it?"

"Yeah, and it's far enough away we can use rockets."

"Good. Go get 'em, Boss Man," Eric yelled as he began to land. When he slowed, a bullet pierced the Plexiglas windshield and hammered into the ceiling behind the two pilots. He instinctively flinched and shouted at Paris, "Son of a bitch that was close, watch the gauges. That round may have hit the engine and I'm not going to get

13

stuck in this little shithole. If something doesn't look right, we're out of here."

Eric continued the approach, and watched the men on the ground drag the dead and wounded toward them through the swaying grass. The skids settled onto the ground and their load of troopers clamored off. While others loaded a body wrapped in a rain poncho, one of the men who left the helicopter was hit immediately and fell into the grass. Two soldiers grabbed him and lifted him back into the helicopter as one of them yelled to the door gunner, "We don't have time to bandage him. Do the best you can."

The two gunships streaked by firing rockets, as soldiers loaded another wounded man into the ship. The air smelled of cordite as they waited for what seemed an eternity. A pathfinder in the trees radioed they were clear and Eric made a hasty take-off. As they climbed out, Eric called for a status check. "What do we have back there, Gary?"

His crew chief quickly radioed, "Pago and I are okay, but we've got a couple of wounded that don't look good."

Eric surveyed the scene and saw that Gary was already out of his door gunner's position and was administering first aid to the soldier who had just been hit.

His crew chief was Gary Jarvis, one of the best in the company. He was from West Virginia and talked with a southern drawl, but behind his country boy image was one of the sharpest minds in the company. Besides being one of the best mechanics at fixing shot-up helicopters, he had become adept at patching shot-up bodies.

Eric motioned for Paris to take the controls, and then asked Jarvis, "How bad is he?"

Jarvis wrapped a bandage around the man's bloody chest and said, "I think he's got a sucking chest wound." He rolled the man onto his stomach and said, "He's not going to make it if we don't get him to a hospital fast." He pointed at the aft part of the ship, and said with finality, "We don't have to worry about that one--he doesn't have a face."

Paris looked at the grisly scene, then back to the front with a grimace.

Jarvis took off his helmet to listen to the other wounded man. He quickly put his helmet back on and radioed Eric over the noise of the rotors. "This guy says he just has a leg wound and wants a cigarette. You got one I can give him?"

Eric took a pack from his pocket and lit one before passing it to the back. Jarvis grabbed the cigarette with a bloody hand and passed it to the wounded soldier. Eric looked to the front and pointed to the right. When Paris turned to the heading, Eric asked, "Can you get us to the hospital? It's on the other side of that hill just ahead."

Paris nodded. "I think so, if my legs will stop shaking."

Eric looked at Paris and said, "You'll get used to it."

With a forlorn look, Paris said, "You think so? Right now I'm wondering how the hell I'm going to make it eleven more months, and you just signed up for another tour."

"I had my reasons."

"Oh yeah, like what?"

"The main reason was when I get back to the States I'll be out of the Army. If I hadn't extended another six months, right now I'd be in Texas instructing at Basic Flight School and you know what a drag that would be."

Paris looked toward his Aircraft Commander and said, "Yeah, but that would be better than going home without a face."

Eric leveled a glare at his new co-pilot and said, "You know Frenchie, you could have gone all day without saying that."

It was still raining when they landed at their home base of Ninh Hoa. Eric shut down the engine and removed his sweat-filled helmet and chest protector. He grabbed a green towel and wiped the sweat from his face and hair. As the rotor blades slowed, he felt the knots in his stomach begin to unwind with them.

He told his crew to secure the helicopter and walked toward the stairs that led to an upper level. The operations office, Officers' Club and barracks area were situated on a natural shelf overlooking the flight line and runway.

15

He climbed the stairs to the upper level and walked the short distance to the Ops office. Despite a ceiling fan and two floor fans, the room always smelled of sweaty bodies and musty plywood. Eric threw his paperwork onto the counter and greeted the Spec 4 charged with signing out the company helicopters. "How's it going, Gil?"

"Not too bad, Mr. Bader," the young man answered, as he took the papers and recorded the time on a clipboard.

Specialist 4th Class Tim Gillick had been in country almost as long as Eric and over that time they had become friends. Gillick looked up from the counter and asked, "How was it out there today, Sir? You look like you could use a little time off."

Eric turned to leave and said, "Good idea, Gil. Why don't you put me in for a few days R & R in Vung Tau?"

"Sure thing Mr. Bader and while I'm at it, I'll see if I can get your DEROS date moved up a few months."

Eric pushed the screen door open and said, "I'll see you tomorrow, Gil."

Gillick called out, "I did hear there's a trip to Dalat in the works and that wouldn't be too bad."

Eric stopped and asked, "How many ships?"

"I think it's only one."

"Then put in a good word for me. I flew out of there for over a month and I already know the terrain."

Eric stopped at the mail room and then sloshed across the muddy center courtyard toward his living quarters. The barracks were divided into small two-man rooms made of plywood and screens, so they looked more like chicken coops than barracks rooms. The screens also assured the occupants could hear and smell everything that happened in the company area at all hours of the day and night.

The barracks area made up two adjacent sides of a quadrangle. The other two sides housed the headquarters offices and the Officers' Club. Eric's room was next to the corner room closest to the O Club.

The corner room was occupied by Chief Warrant Officer Tucker Burdett, one of the few warrant officers to have a college degree.

16

Burdett was the camp scrounger and "dog robber," an aid to the commanding officer whose duties were so varied they defied explanation.

The room on the other side of Eric's was occupied by three young co-pilots who had gotten permission to put an extra bed in their room. Since there was barely enough room for two beds, adding another one meant that the three beds would form one large bed. If the three of them hadn't always been reading letters from their girlfriends, the other pilots would have thought the arrangement to be very strange.

Their names were Carl Wilford, Jerome Milton and Terry Tomlinson. Eric's roommate had promptly nicknamed them Wilford, Milford and Tilford. When they weren't flying, the three of them usually stayed in their room, drinking and reading letters from home. Occasionally, the sounds of crying could be heard coming through the screen.

Eric entered his musty room and threw his flight gear into his wall locker. Stripping to his underwear he sat on his bed and turned on his little Sanyo fan. As he read his mail, the breeze on his wet skin felt as refreshing as a cold shower.

Thirty minutes later, his roommate, Chief Warrant Officer Paul Eason, entered the room. He threw his gear on the floor and began taking off his flight suit. Eason came from Newport Beach, California, and was also twenty-three, handsome and blonde, with an assertive self confidence that most women liked and some men hated. He was the kind of guy who could enter a room full of strangers and in less than an hour everyone would be calling him by his first name. His glib tongue had earned him the call sign Devil, as in silver tongued.

Both men had been in Vietnam for thirteen months, which made them two of the most experienced helicopter pilots in the 48th Assault Helicopter Company.

Eason turned on his fan and said, "I just heard the 281st is loaning us four new co-pilots until we can get more replacements. You and I are going to have to fly with two of them."

Eric looked up from a letter and said, "When are they getting in?"

"In about an hour, if they can make it through the rain."

Eason went to his locker and took out a bottle of bourbon and two tin cups. He poured whiskey into each cup and offered one to Eric. Usually, it was too hot to sit in their room, but the cloudy weather and fans blowing on their bodies made it tolerable. Paul sat on his bed and said, "It sounds like the co-pilots are all cherries, so I doubt if they'll have much info on the other pilots in their company."

It was customary to interrogate visiting pilots about flight school classmates to see who from their class had been killed or wounded and sent back to the States. Paul added water from a canteen to his drink. "I also heard there's a detail to Dalat."

Eric took the canteen and said, "I heard that too. It sounds like only one ship is going?"

"Yeah, which is too bad. It would be great if the two of us could get back there. Dalat was definitely the best time we've had in Nam."

"That's a pretty low bar, but you're right," Eric said, as he got up to look out their screen door. The rain had increased to where it was pelting down on the tin roof and wooden boardwalk outside. Although the rain gave the appearance of cooling things off, it had raised the humidity to where it and the temperature were squared at ninety.

The weather and whiskey gave Eric an unaccustomed feeling of security. It felt good to be done flying for the day. Another one down, he thought. How many more did he have left? There were so many he hadn't started a short-timer's calendar.

Eric turned around and said, "You know, Dev, I've been thinking. Maybe extending our tours might not have been that good of an idea. I wonder if we can still put in for Germany."

Paul waved him off and said, "Hey, we're going to Europe, but not as Green Maggots. Do you have any idea how many rules and regulations they have over there? I've heard it's worse than stateside duty and how many rules do we have here in Nam? Two! Get it up, and get it back!"

Eric laughed and said, "Okay, you're right."

"I know I'm right," Paul said. "And what are we stuck with if we *don't* get Germany? Flight instructing in Mineral Wells, Texas. Five more months of this has got to be better than two years of that bullshit. Now I've heard they may start to teach the South Vietnamese how to fly helicopters. Can you image that? I'll take my chances with Charlie Cong over here, before I'll let one of them try to kill me in flight school."

Eric looked back at the rain. "You've got a point there. It would be a real bitch to go through all this shit in Nam and then get killed instructing in Texas.

Paul finished his drink and asked, "Do you want another one?"

Eric handed him his cup. "What else do we have to do?"

When they had finished another drink, the late afternoon sun was shining and the two roommates decided to see if the new pilots had arrived. The courtyard outside their room had turned into a muddy steam bath and large patches of perspiration were forming on the backs of their clean olive drab t-shirts.

They sloshed toward company headquarters and Paul said, "Another shitty day at Club Mud, Amigo. Only five more months and we'll be out of here and free to do anything we damn well please."

"Like skiing in Austria," Eric added as they reached the Ops office.

Paul opened the door. "Exactly."

Specialist Gillick told them the new pilots had already arrived and were eating dinner. When the two roommates entered the mess hall, they saw six new pilots instead of four. Two of the pilots were distinguished by tan faces and faded flight suits. The other four sat at the table wearing new uniforms and nervous smiles. The visitors were sitting with a group of local pilots inquiring about flight school classmates.

When Eric and Paul joined the group, they were told two of the pilots had flown the others in and were waiting for their crew chief to check an engine warning light before returning to their home unit. Eric waited until his fellow pilots were done questioning the others and then asked, "Is there a Captain Reddick in your unit?"

Both of the experienced pilots stopped eating and glanced at each other, before one of them asked, "Is he a friend of yours?"

Eric shook his head and said, "No, he's definitely not a friend."

The pilot took a bite of ham and said, "I didn't think so, you look too normal to be a friend of that prick."

The pilots at the table chuckled as Eric said, "Then I take it he is in the 281st."

The visitor waved his fork and continued, "No, and there's something strange about the way he left. He was without a doubt the worst flight leader we've had. He was always pushing guys to land in shitty areas, or sending them to hot LZs by mistake. Those mistakes cost us four helicopters. Some of our guys said if he got one more ship they were going to make him an Ace."

Everyone laughed and the pilot continued. "Before he left, the situation was almost mutinous with everyone refusing to fly for him. The CO finally took his command, which really pissed him off. If he'd been in the infantry he probably would have gotten fragged."

Eric asked, "Where did he go?"

"We don't know. One day he just disappeared. Rumor has it he's in Saigon." After a pause the man asked, "How do you know him?"

With a wry smile, Eric answered, "He was going to write me up for being a disgrace to the uniform."

Eric's fellow pilots began laughing and goading him. One of them asked, "You've got to tell us what that's all about."

Reluctantly, Eric answered, "I accidentally let all the water out of his shower."

Most showers in Vietnam were wood-framed cages with fifty-five gallon drums of water on top and a pull-cord to release the water. If the drum had been in the sun, the water would feel warm, even hot.

Eric's co-pilot, Tom Paris said, "That's not enough to write somebody up. This is a joke, right?"

Eric shook his head and said, "Unfortunately not." He pointed at his roommate and said, "It was his fault."

Paul feigned surprise, and said, "Hey, I was there, but it wasn't my fault."

One of the local pilots said, "Why do we find that hard to believe, Eason?"

Paul pointed at Eric and said, "Tell them the story, Dog."

"It all started in the Officers' Club at Cam Rahn Bay. It was my second night in country. I'd met Eason the night before. He had been there for six days. When I walked into the club he was celebrating getting out of the processing center, and bought a bottle of champagne. Before he opened it, he pointed at a velvet painting of Elvis and said, 'I can hit that picture with the cork and I'll bet I can get three to one odds from these guys at the bar. Are you in?'"

Eric pointed at the wall and said, "The painting was about that far away, so I was skeptical, but the Military Payment Certificates still looked like monopoly money, so I said I'd put up a twenty. He not only got three to one odds, he got the others to agree to buy us drinks for the rest of the night if we won. You can guess what happened. He hit the painting and they paid the bet. We drank the champagne, and they bought us three more rounds. We were pretty well shitfaced when we left the bar.

"On the way to the barracks, a Siren went off and the camp started getting mortared. We didn't know where the bunkers were, so we took cover in a canal under a bridge. When I finally reached my barracks, I literally smelled like shit, so I went to the outside shower to rinse off. The last thing I remember was sitting in the shower with a warm stream of water falling onto my head.

"I awoke with someone shaking my shoulder. I was sitting in the shower still dressed in my flight suit. There wasn't any water left, so the guy was pissed. He said he was a captain and he thought I was a disgrace to the uniform. He told me to report to him at headquarters because he wanted to write me up. Of course I didn't do that. Instead, I beat it over to Paul's barracks and took the bunk he was vacating. The next day, I talked an assignment clerk into sending me to the 48th, because that was where Paul had been sent."

Eason interrupted, "When he got here I said, good to see you Bader, you're one bad dog. The name stuck."

The visiting pilot looked at Eric and said, "Let's hope Reddick is on his way out of the country."

When they finished eating, the two experienced pilots left for the flight line while the four new men joined the local pilots in the bar. Eric and Paul began questioning them about how much flight time they had in Nam. After several drinks, two of them became vocal about how they did things in their home unit. The other two were quiet and nervous. The two roommates got bored and walked to the other side of the bar.

An hour later, Captain Al Hutchins entered the club and took his Aircraft Commanders aside to read them their assignments. He turned to Eric last. "Bader, you're going to Dalat with one of the borrowed co-pilots, a Lieutenant Skiles."

The other pilots moaned and Eric said, "What can I say guys." He looked at Paul and said, "I'll be sure and tell your girlfriend you're still alive."

"Thanks roomy, you're all heart," Paul said, before moving down the bar to trade insults with a couple of gunship pilots.

Eric crossed the room to inform his new co-pilot about their trip. He extended his hand and said, "Lieutenant, I'm Eric Bader. You and I will be flying to Dalat in the morning."

The lieutenant let out a whoop and Eric motioned for him to keep it down. He looked around the bar and said, "We'll be leaving at 0600 in ship number 59."

The lieutenant regained his composure and said, "Yes Sir, I'll be there."

Eric lowered his voice and said, "You can call me Eric, Lieutenant."

Skiles shrugged and said, "Okay."

Eric bade him good night, then walked out of the crowded bar into the warm moonlight. In his room, he made himself a drink and thought about his last visit to Dalat.

A month earlier, he and Paul had piloted two helicopters in a five-ship armada. Since they were stationed in Dalat for a month, the Army leased a rambling old house that was part of a defunct French coffee plantation. The house came with an older French woman named Marie Gallant, who served as cook and housekeeper. Madame Gallant's husband had been the director of the plantation. When the plantation closed, the company let them remain in the house as part of his severance package.

Monsieur Gallant died two years later and Marie Gallant decided to stay in Vietnam and operate the house as a bed and breakfast. Besides paying her rent, the Army gave her a generous allowance to serve the pilots breakfast and a bag lunch each day. Most mornings she prepared crepes, fresh eggs, and a bowl of strawberries. She also offered them strong coffee and a shot of brandy. She said she had read that the brandy was a tradition of French pilots dating back to World War I. The U.S. pilots weren't sure about the story, but thought it was an excellent tradition to continue. Life was good at the house with the coffee, crepes and strawberries being far superior to the powdered eggs and chipped beef they were used to being served.

For dinner, Madame Gallant had recommended a French restaurant owned by one of her friends, Monsieur Jean-Luc Aubert. Monsieur Aubert was a widower who had also decided to stay in Vietnam after his wife died. He had a beautiful daughter named Collette who was attending the University of Dalat.

The pilots knew they would not be permitted to date the lovely Mademoiselle Collette, so one night Paul asked if she had any college friends who might want to meet her pilot friends. Collette answered excitedly, "*Oui, oui,* I have two beautiful Eurasian girls I am tutoring in English and French. They are trying to get into the university."

Paul smiled and said, "Well that means Eric and I will have to meet you ladies at a café for drinks and dinner."

Collette agreed. "Why not tomorrow night?"

The following night they all met at an outdoor lake-side restaurant. The weather was almost as beautiful as the two ladies Collette introduced to her friends. There were three weeks remaining in the detail, so Eric and Paul continued to date the girls until they returned to Ninh Hoa.

Eric took a sip of his drink and wondered if his lady would be happy to see him.

The next morning, Eric was in the latrine shaving when he was greeted by four gunship pilots. One of them was the lead Gunnie, Clay Boone. As he stood at the urinal trough, Boone said to Eric, "Hey Bader, I hear you're going back to Dalat. Whose ass have you been kissing? I've never been there and I hear you're on a first-name basis with the locals."

Eric rinsed his razor and said, "You're not jealous, are you Shooter? If you were a nice guy like me and hauled people around, you might get there too."

At six foot three and two hundred and twenty pounds, Clay "Shooter" Boone was the biggest pilot in the company. An earlier helicopter crash had left him with a horseshoe-shaped scar around his left eye which gave him a menacing look. The crash had been so spectacular his fellow pilots said when they found him he was reading the instrument panel from the back side.

His injuries were severe enough to send him home to Louisiana and out of the Army. After six months of flying oil workers to rigs off the Gulf Coast, Boone was so bored he talked an Army recruiter into sending him back to his old gunship unit in Vietnam.

While Eric and Boone were talking, Paul emerged from the showers with a towel wrapped around his waist. As he passed the Gunnies, he said, "Hey girls, I love those green shorts."

He took the sink next to the urinal and eyed Boone, whose boxer shorts were so baggy they reached to his knees. Eason combed his hair and said, "Nice pants, Shooter. Who's your tailor, Omar the tent maker? Why did he put such a big opening in the front when a button hole would have worked just as well?"

Boone scowled through smoke rising from a cigarette dangling from his lips and replied, "You think you're real fuckin' cute don't you, Eason?"

Paul's blond hair was the longest in the company and he continued to flip it with a comb as he said, "A couple of your Joker buddies think so, Shooter. They've even asked me to go to the beach with them. They're so macho and have all those cool patches you guys wear. I just might be tempted to go with them."

24

Boone ignored him and turned toward the showers. Eason pointed at a bottle of Pine-Sol and said, "Hey Shooter, you forgot your mouthwash."

Boone looked over his shoulder and said, "Dickhead!"'

Paul turned to his roommate. "The animals are a little testy this morning. I think somebody forget to feed them."

Eric moved down the row of sinks. "I think you need to ease up on those guys. One of these days you're going to push them too far."

Paul waved him off and said, "Nah, they eat that shit up. They'd miss it if I quit."

Eric wiped his face with a towel. "Okay, it's your neck."

Paul noticed five Slick pilots enter the latrine and said, "So you're going back to Dalat, huh Dog? I wish I was going with you. If you run into those French girls we got next to, be sure and tell mine not to forget me."

One of the new arrivals asked, "French girls? How did you guys meet French girls?"

Paul looked at the pilot. "We did more than meet them, Koz."

Kozlowski looked confused, and asked, "Why are they in Dalat?"

"They're studying at the university."

"But why are French girls over here?" another pilot asked.

Paul looked around the room. "Think about it guys. Who was here before us? The French Army. These girls are the product of all those French-Vietnamese liaisons of twenty years ago. Besides all the French lovelies, there are hundreds of Vietnamese girls up there too."

The Gunnies had walked out of the shower and were listening attentively. Eason eyed them as he continued, "Rumor has it, Ho Chi Minh wants Dalat to be the new capital of Vietnam if they win, so there hasn't been much fighting around there in years. The city was built by the French, so when you're there you think you're in Europe. It's so high in the mountains, the air is cool enough you sometime need to wear a jacket. It's also surrounded by pine trees instead of jungle."

After a moment to let them reflect, Paul continued, "All of the local men are out in the bush trying to kill GIs, so somebody has to take care

25

of all those ladies. Since you dog faces aren't up to it, I guess that leaves my man Eric and me." He laughed and walked out of the latrine.

Clay Boone watched the door close and said, "French girls. *Shee-it,* what would that be like?"

Eric collected his shaving kit and said, "I'll let you know when I get back, Shooter."

As he walked to his room, Eric thought about what Paul had said about Dalat. Most of it was true, except the part about their girlfriends. They were actually waitresses in a hotel bar, but they were French-Eurasians and they did want to go to the university. That was close enough.

Forty minutes later, Eric was on the flight line walking with six other pilots when he saw his new co-pilot. Even from a distance he could see that the lieutenant had a perplexed look on his face. He came alongside and asked, "What's up Lieutenant?"

"Good morning Mr. Bad … uhh, Eric. It's no big deal, but how come nobody salutes me?"

Eric laughed and said, "That's the way we are in the 48th. We're a little more informal than other units." He put his hand on the lieutenant's back. "They still love you though."

As they approached their helicopter, the crew chief was on a ladder examining the rotor blades. Eric yelled up at him, "Are we set to go, Gary?"

"Near as I can tell, Mr. Bader." Eric was glad to have Jarvis along for the trip because he was a cool head under fire.

Eric pointed at the lieutenant. "Gary, this is Lt. Skiles. Lieutenant, Gary Jarvis, our crew chief."

"Welcome aboard Lieutenant," Gary said, as he climbed down the ladder to shake hands.

Eric looked through the wide open doors of the helicopter and called to the door gunner on the other side, "Pago, this is Lt. Skiles."

Tony Pagliano looked up from loading his machine gun and eyed the lieutenant suspiciously. He was a street-smart kid from the Bronx. His brooding dark face and the six months he had spent as an infantryman

26

gave him a look much older than his nineteen years. It had also left him with distrust for anyone with a rank higher than sergeant. With a nod, he said, "Morning Lieutenant."

"Good morning," the lieutenant said as he waved through the empty helicopter.

Eric opened the door to the cockpit and threw in his gear. He turned to the lieutenant and said, "Why don't you give her a military look-over, while I sign the books?" He knew the lieutenant wouldn't find anything after the crew chief had given it a preflight, but the pilots had to sign that the ship was ready to go.

When they were all seated and set for startup, Eric yelled "Clear" and pressed the starter trigger. The starter growled and the rotor blades began to turn. When the pre-takeoff checklist was complete, he raised the helicopter several feet above the ground, and then backed it out of the sandbagged revetment. When they were clear of the walls, he did a pedal turn to the right and nosed it down the runway.

They flew south along the South China Sea. The azure water against the dark green jungle reminded Eric of pictures of Hawaii. I should be there flying tourist around the islands, he thought. What a great life that would be.

When they topped the mountains to their right he turned inland for Dalat. The early morning air became cool enough to close the cockpit windows for the first time in months. Eric leveled off at their cruising altitude and asked his new co-pilot if he wanted to fly. The lieutenant took the controls and asked, "Is this our heading?"

Bader pointed out the windshield and said, "See that mountain at one o'clock? We need to go about two fingers to the right of that."

Over the ship's intercom the two pilots could hear the crew chief and door gunner discussing previous trips to Dalat. Pagliano's mike was intermittent, so they could only understand part of what he was saying.

Eric turned to his crew chief and said, "Gary, Tony's mike is breaking up. See if you can find the problem when we land at Dalat. I think he asked if we're spending more than one night and the answer is no." Gary clicked his mike button twice to signify that he understood.

27

Twenty minutes later, they crossed another ridge and the mountainous jungle changed into rectangular tea, coffee and rubber plantations. A lake and city came into view and the lieutenant asked, "Is that Dalat?"

"That's it," Eric said. "The airport is on the bench to the south." Eric shook the controls and said, "I'll take it from here, Lieutenant."

Eric circled the airport to check for other traffic. When there wasn't any, he carefully set the Huey next to the jet fuel pump. He killed the engine as two Green Berets walked toward the aircraft. He jumped down from his seat and introduced himself. After a short conversation he turned to his crew and yelled, "I'm going to get our assignment. We'll fuel when I get back."

Eric and the soldiers walked up a dusty road to a hut on a small hill. The rest of the crew got out of the helicopter and stretched. While they were enjoying the cool, quiet isolation of the mountain airstrip, a Specialist 4th Class approached and said, "If you guys want fuel, you'd better get it now. I'm leaving for town and I have to lock the pumps while I'm gone. Somebody's been helping themselves to our fuel when nobody's here."

Jarvis pointed up the road and said, "Our Aircraft Commander is getting the mission right now. Can't you wait until he gets back, so we'll know how much fuel to put on?"

The attendant pointed toward a Jeep and said, "See those two guys over there? They aren't going to wait much longer and it's a long walk into town if they leave me."

The lieutenant interrupted and said, "We know we're probably going to need fuel, Gary, and we may need a lot. Let's show a little initiative and get it done, so this man can get on his way."

Jarvis frowned and said, "I don't know about that, Lieutenant. I think we should wait."

In an authoritative tone, Lieutenant Skiles said, "I'll take responsibility here. Let's just run it up to three quarters full and be done with it."

Gary shrugged and said, "Okay, you're flying it. Can you watch the gauge while I fuel it? Let's just put on half a tank."

The lieutenant shook his head. "No, I'd prefer not to turn on the battery. I'll fuel it by looking down the filler spout until I see foam."

Gary walked toward the pump and said, "Okay Lieutenant, she's all yours." At the pump he said, "I still don't think this is a good idea."

The attendant turned on the fuel valve and said, "He sounds like a know-it- all to me."

The lieutenant concentrated on the fuel coming out of the high-pressure nozzle. Halfway into the fueling, the lieutenant's eyes were drawn toward two college girls as they sauntered past the helicopter. The sight of the girls in their tight fitting *ao dai* dresses distracted him long enough for the tank to fill and blow fuel over him and the helicopter.

The shocked lieutenant gasped and wiped the fuel from his eyes. In a polite voice the attendant asked, "Do you need any more, Sir?" His friends in the Jeep were laughing and pointing at the helicopter. The two girls looked at the scene and giggled, covering their mouths.

The lieutenant shook his head as he used his shirt tail to wipe the fuel from his face. The attendant took the nozzle and rolled up the hose. After he locked the pump, he ran to the Jeep where his buddies were still laughing.

Gary took a greasy towel from under his seat and began wiping the excess fuel off the side of the helicopter. The lieutenant took off his Nomex shirt to wipe the fuel from his hair and said, "I'm not used to that fast a pump."

Eric walked down the hill waving a map. "Looks like a piece of cake. We just need to move eight Greenies and three hundred pounds of gear from one hill to another. They're both within twenty minutes, so we'll fuel when we get back."

As he approached the helicopter, his crew lowered their eyes and began kicking the dry, red clay. Eric looked at the lieutenant and for the first time noticed his wet shirt and pants. He spun around to look at the ship and saw the clean area where Jarvis had wiped off the fuel.

Oh no, tell me they didn't fill it, he thought. He looked at Jarvis and asked in a flat voice, "It's topped isn't it?" Gary nodded and looked at the lieutenant.

In an apologetic voice, Skiles said, "I'm sorry Eric. I wasn't used to that fast a pump."

Eric turned away and looked at the surrounding mountains. His nice day had evaporated. Now he had to extract eight guys and their gear, with a helicopter filled to the gills with fuel. He turned to glare at his co-pilot and asked, "Do you think this Huey will get off the ground with us four, eight Green Berets, three hundred pounds of gear, *and all that goddamn fuel*?"

With an anguished look, the lieutenant said, "Probably not Sir--uh, but I can get the performance chart and check it out."

Eric yelled, "Check it out! Check *what* out? Do you have any idea how far off that chart we'll be?"

The lieutenant looked at the ground and said, "Probably pretty far."

Eric stepped closer to his co-pilot and said, "You've got that right, Lieutenant. Lucky for you, I've got a plan. We'll do it in two trips and take the gear on the last trip." He turned to his other crewmen and said, "Let's get the hell out of here, guys. We're already late."

Eric was still agitated as he took his seat and slipped his chest plate under his seat belt harness. He checked to see if the others were ready and saw Jarvis and Pagliano belted into their side-facing door gunner positions. His co-pilot was swearing and frantically trying to put on his shirt.

Eric turned back to the instrument panel and pressed the starter trigger. When they reached idle RPM he checked to see if the lieutenant was ready. His co-pilot finally had his shirt on and was reaching for his seat belt when Eric stopped him. "They say we may take enemy fire, so you'd better put on your chicken plate."

The rest of the crew had theirs on, so they all watched as the lieutenant swore and slipped the ceramic armor plate under his shoulder straps. When his co-pilot was finally ready, Eric asked, "Do you have a pistol?"

Skiles pointed at his helmet bag and Eric said, "Let me see it." His co-pilot handed him a holstered .38 caliber revolver and Eric took the pistol and placed it in the lieutenant's crotch. His surprised co-pilot stared at the pistol as Eric said, "You have to keep it somewhere, so you might as well put two pounds of hard cold steel between the enemy and your family jewels."

Eric brought the screaming turbine engine up to takeoff power and then nosed the loaded Huey down the runway. As he circled the town to gain altitude, the crew watched as shrines and pagodas slipped under the ship.

"There's the university, Mr. B," Gary said excitedly.

Eric looked back at his crew chief and said, "You guys can check it out tonight."

When they reached their cruising altitude, Eric trimmed the aircraft and said, "I love your cologne, Lieutenant. Did you get that stateside, or can I get it at the PX?"

The lieutenant glared at his AC and said, "Very funny."

Eric turned his attention back out the windshield and struggled to find the Cam Dao River. He gazed at the giant teaks and tangled vines that made up the impenetrable vegetation passing below the helicopter. He knew if the engine malfunctioned while they were over that kind of terrain they would be swallowed without a trace.

He felt a tension slowly rise when he couldn't distinguish one river from the next. There were too many small creeks and hills and not enough solid landmarks. He studied the map and decided on a river that looked right and made a turn to follow along its southern bank. He knew he had been picked for this detail because of his experience and knew it would be his last if something went wrong.

He glanced from the windshield to the map as his co-pilot asked, "Where the hell are we supposed to land out here?"

"They say it's a good landing spot on a grassy knoll," Eric said, then called the ground troops. "China Fog, this is Blue Star 59."

A trooper answered quickly, "Blue Star 59, China Fog." The call was loud and clear, so they were close. It was also whispered, which meant there were probably enemy troops nearby.

31

Before Eric could respond, the soldier called again, "We hear you Blue Star. If you head to the southwest you should be coming toward us."

Eric called back in an apologetic voice, "Roger, China Fog. There's been a slight change of plans. Instead of taking all of you on one trip, we'll be making two trips of four, with the gear on the last trip."

The grumbled response communicated to the aircrew that the man was not happy about the change. "Ahhh ... Roger that, Blue Star."

"Are you guys ready?" Eric asked, quickly.

"Affirmative, we've got you in sight. Continue on your present heading and you'll see us."

All eyes turned forward, as Eric asked his crew, "Anybody see something that looks like an opening?"

His co-pilot strained to look out the windshield and replied, "Are you kidding?"

Eric called the ground again, "China Fog, give me a Goofy Grape and a Laffy Lemon."

When his co-pilot looked at him inquisitively, he said, "Smoke grenades."

The smoke could be seen for miles and worked fine for awhile, until the Viet Cong captured a radio and a few grenades. The enemy monitored the calls for smoke and the color requested and then popped that color, leading an unfortunate flight crew into an ambush. The American pilots countered by calling for a combination of colors, increasing the chances the VC would not be able to comply. When a wrong combination was discovered, gunships were called in to thump a sure thing.

The Viet Cong eventually caught on, and the aircraft crews were again forced to devise a different means of identifying the various colored smokes. Knowing only an American subjected to mass marketing would know the correct colors for the flavors of a children's drink, they began using the flavors instead of colors, and once again gained the upper hand in the smoke grenade game.

"There they are at one o'clock," Eric said, as he banked toward the purple and yellow smoke. He approached low, just above the trees. At that altitude they were safer, but it made it harder to see the landing zone.

With the opening still not in sight, Eric began to flare the Huey to begin a descent toward the base of the smoke. With the ship's nose high, it began to shudder more than normal due to the heavy fuel load. As they continued their descent, the smoke swirled around the helicopter, making strange whirlpools and vortices. They finally punched through the smoke and the clearing came into view.

"Shit, it's elephant grass," Eric yelled as he fought his bucking helicopter in a near-vertical descent. Elephant grass got its name because it could be high enough to hide an elephant. Its tall blades made the ground hard to find and could give a pilot vertigo as it swayed in the downwash from the rotor blades.

Eric saw a place that the troops had trampled down and maneuvered his rapidly falling helicopter to that spot. He called his door gunners. "Get ready to go hot. We don't know what we have down here." Eric hunched over the controls, and the crew knew this was not a normal landing.

Over the clearing, Eric pulled pitch into the blades to start their flare. The ship groaned as it tried to overcome a combination of too high an altitude and far too much weight. When he realized he could no longer slow their descent, Eric exhaled in disgust and yelled, "Hang on."

Dust flew as they hit the ground and the rotor blades flexed down and clipped the tall grass. As the blades flexed back up, Eric didn't feel anything unusual in the controls, so he was fairly certain the blades hadn't knocked anything off the tail section. He glared at his ashen-faced co-pilot and said, "Love it." He quickly turned to his two gunners and said, "Get 'em on board guys, load 'em up."

Gary and Tony waved frantically to the awaiting grunts, while the lieutenant looked at the gauges with sweat dripping from his face.

Eric looked out his side window and noticed all eight soldiers wallowing toward the helicopter. He thrust his arm out the window and held up four fingers. The gesture was understood and only three of them continued toward the ship. Three others returned to crouch behind their pile of gear and scanned the tree line. The remaining two argued over the noise of the helicopter.

"Christ, what's taking them so long," Eric muttered as he watched them yell at each other. As if they heard him, one of them walked to the helicopter. The man climbed onboard to the distinctive crack, crack, crack of enemy AK-47 assault rifles.

"Tony, go hot on that tree line," Eric said as he prepared to lift off.

Tony's machine gun was spitting tracers before Eric finished the sentence. The four men on the ground began firing from behind the pile of gear. The gunfire was increasing, as Eric lifted the helicopter to a hover.

"Here they come, Mr. Bader," Tony screamed into the intercom.

Eric looked out his right window and saw six slinking figures coming toward them. Tony fired a short burst, hitting two of them. The others dropped out of sight into the grass. As they began moving forward, Eric caught sight of the four remaining American soldiers frantically sprinting toward the ship. The men knew all eight had come in on a helicopter, so they figured all of them could go out on one.

"Wait, wait," a sergeant in back yelled. There was another burst of enemy fire, as one of the soldiers on the ground spun around and went down. One of his companions knelt over him as the other two returned fire.

"Now there's four coming from my side," Gary yelled, between bursts from his machine gun. "They must not have heard what Uncle Ho said about fighting around Dalat."

Eric's mind raced as tracers whizzed around the helicopter. He had to decide whether to go or not. He knew the proper military decision was to get out fast, saving the Huey and the lives of the men on board. If he took all eight, he risked a crash that could kill them all.

He glanced at his co-pilot. The lieutenant's frightened expression said, come on, let's get out of here. Eric knew there was no help there. He wished he was a co-pilot and could let some cool, experienced AC get him out of this mess.

With the situation deteriorating around him, he knew he couldn't leave the remaining men. He reluctantly lowered the collective and set the ship back down. When they were on the ground, Gary jumped out to help load the wounded man. As he did, there was another burst of AK-47 fire and the sound of bullets hitting metal.

"We're hit, Mr. Bader," Jarvis yelled.

"I know, Gary. Find out where, *fast!*"

Jarvis was still outside the ship with his helmet attached to the intercom by a long cord. He looked up at two shiny streaks in the OD paint of the tail boom and yelled, "They look like skin hits to me, let's go."

With everyone on board, Eric pulled the loaded Huey back to a hover. As they moved forward, the rotor blade RPM began to bleed off and dropped below minimum operating range. The controls became sluggish as a warning Siren blared and an amber light flashed "LOW ROTOR RPM."

Eric knew he had to set the ship back down and landed before they fell from a five foot hover. The ship had moved far enough forward to be out of the tramped-down area and was engulfed by the waving elephant grass. "Shit, now I can't even see out," he yelled. "Those gooks will be on top of us in no time. You gunners fire off periodic bursts to keep them from moving in on us."

The frightened troops in back stared at the swaying grass and yelled, "Let's go. Come on, let's get the hell out of here."

Good idea, Eric thought. Tell me how and I will. He wiped the sweat from his eyes and thought, why didn't I stay in school. College was so easy. I could be on the Dean's list, chasing skirts and having fun with my buddies. Now what do I do?

He looked out at the swaying grass and remembered that when they had landed, the hill dropped off sharply just ahead of them. The question was, how far did they have to go to get to that point? Over the intercom, Eric said, "Gary, I think if we can make it another forty feet we'd be at a point where this hill drops off, but we can't get above this grass and we sure as hell can't plow through it."

35

While he was talking, his fingers nervously fingered the controls and his left thumb hit a small button on the top of the collective. He turned to his crew chief and said, "Maybe we can beep our way out of here with the fine-tune switch?"

The button he'd touched was a motorized switch that allowed the pilot to fine tune the RPM to keep it within operating range. If he held it forward, it could advance the RPM over maximum red line, boosting the power. Eric had never intentionally advanced the RPM over red line, but he was ready to try anything to get them off the hill. He knew it could also possibly damage to the engine, so he said to his crew chief, "Gary, I don't know what this will do to your helicopter, but I'm going for it."

Gary yelled back, "I don't care, beep the shit out of it. Let's just get the fuck out of here."

"You've got it," Eric said, as he pushed forward on the button and raised the collective. The heavy ship rose slowly and began chopping its way through the thick grass. The beeper had worked. They were several feet higher and moving forward.

Eric's eyes froze on the tachometer as he watched the rotor RPM deteriorating toward minimum range. When he looked outside, he could see the edge of the clearing just ahead. The obnoxious Siren began blaring and the amber low RPM light flashed its ominous warning. His eyes moved back and forth from the tachometer to the edge of the clearing.

Which would they hit first, he thought, minimum RPM, or the cliff's edge. As they approached the rim, the grass was much shorter, but the ground was covered with boulders. When the hill began dropping away, Eric blurted, "I'm going for it."

The RPM dropped below red line as he pushed the stick forward. The final edge was only a ship's length away when he realized they were *not* going to make it.

"Oh shit, hang on!" Eric yelled as the back of the skids hit the rocks. He felt his seat belt cut into his legs as the helicopter ricocheted off the cliff. They had cleared the ledge and the two pilots were staring directly at the bottom of the canyon. The soldiers in the back were screaming and holding on to each other to keep from falling out of the open doors.

Eric looked from the bottom of the ravine to the instrument panel. The ship was gaining airspeed rapidly, but was still in the minimum range for rotor RPM. The only way to increase RPM was to lower the collective and flatten the pitch of the rotor blades. He knew that would cause them to fall even faster, maybe too fast to be able to stop their descent before crashing into the trees below.

There wasn't a choice, so he bottomed the collective and guided his falling missile toward the deepest part of the ravine. The airspeed was approaching maximum red line, when the rotor RPM slowly climbed back into normal range and he began to feel more like a driver than a passenger.

They were two hundred feet above the trees when the moment of truth arrived. Eric pulled back on the stick to slow the airspeed and simultaneously raised the collective. The increased pitch in the rotors slowed their descent and the ship groaned as the blades began taking a bigger bite of air.

They leveled off and Eric began breathing again. He was exhausted and his knee caps were quivering. Knowing the spasms would subside in a few minutes, he flew on in silence with his boots pulsing on the pedals.

His co-pilot turned toward him and asked, "Do you guys in the 48th always fly like that?"

Eric looked at Skiles and said, "Yeah, when we have to, like when we're *overloaded* with fuel."

The lieutenant turned to look nervously out the windshield as Pagliano said, "I can't believe we're not fucking dead."

Eric called his crew chief. "Gary you have to fix Tony's mike. It's starting to get on my nerves."

"You bet," Gary replied. "I'll fix it as soon as I change my pants."

Eric laughed and asked, "How does it look back there? Is everyone still on board?"

"Yeah, they look a little shaken up, but they're all here."

"How's the guy that got hit?"

"He's a lucky man. The bullet knocked the wind out of him, but it's stuck in his flak jacket."

"That is lucky," Eric said, then asked, "Does the sergeant still want to be dropped off at the other hill?"

Gary checked and said, "He says they have to go back to Dalat because they don't have no gear, no more."

Eric turned to the back and chided his friend. "No gear, no more. Does everybody in West Virginia talk like that?"

Gary grinned broadly and answered, "Just the ones that get drafted." He paused and said, "Do you mind if we fly a little higher on our way back? I don't want any more work on this ship than I already have."

"No problem there, Gary," Eric replied. He turned to his co-pilot and said, "Lieutenant, would you like to fly us back to the airstrip?"

Lt. Skiles took the controls and said, "I'd love to. It'll make me feel like I've done more than pray." He turned toward Dalat and asked, "How does this look for a heading?"

Eric took off his sweat-soaked chest protector and scanned the horizon. He pointed and said, "Steady as she goes, Lieutenant."

Back at the airstrip, Eric shut down the engine and took off his helmet. When he opened his door, one of the soldiers came to the front and said, "Thanks for coming back for us."

"Yeah," Eric said sullenly as he climbed down from his seat. As the man walked away, he mumbled to himself, "If it hadn't been for our screw up, you would have been on board to begin with." He knew there would be some flak over leaving their gear, but luckily, they had carried their weapons and ammo on board. He also knew he could probably kiss this sweet deal goodbye, but with the Army you never knew. He slipped off his flight gloves and angrily threw them into his helmet.

Gary approached with a ladder and said, "It'll only take a few minutes to check the bullet holes. Then I'll take a look at Tony's mike." He pointed at the skids and said, "The remodel job you put on those will have to wait until we get back to the unit."

Five minutes later, Jarvis climbed down from the ladder. "It doesn't look like the bullets hit anything important. Now I'll have a look at that mike."

"Okay, I'll try and find a ride into town," Eric said. Before he left, Eric noticed his co-pilot was busily writing the flight times into the aircraft logbook.

Eric walked to the highway and flagged down a deuce-and-a-half, then asked the driver if he would take him and his crew to the 145th Engineering compound. The driver nodded and Eric walked around to the back of the truck. His legs were still weak as he climbed up and sat on a side-facing bench seat.

Pagliano climbed up and sat on the bench opposite Eric. After lighting a cigarette, Eric threw the pack to Tony, and began to laugh. "Well Pago how did you like that flight?"

Tony caught the pack and said, "I'll tell you what Mr. B. That was one hell of a helicopter ride. It even beat the Cyclone at Coney Island."

"Yeah, I'll bet it did. That must have been some sight for you and Gary, hanging there in your door gunner seats."

"Tell me about it. It scared the hell out of me and I'm fearless." They both laughed the giddy laughter of survivors who had faced death and won.

Pagliano tossed the pack back and looked over his shoulder. When he saw the others were still at the helicopter, he said, "We've got to ditch the lieutenant, or he's going to spoil our fun."

"I know. What do you guys have planned for the night?"

"We thought we'd start at the Steam and Cream, and then try to hustle girls at the college."

Eric smiled as he remembered similar visits to the massage parlor. "Okay, after we get cleaned up, I'll take the lieutenant to the Hotel Dalat. That will give you two enough time to hit the steam bath and get something to eat. When you're done, meet me at the restaurant on top of the hotel. If I get lucky with my girlfriend, I'm going to need you to take the LT off my hands. You can take him back to the barracks and dump him."

"Sounds like a deal," Tony said as the other two approached the truck.

At the Engineer's compound, Eric returned from the showers to find his co-pilot already dressed and sitting on his bed checking his .38 caliber revolver. After slipping the pistol into a shoulder harness, he put on a survival vest to conceal the holster. Eric dried his hair with a towel and said, "Jesus Lieutenant, we're just going into town for dinner, not out on a long-range patrol."

The lieutenant took the pistol out of the holster and held it in front of him.

"I know that, but no gook is going to get the upper hand on Sam Skiles without a fight."

So he does have a first name, Eric thought. He had been calling him Lieutenant all day, hoping Skiles would suggest they use their first names, but he never did.

When Eric was dressed, they walked to the compound gate and waved down an old papa-san in a Lambretta. The man agreed to take them to the Hotel Dalat for a dollar. The pilots climbed into the back of the three-wheeled motorbike then sat speechless as the old man maneuvered the Lambretta wildly through various types of motorized and animal-powered vehicles. The roadway was crowded with motorbikes, Army trucks, buses, Vespas, bicycles, ox-drawn carts and an occasional French sedan.

After several near misses, Eric was relieved to see the hotel come into view. He thanked the man and gave him a dollar in MPC. The bar and restaurant were on the roof of the hotel. Half of the bar was an open veranda overlooking the town market. As they walked to a table by the railing, Eric spotted the girl from his last visit to Dalat.

She wore a sleeveless, black *ao dai* dress cut up the side. Both men admired her long legs as she cleared a table and walked to the bar. The lieutenant said, "She's so tall."

Without taking his eyes off of the girl, Eric said, "She's half French. Wait until you see her face. She's beautiful."

The girl turned around and noticed Eric's wave. She burst into a bright smile and said, "Lieutenant Bader. It's so nice to see you again."

Eric stood and gave her a hug and turned to introduce her to his co-pilot. The lieutenant was still sitting at the table with a befuddled look on his face.

"Kathy, this is Lieutenant Skiles."

The lieutenant quickly stood and shook her hand. "I'm very pleased to meet you." Then into Eric's ear he whispered, "What's this, Lieutenant Bader?"

Eric looked at him and said, "I tried to explain it the last time I was here. Kathy, you remember, I'm a Warrant Officer."

"Yes, I know you officer," she said, tugging at the CW2 bar on his collar. "You Lieutenant, it says so right here." Eric looked at the lieutenant and shrugged.

The girl asked, "What you want to drink? I have to go, I very busy."

"I'll have a bourbon and water," Eric answered.

"Same here," Lt. Skiles said.

When the girl returned with their drinks, Eric asked her, "Do you still get off at eight?"

"Yes," she answered with a worried look. "But I cannot go with you tonight. We go out tomorrow night, okay?"

Eric shook his head and wondered if the day could get any worse. "I won't be here tomorrow night. I thought we could go to dinner tonight."

"That is where I go. To birthday dinner for my sister."

Frustrated, Eric said, "Dinner won't last that long and I only have this night. I could wait for you at your apartment."

The girl looked at the lieutenant and then back at Eric. "Okay, I get my key."

Lt. Skiles asked, "Her name is Kathy?"

"Yeah, I take it you haven't met too many Vietnamese bar girls."

"She's my first."

"They like to use American names. She won't tell me her real name."

The lieutenant paused and said, "I'm sure you must know the Vietnamese word for Warrant Officer."

Eric stared at the lieutenant and said, "Yeah, its *Chun Wi*. What's the point?"

"The point is, you warrants disparage us other officers until it's to your advantage to be mistaken for one. What did you do, conveniently forget the word when you were trying to explain the difference?"

"No, I told her, but it's a military term. She didn't understand it any more than she did the English version."

"And the explanation didn't go any further because you didn't want to sound inferior to the lieutenants and captains she probably dates when you're not here."

Eric studied the lieutenant's face before he said, "Something like that."

Skiles smiled smugly and said, "So the great Eric Bader is human after all."

"What the hell is that supposed to mean, Lieutenant?"

"The way the other pilots talked last night I thought I must be flying with one of the world's greatest aviators."

Eric was getting angry and said, "That was the liquor talking."

"Maybe so, but they still have a lot of respect for you."

"I also have twice the time in-country and three times the missions." After a short pause Eric said sarcastically, "Maybe when you have that much time they'll think the same about you. Hell, who knows, they might even start to like you."

The lieutenant's eyes narrowed as he returned Eric's glare. The two men drank in silence until Kathy returned with more drinks and the key to her apartment. "I leave now. I see you in two hours."

Eric smiled and said, "Okay, have fun."

As they watched her leave, Skiles said, "Are you really going to her place? Alone!"

"That's the idea, Lieutenant."

"Do you realize how many things can happen to you?"

"Right now I can only think of one."

"What if you're attacked on the way? I thought we're supposed to stay together."

42

"We are, but there are some things a guy would like to do without his buddies. Besides, her apartment is just on the other side of the town square. Gary and Tony will be here to get you back to the barracks. Let's order something to eat."

Lieutenant Skiles looked for a menu and asked, "Can you help me order. I haven't eaten outside an Army mess hall since I got to Vietnam."

"Sure, they just have two main dishes. One is a boiled duck with vegetables and rice. The other is a Vietnamese beef noodle soup called *Pho*. It's spelled PHO, but pronounced 'fuh'. That's what I like."

Skiles asked, "What's in it?"

"I wondered that too, so I asked the manager. He's a hustler that goes by the name of Jimmy Hoa. He'll come over when he sees us. He said they boil beef bones with a bag of Vietnamese spices. Then they take the bones and spices out of the water and add rice noodles, thinly sliced beef, charred onions, and ginger, then they simmer it again. Don't look so worried, it's good. Let's get a couple bowls."

An older woman brought the bowls out from the kitchen, followed by a young girl carrying a tray with a bottle of chili sauce and small bowls of cilantro, scallions, and bean sprouts.

The two men had just started eating, when manager Jimmy Hoa entered the bar dressed in a maroon silk shirt and black pants. He saw the two pilots and walked up saying, "Hey Mister Eric, how are you? You have new friend. Where is Mister Paul?"

Eric shook Hoa's hand and said, "Paul isn't on this trip. This is Lieutenant Skiles."

The two men shook hands and Jimmy asked the lieutenant, "How you like my *Pho*?"

Skiles wiped his mouth with a napkin and said, "It is very good. This was the first time I've had it."

Jimmy smiled broadly and said, "Good, good. I know Mister Eric likes it. He has it many times."

Eric asked Hoa, "I've been meaning to ask, where do you get your beef? I haven't seen too many cattle ranches in Vietnam."

Jimmy answered, "No, no beef farms in Vietnam. Here people have cows with … how you say with a rope?"

Eric answered, "Tethered to a stake."

"Yes, the cows are tethered in back of houses." Hoa pointed at the bowls and said, "This is special beef. I was in Saigon and bought beef from Australia."

Skiles asked Eric, "Didn't I read where the Aussies got caught adding kangaroo meat to their beef exports?"

Jimmy Hoa chuckled nervously, and said, "Not so here. No kangaroo meat in my food, only number one beef."

Eric looked at Hoa and said, "I don't know Jimmy. I think I saw a couple of chunks trying to jump out of my bowl."

Jimmy laughed loudly and said, "That good joke, Mister Eric. You funny man."

Gary and Tony arrived as the two pilots were finishing their meal. Eric welcomed them and then bid the lieutenant goodbye before grabbing his bag and leaving the hotel. He walked through the deserted market place with its lingering smells of rotting fruit and vegetables. Past the square, he walked down a narrow passageway and climbed a rickety wooden staircase to Kathy's apartment.

The room was small, but tastefully decorated with rice mats and bamboo curtains. A bird fluttered excitedly in a small wooden cage as he walked around the room. There wasn't a refrigerator, so he looked for the Coleman cooler Kathy used instead. Inside, three cans of Budweiser floated in warm water.

They're not cold, he thought, but at least they're American. Probably left by one of the real live officers the lieutenant was talking about. He opened the can and remembered a bottle of brandy he had bought at the PX. He took the bottle out of his overnight bag and placed it on a counter next to a picture of Kathy and a Vietnamese girl.

He turned on a small lamp and tried to read the inscription written across the bottom. He thought it probably said, "To Lien, with Love, Mai." So her name was Li, he thought as he looked at the picture and marveled at how pretty she was. If she were anywhere else she could be a model.

He sipped his beer and looked at the bottle of Courvoisier. The last time he was in Dalat he had asked if he could bring her something. A bottle of French brandy was what she had requested. He wondered if it was some kind of link to her lost father. She had grown up an outcast in her own country. They were called "Dust Children" because most of them lived on the street. He was taking a prophylactic out of his overnight bag when he heard a soft knock.

He opened the door and said, "Hello Lien. How was your dinner?"

The girl looked surprised and asked, "How you know my name?"

Eric pointed at the picture. "Is Mai your sister?"

"Yes," she answered defensively.

Eric walked to the picture and said, "She is very pretty, but not as beautiful as you."

"Oh no, she is much more pretty than me," Li protested.

"She may be to some people, but not to me. You also have a nice name. Why do you use an American name when you have such a pretty Vietnamese name?"

"All the girls have American names."

"So I've noticed," Eric said as he crossed the room and picked up the bottle of Courvoisier. "I brought this for you. Do you want some?"

"Not now, thank you." Li went to the counter and lit a josh stick and some candles.

"Did another soldier help you with the name Kathy?"

"Yes, it was old boy friend," she answered as she lowered her eyes.

"Am I a boy friend?"

Li looked up and said, "Yes, you numbah one boy friend. You be only boy friend you here more."

Eric laughed and thought that he couldn't ask for much more than that. He sat on a thin mattress and muttered, "The way things went today, I could be here a lot less."

With a quizzical look, Li asked, "What you say?"

"Oh, nothing," he answered.

She sat next to him and asked, "Last time you here, your friends all the time call you Bad Dog or Mad Dog. What that mean? I know mad,

45

and I know dog and you not angry dog."

Eric laughed and said, "Pilots have other names like you girls."

"But what that mean?" Li asked again.

"It means crazy. You know *dinky-dow*."

Li giggled and said, "You not *dien cai dau*."

He pulled her down and kissed her. "Yes I am, I'm *dinky-dow* about you."

After they made love, Li fell asleep with her head on Eric's chest. Her soft breathing and the smell of jasmine in her hair soothed him. He fell asleep thinking he had been in-country too long. He was starting to like it.

At dawn he was awakened by the singing of the little bird in the wooden cage. He thought he could get used to this--waking next to a beautiful woman and a bird singing. There were other things he would like to do that day, like a walk with Li along the lake and then lunch at a waterfront café. The types of things lovers did elsewhere in the world. Instead, he raised himself onto his left elbow and whispered, "I have to go."

"I know," Li answered softly, pulling his head down and kissing him.

He kissed her back and said, "Maybe I can stay a little longer."

Thirty minutes later, he left her apartment and walked across the street to the market. He found an old woman setting up a fruit stand and bought two bananas. Next he found another woman selling fresh bread and sweet rolls. He picked out a roll and then hired another papa-san to take him back to the Engineer's compound.

As he rode in the open-air cyclo, he ate the roll and thought about Li. He wished he could stay a week. He thought of taking her to Paris. There were a hundred things he wanted to do. Flying to a grass-covered hill, where Charlie Cong was waiting to blow him into another lifetime, wasn't on the list.

The delivery of the eight Green Berets to a new LZ was uneventful, and a light rain began to fall as Eric reluctantly turned toward Ninh Hoa. Back at his home base, he realized the heat of the coastal lowlands was even more oppressive after being in the relative cool of the mountains.

He climbed the stairs to the barracks, and wondered if he would ever see Li again. Probably not.

As he approached the barracks, he noticed a yellow short-haired dog get up from in front of his room. Eric reached down to pet him and said, "Where'd you come from little fella?" The dog had the face of a Lab, a muscular body and a tail that curved toward its head.

Eric opened the door and held it for the dog. When they entered the room, Paul said, "Well if it isn't the Dalat Kid. How'd things go?"

Eric threw his gear on the floor and said, "It could have been better. Dalat was as good as ever, but the flying got all dicked up. I doubt if I'll be going back there again."

"What happened?"

"The stupid ass co-pilot I was flying with almost got us killed. I'll tell you about it later. What's the story on the dog? He looks like he's made himself at home."

"Yeah, I picked him up yesterday. I was inserting troops into a jungle opening when I saw this yellow head come bounding at me in the grass. I wasn't sure what it was at first, but through all the noise and rotor wash, this little guy runs right up to the ship and jumps in. Then he plants himself in the middle of the deck and looks at me as if to say, I'm getting the hell out of here. Apparently somebody had taken him into the bush on a chopper and he figured he was getting out on one. I call him Jungle Dog."

"Good name," Eric said petting their new pet. "I think he's a good addition to the hooch, but we'll have to feed him scraps from the mess hall. I haven't seen any Alpo at the PX."

Eric was about to ask Paul if anything else had happened, when the screen door opened and their next door neighbor walked in carrying a small cooler. Tucker Burdett pointed at the dog and asked, "Where'd you get him?"

Paul petted his dog and said, "I found him out in the field, or maybe you could say he found me. His name is Jungle Dog."

Burdett opened a folding chair and said, "That suits him." He reached into the cooler and said, "I'm back from Saigon and thought you guys might enjoy the best beer in the Orient." He produced two icy bottles of San Miguel and offered them to his friends.

Eric took a bottle and asked, "What were you doing in Saigon?"

"I had to get one of our ships out of maintenance and do a little business for the CO. Of course I had to do a little business for myself." Burdett got up and walked toward the door. "I've got something to show you guys."

He returned with an AK-47 assault rifle. "I bought four of these at twenty bucks a pop. I also picked up six M-16s for four dollars each if you guys want one."

Eric took the AK and examined it. "Isn't that great, an enemy rifle goes for twenty dollars on the black market and one of ours only costs four."

Paul took the rifle from Eric and put it up to his shoulder. "That's because you have to kill a VC to get his rifle. All you have to do to get a case of M-16s is bribe the right Vietnamese supply sergeant."

Burdett took the rifle and said, "That's true, but it wasn't me who did the bribing. I'm only the middle man."

Eric wiped the beer bottle across his forehead and asked, "What are you going to do with them?"

"I'll sell the Mattie Mattels to our own guys for cost and then dump the AKs on some REMFs at Cam Rahn Bay for two hundred bucks each."

Paul took a sip of beer and said, "That's a pretty good profit, Tuck. What do those guys think they're going to do with them? They can't take them home."

Burdett grinned and said, "You guys know that and I know that, but those dumb fucks don't know that."

They all laughed and Burdett said, "What a war, huh? I think I'm actually going to miss it. I only have four more months and then I'm out of here. After a month at home I'll be moving to an island in Indonesia to start a helicopter operation. I'm going to need a few good pilots and you two are on the top of my list."

Eric started to protest and Burdett cut him off. "I know you two are going to Europe when you leave here, but what will you do after a winter of skiing?"

Eric was about to answer, when his co-pilot, Tom Paris, opened the screen door. "Hey guys, four newbies just got in and they're already in the club. Shooter's about to start with the Blue Star specials, so we'd better get down there."

Burdett stood and said, "Keep the beers, there are more where those came from. We still need to talk about what you're going to do after next winter."

The four pilots walked out to the sound of crying coming from the room next door. Paul put out his arm and said, "Hold on. I've got to jack up those dickheads." He walked to their screen door and yelled, "Buck up in there you wienies. There's a war going on out here and you're going to get greased if you don't toughen up."

He rejoined the others and asked, "How in the hell did those three goofballs make it through flight school? The way they were flipping guys when I went through, I was lucky to graduate. They must have lowered their standards."

The Officers' Club at the 48th Assault Helicopter Company was one of the best in South Vietnam, with a mahogany bar and mirror that ran the length of the bar. The club was run by a pretty Vietnamese woman the pilots nicknamed Baby-San because they couldn't pronounce her real name. All the men knew that she and the other barmaids were off limits, no matter how much they may have wanted to take them back to their rooms.

When the four friends entered the club, Clay Boone was holding court with the new pilots lined up with their backs against the bar. A dozen veteran pilots stood around the bar waiting for the show to begin. Baby-San was conspicuously absent because she hated participating in the Blue Star specials. Behind the bar was a Gunnie named Little Eli Asarian.

Clay Boone explained that Little Eli was going to build four identical drinks made up of a shot from every bottle behind the bar: vodka, gin, bourbon and rum, topped off with a shot of crème de menthe to make it more palatable. In the past, most of the men who were able to get the drink down ran out of the bar and threw up.

There was an opening in the gunship platoon, so Boone was appraising the applicants. One of the new pilots was his size. He stopped in front of the man and said, "You look like you'd make a good Gunnie. Do you have anything against being in a gunship?"

The new pilot answered in an assured voice, "No, I thought you'd put me where I'll fit in best."

"I think you'll fit right into a gunship. You look like a tough guy and we like tough guys in the guns." Boone extended his hand and said, "I'm Clay Boone. My guys call me Shooter."

The pilot shook his new unit leader's hand and replied, "Good to meet you Shooter. My name is John Lambi."

"Lambi, what kind of a name is that?" Boone asked. " Have you ever been called namby-pamby, Lambi?" The bar erupted in laughter, and Boone grinned toward the crowd.

Lambi waited until Boone turned back to him and answered, "Not that I can remember. If they did, they only did it once."

With a nervous laugh, Boone said, "Yeah, I suppose so. You look like you may have played some ball, Lambi. Did you play college football?"

"I was a starting offensive guard for Colorado State."

"Colorado!" Boone said, excitedly. "That makes it easy for me to come up with a call sign. You look like a Buffalo and it has a nice Gunnie ring."

Lambi shook his head and said, "I hate the Buffalos. They were at Colorado U, our arch rivals at State."

Boone waited for the ooohs and ahhs to die down before he asked, "What were you called at your school?"

"We were the Rams."

Clay Boone shook his head and said, "No, Ram doesn't do it for me. Listen Lambi, I need to explain something. This is not a democracy. This is the U.S. Army and I'm in charge. What I say goes and it doesn't matter what you want. I like the name Buff, so that's your call sign, okay?"

Lambi smiled for the first time and said, "Now that you've explained it, I can live with Buff."

Shooter patted his new pilot on the shoulder and said, "That's more like it. You're smart Lambi. You'll be a good Gunnie."

Boone pointed at the crowd and continued, "We all have call signs so Charlie doesn't know who's flying our helicopters, especially if one gets shot down. Hell, I've named every Gunnie in here. I've even named a few Slick pilots, but I usually don't give a shit what they're called."

Boone pointed at the pilot closest to him. "Take Dan 'Mako' Sharkey here. His name was a no brainer. Next to him, is my main man, Pete 'Boss Man' Barnes. He and I started as Gunnies over two years ago. We keep extending our tours because we don't have anything else to do. Then there's James 'Slyde' Cornelius, one of the few Gunnies with a college degree. After he graduated in music, he got a cushy job in an Army band playing the trombone. With only three months left in his enlistment, he decided he wanted to fly helicopters. So what did the crazy son of a bitch do, he signs up for flight school. I had to pick a guy with balls like that for the guns."

Boone moved down the line of pilots. "Now, here we have Tucker Burdett. He's one of the few Slickies I named. His call sign is 'Friar Tuck,' but most of us call him Tucker, because some day he's going to own a helicopter company in Indonesia and we might want to fly for him."

He pointed to the back of the room where two young pilots sat alone. "Back there are two of the toughest guys you are going to meet. I call them Sphinx and Zombie. They don't say much. They just sit there drinking and staring like two twenty year-old assassins. For R & R they wanted to go out on a Long Range Reconnaissance Patrol. The Army said no, so they went to Bangkok and got laid instead."

Boone turned around and pointed at the bartender. "Then there's my good buddy, Little Eli here. He's only five-seven, but he's tougher than six Slick pilots. He grew up in Fresno, where he spent most of his youth either playing pool, or boxing in a gym. All that time earned him a state billiards championship and he got pretty far in the Golden Gloves, didn't you Eli?"

Eli shook his head. "It wasn't far enough Shooter, and I was only city eight-ball champ."

Boone nodded in appreciation and said, "That's good enough for me. He's also undefeated on our pool table here in the bar." Boone pointed at the bottles behind the bar and said, "That's enough talk, it's time for drinking. Eli, start mixing the Blue Star specials. These newbies look thirsty."

Little Eli placed four plastic glasses on the bar and poured a shot from each of the liquor bottles into the glasses. With a flourish, he floated an ounce of crème de menthe on top, then stirred the drinks. Boone picked up a glass and handed it to the first pilot in line. "Okay cherry, down the hatch. If you don't drink this, you will be catching shit from me for the rest of your life."

The worried pilot tried to get the drink down in one try, but came up short. Wincing, he tried again. When he finished, the young man ran for the door as the crowd booed.

The next pilot picked up a glass and was able to get the drink down. He tried to stay in the bar, but soon ran for the door. Before he could make it, he vomited on the floor to jeers from the crowd. The third pilot had the same result as the first.

That left John Lambi confidently standing at the bar with his drink in his hand. He took a large swig, wiped his mustache and set the glass on the bar. As the crowd waited in anticipation, Lambi said, "Not a bad concoction Shooter. I'll drink it, but not all at once. Hell, I drink that much booze in a night, anyway."

Boone turned toward the crowd and said, "That's why I like this guy. I told you he was smart." He patted his new pilot on the back and said, "Welcome to the Jokers, Lambi. I'm going to train you myself."

Little Eli got Boone's attention and said, "Shooter, remember what the CO said about our gunships going out so heavy. He doesn't want any more big guys in the guns. He'll go ape shit when he hears you two are flying together."

Boone waved off the comment and said, "Screw the Old Man. I'm running the guns and if I say I'm going to train this guy, I'm going to do it. Tell the Major I'll take off a couple of rockets to lighten the load. You know I'm such a good shot I don't need all of them anyway."

When the laughter died down, Boone said, "Eli, go get Baby-san. We need some real drinks in here and the first round is on me."

Two weeks after the Blue Star Special initiation, Eric watched as four sweaty infantrymen loaded his helicopter with supplies. He and Tom Paris were flying food and ammunition to outposts surrounding the Phan Rang Air Force Base. The weather was clear and the flying had been uneventful. It was one of those light duty days the pilots relished.

They were about to leave on their last trip of the day when an infantry captain ran up to the helicopter and yelled over the rotor noise, "You've got to unload this stuff. I've got an emergency. One of my patrols just tripped a booby trap and a medivac is too far away. I need you to pick them up and get them to a hospital, fast. I'll go along and show you where they are."

Eric motioned to his door gunners and they began throwing the supplies from the ship. The captain climbed on board and thrust a map between the two pilots. "They're right here. They say there are two KIAs and three wounded. I'd like to get them all out on one trip."

Eric yelled, "We can do that."

When the ship was unloaded, the crew chief gave the infantry captain a flight helmet connected to the ship's intercom system. After takeoff, Eric turned to the captain and asked, "Are they taking enemy fire?"

The captain shook his head. "No, they say it was a Claymore set to go off waist high."

Eric winced and said, "Oh shit."

The captain furrowed his brow and said, "Yeah, they say the wounded are in pretty bad shape."

A Claymore was a powerful crescent-shaped mine with a long detonator cord, designed to explode forward, used by the infantry to secure their night defensive positions. If the soldiers were attacked and in danger of being overrun they would deploy the Claymores, sending hundreds of pellets toward the advancing enemy. Unfortunately, some of the unexploded mines had been captured by the Viet Cong and were being used against American forces as booby traps.

53

Eric asked the captain, "Where do you want us to take them, Sir?"

"The hospital at Phan Rang Air Base is the closest. I had my company call them so they're expecting us."

Eric clicked his mike button twice to signify he understood. He could see the clearing and was already starting his approach. The dead and wounded were laid out on top of their rain ponchos. Eric turned to his co-pilot. "You better brace yourself, Tom. This is going to be ugly."

When they were on the ground, the captain and Pagliano jumped out to help load the bodies. Eric watched through his cockpit window. The last man to be lifted into the ship weakly raised his right hand and waved a peace sign to his comrades.

The captain and door gunner climbed back onboard and Eric took off for the Air Base. Even with the doors open the ship was soon filled with the metallic smell of fresh blood. When he leveled off, Eric could hear a banging coming from the rear of the ship. The severity of the wounded had unnerved him and the sound was grating on his nerves. He yelled to his crew chief, "Gary, find out what's causing that goddamn banging."

Moments later it stopped and Gary said, "I found out what was making that racket, Mr. B. This guy's arm was hanging out the door." Eric turned to look toward the back. The man's hand had been completely severed from his arm and was dangling by a tendon. Eric winced and looked at Paris who was staring at Gary and the man's hand.

They both turned to the front and Eric called the Air Base. He had never been there, so he asked the tower for assistance in finding the hospital. The tower quickly directed him to the helipad and cleared him to land. When he started his approach, a large crowd rushed from the hospital. Most of the doctors and nurses loaded the wounded onto gurneys and rushed them toward the hospital. It was unusual for an Air Force hospital to have a helicopter full of wounded and dead landing at their helipad, so some of the bystanders began taking pictures. The four man helicopter crew was dumbfounded.

The infantry captain jumped out and yelled, "Keep it going. I'll be right back."

Eric watched the group enter the hospital. "Christ, look at those people," he said, exasperated. "I don't think they've ever had a medivac in here before."

"At least not one this bad," Paris added.

One of those with a camera was a stocky nurse who continued to snap pictures as she followed the others, and then returned to take pictures of the bloody helicopter deck.

As the aircrew waited in the idling helicopter, Paris said, "Get a load of this. She must not have gotten enough gore the first time around."

"I don't believe this shit," Eric said.

The captain ran out of the hospital and climbed on board as the nurse maneuvered for another picture. He yelled that he wanted to go back to his base camp and then slumped on the back seat, not bothering to put on the flight helmet. He leaned back and closed his eyes, fighting back tears.

Eric barked to Paris, "Get us a takeoff clearance."

Paris called the tower and then pointed out the window. "Don't you think we better warn Big Nurse?"

Eric shook his head and pulled in pitch for takeoff. When Paris realized what he was doing, he said, "Oh no, don't do it Dog. You're going to get us in trouble."

The downwash whipped up the nurse's skirt as she ran bent forward toward the hospital.

When she was clear, Eric made a maximum performance take off. As they climbed out of the area, Paris looked down at the nurse who was glaring at the departing helicopter. He turned to the front and said, "You've done it this time, Dog."

Eric feigned surprise and said, "Why's that, Frenchie?" He glanced toward the back and asked his two door gunners, "Did you guys see a nurse out there?"

Both men shook their heads, and Gary said, "Why would a nurse be outside with all those wounded inside?"

"That's what I thought," Eric said, and looked at his co-pilot.

Paris turned to his Aircraft Commander and said, "Okay, I didn't see anyone out there either."

The sun was about to set when Eric and Paris returned to their base. As they left the flight line they were told a boxing match was taking place near the volleyball court. They climbed the steps to the upper area and saw that the bleachers were filled with a cheering crowd.

Someone had used the volleyball net and a rope to form a makeshift boxing ring. They added sand from the volleyball court to soften the fall of anyone knocked down.

As the two men approached, Paul met them and said, "You guys need to avoid this goat rope. Get up in the bleachers and hide out. Shooter and Little Eli have organized a tournament. Last man standing is the winner. Eli just got back from Sydney where he bought new boxing gloves. He and Boone say they are disqualified because of previous boxing experience, so they each put up fifty bucks for prize money. The winner gets seventy-five dollars and the runner up twenty-five."

Eric asked, "Have you been in it?"

Paul frowned at his roommate and asked, "Are you kidding? I told Boone I was too good-looking to get involved in a boxing match, so I'm corner man for the Slickies. My co-pilot Nick Bookman is up next against Sharkey's co-pilot Jay Norse. Boone and Eli have been trying to go with Gunnie against Slickie. The winner keeps moving on until he loses."

The two combatants climbed into the ring with Little Eli who wore a white shirt and a black bow tie to play the part of referee. Eli explained the rules. "Listen guys, I want this to look like a boxing match and not grab-ass wrestling. No hitting below the waist and when I say break, I want you to break. Is that understood?"

The two pilots nodded and touched gloves. The bell rang and they began throwing punches, to the cheers of the crowd.

Paul reached into a cooler and grabbed two beers. "Here, take these to the bleachers. I've got to get back to my corner."

The round ended with the timer banging a frying pan with a hammer. Eric and Paris watched from the side of the bleachers as Paul placed a chair in Bookman's corner and said, "Good job Bookie. You're looking good. You can take this guy. He's tired from his last match and the heat's getting to him. I noticed he's starting to let his right hand down and he doesn't know you're a lefty. The next time he lowers it, pop him with a hard left jab."

Bookman nodded as Paul poured water from a canteen into his mouth and over his head. The two boxers stood and walked to the center of the ring. Little Eli started the round and the two boxers began swinging. Most of the time they were just hitting each other's gloves, but then it looked like Norse's right hand was starting to weigh a ton. He let it down long enough for Bookman to hit him on the jaw. Norse lost his balance and fell onto his back. Eli counted him out as he rolled over onto his hands and knees.

Nick Bookman lasted through two more opponents, before he was knocked down and was too exhausted to get up. A dozen matches later, Dan Sharkey was becoming the favorite. At six foot four, Sharkey was the tallest man in the company with the longest reach. During his first five matches, no one had laid a glove on him.

Boone had saved Pete Barnes to be Sharkey's final opponent. Barnes was tough, but was two inches shorter than Sharkey and didn't have the reach. During the third round, Barnes fell victim to one of Sharkey's sharp punches.

Boone was about to crown Sharkey the victor, but decided to look over the crowd to see if there was anyone he had missed. When he spied Eric, he yelled, "Hey Dog, come here. We need to see if a Slickie can take Mako."

Eric started to protest, but the crowd began chanting, "Go Dog, Go Dog." He realized he didn't have a choice and walked to the side of the ring and took off his shirt. Paul put the gloves on him and said, "Look, this guy is good, but he's also been in this heat for almost an hour. He has to be tired. It's just a matter of time before he lets his guard down and you can pop him like Bookman hit Norse."

Paul put a canteen up to Eric's mouth. "Drink this so you stay hydrated. You can take this guy and then we'll have seventy-five bucks for a party. Just stay away from him until you see an opening. When you do, hit him with all you've got."

Bader eyed Sharkey on the other side of the ring and said, "All I'm worried about is how to keep from getting killed."

Paul ignored the comment and said, "Go out and wear him down."

The round began with Eric moving around the ring doing his best imitation of Muhammad Ali's float like a butterfly dance. Sharkey soon grew tired of the performance and moved in to close it out. A flurry of Sharkey's punches hit Eric's gloves and stomach. The round ended to cheers.

When Eric was seated, Paul poured water on top of his head and said, "You looked good out there, Dog. Those last punches must have tired him out. He won't last much longer."

Eric panted and said, "I hope so because this is a lot harder than it looks. What do you want me to do, let him keep pounding me, so it will wear him out?"

"Yeah, that's exactly what I mean."

Eric nodded and walked to the middle of the ring. The second round started with Sharkey moving in with another volley of jabs. Eric danced away and then moved in to throw punches to Sharkey's midsection. When Eric backed off, Sharkey threw a hard punch that Eric was able to duck and then land a left jab to Sharkey's jaw. The round ended to more cheers.

Paul poured water into Eric's mouth and said, "Nice shot, man. That's what I was talking about. He's slowing down, so this is the round you nail him."

Eric spit the water out and said, "Do you know how heavy these fucking gloves are? It feels like I've got ten-pound weights tied to my arms."

Paul poured water over Eric's head and said, "Just think how heavy Sharkey's gloves must feel. This has to be his twelfth round. It's only your third, so go get him."

The round started with Sharkey landing several jabs to Eric's stomach. Eric moved away and danced around until he saw Sharkey let his left glove down. He moved in and hit him on the jaw with a hard right jab. Sharkey staggered back and landed on his butt. It was the first time he had been knocked down and the crowd cheered wildly. He quickly rolled onto one knee and remained kneeling until Little Eli counted to seven. Sharkey jumped to his feet before the count of ten and stared angrily at his opponent. The round ended with Eric thinking he was looking into the eyes of an angry shark searching for a kill.

Paul planted a chair at his corner and said, "Way to go, man. I knew you could take him and now you've got him."

Eric sat on the stool and shook his head. "I don't think so. You didn't see the look in his eyes. Now he's pissed off and he's really going to come after me." Eric swallowed water from the canteen and pointed across the ring. "Look at Boone over there. I'm sure he's telling Sharkey it's time to finish this thing."

Paul poured water over Eric's head and said, "I'm sure he is, but it's going to be *you* who does it. He'll let his guard down again and then you hit him."

Eric rose from the chair and said, "I'll give it my best shot."

The fourth round started with Eric trying to stay away from Sharkey as long as he could. When his opponent moved in, Eric put up his gloves and moved from side to side looking for an opening, but there was none. With a menacing look, Sharkey moved in with another volley of quick jabs. One of the punches reached around Eric's left ear and flicked him on the head.

Eric didn't know what hit him. The next thing he saw was sand coming up to meet his face. He tried to use his arms to break his fall, but they wouldn't move. Before he hit the ground he thought, this is going to hurt.

He was awakened by the acrid scent of ammonia. A medic knelt next to him waving smelling salts. Paul was on his other side slapping his face and saying, "Wake up, Dog."

When he was conscious, the medic and Paul helped him to a sitting position. Clay Boone stood in the middle of the ring telling the crowd he was going to award second place to Bader because he was the only one to lay a glove on Sharkey.

Paul and the medic helped Eric to his feet and Boone moved between the two combatants and raised their arms. The crowd was still hooting as a crew chief named Clarence Hilton entered the ring with a Polaroid camera. Hilton motioned for them to move closer and yelled, "We need a picture."

Sharkey was on the right, Boone was to his left and Eric was between him and Little Eli. Eric fought the urge to vomit as Hilton said, "We need two more pictures, one for each boxer and one to hang in the mess hall."

When the picture taking was finished, Eason and Paris helped Eric leave the ring. Paul asked his roommate, "How are you doing?"

Eric answered, "Get me out of here, I think I'm going to hurl."

Paul wiped Eric's face with a wet towel and said, "You were looking real good, man. I thought you had him."

Eric stumbled and said, "I thought so too, right up to the point where I went to wipe sand off my face and discovered it was the ground."

Paul laughed and said, "I think a famous author said that, but you said it better." As they walked into the latrine, Paul said, "A shower will fix you up and you'll be good as new."

Eric turned on the water and said, "I don't think so."

After the shower and some fresh clothes, Eric felt well enough to accompany Eason and Paris to the club. When they entered the bar, Eric was greeted by cheers. He noticed Sharkey moving toward him and wondered what the tall gunship pilot would say.

Sharkey extended his hand and said, "Nice job, Dog. You put up a good fight. I felt those punches you threw."

Eric shook his hand and said, "Thanks Mako, that was a sneaky punch you hit me with."

Sharkey laughed and said, "I didn't even know what I did. I was surprised when you went down."

Eric turned to the others that were gathered around and said, "I'm here to tell you, if any of you think Sonny Liston took a dive in the second fight with Muhammad Ali, you're wrong. They said Muhammad clipped him behind his left ear with a right jab. That's exactly how Mako hit me and it was lights out."

While the other pilots discussed the matter, Clarence Hilton approached with pictures and handed one to Eric and Sharkey. Eric smiled at the picture and showed his roommate. Paul laughed and said, "You look like shit. You're covered from head to toe with sand."

Eric grabbed the photo and said, "If you think I looked bad, I *felt* even worse." He moved away saying, "Where's Boone? He owes me twenty-five bucks for coming in second."

The next day Eric sat in his helicopter with a throbbing headache. He was just outside the village of Khanh Dong where a stray mortar shell had wiped out one of the town's wells. Four infantrymen unloaded fifty-five gallon drums from his ship. The drums had been loaded with a fork lift, but these men didn't have that advantage as they unloaded the barrels onto the bed of an old Datsun pickup. Eric was flying in potable water to tide the village over while Army engineers repaired the well.

During the unloading process, a teenage boy approached the helicopter with a piece of paper. Eric turned to Paris and said, "What do you think that kid wants?"

The boy handed Eric a note through his open cockpit door and then saluted before walking back toward the village.

Eric read the note and laughed. He passed it to his co-pilot who laughed and asked, "Are you going to do it?"

"Sure, why not? He seems like a good kid. He's obviously been studying English."

When Eric finished flying and returned to his room, Paul was drinking beer and listening to Jimi Hendrix on their Akai reel to reel tape player. Hendrix was singing "All along the watch tower." Eric stowed his gear and asked, "Does it get any better than Jimi doing a Bob Dylan song?"

Paul smiled and said, "If there is, I haven't heard it. How was your day?"

"It was like having a day off. We spent the day hauling fifty-five gallon drums of water to the village of Khanh Dong." He took the note from a shirt pocket and handed it to his roommate. "This was the only interesting part of the day. A teenage boy gave it to me."

Paul took the note and read:

Dear Mr. Pilot,

How are you? Thank you very much for carrying drums of water for us. By the way, I want to make a scrap book, so I need Playboys where the pictures are. Would you mind taking me the magazines so soon as possible? If you can do, I will give you C-rations and I have a sister who is going to run for a beauty contest. How about keeping company with her? Now my name is Thanh Van Dieu. Please get in touch so soon as possible.

Sincerely,

Thanh Van Dieu

Paul chuckled and asked, "Are you going to give him a couple?"

Eric took the note and said, "Yeah, he looked like an okay kid and the articles will help with his English."

"Yeah right, I'm sure that's what he has in mind," Paul said. "The kid is also pimping his sister."

Eric laughed. "Like I'm going to get to meet her. I figure it's my way of helping the war effort. If the kid sees what capitalism looks like, he may not become a Viet Cong."

Paul smiled. "I'm sure Hugh Hefner will be happy to hear he's doing his part in this war."

The next afternoon, most of the flight crews returned early ahead of a massive thunderstorm. With so many pilots in camp, they decided to have a volleyball game. Many of the players stripped to their shorts and bare feet, while others took off their shirts and played in pants and boots.

The games were supposed to be played by traditional rules, but usually denigrated into jungle ball. This time the games were a revenge match between the Jokers and Slickies. The Slick pilots were about to win the third and final game, when a heavy rain drove everyone for cover. Eric and Paul ran for their room and were toweling off when there was a knock on their screen door.

Paul yelled, "Come in," and a short Specialist 4th class with a Nikon camera strapped around his neck entered the room and asked, "Are either of you Eric Bader?"

Eric appraised the kid and said, "That would be me."

The young man said eagerly, "Mr. Bader, I just came from the first sergeant's office and he told me you're the officer in charge of athletics and recreation."

"That's true, what do you need?"

"I think our company needs a photography club. I used to work in my dad's photo store, so I know how to develop film. If I had a darkroom, I could teach other guys how to do it. Do you think we could get one?"

Eric glanced at Paul before answering. "Listen, I've been in charge of athletics and recreation for more than a year and I haven't had anybody ask about a photography club. I don't think we need to go to the expense of a darkroom for only one guy."

The specialist protested, "The first sergeant said he would approve it and I'm thinking once I get it set up, other guys will want to learn how to use it."

Eric sighed and said, "Okay, I'll see what I can do. What's your name and where do you work?"

"My name is James Newton and I work in the commo bunker. I'm a radio specialist. The guys I work with call me Neutron."

Eric put his hand on Newton's shoulder and walked him to the door. "Okay Neutron, I'll talk with the first sarge and see what we can do for you."

When the Spec 4 was gone, Paul said, "You've got a live one there, Pal."

Eric looked out the screen door and said, "Yeah, as if I don't have enough to do, now I have to deal with that guy." He opened the door and said, "I better find out what Top told him."

First Sergeant Harold Andrews was one of the most competent men

63

Eric had met in the Army. He commanded the respect of everyone, whether above or below him in rank. He had been too young to serve in World War II, but was stationed in Japan during the Occupation and had married a Japanese woman. When the Korean conflict erupted, he was one of the first to volunteer for combat and had come home highly decorated.

He made a career in the Army and was on his second tour in Vietnam. He and Eric had become friends when they discovered they were fellow Arizonans. Eric knocked on his office screen door and said, "Good afternoon Top. How are things going?"

Andrews looked up from his desk, and said, "Not too bad Eric. Come in and sit down. I suppose you're here to talk about Specialist Newton."

Eric sat on a gray folding chair and said, "Yeah, I thought I better hear what you told him. Did you authorize a darkroom?"

"Yes, if he can find one. In exchange, I told him he would have to run the movie projector. I know how much you hate that job. I also told him I would send him to a three day course on projector maintenance."

"That sounds good to me, Top. I really would like to get rid of that responsibility. Don't send him before Saturday though. We have a John Wayne western and I'd like to get him familiar with our projector."

"Okay, I'll send him next week. Maybe he can pick up a newer model when he's at the school."

Eric stood and said, "Good idea, let's talk more when he gets back."

The following Saturday Eric was showing his new charge where to place the movie projector when Newton asked, "Mr. Bader, when I get my darkroom, do you think I could go out on some flights with you? I'd like to get some action pictures and try to sell them to a magazine."

Eric didn't respond and Newton continued the questioning. "Would I be able to fly the helicopter? I've always wanted to see what that's like. I was going to apply for flight school, but my mother sent me to a psychologist when I was in high school. I was having behavioral problems and I thought that would probably wash me out of flight training."

Eric thought there were a few other issues that would have washed him out, but he didn't tell him. He opened the door to the storage shed and said, "Sorry Neutron, but only authorized personnel can ride in a mission helicopter. On the other hand, when you go to Saigon you'll probably be riding in one of our transport helicopters and you can take pictures then."

"Oh yeah, I'll do that. Thanks, Mr. Bader."

"Good, give me a hand with this sheet of plywood. We need to hang it white-side out on an outside wall of the O Club."

Twenty minutes later, the film had been loaded and was ready for viewing. While the audience took their seats, Eric pulled Newton aside. "I want to warn you--these guys have been drinking and will get a little rowdy when the film breaks. They'll also probably call you nasty names, but don't let that bother you."

Newton looked worried and said, "Okay, I'll try and fix the film as fast as I can."

Eric slapped him on the shoulder and said, "That's what I want to hear, now let's get this show started."

The film ran fine for thirty minutes before the screen turned brown and the movie stopped. The crowd jeered and began throwing beer cans at the wall. Newton hurriedly began to splice the film as the viewers left to buy more drinks. It was spliced in five minutes and the movie resumed with Indians attacking a line of covered wagons. After several minutes, the Indians stopped their attack and regrouped on top of a hill. During a close up of the Indians, two loud thuds were heard followed by laughter when the crowd noticed two arrows stuck in the wood screen. The Indians resumed their attack and two more arrows hit the board. Eric joined in the laughter as he remembered two crew chiefs had checked out archery equipment the day before. He removed the arrows and the film ran without incident for the rest of the night.

The following week was uneventful until one morning Eric walked toward the revetments and saw his crew chief on a ladder looking into the engine compartment of his helicopter. Eric shouted, "Do we have a problem Gary?"

Jarvis looked at Eric and said, "Yeah, the fuel pump is leaking. It's going to take at least two hours to change."

Eric dropped his flight gear and said, "Okay, I'll see what Operations wants us to do."

Ten minutes later he returned and said, "I've been assigned another helicopter. I'm supposed to take Tom and Pago and another door gunner, so you can keep working on this ship. They may send you out with another crew when this ship is ready. Copeland and Hurst just got back from R & R, so it will probably be them. I told Operations this is not a permanent situation."

Gary waved a wrench and said, "Thanks Mr. B. I don't want us to get split up either. I'll see you tomorrow."

Eric took off and headed for the Dau River Valley to participate in an assault near the town of Son Hoa. After he landed he was informed that he was being held in reserve along with three other ships. Paul was there lounging with a squad of infantry troopers who had made sun shelters out of their rain ponchos and bamboo poles.

Eric spotted his roommate and joined him under the makeshift tent. After reading and napping for an hour, a flight of six Hueys came into the staging area to pick up more troops. When the soldiers were loaded, the flight lifted off of the dusty airstrip blowing jet fuel exhaust fumes through the area.

Paul coughed and said, "You know Dog, I always wanted to fly jets. Somehow this isn't what I had in mind." Eric chuckled and went back to his novel. It was too hot to talk.

Within the hour, the Dustoff medical evacuation helicopter departed and flew in the direction of the assault. An infantry sergeant yelled, "We better get ready. They must be taking casualties."

While they waited, the only call that came was to announce the return of the first sortie. After the helicopters shut down, a pilot named Ron Koss spotted Eric and Paul under the tent and said, "I've got bad news, guys. I just heard one of our ships went down hard. Copeland and Hurst were flying."

Eric sat up and said, "Oh shit! Those guys were in my ship. Was Jarvis the crew chief?"

Koss looked at his clip board and said, "I didn't look up the other numbers." He flipped a page and searched for the names of the other two crewmen.

To prevent giving the names of those killed or wounded over the radio, the company clerks made up lists of names matched to numbers. The numbers would then be radioed back to the unit instead of the names.

When he found the numbers, Koss said, "The other two crewmen were Jarvis and Hightower. If it's any consolation, all four were WIAs."

Eric frowned and said "Did you say it was pretty bad?"

"Yeah, I heard the ship cart-wheeled, so the crew is in bad shape. The Dustoff took them to the field hospital at Lai Khe."

Paul turned to his roommate. "It sounds like your trusty steed is history."

Eric stared blankly and said, "Yeah, I don't mind losing the ship, I just hope the crew is okay."

An hour later the call came for reinforcements, and all ships were launched. After the sortie, two wounded men and two KIAs were loaded onto the floor of Eric's ship to be transported to the hospital at Lai Khe. At the MASH unit, medics hurried out and loaded the wounded onto gurneys. The two dead men were placed on stretchers and carried to the side of the hospital.

When everyone was clear, Eric moved the ship several hundred feet off the helipad. While the rotors wound down, he told his co-pilot, "I'm going to check on our downed aircrew. Keep the radio on in case they have something else for us."

Paris nodded as Eric unfastened his seat belt and jumped out of the ship. To avoid passing through the emergency room, Eric walked around the side, past Graves Registration. Workers from GR had placed the dead soldiers on a cement slab and were spraying them with high-pressure hoses. Next to the slab was a pile of bodies in dark-green body bags.

Eric looked at the pile and imagined his own body in one of the bags. He shuddered and thought he had to quit thinking like that. Guys who did were usually the next ones to get killed. He quickened his pace because the place gave him the creeps.

He entered the cool, air-conditioned hospital and almost ran into a medic in a green surgery gown. When he asked about his fellow airmen, the medic pointed at a pair of swinging doors and hurried into the operating room.

The room was long and narrow, with a row of beds on each side. Eric walked down the aisle checking the faces of the men in the beds. As he approached the end, he recognized Hightower, the door gunner, a tall black man who had flown with Eric on several occasions. His leg was in a cast and attached to a traction device. He was asleep, so Eric couldn't ask about the others.

When he turned around, a cute nurse dressed in green fatigues walked toward him and asked, "Can I help you find someone?" Her name tag read "Chapman" and the insignia on her collar indicated she was a first lieutenant. Before he answered, the nurse noticed the wings on his flight suit and said, "I'll bet you're looking for the helicopter crew that came in today."

Eric pointed at the door gunner, and said, "So far I've only found one. Are the others in another room?"

With a sympathetic look the nurse said, "No, the other two are right here."

Eric couldn't believe he had been standing next to his fellow pilots and didn't know it. The nurse walked between the two beds and plumped up the pillow of the man nearest Eric. As she moved to the other bed, she said, "They look pretty bad now, but they'll be okay."

"Pretty bad," Eric blurted. "I can't tell who's who."

He walked to the one closest to him and figured it must be Copeland, but he had to check his identification band to be sure. His cheeks and eye lids were swollen, and his nose had a tube running into it.

Eric turned to the nurse and said, "I just had breakfast with these guys and now I don't even recognize them."

While Eric was checking the ID of the other man, he suddenly remembered the nurse had only mentioned two others. In a hesitant voice, he said, "You said there were only these two. What about the crew chief?"

"I'm sorry," the nurse said softly. "These three are the only ones they brought in here."

Eric quickly looked in the direction of the pile of bodies and thought that Gary's luck had run out. Lt. Chapman saw his worried look and said, "It could be that he wasn't injured badly enough to be admitted. Give me his name and I'll go check."

"His name is Jarvis, Spec 4 Gary Jarvis," Eric answered, trying not to choke up.

The nurse spun around and said, "I'll be right back."

"Thank you."

As he watched her leave, he wondered what the chances were that Gary was uninjured, considering the way the other three looked. While he waited, he envisioned his friend lying in one if the body bags and thought of pictures he had seen of Gary's wife and little boy. Now there would be a dark green Army sedan driving up to their house. A uniformed officer would get out, walk toward the door and his wife would be told.

While he waited, he tried to recall if this was the third or fourth time Gary had been in a crash. The guys in his company had nick-named him "The Cat," because of his close calls.

A few minutes later, the doors opened and Lt. Chapman returned with a smile. "Your friend is okay. He just had a badly sprained ankle and some minor contusions."

"All right," Eric said, trying to keep his voice low. He gave the nurse a hug and then realized what he had done. He took a step back and said, "Sorry, I got a little carried away."

The nurse smiled. "That's okay. I understand."

For a few seconds they looked into each other's eyes. Their jobs didn't afford many chances for celebration and they enjoyed the moment. Eric extended his hand and said, "I'm Eric Bader."

The nurse shook his hand. "Hello Eric Bader. I'm Cheryl Chapman, nice to meet you."

"Great to meet you," Eric said, as he continued to look into her eyes. Then he glanced toward the door and said, "I guess I better go. Thanks for the help."

"You're welcome. It was nice to have good news for a change. There have been so many times when I've had to tell somebody their friend didn't make it."

"I can imagine what that's like," Eric said. He pointed at the injured crewmen and said, "I can see our guys are in good hands."

Lieutenant Chapman smiled and said, "Thank you. We try to do our best."

As he walked out of the cool hospital into the hot steamy night, he couldn't stop thinking of Cheryl Chapman. Even in her OD jungle fatigues she looked good. He imagined what she must look like with makeup and dressed in civilian clothes.

It was almost dark as he walked past the two guys from Graves Registration. He could just make out their silhouettes next to the dark-green pile of body bags. They were sitting on a bench smoking cigarettes. He continued toward his helicopter and thought, what a shitty job they had. Then he realized it kept them out of the field. He had never heard of anybody getting greased while they worked at GR.

By the time they flew back to their base, it was late. As they climbed the steps to the barracks, Bader said, "I'm going to the club for a couple of beers."

"Sounds good to me," Paris said.

Inside the smoke-filled bar, the two men joined Paul and five other Slick pilots. After Eric told them about his trip to the hospital, Paul took Eric aside and said, "I'm glad you have good news, because what I have is all bad. You know the captain you had a run-in with at the processing center in Cam Rahn Bay?"

"You mean the shower guy. What about him?"

"The CO was just in here introducing him as our new platoon leader."

"You mean Reddick is *here*?"

"That's his name, and the major said he was with the 281st. Hopefully, he has a short memory."

"Let's hope," Eric said, as he signaled to Baby-San for a beer. The pretty bartender walked toward him wearing a tight *ao dai* dress and handed him a Budweiser.

Eric took a sip as Paul said, "You're not the only one who has to worry. I have a premonition that little prick is going to make everybody's lives miserable."

The next morning Reddick appeared on the flight line, and walked up to a group of warrant officers. In a hostile voice, he said, "Things are going to start shaping up around here starting right now. I see multiple breaches of regulations all over this place. I see long hair and mustaches growing over lips. There are sideburns below ear lobes, and some of you haven't even shaved this morning. What's the problem, gentlemen? Are you too hung over?"

The pilot closest to him had hair coming out from under his ball cap. Reddick yelled at him, "Look at your hair. Is that what you call regulation length?"

The man protested that he hadn't had a day off in weeks, and Reddick flew into a rage. "I don't give a rat's ass, Mister. Get it cut today. Is that understood?"

"Yes Sir," the man answered crisply.

Reddick addressed the group and said, "That goes for the rest of you. Is that clear?" When they answered with a cursory "yes Sir," Reddick screamed, "What was that?"

Knowing they weren't going to get rid of him until they played along, the group yelled, "*Yes Sir!*"

With a thin smile Reddick said, "That's more like it."

As he walked away, Tom Paris asked Eric, "Who died and left him king of the assholes?"

During the following week Reddick was the central topic of conversation. He had been especially hard on the crew chiefs and door gunners. The officers had the benefit of Vietnamese hooch maids who cleaned their clothes and shined their boots. Without the same service, the enlisted men tended to be rougher around the edges.

After several weeks of grumbling, Eric decided to talk with the gunship pilots. The next evening he said to Paul, "I need to talk with Boone about what we're going to do about Reddick."

Paul said, "You're going to talk with Boone? I don't think we're that desperate."

Eric opened the door to the club and said, "I think we are."

Clay Boone, Dan Sharkey, Pete Barnes and John Lambi were standing in front of the bar. As the two roommates walked toward the group, Paul called to Boone, "What's happening Shooter? How's the eye?"

Boone gave Paul a menacing look and growled, "Not too bad, Eason. How's the mouth?"

Paul laughed, and said, "It's too bad that frontal lobotomy didn't work out Shooter, it might have done wonders for your personality."

Boone stepped in front of Eason and said, "Why don't we put the gloves on and settle this right now?"

Paul walked past Boone and said, "No way Shooter. I learned a long time ago never to get into a fight with an ugly man. You don't have anything to lose."

Eric stepped in and said to Boone, "We need to talk."

Boone pointed at a table and said, "Over there."

The three other Jokers followed them to the table. If there was going to be a meeting, they wanted to be a part of it. Usually the Gunnies and Slickies were segregated like boys and girls at a junior high dance, so the other pilots watched the meeting with interest.

When everyone was seated, Clay Boone lit a cigar and asked, "What's on your mind, Dog?"

"I want to volunteer for the guns, Shooter. I hear it's a lot of fun."

Boone laughed and said, "That's good Bader, you're a real comedian." He took a puff on his cigar and said, "Okay, I can guess why you're here. You want to talk about Reddick. The little prick better watch how he treats the enlisted men because I've got door gunners who would just as soon shoot the bastard, as look at him." He glanced over his shoulder at Sphinx and Zombie and said, "Not to mention a couple of my pilots."

Eric looked around the table and said, "If we can get the right people to believe that, we may be able to get rid of him."

Boone blew a smoke ring across the table and asked, "Just how are we going to do that?"

Eric waved the smoke away and said, "When the infantry get a particularly bad officer they do what they call disappear him. The word gets out if that officer doesn't get a transfer, it may not be good for his health. They usually get transferred. Our biggest problem will be getting the new major to believe the threats. He's still pretty green, and all Reddick has done is jack us up for having long hair and dirty boots. We've been getting dinged on that for years, but this guy's an asshole. He puts people on edge and that's dangerous."

Boone leaned across the table and said, "That's right and if he jacks the wrong guy one more time you won't have to worry about anybody believing the threats."

Eric stood and said, "Let's hope it doesn't come to that. We want to get rid of him, not send him home in a box."

The next afternoon, the sun was setting behind a large bank of cumulus clouds as Eric and Paul approached their home field in an eight-ship group. When they were on the ground, the two roommates walked out of the revetments together. Eric was the first to see Gary Jarvis hobbling toward them on crutches. Eric nudged Paul and said, "Look who's there." It was the first time he had seen his old crew chief since the accident.

After the two pilots greeted him, Gary asked, "Do you guys have a minute? I need to talk with you."

"Sure Gary, you know that," Eric said as they approached the stairs. "Let's go to our room."

While Jarvis struggled up the steps, Paul said, "I'll go to the club and get a six pack. See you at the room."

Eric said to Jarvis, "I was really glad to hear you made it through another one, Gary. How many crashes have you been in?"

As they continued to climb the stairs, Jarvis said, "This was my third. That's why I need to talk with you."

They reached the room and Eric held the door open for Gary and Jungle Dog. Jarvis leaned his crutches against the wall and sat on a folding chair. "I need some advice, Mr. Bader."

Paul walked in as Eric said, "We'll do anything we can to help."

Gary took a beer from Paul and said, "Thanks, Mr. Eason." He looked at both pilots and said, "Since I've been in Nam I've survived three accidents. Then there was that ricochet off the cliff by Dalat. I really thought we had bought it that time." He took a sip of beer. "I don't think I can take another close call. Sooner or later, my luck is going to run out. You've got to realize, I've got a wife and kid waiting at home and I have to think about them. That's why I'm going to take myself off flight status."

Eric glanced at Paul before he said, "You can't do that without permission, Gary."

"I know that and I don't care. I'm too spooked to go out on any more missions."

Paul sat on his bed and said, "If you quit flying you'll be burning shit until you leave the country."

Jarvis turned to Paul and asked, "Have you ever heard of anybody getting killed while they were burning shit?"

Paul smiled and said, "No, I can't say that I have."

"Hopefully it won't come to that," Gary said solemnly. "Can one of you talk to the first sergeant and see if he can give me a non-flying job until I DEROS? I don't care what it is—just as long as I can stay on the ground."

Paul turned to Eric. "You know Top better than anybody, what do you think?"

"I can't promise anything, but it's worth a try. I'll see what I can do."

With a relieved sigh, Gary said, "That would be great Mr. B. I'd really appreciate it."

Eric finished his beer and tossed the can into a waste basket. "Right now is as good a time as any. I need to talk with him about Newton anyway."

As he walked toward the Headquarters building, Eric thought that he was having enough problems getting through his own war without having to worry about someone else, but there wasn't anybody more deserving of his help than Gary Jarvis.

Eric knocked on the first sergeant's door and said, "Good afternoon Top."

Andrews called out, "Come in Eric and have a seat."

Eric sat on a gray folding chair and Andrews held up a box. "My wife just sent this to me. She loves having me here in Nam. It gives her a chance to stay with her mother in Japan for a year. I usually get over there a couple of times on R & R."

"Sounds like a good deal to me," Eric said, as he watched his first sergeant empty the contents into a bowl. Eric asked, "What is that stuff?"

"Japanese appetizers," Andrews answered. "It's mostly dried squid. The little yellow things are bread sticks." Andrews handed the bowl to Eric. "Try some, they're pretty good."

Eric took a squid and a few bread sticks and set the bowl on the desk.

Andrews happily munched on a squid. "The green stuff is dried seaweed. It's supposed to be full of minerals and vitamins."

"I'm sure it is," Eric said as he took a bite of squid.

The first sergeant reached into a drawer and took out a bottle of sake. "You're done flying for the day aren't you?"

Eric nodded as he continued to nibble on the squid. Andrews poured them each a glass of the Japanese wine. "I would imagine you're here to talk about Specialist Newton."

"Yeah, that and something else, but let's start with him."

Andrews took a sip of wine. "He hasn't gotten off to a good start. He was supposed to go to Saigon for three days and stayed six. I chewed his ass and told him if he went AWOL again, he'd be spending time in the stockade."

"Did he bring back a projector?"

"No, he said he couldn't find one, but he did manage to find chemicals and a printer for developing film. Now he says he needs a darkroom."

"How the hell can we put together a darkroom in this place, Top?"

"He says if he can find the right space he can make it happen."

"Okay, I'll see what I can do, but I've got a bigger problem than that. I need to talk about Gary Jarvis. He's one of our best crew chiefs, but this last crash really screwed him up. He says he can't fly any more missions."

Andrews frowned and leaned back in his chair. His thin, angular face had been sculpted by two wars. When he was serious, it made him look even more severe. He ran a hand through his gray flat top and said, "I know Jarvis has been through a lot, but who hasn't? I just can't take him off flight status because he's been shot down a couple of times. Do you think we can talk him out of it?"

"I don't think so. Not this time, and it's been more than a couple times. This last crash was his third and I think he's lost his nerve. Don't you have a job here at the base? He only has five months left in-country."

Andrews looked at a clipboard and said, "I do have a mechanic about to DEROS. He's been on the recovery team, so Gary would still have to fly, but it would just be to recover a downed ship every once in awhile. It wouldn't involve combat missions."

Eric smiled and said, "That would be great Top. I know Gary will really appreciate it."

"Tell him to report to me in the morning." Andrews pointed at the bowl of appetizers and asked, "Do you want any more?"

Eric shook his head and said, "No thanks, but I'll have another glass of that sake."

Eric returned to his room and was listening to a Doors album, when Paul said, "It looks like your man from the planet Kodak is headed our way." Paul jumped off his bed and said, "I don't need to listen to his problems. I'll see you at the mess hall."

Paul held the screen open for Newton, who walked in and said, "Hi

Mr. Bader."

Eric pointed at a chair and said, "Hello Neutron. How was your trip?"

Newton sat on the chair and said, "Good, I learned a lot and met an old friend from basic training."

"Top told me you were late coming back. You didn't make a very good impression with the boss. I wouldn't cross him again."

"Don't worry, I won't. I do have good news. I found a place that will work as my darkroom. It's an empty storage room that no one is using at the end of my barracks. I think I can cool it down with ice blocks and a fan."

"If there isn't anything in it, you can probably use it," Eric said. "I'll see you Saturday night for the movie. I want you to run the projector this time."

"Thanks Mr. Bader, I'll be there." Newton stood and left the room.

It had been a month since Captain Reddick joined the company and Eric and Paul had managed to avoid a confrontation. One morning the inevitable happened as the two of them left the mess hall. Eric saw Reddick and said, "Be sure and salute the prick, so he doesn't have an excuse to stop us."

In a disgusted voice Paul said, "Saluting isn't going to help. He's going to be all over me when he sees the length of my hair."

"I hope he doesn't recognize me."

"Don't worry Dog, I'll handle everything."

"That's what I'm afraid of."

Reddick returned their salutes and stepped in front of Eason. "Your hair's getting a little long, isn't it soldier?"

Paul answered, "Yes Sir, I've been busy and haven't had the time to get to a barber shop."

Reddick looked at Paul's name tag and sneered, "Well Mister Eason, let's see that you get it cut today. Is that clear?"

"Yes Sir."

Satisfied, Reddick turned to Eric. Not finding anything wrong, he walked around him, then glanced back and said, "Don't I know you from somewhere?" He looked at Eric's name tag and said, "Bader, I know we've met before. Was it the processing center at Cam Rahn?"

Eric leveled a stare at Reddick and said, "Why does it matter now?"

Reddick's mouth twitched as he said, "Because if I remember correctly I gave you a direct order and you disobeyed me. That's why it matters."

Paul stepped in front of Reddick and said, "Oh come on Captain. That was a long time ago. We were all one-week wonders back then. This war changes people and from what I've heard you aren't anybody to be digging up skeletons."

Reddick glowered at Paul. "Just what the hell does that mean?"

"For starters, the pilots in your old company said you're a marginal flight leader."

"Is that so?"

"Yeah and that's not all."

Reddick got into Eason's face and asked, "What else did they say?"

"They said you're an asshole and from what I've seen you haven't done anything to dispel that either."

"That does it. You're on report."

Paul threw his hands up and said, "What for, Captain? You asked me what they said and I told you."

Reddick poked his finger into Eason's chest, and yelled, "You haven't heard the last of this, pal."

While the two roommates watched Reddick stomp away, Eric said, "You've done it this time, Dev. You're going to catch a lot of grief."

Paul turned toward their room and said, "What's he going to do, cut off my hair and send me to Nam?"

Eric chuckled at the old joke and said, "He could get some of your pay."

"What, an Article 15? I'll have the guys at HQ tear it up before the ink's dry." Paul slapped Eric on the shoulder and said, "What are you worried about? I took the heat off of you, didn't I?"

Eric grinned at his roommate and said, "You definitely did that."

That afternoon, Paul and Eric were leaving the flight line when they were greeted by a company clerk. "Excuse me Mr. Eason, you're to report to the XO's office."

"Did he give you a time?"

"No, but I would imagine he meant right away."

"Tell him I'll be right there."

Paul turned to Eric and said, "I better get changed."

At their room, Eason dug through his foot locker for a new flight suit. Before reporting to the XO's office, he went to the barber shop and had his hair cut into a flat top. Back at the barracks he greeted Eric. "How do you like my new look?"

Eric laughed and said, "It's about time you cleaned up your act. Good luck with the XO."

Paul opened the door and said, "You know I like a good fight."

Twenty minutes later, Paul returned sporting a big smile. When Eric saw him, he said, "It looks like things went well."

"Oh yeah," Paul said, taking off his new flight suit. "As soon as Captain Hart mentioned Reddick's name, I went on the offensive and started dropping dimes on him. I told Hart everything the guys in the 281st had told us. Then I described how bad he was treating our guys. I even said if Reddick doesn't get transferred it may not be good for his health. Before I left there were some major doubts in our executive officer's mind about Captain Reddick."

"Did he say what they're going to do to you?"

"Hell no! He was too busy worrying about what I said. I told you I would get rid of that little weasel and I will. Let's go to the club, I need a drink."

When they entered the bar they were surprised to see their three young neighbors sitting at a table. Paul approached the three co-pilots and said, "Well if it isn't Wilford, Milford and Tilford. What brings you guys out? Did you finally decide to join the real world?"

Two of the pilots pointed at Wilford who was slumped over a letter. When he spied the dispatch, Paul said, "What happened Willy? Did you get a Dear John?"

Wilford nodded as Paul placed a hand on his shoulder. "Hey man, don't take it so hard. You aren't the first one to get a DJ and you definitely won't be the last. You've got to get over it as soon as you can, or you're going to be thinking about her when you're supposed to be doing your job and you could let somebody down."

Wilford stared up at Eason and didn't respond. Paul walked toward the bar, saying, "Hey, I tried."

The evening wore on with the three roommates ordering round after round. The other pilots in the bar watched and wished they could get their hands on the letter. Eric and Paul left the bar early. It was raining heavily as Eric said, "Tomorrow will not be a good day for the three amigos."

Jungle Dog usually slept outside, but because of the rain, they let their dog sleep on his indoor mat. At 0230, the roommates were awakened by the sound of growling and toenails scratching the wooden floor. Eric turned on a light and saw Jungle Dog violently shaking a rat. He jumped out of bed and coaxed the dead rat out of their dog's mouth. When he threw it outside, JD wanted to go after it. Eric pulled him back and grabbed a bag of dog biscuits his parents had sent him. He gave JD two of them and then went back to bed. "It was our lucky day when you found that dog," Eric said.

Paul turned off the light and said, "I'd like to take credit, but if you'll remember, I didn't find him, he found me."

The next day was a down day for Eric, so he was able to sleep in. He had flown for fifteen straight days and had earned it. The executive officer had ordered it, not to do Eric a favor, but because Captain Hart wanted him to work in the company area. Although it felt good to stay in bed, Eric knew he could never get back to sleep. The heat was rising and he heard the screeching brakes of the truck that brought the hooch maids to the company area and they would soon start cleaning the barracks.

A few minutes later he heard the familiar sound of rubber thongs slapping the wooden walkway outside his room. He was about to get out of bed when the screen door opened and a homely young woman stepped inside. She was surprised to see Eric and asked, "Why you no fly?"

Eric patted the bed and said, "Because I wait for you to come here and boom-boom."

The woman giggled as she picked up two laundry bags and left the room.

Eric got out of bed and muttered, "You know you've been here *way* too long when you're trying to jump a hooch maid."

He grabbed a towel and his shaving kit and left for the latrine in his boxer shorts. It felt good to have a day off and he allowed himself a thought of the States. He wondered how good it would feel to be home with more than one day off. He quickly put it out of his mind because he still had five months to go before it could happen. Today he had to straighten up the ammo dump.

When he neared the latrine he could smell the shit-burning detail. Usually, he was flying before someone started the odious task of burning feces with diesel fuel. Two mama-sans were squatting in the sink room over a pile of dirty flight shirts. They had been looking through the pockets and when they saw Eric, they quickly hid a black government pen and several bills of MPC under a laundry board. Eric greeted them in Vietnamese before going into the shower.

Fifteen minutes later he was in his room hoisting his weathered Nomex flight shirt. His name tag was faded and coming unsewn. The Chief Warrant Officer bars on the collar were also unraveling. It was a shirt that spoke of what he had seen and done. Rank still had clout, but time in-country carried universal respect.

He dressed in a green T-shirt, pants and a ball cap. As he walked out of the room, he wondered what guys back home were wearing. When he left the States, it was paisley shirts and bell bottomed trousers. Now all he had to go on were glimpses of stateside life in magazines.

He walked by the O Club and decided to stop for a cold drink before heading down to the ammo dump. He pushed the wooden door open and the sunlight highlighted the slumped figure of Carl Wilford sitting at the bar. The young man shielded his eyes and mumbled, "Hey Eric."

Eric sat on the stool next to him and said, "What's up Willie? I'm glad to see you're still alive."

"Just barely," Wilford said weakly.

Eric ordered a Pepsi and said, "I'd have a beer, but I doubt they have any left."

The chubby co-pilot had always seemed depressed, but now he had a reason. With his head in his hand, Wilford said, "I guess I really made a fool of myself last night."

Eric didn't comment and Wilford continued, "I feel so lost and hurt without her. What would you do if you were in my place? You always seem to have it all together."

Eric's nice day was starting to fade as he turned to Wilford and said, "Listen Willie, what you need is to get laid and the sooner the better. Take your R & R and head for Thailand. Have you ever heard of a Bangkok basket? A week of that and you won't even remember old what's her name."

Wilford straightened from his slouch and stared at Eric with his mouth agape. He found his voice and said, "What are you talking about?"

"What I'm talking about is you can't pack this around with you forever. You've got to get over it. If you don't keep your head in the game you're going to get killed and maybe take somebody else with you. You need to forget her and the sooner the better."

In a screeching voice, Wilford said, "That's easy for you to say. You've probably never had a love like me and Penny."

Eric nodded and said, "You've probably got that right. Listen, the operative word here is *had*. You've got the letter. It's over." Eric was about to leave when he noticed the letter was a bookmark in the paperback on the bar.

He decided to stay and Wilford turned to him and asked, "Why would she want to throw away all that we had together, just so she can start over with some other guy? And why would she do this to me now that I'm over here? What if I do something stupid while I'm thinking about her and I get greased?"

Eric looked at Wilford in the mirror behind the bar and thought, that's not too hard to imagine. He was getting tired of the soap opera and said, "That's what I've been talking about. Look Carl, you're not the first guy this has happened to and it's not the end of the world. You need to get over this lady."

Wilford ignored the comment and opened the letter. "I've read it over and over a hundred times and the part that kills me is this. Listen to this, Eric. She actually says, there's nothing I want more than for you to share my happiness. How could she say something like that?"

Eric peeked at the letter and said, "Sounds like a pretty strange request to me."

When Wilford lost himself in reading, Eric cleared his throat and said, "Listen, I realize this is really personal, but maybe a disinterested party may be able to find something between the lines, so to speak. I've read a dozen of these letters and sometimes a woman doesn't really mean what she says. It's worth a try."

Wilford looked at him and said, "Do you really think so?"

Eric knew he was close to reading the letter and said, "Sure, I might find something you've been missing."

Wilford slowly handed over the letter and Eric couldn't believe his luck. All of the pilots in the company wanted to read the letter and now he had it in his hands. Usually when other men got a Dear John letter they were more than happy to have other guys read it. Some even sent their letters to the battalion newspaper to try and win the hundred dollar prize for best Dear John.

Eric pointed at the salutation. "Dearest Carlton, is that your real name?"

"It's Carlton Wilford the Third."

Eric looked at Wilford and said, "That fits. Did she ever use dearest before?"

"No she always used dear."

"That's what I thought. You know you're in trouble when they start like that." Eric turned back to the letter.

83

Dearest Carlton,   *Friday night*

You don't know how awful I feel about not writing you this past month, but at least I have a good excuse. I'm living in New York City and don't have a minute to myself anymore. I'm going to a clothes buyer's school on Madison Avenue and it's the best in the world. It has girls from all over the country, with an enrollment of less than 200, so as you can guess it's a hard school to get into and very difficult to stay in! As part of our training we have to work in the stores and I'm working at Macy's. I'm an assistant buyer, which is an executive supervisory position that pays $90 per week. Not bad, huh? I love the work, even though I'm worn ragged by the end of the day. It's really very exciting. New York is a lot different than Atlantic City.

Eric looked up and asked, "Are you from Atlantic City?"

Wilford shook his head. "No, we met there while we were working at a resort the summer before last."

Eric looked back at the letter and said, "She's done a nice job of chatting you up, but something tells me she's about to lower the boom."

Wilford let out a mournful, "Yeah," and went back to slumping while Eric went back to reading.

Now that you know what I'm up to, and that I'm still alive, I've got some more news to tell you. I hope you know me well enough to accept this news with a warm heart. I'm engaged to be married and I have been since the end of May. I've wanted to tell you for such a long time, but just didn't know how. You and I had a lovely and memorable summer together, so full of love and joy, but it has all faded into the past and now it only exists as a memory never to be forgotten.

I'm in love with a wonderful guy and I have decided to share my life with him. This is the happiest time of my life and I hope you can be happy for me. There is nothing I want more than for you to share my happiness. I know someday you will find a wonderful woman who is destined to fill your life with love and happiness.

84

Well Carl, please write again soon. I love hearing from you and I promise to answer your letters. Please never forget me, because I will never forget you. Love, Penny

Eric set the letter on the bar and said, "I have to admit that's quite the letter. The lady can write, but I'm afraid its curtains for the two of you."

Wilford grabbed the letter and blurted, "What about her wanting me to continue to write? Doesn't that mean there might be some hope?"

Eric shook his head. "Nah, that's her way of easing her conscience. She's done her homework on this one. She wants you to think she still cares, but the last thing she'll want, after she's married, are letters postmarked Southeast Asia showing up in her mailbox. The cold hard truth is your relationship is over and the sooner you get it behind you the better. It could have been worse--think of all the poor bastards who are married and get a letter like this."

Wilford turned toward Eric and said, "Oh yeah, like that makes me feel better."

"Okay so it doesn't. Look, you asked me what I thought and I'm telling you. Take your two buddies to Thailand and have a good time."

Wilford didn't respond, so Eric continued, "Listen, here's an idea. If you want to get back at her, you could send this letter to the battalion newspaper and enter it in the 'Bitch of the Month' column. I've seen a lot of Dear Johns in there and this one could be a winner. If it is, you can write and tell her the letter was so good it won a hundred dollar prize."

Wilford looked horrified. "Are you crazy? I couldn't do that."

Eric shrugged and said, "It was just a thought. Look, I've got to get down to the ammo dump. Try and pull yourself together before you have to fly. I don't want to hear that you got greased because you were thinking about this."

Eric spun around on the stool as the door opened and flooded the bar with sunlight. He squinted into the bright light and recognized the profile of his roommate coming through the door. Paul walked toward the bar and said, "Good morning gents. How are you feeling Willy? That wouldn't be your Waterloo you're holding is it? Are you going to let me read it?"

Wilford stomped toward the door and snapped, "It's personal Eason. Not that you would know anything about that."

The door closed behind him and Paul said, "Sheesh, touchy little troll." He motioned to the bar girl for a soda and asked his roommate, "So how come you're not down at the ammo dump getting it all cleaned up like the XO wants?"

Eric said, "I could ask you the same question. Why aren't you out fighting the war like the Army wants?"

Paul took a stool and said, "Ship wouldn't start. The mechanics are looking at the fuel control unit. It may be a while, so I came up here to cool off. I figured I'd find you."

Eric took a sip from his can and said, "One doesn't want to rush things on his day off."

Paul asked, "Did you get to read it?"

"Yeah, and it's pretty good. I think it could win the hundred bucks, but we'll never get it away from Wilford. Even if we did, he would have a shit fit if we sent it in. He's taking it pretty hard and we don't want to push him too far. Remember the clerk that killed himself when he got a Dear John."

Paul nodded. "I don't think Wilford has the cajones to do that, but we better not risk it."

Eric finished his Pepsi and stood. "I guess I'd better get down to the ammo dump." He grabbed Paul in a headlock and said, "Give me a Distinguished Flying Cross, or I'll rip your head off."

"All right, all right!" Paul pleaded. "You're breaking my neck!"

"Then I get a DFC?"

"Only if you let me sleep with the Colonel's twenty year old daughter."

"Deal," Eric said, releasing the headlock. Paul straightened up and they both laughed. Neither of them knew whether the Colonel even had a daughter.

Paul rubbed his neck and said, "You better get your rockets in tip-top shape because rumor has it we've got six ships headed north. It sounds like they could be there awhile."

"On my way," Eric said as he pushed the door open.

Approaching the gate to the ammo dump, Eric wondered if he would be the first one there. The site didn't have full-time workers, so once a month he was ordered to take a couple of enlisted men and straighten it up. The ammo dump was a prize target for enemy mortars, so it was bermed on all sides with a ten-foot-high dirt wall. The gate was marked with four no smoking signs in English, Vietnamese, French and Korean.

He walked through the gate and saw the two door gunners who had been assigned to his detail. They were the company screw-offs who were continually in trouble and frequently assigned menial details. One was a white guy nicknamed Snake, the other a black man called Blue. Eric didn't know if Snake was called that because he liked snakes, or because he was so skinny.

Both men had their shirts off and the one called Snake had tattoos covering most of his upper torso. They were sitting on a stack of rockets sharing a marijuana cigarette. When they saw him, Blue flicked the lit joint and said, "What's happenin', Mr. Bader?"

Eric stood over them and Blue said, "What ya gonna do, cut off our hair and send us to Nam?" The two door gunners laughed and slapped their thighs.

Eric waited until he had their attention and said, "Lucky for you two I needed help this morning, so it got you out of a shit burning detail." He walked away knowing he should turn them in, but it had been done before with no consequences. Plus, he needed the help, so he went to a small shed and found the clipboard with the inspection gigs that needed to be corrected.

He returned and told his two helpers, "It looks like almost a day's work, so we better get started."

Blue looked up and let out a loud, *"Shee-it."*

Eric ignored him and said, "If you'll notice, those rockets you're sitting on are pointed the wrong way. When they were unloaded some pinheads pointed them at the barracks. We need to move them to the east wall anyway, so be sure the warheads are pointed at the berm, okay?" He got their agreement and added, "I'm going to staple up a few more no smoking signs. The ones we have don't seem to be working."

Both men stood and began carrying rockets toward the east wall. Eric removed his shirt and started stacking the rockets in neat rows. He wasn't required to help, but he enjoyed the physical work. The animosity between him and the two door gunners quickly passed as they became engaged in the mindless, sweaty production of moving hundreds of rockets and crates.

By late afternoon they had finally completed all of the inspection requirements and were left with one crate of outdated M-60 machine gun ammo, and four hand grenades. The outdated ammo was supposed to be disposed of by flying a helicopter out to sea and dumping it into the ocean, but it was a lot more fun to load the old ammo into the machine guns and shoot at sharks, or anything else unfortunate enough to be swimming near the surface. Sometimes, they would go out on airborne deer and pig hunts that produced enough meat to stage a company barbeque.

As officer in charge of the ammo dump, Eric could choose who would dispose of the outdated munitions. Eric and Paul usually traded off flying, because it was the only time they were able to fly in the same helicopter. Almost everyone in the company liked hunting, so the role of the shooters was greatly coveted.

Eric went to the club to look for volunteers. The bar was mostly empty except for two Slickies at the bar and the two young guns, Sphinx and Zombie, at their usual table. Eric knew they would want to go out and shoot at things, so he approached their table. The Gunnies weren't used to a Slick pilot wanting to talk with them, so they gave him a suspicious look. Eric stood over them and said, "Good afternoon guys."

Sphinx set his beer down and asked, "What's up, Dog?"

"I just cleaned the ammo dump and I have a crate of M-60 ammo I need to get rid of. I figure you two would want to go out and shoot it up."

Both men grinned and Sphinx said, "You bet. How soon can we leave?"

"We have to wait for Eason, so let's meet on the flight line at 1800."

Zombie raised his beer and said, "We'll be there."

Thirty minutes later Eason landed and walked up the flight line. Eric was on the deck of his helicopter loading a machine gun, when Paul asked, "Are we ready?"

"Yeah, our shooters should be here any minute. I invited Zombie and Sphinx to join us."

Paul's eyes bugged out as he said, "Are you nuts? Why those two crazies?"

"I think we need to start an alliance with the Jokers."

Paul threw his gear on the co-pilot's seat and said, "I don't agree, but it's your show."

Eric stopped Paul before he climbed into his seat and said, "Watch what you say while we're flying. The privacy switch on the intercom is broken, so they'll be able to hear everything." Paul nodded as the two Jokers approached the ship.

The shooting started when they found a twelve-foot hammerhead shark swimming near the surface. Zombie nailed it with a barrage of machine gun fire. When the shark was hit, it rolled onto its back. Zombie fired again at the shark's white belly. Two red holes appeared in its stomach and Eric thought, this guy is good. The shark continued to roll and Sphinx yelled, "Hey Dog, hard left turn so I can finish him off with a couple grenades."

Eric leveled off and said, "I don't want to do that. If they go off above water they could hit the ship."

Sphinx waved a grenade and said, "Then get lower and it'll go off under the surface like a depth charge."

Eric started a left turn and said, "Okay, but I'm not going to do it from a hover. I'll fly out and come back. You can each drop a grenade when we fly over the target."

The explosions went off as planned and both Gunnies asked for another run. Eric did a one-eighty and lined up on the dying shark. Two more grenades were dropped and Eric thought that was enough shark killing for the day. He turned toward the west and told the others they were headed for Free-Fire Island.

The island had once been the site of a thriving fishing village until it was wiped out by a typhoon five years earlier. All that was left were abandoned bamboo huts and a few mud buildings. The deserted houses stood on the beach, with the center of the island covered by jungle.

Eric told Paul to take over flying, so he could look for a target for his M-79 grenade launcher. The M-79 looked like a sawed-off shotgun and fired a shell which exploded upon impact.

Paul made a run along the west side of the island with Sphinx strafing the abandoned buildings with his machine gun, debris flying everywhere. Eric told Paul to reverse course, so he and Zombie could fire their weapons.

As they lined up on the beach, Eric said, "Move closer, I'm going to try and put a grenade into the window of that mud building."

Zombie started firing as Paul skimmed just above the sand. Eric put a shell in his grenade launcher and aimed it out his side window. As they approached the building he fired. He missed the window and the grenade hit the wall with such force it rocked the helicopter. Eric turned to Paul and said, "Okay, I think that's enough of that shit. Let's move to the other side of the island and see what's over there."

Paul clicked his mike twice and initiated a climbing right turn. When they passed over the palms in the middle of the island they saw three wild boars running along the beach. Paul maneuvered to fly on their left and Eric yelled, "We've got pigs on the run, Zombie. They're coming up on your side."

The young Gunnie lowered his helmet visor and leaned into the slip stream. "Roger that, I've got them in sight."

Paul slowed to provide a better shot and Zombie hit the trailing pig with a short burst from the machine gun. Sphinx got out of his seat and yelled, "Eric, give me your M-79. I want to shoot one."

Eric loaded a round into the weapon and handed it back. Sphinx knelt in the door and fired the grenade launcher. The round landed in front of the lead pig, knocking it down and turning the other one toward the trees.

Zombie yelled, "Eason, go to a hover, so I can shoot that last pig." Paul flared and Zombie nailed the boar with his machine gun. The two Gunnies whooped and slapped hands as Paul turned out over the water.

Sphinx handed the grenade launcher back to Eric and said, "Thanks Dog. We need to land and pick up one of those pigs for a barbeque. Let's take the one I got with the grenade. It looked like the youngest one."

Eric signaled for Paul to circle and land on the beach. When they were on the ground, Eric told Paul, "Stay here and don't shut down. I don't want to have a problem with a start."

Paul laughed and said, "No worries there. I don't want to have anything to do with that damn pig."

Sphinx jumped out and began gutting the pig with his survival knife. When he finished, the two Gunnies and Eric dragged the wild boar to the ship. It took all their strength to get the bloody, slippery pig up and onto the helicopter deck. When they finished, they were covered with blood and mud.

Paul looked back from his pilot seat and yelled, "Are you guys having fun, yet?"

The three pilots nodded before climbing back on board. When they were buckled in, Paul took off and Eric said to the two shooters, "Get rid of all of your ammo. We need to get this pig to a cooler as fast as we can."

The two Gunnies emptied their machine guns and Zombie said, "That's all there is Dog, thanks for the fun."

Back at the base the Gunnies jumped out and Sphinx said, "We'll find something to haul this pig to the mess hall where we can butcher it."

Eric climbed down from his pilot seat and said, "Good, I want it out of my helicopter as soon as possible."

When Eric turned around, his new crew chief walked up and

motioned for him to move to the rear of the helicopter. Nacho Quintana pointed at a shiny gash in the tail section and asked, "How the hell did that happen?"

Eric looked up at the six inch rip in the tail boom and said, "Something must have blown back on us when I hit a building with my M-79 grenade launcher."

Quintana looked incredulously at his Aircraft Commander and said, "You were shooting an M-79 grenade launcher at a building from a *moving* helicopter? What the hell was going on out there, Boss?"

In an apologetic voice, Eric said, "I guess it was four guys out doing stupid shit."

His new crew chief glared at him before he walked away muttering, "Just what I fucking need, another hole in my helicopter."

Ten minutes later Clay Boone pulled up in a Jeep and said, "Bader, I'm taking charge of that pig. I've cooked a few hogs on my father's farm in Louisiana and he just sent me a box of spices that I call Cajun napalm. It's perfect for this kind of game meat."

"Sounds good to me, Shooter," Eric said as he walked to the side of the helicopter. "Back up here and we'll roll it into the the Jeep."

When the wild boar was loaded, Eric jumped into the front seat for a ride to the mess where he could watch Boone and Sphinx butcher the wild pig. The two Gunnies used butcher knives, a machete and a meat saw to cut it up. Eric was amazed at the skill of the two men as they cleaned and dressed the kill. When they were finished, the meat was transferred to aluminum pans and placed in a walk-in cooler where Boone said it should marinate for about a week.

Six days later it was cooked on two fifty-five gallon drums that had been cut in half and made into barbeque grills.

The marinade was a success and to everyone's surprise, the meat was tender and tasty. The mess cooks added baked beans and potato salad, and First Sergeant Andrews supplied the party with four cases of beer. Paul brought his Akai reel to reel and played Jimi Hendrix, Dylan and the Doors.

Eric looked around at the festivities and said to Paul, "Do you notice who is conspicuously absent?"

Paul frowned and said, "I wonder where the little prick is hiding."

They walked to the garbage can that was filled with iced beer, and were approached by Sphinx. He handed Eric a tusk from the wild boar and said, "It took me half an hour to hack this out of that damn pig with a machete. I want you to have it as thanks for letting us go on the flight."

Eric took the tusk and said, "Thanks Sphinx, I appreciate that. It was your idea to bring that pig back for a party and it was a good one."

What had started as an ammo demolition mission, finished as the best bash of the year.

The next day, Eric was leaving the Ops office when he heard the familiar voice of Tucker Burdett. "Hey Eric, wait up. I've got bad news about your boy Newton."

Eric turned to his friend and said, "Listen Tuck, he's not my boy. I don't even like the guy."

Burdett waved off the comment and said, "It doesn't matter now because he won't be coming back."

"Why's that?"

"He's gotten himself into a lot of trouble, that's why. It's fairly unbelievable actually. He had the day off and went to the beach. Apparently, he was taking landscape photos when he came to the area that's fenced off for females. When he started taking pictures of nurses in bathing suits, two of them went for the Military Police."

Eric stared with his mouth agape as Tucker continued. "It gets worse. After the picture taking, Neutron decided to go skinny dipping right in front of the nurse's area. He was naked as a jay bird just as two cops showed up. Instead of giving up peacefully, Newton charged them."

"What?" Eric said. "That guy couldn't take on two of the nurses, let alone two MPs. What the hell was he thinking?"

"I don't know, but it gets worse. Somehow Newton got a pistol away from one of the MPs and shot him in the thigh. The other one finally subdued him and put cuffs on him. The only good news was there were ten nurses to administer to the wounded guy."

With a perplexed look, Eric asked, "Are you sure we're talking about the same guy that's been running the projector for me? I can't believe this."

Tucker nodded and said, "You need to talk with Top. He knows what happened after they took Newton to the gooney pen."

Eric turned toward HQ and said, "I'll see you when I get back. I still can't believe this."

He entered the first sergeant's office and asked, "What the hell's going on, Top?"

First Sergeant Andrews motioned for Eric to sit and said, "I've been around the Army a long time, and I've never seen anything this crazy. The kid was a little weird, but I never saw this coming. Did Tucker tell you what happened on the beach?"

Eric nodded and Andrews continued, "It got worse when they took him to the hospital. A shrink wasn't available, so they put him in a private room with a guard stationed outside. They gave him some food and when the guard went in to check on him, Newton was standing in the toilet with a fork in an open light socket. Now he's sedated and in a straight jacket."

Eric sat stunned as Andrews pushed an envelope across his desk. "Take a look at these. Newton gave them to me last week."

Inside the envelope were six large black and white photographs. One showed a shirtless door gunner loading ammo into his machine gun. Another was a picture of a loaded gunship displaying the Joker emblem. Three were taken inside the helicopter on his trip to Saigon. The last photo was a close-up of Eric, wearing his helmet and sunglasses, looking out an open cockpit window.

Eric looked up at his first sergeant and said, "These are good. The kid knew what he was doing. Too bad he screwed up."

Andrews pointed at the pictures and said, "You can have them."

Eric put the pictures back in the envelope and got up to leave. "I feel pretty bad about this, Top. What the hell do you think got into him?"

"Who knows," Andrews said, as he rubbed his gray flattop. "Don't worry about it. It's one of those crazy things that happen when you put young men into war."

The next day, the CO invited Captain Reddick to fly in the Command and Control ship. The flight was comprised of four Slicks, two gunships and a light scout helicopter. The mission was to support a cavalry unit with five tanks and four armored personnel carriers.

Eric and Paul were two of the Slick pilots. A friend of theirs, Patrick Ellis, had been recently assigned to fly the scout helicopter and was having trouble complying with Command and Control requests. After an hour of criticizing the scout pilot's technique, Reddick told him to land, so they could trade places. When the two helicopters were on the ground, Reddick walked to the small OH-23 Hiller that served as the scout.

Although the OH-23 had room for three people, it was usually flown single pilot with one crew chief/door gunner. Reddick climbed into the small helicopter, and Ellis elected to ride in one of the tanks rather than join the major in the command ship.

The flight watched as Reddick flew above the jungle at tree-top level. He spotted several occupied bunkers and called in gunships to hit the area with rockets. The cavalry engaged the VC in a short battle with most of the enemy killed, or driven into the jungle.

When the sun began to set, Reddick called that he would be landing to pick up the pilot he had left on the ground. Ellis jumped into the small helicopter and Reddick made a rushed takeoff. While they were climbing out, Ellis radioed they had a low fuel situation. The command ship radioed they would follow the scout back to base. Twenty minutes out of Ninh Hoa, the engine quit. The flight heard the distress call and watched the scout helicopter descend toward a clearing. Dust flew as it hit hard and listed to the right. Ellis radioed that everyone was okay, but they had broken the right skid and damaged the tail rotor.

The major angrily acknowledged the transmission and called the lead Slick to pick up the air crew. He called the gunships and asked if they could stay and cover the downed ship. When the lead Joker radioed they could only stay for twenty minutes, the major radioed, "Okay, stay here as long as you can. I'll call a recovery ship. Hopefully, they can get here before dark."

The flight turned for home and Eric noticed another ship fly alongside. It was Eason who held up five fingers. Eric acknowledged the gesture with two clicks of his mike. Reddick had wrecked his fifth helicopter. He was now an Ace.

The Slick pilots waited outside the revetments for Ellis. On the way to the club, their friend told them he and the crew chief had tried to warn Reddick about the low fuel situation, but he said he was flying and he was sure they had enough fuel to make it back to their base. The question arose as to whether this should count as Reddick's fifth crash because the damage hadn't been that substantial.

The group had just reached the top of the stairs when someone yelled that the recovery helicopter was thirty minutes out. All of the pilots went into the O Club for drinks and then gathered on the terrace to watch the recovery ship approach with the scout helicopter slung underneath.

In the growing darkness the pilot misjudged his altitude and flared too low, causing the scout helicopter to hit the ground and bounce. The pilot jettisoned the load and it rolled twice before coming to rest, totally demolished. When the dust cleared, the pilots on the terrace cheered, and Eason said, "That's what I call a confirmed kill."

The following afternoon Eric entered his room and found Paul kneeling on the floor working on a poster. He stowed his gear and then lit a cigarette to study his friend's work. He read the inscription and said, "Isn't that hitting a little below the belt?"

Paul turned to his roommate and said, "Hell no, this is part of my plan to get rid of that prick. What the hell are you smoking? It smells like shit."

"Tastes like it too. It's a Ruby Queen."

Paul frowned at his friend and asked, "Why are you smoking a fucking Vietnamese cigarette?"

Eric threw the butt outside and said, "I figure it's time to get back into shape. It's part of my tobacco end game. I've told my brain it can have all the nicotine it wants, as long as it comes from one of those little turds. They taste like you're smoking dirt. So far I'm down to three a day."

"I'm glad to hear it," Paul said, as he stood and handed Eric a pencil. "You know how to draw. I need a ribbon and a medal at the top of this."

Eric pushed the pencil back and said, "There is no way I am getting involved in that thing."

Paul pushed it back and said, "You already are. I need something like that Blue Max we saw in the George Peppard movie last month."

Eric reluctantly took the pencil and knelt down in front of the poster. "Where are you going to hang this?"

"In the O Club of course."

Eric turned to his friend. "That's crazy. You won't be able to get this in there without someone seeing you."

"I've already figured that out. Remember who's going to be officer of the day this week, or should I say officer of the night?"

Eric waved the pencil. "Oh no, there is no way I'm going to sneak this into the O Club."

"You won't have to. When you're making your rounds, you slip me the key and I will."

"But they'll suspect me right away."

"No they won't. Everybody knows you're too nice a guy to do something like this."

"Yeah right," Eric said as he started drawing a ribbon.

When he finished, Paul said, "Good job. I'll take it from here."

Three days later, the first pilots to enter the Officers' Club were greeted by a poster sporting a bright yellow medal and a red ribbon. The inscription read:

For having downed five aircraft
Robert L. Reddick is awarded the
The Honorary Title of Ace

Eason and Bader entered the bar, followed by Pete Barnes and Dan Sharkey. When Barnes saw the poster he laughed and said, "That's funny, Eason. I have to admit you have balls."

Paul waved him off and said, "Don't look at me."

Other pilots drifted into the club and laughed at the poster. Eventually, the word got to Reddick and he stormed in and tore it down. He wheeled around and yelled, "Who the hell is responsible for this?" The crowd remained silent and he said, "I know who did it, where's Eason?"

Eason and Bader had been sitting at the far end of the bar waiting for Reddick to challenge them. Without getting out of his seat, Eason said, "I've been flying since seven this morning. How could I have done it?"

Reddick was visibly shaking as he screamed, "I know you did this you bastard and you're not going to get away with it." Reddick stomped toward the door and the other pilots began to heckle him. When he was gone, the pilots turned to Eason and clapped.

Eric leaned toward his roommate. "We need to get out of here. It won't take much of an investigation to figure out I had the keys to the club last night."

"What are they going to do?" Paul asked. "They're way too short of pilots to ground us. Don't worry-- this is all part of my plan."

Eric stood and said, "I'm happy for that, but I think we still need to leave."

Reddick was not seen for several days and there was a rumor he had been sent to Cam Rahn Bay on temporary duty.

Eric and Paul were walking across the center courtyard when they were joined by Tucker Burdett. "Let's go to my room," he said. "I need to fill you in on what I just heard." Burdett handed them each a frosty Budweiser and said, "Eason, I don't know how you do it, but you're going to get away with another one. I don't think there's a pilot in the company who doesn't think you put that poster in the O Club, but from what I just heard at HQ nobody cares."

Burdett took a sip of beer. "The XO doesn't like Reddick because he's usurped some of his duties and the CO is mad as hell because Reddick crashed one of his helicopters. The accident is already raining piss down on the major from Battalion. I think I can safely say, there won't be any repercussions from your little art work."

The two roommates exchanged glances as Tucker continued. "I've got something else to tell you. The other day I said I was selling AK-47s to guys in Cam Rahn. Now I've decided to send twenty of them to Indonesia. I figure if I'm going to run the biggest private helicopter operation in Asia, I'm going to need protection. At ten pounds each, twenty of them will weigh the same as a corpse. I plan on wrapping them in packing, placing them in a coffin and shipping them to Jakarta through Hong Kong. You just have to bribe an airline load master and the right officials to pull it off."

Eric interrupted his friend and asked, "Tuck, isn't there a revolution going on in that county? You'll be in big trouble if you're caught."

Burdett shook his head. "The key is having someone trustworthy to take possession of the goods. My best friend and future business partner still lives there. He's an Indonesian named Zaki Salim, and I've known him since we were eight years old. His dad and mine were oil company engineers for Standard Oil, so we were in the upper class of Javanese society. We even had our own baby elephants for pets. It was the best time of my life. But when I was fifteen we left Indonesia for southern Louisiana. My father said it was a promotion, but it wasn't for me. I promised my friend Zaki I would return.

"I'm telling you this because I want you guys to fly for me. I plan on catering to the oil business, because I've been around it my whole life. I was even born in an oil field hospital outside of Bakersfield. The summer before I left for college my father got me a job in a drilling pipe yard. We called it rolling steel. If you think Nam is hot, you haven't seen hot until you've spent a summer moving pipe in southern Louisiana. The summer before I graduated, I was working on an off-shore oil rig. While I was flying out to the rig I started formulating a plan to own my own helicopter company. I knew the oil business, but I didn't know

99

anything about helicopters. Now I do, and I'm ready to implement my plan. I want you two as my first pilots."

Eric was the first to talk. "That's a good offer, but it will have to be after we spend the winter skiing in Austria."

"I know that and I also know after a winter in Europe you guys will be low on funds and will need jobs. It's going to take me at least eight months to get things running, so if you're there by fall the timing should be perfect."

The two roommates got up to leave and Eric said, "We'll keep you posted, Tuck."

Storm clouds were piling up on the horizon several days later. Eric was in his room putting a new music reel on their tape player when Paul came in and angrily threw his gear on the floor. "That fucking Reddick has done it this time."

Eric turned and asked, "What has he done now?"

"He almost got a bunch of us killed, that's what. We were going into what we were told was a secure area. As we started into the clearing, we were hit with one of the biggest ambushes I've ever seen. They were on both sides of us. Luckily, they started shooting early, so nobody landed and we were able to get out with only minor injuries. On the way back, one of the ships radioed that his crew chief had been in that same LZ yesterday. Apparently Reddick was showing a new lieutenant where there was going to be a big insertion. The VC figured it out and were waiting for us."

Paul kicked the screen door open and said, "I've heard the bastard is in the club. I'm going to have it out with him."

Eric followed him out. "I'm going with you."

As they entered the bar, Eason yelled, "Captain, you son of a bitch, you almost got me killed."

Reddick turned to face him. "You'd better watch how you talk to a superior officer, pal."

A new lieutenant who had been sitting with Reddick got up and hastily left the bar. Eric knew Paul would punch his rival at any provocation, so he pulled him aside and walked ahead. Reddick stood and said, "What the hell are you raving about?"

Paul yelled, "I'm talking about you landing in the same clearing as our insertion today. As long as you were there, why didn't you put up a sign that said, hey Chuck, we're having a party, bring friends."

Reddick smiled derisively and said, "What's the matter Eason, losing your nerve?"

Paul pushed Eric aside and yelled, "You're goddamn right I am, but at least I had some to begin with."

"Are you saying I don't?"

"That's exactly what I'm saying."

With a menacing look, Reddick lunged at Paul with a hay maker that would have sent Smoking Joe to the canvas. Paul's reflexes were still combat-quick and he leaned back, avoiding the punch. Reddick stumbled forward which allowed Paul to grab his shirt and throw him into a table.

Eric quickly jumped in between the two and said, "Take it easy guys, let's try and talk this out."

Reddick regained his footing and lunged at Eric with another punch. Eric ducked below the swing and threw a shoulder into Reddick's chest driving him backward onto a small table and lamp. The table collapsed under his weight and Reddick hit his head, knocking him unconscious.

While everyone cheered, a Gunnie took out a Buck knife and cut the cord from the broken lamp. Extending it to Eric he said, "I think we need to tie him up."

Eric looked at the cord and said, "I don't think we want to go that far. He'll really be pissed when he wakes up."

Paul grabbed the cord and said, "I think we should. You tried to reason with him and he went berserk."

Paul used the cord to tie Reddick's hands as another pilot found some tape and bound his legs. When they were finished, everyone stood over Reddick. He quickly recovered and began to scream that he was going to kill everyone if they didn't untie him. Eric pulled Paul aside and said, "You're the one with the bright ideas, now what do we do?"

Paul shook him off and said, "I don't know, but for now I think he's better off tied up. I'm going to watch the door to see whose coming." Paul looked out the door and called to Eric, "Hey Dog, come here. I just saw the new flight surgeon go into his room. Maybe he has something to calm Reddick down."

Eric looked out the door. "I'll go ask him. You stay here and keep a lid on this mess."

The company doctor was just out of medical school and had only been in Vietnam a month. Eric knocked on his screen door and explained how an officer in the club was threatening to kill people. The doctor rubbed his short brown hair and stammered, "Well, I don't know. I never saw anything like that in med school. What do you want me to do?"

Eric pointed at the bar and said, "You have to do something, Doc. We had to tie him up and now he says he's going to kill us."

The young doctor looked toward the club and said, "I guess I could take a look at him."

Eric opened the screen and said, "Thanks Doc, do you have a tranquilizer?"

"Not with me," the doctor said as the two of them hurried toward the bar.

When they walked through the door, Reddick yelled, "There's one of the bastards that did this to me. Bader, you're a dead man. Doc, I'm perfectly sane and these bastards have tied me up. They're going to pay for this and you will too if you touch me."

While the doctor was appraising the situation, Eric whispered into his ear, "It looks like combat fatigue to me."

Reddick continued to rave as the doctor walked to an old crank telephone and made a call to the dispensary. Five minutes later a burly medic appeared at the door with a syringe. Everyone stopped talking and stared at the medic. Reddick broke the silence by yelling, "I'll kill you if you touch me with that."

The medic ignored the threats and walked up to Reddick. Everyone watched as he knelt and administered the shot into Reddick's right arm. When Reddick lost consciousness, the medic walked toward the door saying, "Crazy fuckin' pilots."

The doctor stood over Reddick and said, "He'll sleep for about eight hours, so you better take him to his room."

There was an uneasy silence after the doctor left the bar. Clay Boone finally said, "Hey, the prick got what he deserved. We all saw him throw the first punch and then he just went nuts. Bader, you even tried to stop him. If we stick together nothing will happen."

Two Jokers untied Reddick and carried him to a couch by the door. One of them folded his arms across his chest which made him look like a corpse in a coffin. Everyone returned to the bar for a round of celebratory drinks. Captain Asshole had been defeated.

"Did you see the look on his face when he saw the size of that needle?" Boone asked with a big grin.

Paul laughed and said, "That was the best part. The guys in the 281st will love this story."

Eric glanced at Reddick lying on the couch and said, "I hope we didn't get the new doctor in trouble."

Boone protested. "We didn't have a choice. You heard the threats. He said he was going to kill us."

The discussion continued until a group of other pilots arrived. They had spent the day loitering near a mountain village. During their down-time Dan Sharkey bought a pet monkey. He walked into the bar with the monkey on his shoulder and said, "Gentlemen, meet our new mascot. His name is VC."

The pilots laughed and crowded around as Sharkey set the monkey on the bar and ordered a beer and a bowl. He poured a splash of beer into the bowl and offered it to his new pet. The monkey looked around nervously before drinking the beer. When he finished, Sharkey unhooked the monkey's leash and it ran down the bar. After several trips up and down the bar, the monkey jumped down and ran across the room to where Reddick was lying on the couch. He climbed onto Reddick's stomach and began emptying his shirt pockets. He found a pack of cigarettes and took one out of the pack and began to roll the cigarette in its paws. As the monkey emptied the cigarette, the tobacco fell onto Reddick's chest.

Everyone enjoyed the monkey's antics until the old crank telephone rang. They all stopped talking and stared at the phone. It was rarely used, so it had to be an important call. Baby-san moved to answer it, but Paul cut her off and picked up the receiver. "Officers' Club, Eason speaking."

The caller was Lieutenant Jack Cates, a friend of Eric and Paul's. In a hurried voice he said, "Paul this is Jack."

"Yeah Jack, what's up?"

"I'm at HQ and I just heard the new doctor telling the CO about a captain that had to be sedated. He mentioned Eric's name, so I thought I'd better warn you. The Old Man just stormed out of here headed your way."

"Thanks Jack, we'll be ready."

He hung up the receiver and advised the others. They decided there wasn't enough time to take Reddick to his room, so they waited in front of the bar and braced for the worst. The major threw the door open and demanded to know what was going on. He focused on the group standing by the bar and didn't notice Reddick lying on the couch behind him.

He slowly paced in front of them and said, "I heard you guys have been harassing an officer in here, and it got out of hand." He accentuated the word "officer" to emphasize the difference between commissioned officers and warrants.

Before the major could continue, the monkey began to screech. The CO turned toward the noise as the monkey emptied another cigarette and stacked it in a neat pile on Reddick's chest. The major whirled back toward the bar and said, "Okay, which one of you jokers is responsible for this?"

Someone in the back yelled, "It wasn't a Joker that did it, Sir."

The pilots stifled laughs as the major glared at the group and then stormed out of the room. When the door closed, Eason said, "I think it's time to get Sleepy to his room."

Several minutes after they had deposited Reddick on his bed, the

104

door opened and the Executive Officer entered the club. Captain Hart looked around the bar and asked, "Who's going to tell me what went on in here?"

Everyone began telling him how Eric had tried to break up a fight between Reddick and Eason, but Reddick had thrown punches at both of them. They were all in agreement that the only thing they could have done was to have the doctor give him a sedative. When the stories died down, the XO asked, "Where's Captain Reddick now?"

Paul stepped forward and said, "We took him to his room, Sir. The doctor said he'll be okay, but he'll probably sleep for awhile."

Hart nodded and then walked out the door. As it closed, Eric said, "It's going to be our word against Reddick's and the odds are thirty to one in our favor."

Paul turned toward the bar and said, "Let's have a drink. Baby-san, set a round up on me."

Sharkey set his monkey on the bar and poured more beer into the bowl. As it lapped up the beer Sharkey said, "You put on a good show tonight, VC."

The morning after what was to become known as the Monkey Caper, Eric was jolted into consciousness by four loud explosions. His mind cleared as he tried to remember if the rounds sounded like incoming, or outgoing. They were followed by another volley and he realized the rounds were the sharp, high-pitched sound of outgoing artillery and not the low-pitched thump of incoming mortars.

He swung his legs off the bed and took a drink from a canteen. Paul entered the room and asked, "Do you feel as bad as I do?"

Eric looked at his roommate and said, "I'm sure I do. Are you going to the mess hall?"

Paul took a shirt from his locker. "No, I've already had a Gunnie's breakfast."

Eric looked quizzically at his roommate. "What's that?"

"A cigarette, two aspirin, and a puke."

Eric chuckled. "Don't start with the jokes. It hurts too much to laugh." In a serious voice, he asked, "How much trouble do you think we're in for what we did to Reddick?"

"I think it'll blow over in a few days, providing Reddick doesn't make good on his promise to kill us. I'm not too worried though. He knows the Army would bust him down to private and send him to Leavenworth."

"Thanks for the encouragement," Eric said, as he grabbed his shaving kit. "I think when we're done flying, we better see if we can get ourselves on the long term detail to Ban Me Thout. A few weeks away from here wouldn't hurt."

"Good idea. BMT would be a good place to hide out."

On the flight line, they were greeted by a handful of pilots offering their support. Captain Reddick was conspicuously absent and everyone speculated on how he would react when he saw Eason and Bader.

Eric had a light schedule, so he was back in the revetments by five-thirty. After telling his crew to secure the ship, he headed for company headquarters. He decided to go straight to the Executive Officer because he trusted Captain Hart and knew if there was going to be trouble the XO would tell him. As he entered his office, Eric saluted, and said, "Good afternoon Sir."

Captain Hart pointed at a chair and said, "Let me guess, you want to volunteer for Ban Me Thout."

Eric sat down and said, "Yes Sir, I would appreciate you putting me on the list."

"Oh you're on the list all right. The major made sure of that this morning. You didn't exactly make a good first impression with the new CO, Bader. I have a feeling you and Eason are going to be on every shit list that comes along."

"Shit list," Eric said, surprised. "I thought BMT was a good deal."

"Some people might think so, but I'm not so sure. You'll be resupplying outposts in Cambodia."

"Cambodia!" Eric exclaimed. "I thought we weren't supposed to be there."

"We aren't, so don't tell anybody. They're also predicting heavy fog in the area, so that ought to make things interesting."

"Yeah, it should," Eric said. "What about Eason, is he going?"

"No, I think you guys need some time apart." Hart leaned across his desk. "Listen Eric, you and Eason are two of my best pilots and I like you guys, but I'm not going to stand for anymore of the bullshit that's going on between you two and Captain Reddick. Is that understood?"

"Yes Sir."

The XO leaned back and said, "Good luck in Ban Me Thout."

"Thank you Sir," Eric said, as he stood and left the office.

Eric was almost to his room when he saw Reddick leave for the latrine with a towel wrapped around his waist. He looked ashen and weak. When he saw Eric, he sneered, "You bastard! I'm going to get you for this and that goes for your asshole buddy."

Eric turned away without saying anything. He wasn't worried about Reddick, but he was glad to be leaving just the same. He entered his stifling room and took off his shirt and poured water on a towel. He turned on his fan and placed the towel over his head. It felt good to lie down for a badly needed nap.

He had been sleeping for half an hour when Paul entered the room and stowed his gear in his locker. "I just heard there's a briefing for those going to BMT and I'm not one of them. I take it you couldn't talk Hart into letting me go."

Eric removed the towel and said, "No, he said he was going to keep us apart for awhile. He also said he didn't want to hear anything more about either one of us."

"So apparently there isn't going to be any action taken against us?"

"I don't think so. He would have mentioned it if there was."

"Has anybody seen Ace?"

"Yeah, I just saw him leave for the latrine. He looked pretty bad. He said he was going to get us."

"I'm shaking in my boots."

"I know, but stay away from him anyway. Captain Hart was pretty mad, and it sounds like the CO is even more pissed."

"Okay, I'll be good. I just wish I was going with you."

"So do I," Eric said, as he sat up and splashed water on his face. He toweled off and got up to comb his hair. He put on a clean T-shirt and walked toward the door. "I'll see you at the mess hall after the briefing."

Inside the briefing room, the Jokers were hooting and laughing. The lead Gunnie was Pete Barnes, with Dan Sharkey as his trail.

The mission would be comprised of four slicks and two gunships, temporarily assigned to the 155th Helicopter Assault Company in Ban Me Thout. Captain Al Hutchins was the flight leader and began the briefing. "Men, the 155th has sustained a number of casualties and don't have enough flyable helicopters to support all of their area of operation. Our six ships will stay in BMT until the 155th can acquire new ships and pilots. They expect it will be at least two weeks before they will be back to operational strength.

"Fog is predicted for the area and as you know there aren't any refueling stops along the way. We will have just enough fuel to fly the ninety miles to Ban Me Thout, take a quick look for the airport and if we can't find it, fly back here to Ninh Hoa. Takeoff is set for 0600 hours. I'll see you then."

Eric figured he had a few things going for him. Al Hutchins was a good flight leader, and his co-pilot was Tom Paris. He also had his regular door gunner Tony Pagliano. His new crew chief was Nacho Quintana, one of the best in the company. It was always good to have an experienced mechanic on an extended detail.

Ignacio "Nacho" Quintana had grown up in El Paso, Texas, the son of an Army sergeant stationed at Fort Bliss. Besides his Army duties, his father owned a lawn mower repair shop. Quintana had grown up working on the engines and was raised bilingual, English and Spanish. In high school he studied French, so when he graduated he was fluent in three languages. After graduation he joined the Army and became a helicopter crew chief. Despite having a pocked face, he was considered ruggedly handsome and was a favorite with the ladies.

Eric left the briefing more worried about the fog than the enemy action they might encounter. He always felt if the enemy knocked out his engine, he could put his ship down in a place where he and his crew could survive and be rescued. If his engine quit over fog and he had to descend into it, the trees would tear his helicopter apart before he could do anything about it. Even if they survived the crash into the jungle, the probability of capture was high.

In the morning, Eric let Paris start the ship. Tom had been doing well and Eric was about to recommend him for Aircraft Commander. Paris usually did the flying, but Eric decided he would back the helicopter out of the revetment himself. The ship would be heavier than normal and he didn't want to let anything jeopardize the mission.

The revetments consisted of three sandbagged walls running six feet high along each side, and in front of the helicopter. It was designed to keep small-arms fire and mortars from damaging the helicopters during an attack. Moving the helicopters in and out of the revetments was at best a tricky situation and at worst downright scary. The air washing down from the main rotor would bounce off the walls, causing the tail of the helicopter to wag back and forth. Having the tail rotor strike the wall was the pilot's greatest fear. If the wind was blowing, or other helicopters were hovering nearby, the procedure was even more hairy.

Each pilot developed his own style for operating into and out of the revetments. Eric usually liked to use what was known as the pop-up. He got the ship light on the skids and then pulled straight up to about ten feet before backing into the departure lane. Eric liked it because it minimized time in the danger zone.

The other method involved hovering between the walls of the revetment and then carefully backing out. This technique took a myriad of control inputs, as the helicopter tried to yaw, buffet, and roll. It was mainly used when the ship was too heavy to do a pop-up. With the extra fuel on board, Eric would have to use the back-up method. He turned to his co-pilot and Paris read his mind. "She's all yours Skipper."

Smart kid, Eric thought, he knows he's about to be promoted to Aircraft Commander. Why risk the embarrassment of tearing a helicopter apart in its stall. Eric took the controls and radioed the flight leader. "Lead, Chalk One is up."

"Thanks One," Capt. Hutchins called back. "How about the guns? Are you guys up?"

"Yeah, we're up."

"Chalk Two, how about you, are you up?" When there wasn't an answer, Hutchins said, "Three, I've got you in sight. Two, are you up? We're burning fuel Dawson, are you coming or staying?"

"Yeah, yeah, Two's up. Sorry, we had a little problem on the start."

"Okay, Lead's coming out. Slicks go loose trail with the guns to follow."

The flight backed out and then wallowed off the ground in a gaggle of four slicks and two gunships going to war in new country. After they leveled off at their cruising altitude, Eric motioned for Paris to take the controls. "It's all yours Frenchie, I need some coffee." The air was cool as he took his Thermos and poured them each a cup.

They were crossing the coastal mountain range with a large peak named Chu Mi, or Big Charlie sticking up on their right. Past the mountains, the central highlands unfolded as the dark green jungle gave way to brilliant light green grass and rice paddies.

At the halfway point, the flight's worst fears were realized. A layer of ground fog appeared to extend all the way to their destination. The fog started at ground level which meant there would be no way to sneak under it. Without terrain features, or a navigational beacon to guide them to the Ban Me Thout airport, they would have to use what pilots call dead reckoning. The flight leader would take up a heading that he thought would take them toward their destination and would use airspeed and timing to judge when he thought they were over the airport.

When he thought they were nearing the airfield, Captain Hutchins radioed the control tower, "BMT tower this is Blue Star 64, a flight of six helicopters, request your weather conditions."

The controller answered, "Ban Me Thout weather, estimated ceiling one hundred feet, zero visibility, fog, wind calm, altimeter setting 29.82, occasional breaks in the overcast."

Hutchins answered, "Roger tower, we're going to have a look."

When he thought they were over the airport, Hutchins radioed the flight, "Okay guys, fan out and see if you can find something that looks like a runway."

If they didn't find it soon, they would have to go all the way back to their home base. Fortunately, the fog wasn't as thick in this area and occasionally they could see green vegetation through thin spots in the layer.

Suddenly one of the flight members radioed excitedly, "I've got an airport ramp below me and I'm going to have a look."

They all knew the voice and his position in the flight. It was Dave Dawson in Chalk Two and he had already begun a descending spiral. The sucker hole proved too small for the radius of his turn and he became enveloped in the fog. Dawson radioed that he had lost sight of the ground and was climbing back up.

Bader had been the closest to Dawson and was looking down into the hole. The rotor blades from the ascending helicopter stirred the fog enough for Eric to make out an airplane wing. Using it as a focal point he descended and called his flight leader. "Lead, Chalk One has the ramp and an aircraft. I'm going to try and get under this stuff."

Hutchins clicked his mike twice to signify he understood. The rest of the flight circled like buzzards awaiting their turn.

As Eric descended, Hutchins called the controller, "Tower, Blue Star flight of six is starting our decent to the field."

The tower advised against it, as he was still reporting zero visibility. Hutchins lied that they could see the field on the southern end.

The controller reluctantly said, "Okay, you're cleared to land, but only if you can maintain visual flight rules at all times."

"Roger Tower," Hutchins said.

Eric was halfway down and straining to keep the small Cessna in sight. At times it got clearer, then almost vanished. At last he could make out the ramp and a couple of other airplanes. He was fifty feet high when he broke out of the fog. He flew behind the two airplanes and radioed, "Hutch, I'm below the fog and I have a fifty foot ceiling."

The fog thinned as each ship stirred the air on the descent to the

111

airport. The controller became suspicious and asked, "What's taking you guys so long?"

"We have three down and three descending," Hutchins replied. When they were all down, he called again, "Tower, all six ships are on the ground."

"Glad to hear that," the controller replied. "I can hear you out there, but I can't see you."

The crews secured their ships and then assembled at their flight leader's helicopter. Everyone admitted that pushing weather that bad had been a dumb thing to do. With a sheepish grin Hutchins said, "I guess we better report to Operations, if we can find it."

Everyone laughed, as they began walking across the field. When they passed the control tower, they realized they had landed one hundred yards away. Hutchins pointed at the tower cab and said, "That controller is really going to be pissed when the fog lifts and he sees we're parked on the other side of the runway."

At Ops they were given a welcome and were told that because of the fog, there wouldn't be any missions that day. They were shown their quarters and introduced to a pilot who was recovering from an arm wound.

The pilot briefed them on the action his unit had seen the previous week. He also mentioned the company area had been mortared for two nights. One of the rounds had landed in their swimming pool. Eric looked at the hole in the empty pool and thought it was too cold for swimming, but it would be great for sleeping. He hadn't slept under a blanket since he left the cool air of Dalat.

After showing them the company area, the local pilot led them to the company break room. The pilots spent the rest of the day trying to combat boredom by playing ping pong, pool and poker. After lunch, Eric found the novel *The Drifters* and spent two hours reading before he fell asleep. He was awakened by Tom Paris, who told him everyone was going to an early dinner.

While they were eating, the pilots discussed whether they should go into town. Even though the village was just outside the gate, it had been declared off limits. The local pilot had told them some of the men in his company ignored the order and hit the bars anyway. He said community relations were somewhat strained, because the mortars that had hit the base came from the vicinity of the village.

The Jokers were up for going into town, while the Slick pilots opted for beers at the Officers' Club. Pete Barnes got up from the table and said, "What's the matter Slickies, are you afraid a dink might shoot you? I thought we were here to kick some ass." He patted his holstered pistol and said, "If any of them gives me shit, I'll shoot them. A kill's a kill, the way I see it." The Gunnies laughed as Barnes stuffed a cigar in his mouth and led the others out of the mess hall in a trail of smoke.

The next morning Eric was in the latrine shaving before first light. He was the only one there and wondered if he was early or late. Whichever, he didn't care. It was nice to have a latrine to himself. For a moment he thought the Gunnies may have gotten into trouble, but then decided he would have heard them shooting up the town if they had.

He walked outside dressed only in his Army underwear and shower thongs. Like all pilots, the first thing he did was check the sky. The first traces of predawn light showed the fog had lifted. It would be a good fly day.

He was walking along a dirt path when something cold and wet ran up the back of his leg. He jumped forward thinking it was a snake and probably a bamboo viper. If it bit him he would only have minutes to live. He spun around and was relieved to see he had been caressed by the trunk of a baby elephant, chained to a tree. Eric petted it and said, "Hey little guy, where's your momma? I'll bet you're hungry. I'll see if I can find you something at the chow hall." There was a dollop of shaving cream on the little elephant's head, so Eric figured the Gunnies were already up.

He entered the mess hall and saw it was empty except for the four gunship pilots. They had finished eating and were drinking coffee and smoking cigars. Eric took a tray of powdered eggs, chipped beef toast and coffee to their table. As he joined them, Barnes said, "Up pretty early for a Slickie aren't you Dog?"

The other Jokers laughed dutifully as Eric looked across the table at Barnes and said, "Yeah, I just couldn't help myself, Pete. I woke up with this irresistible urge for green eggs and cigar smoke."

Barnes drew on his cigar and said, "That's funny, Bader, you're all right. You should have joined us last night. We had a good time."

"Oh yeah, I figured the MPs probably caught you sneaking off base."

A cloud of blue-gray smoke curled up to a bare light bulb as Barnes looked out the window and said, "It looks like a good fly day. I hope we see some action. I need to finish off the third row of little pointy hats on the side of my gunship."

Eric took a bite of eggs and said, "You never let up do you, Pete?" Barnes wasn't such a bad guy, he thought, but he did get carried away with the macho Gunnie mentality. The truth was, there wasn't anybody Eric would rather have flying cover for him than Pete Barnes and his wingman Dan Sharkey.

An hour later the pilots attended a briefing at Air Operations. The room was sparse with a map, chalk board and gray folding chairs. An Army captain told them they would be flying to Bu Prang, a remote village next to the Cambodian border. He warned there was a problem at Bu Prang because they had recently run out of fuel. That meant the flight would have to return to Ban Me Thout to refuel. He explained that two Special Forces outposts in the area were under siege. The 155th hadn't been there in a week, so they were both short on supplies and ammunition.

The crews walked out of the briefing room looking like confident ball players coming out of the tunnel for a big game.

On the flight to Bu Prang the weather was clear and the airstrip easy to find. As they made their approach for landing, Eric pointed at a wrecked C-130 transport aircraft off the end of the red dirt airstrip and said, "Looks like somebody ran out of runway." The aircraft was lying on its belly with all four engines removed.

The helicopters shut down and the pilots were transported to a heavily fortified compound surrounded by concertina wire and land mines. It was a serious looking place and even the gunship pilots took on a solemn mood. The group was led into a room where a grim-faced Special Forces major looked at each pilot before he said, "Men, this mission is to resupply an outpost inside Cambodia. I need to inform you the U.S. government denies any involvement in that country. If any of you are unfortunate enough to be shot down and captured, your government will deny you ever crossed the border. I know that sounds harsh, but that is the way it is in this political environment." He looked into the eyes of every man again and said, "Good luck gentlemen and good flying."

The pilots thought of the obvious as they followed the major out of the room. With the remoteness of the area, there would be little chance of rescue if anybody went down in "Indian Country."

Thirty minutes later they lifted off in a trail formation just above tree-top level. Their contact at the outpost was Lizard Six. When they were within radio distance, Captain Hutchins tried to contact him, with no reply. A minute later he tried again. Lizard Six answered, speaking fast. "Helicopters, we are under heavy fire from all sides. We need ammo fast, or we've had it. How far out are you?"

"About five minutes," Hutchins said. The truth was, they were flying a heading over thick jungle and didn't really know where they were in relation to the outpost.

"You've got to hurry. We're about to be overrun. I'm going back underground." His second call was louder, so they were getting closer.

A few seconds later, the outpost came into view and Barnes radioed, "Lead, Jokers have the clearing and we're armed and hot."

"Okay, you guns form up," Hutchins said. "I want the Slicks to climb up to five thousand. Dog, call the commander at Bu Prang and tell him what we've got and tell him to order a couple of fast movers."

"Roger Lead," Eric said, as he raised the collective and started a climb. As he did, the gunships streaked by on their way to the target.

Barnes called the compound. "Lizard Six, this is Joker Six-nine. How many enemy you got down there?"

"The last time I checked, it looked like it might be a whole company of NVA."

When they got closer, the flight could see a column of enemy soldiers marching up a hill toward the outpost. Barnes called their contact and said "Okay Lizard, I've got them in sight. We're coming in hot." He called his trail gunner. "Cover me, Mako."

"Right behind you, Boss Man," Sharkey radioed back.

Gray explosions began ripping the hill, as rockets streaked from the diving gunship. Barnes excitedly called the flight, "The gooners are skyin' out. I've got the bastards on the run and I've never seen so many."

The Slick pilots watched from above, as it appeared Barnes was getting too close to the enemy before starting his break. A gunship never flew directly over the target while on a firing run. The lead ship always made a hard turn before reaching the target, to allow the trail ship to cover his exposed turn. Then the lead hurried into position to cover his trail's break.

Barnes continued his run, firing rockets and mini-guns simultaneously. When Sharkey saw Barnes was late for his turn, he yelled into the radio, "Break it off Boss! Break *now!*" He had already started firing in anticipation of his lead gunner's break, but Barnes never turned. Sharkey didn't have anybody to cover his break, so he started his break early.

They all watched as Barnes continued to fire all the way to the target. Suddenly, a small trail of smoke came from the gunship. "We're hit, we're hit," Barnes screamed, as a fire broke out in his helicopter.

Eric saw a small clearing ahead and to the right of the gunship and called, "Turn to your two o'clock Pete, there's an opening at your two." Eric knew they couldn't land in such a small area, but it was better than crashing into the tall trees. The burning ship made a shallow turn to the right before it burst into a fireball and fell into the jungle directly below Eric's helicopter.

The flight leader's voice cracked as he said, "Lizard Six, we just lost a gunship. Are you still there?"

Eric knew Hutchins had to be as shaken as himself, but he kept his cool.

"Yeah, we're still here and it's real quiet. I think you drove them off."

"Good, I'm going to recon the crash site and then we'll drop off your supplies." Hutchins called his remaining gunship and asked, "Mako, how many rockets do you have left?"

"I've got eight pair," Sharkey answered softly. He had just seen his best friend get killed, but he too kept calm.

Hutchins circled the crash site, and then switched to a frequency that only the helicopters could hear. "Are you guys ready to unload this stuff and get the hell out of here?"

There was a short pause as everyone thought of the obvious. The enemy had managed to knock down a speeding gunship under a withering barrage of gunfire. How easy would it be for them to knock down a hovering slick while it unloaded its cargo? Eric broke the silence. "I think that's why we're here, Hutch."

"That's right," Hutchins said. "I'll go first. If we take heavy fire we leave. Mako, cover us."

"You've got it," Sharkey said, as he made an intimidating run at the hill.

When the gunship didn't draw fire, Hutchins started his approach to the compound. As he hovered just above the ground, his right door gunner fired at the tree line while the crew chief tossed the cargo from the left side of the ship. As they left the clearing, Hutchins radioed, "Taking fire, taking fire."

Before he started his descent, Eric glanced at his co-pilot. Under different circumstances he would have laughed. Paris had his six-foot frame curled into a tight ball inside his armor-plated chair. Eric said, "You're supposed to be in a position to take over if I get hit."

Paris looked up from his crouch and said, "First somebody has to *be* here to take control."

Eric looked toward the front and said, "I don't blame you. I'd do the same if I could." He lowered the collective and began his approach to the clearing. His right door gunner's machine gun started its loud chatter. He hovered just above the ground and glanced over his left shoulder to watch as Quintana threw boxes out of the ship. When he turned to the front, a bullet pierced the Plexiglas windshield and knocked out the side window of his co-pilot.

Paris moaned in pain as Eric yelled, "Taking fire, we're hit. Do you see 'em Mako?" Eric glanced at his co-pilot and asked, "Are you all right?"

Paris was holding the left side of his face with a gloved hand and said, "It feels like I took some shrapnel."

Eric checked his face and said, "Looks like the bullet creased your chin too. When we're out of here I'll have Nacho put a compress on your wounds."

"Does it look bad?"

"No, the scar will make for a good story."

Sharkey's calm voice came over the radio. "I've got the bad guys and I'm on a run." The gunship fired four rockets to Eric's right. The explosions were so close they rocked the ship.

Eric continued to hover as he glanced to the back and watched his crew chief kick the last box out of the helicopter. He yelled for Quintana to hold on and quickly hauled ass out of the compound. When he was clear, Chalk Two and Three made their deliveries with minimal fire taken. Sharkey's rockets had done their job.

As the last ship climbed out of the LZ, Hutchins called the ground, "There you go Lizard, that's all we've got."

"Thanks guys, you really saved our asses."

Hutchins circled the compound and said, "You should have some jets here in a few minutes to bomb the trees. It looks like there are still enemy moving around down there. Good luck."

"Roger that, thanks again."

Hutchins called his flight. "I need a status report. Chalk One, how bad were you hit?"

"A bullet knocked out Frenchie's side window and he has cuts on his face, but he's hanging in there."

"Mako, how about you?"

"We took a couple of rounds to the belly, but all our vitals are good."

Hutchins called the other two and they reported no hits. He called Eric and said, "Okay Dog, let's recon the crash site one more time."

"Roger," Eric radioed as he followed his lead to the site. The only indication there had been a crash were smoldering pieces of aircraft stuck on top of the trees.

As they circled the area, Eric radioed, "Even if someone survived the explosion they wouldn't have survived the fall. Those trees are at least a hundred feet tall."

"Yeah, I was thinking the same thing. Let's get out of here," Hutchins said softly.

It started to rain as Hutchins took up a heading for Bu Prang. There was none of the usual chatter between crews as they flew back to the airstrip. The field came into site and Hutchins called the base, "Bu Prang Ops, the helicopters are five minutes out. We need a medic to meet the flight to look at one of our pilots."

The major radioed that he and a medic would meet them at the airstrip. After they landed, the pilots climbed out of their helicopters and followed the major into a tin-roofed hut. An Army medic examined Paris, as the major turned to Captain Hutchins and asked, "How was the mission?"

Hutchins let out a sigh and said, "We got the supplies to your compound, but we lost a gunship."

The major grimaced and said, "My condolences, men. Any chance of survivors?"

Hutchins shook his head solemnly as they all listened to the rain beat rhythmically upon the tin roof. The major looked at the men assembled around him and said, "I know it's been a long day men, but I've got one more mission for you."

He walked to a map and pointed. "We have a patrol of twelve men under heavy fire. They estimate the enemy force to be about twenty NVA. They're holding them off, but they say they don't have enough ammo to last through the night. Unfortunately, we still don't have fuel here, so when you get them out, head straight for BMT and return here in the morning."

Eric couldn't believe what he was hearing. It was late afternoon and their fuel tanks were less than half full. He knew everything would have to go perfectly to pull it off, and how often did that happen. Never.

Hutchins turned and faced his pilots. No speech was necessary, so they followed him out of the shack. They slogged toward the flight line through sticky red mud with slumped shoulders. They were no longer the confident athletes who had walked out that morning. Pete Barnes had been a major contributor to that confidence and most of it had crashed into the trees with him.

They had to wait to depart while Sharkey's crew chief finished tightening screws on an underside panel. The ship had taken two rounds to the belly with no apparent damage to the flight cables.

The rain was lighter as they took off, but ground fog was beginning to form over the steamy jungle. As they crossed back into Cambodia, Captain Hutchins tried to call their new contact, with no luck. He tried again and received an answer with the sound of gunfire crackling in the background.

"Helicopters, this is Tall Snake. It sounds like you are to my south, come north." Hutchins made a right turn and the others followed in a zigzag trail.

"Helicopters, this is Tall Snake, now it sounds like you are to my east. Come west." The flight turned into the setting sun.

"Okay helicopters, I've got you in sight, turn to your three o'clock position."

When Hutchins began a right turn, the grunt screamed, "No, no, you're turning the wrong way!"

Hutchins growled into the radio, "Listen Snake, we're burning valuable fuel. Do you want us to turn to our *right or left*?"

"Turn left and you'll be coming right at us. When you get closer, we'll move to a grass clearing." As the flight made the turn, they could make out a small opening that was lighter than the surrounding jungle. When they made the turn, the grunt said, "You're coming right at us."

"Good, pop a Goofy for me," Hutchins radioed.

He lined up on the purple smoke and asked, "Which direction is the fire coming from?"

"The tree line to our west. Right now it's just small-arms fire."

Sharkey jumped in, "I've got it Hutch and I'm going in hot."

"Okay Mako, cover us. There are only twelve of them, so just two of us need to go. I'll take six, Chalk One you get the rest and we'll get the hell out of here."

Eric reduced pitch to begin a descent and asked his co-pilot, "How'd we get so lucky to be Chalk One?"

"Probably all your clean living," Paris answered.

Hutchins continued the descent and called the ground. "Snake, we're coming in. Get your men into two groups of six, fifty feet apart."

"Roger that," the trooper answered in a relieved voice.

When the lead ship landed, green and red tracers came at it from the tree line. Hutchins yelled into the radio, "Taking fire. We're taking fire from our two. Go get 'em Mako." Sharkey began hosing down the area with his mini-gun, shredding trees and brush.

Pagliano began firing over the heads of the men rushing to get on board, as Eric flared for a landing behind the lead ship. In their haste, the troopers jumped on the skids before the helicopter had touched down.

A mortar round landed a few meters to their left, as Eric fought his bucking ship to the ground. The round rained dirt onto the helicopter as Quintana yelled, "We're hit."

"How bad?" Eric yelled, looking over his left shoulder.

The thick air smelled of damp jungle and cordite as the troopers clamored on board. His crew chief was hanging out of the left door and said, "We've got a six-inch rip in the tail boom." When he sat back down, Quintana yelled, "She's still running, let's go!"

Another mortar landed as they lifted off the LZ. Eric called Hutchins, "Lead, we took a hit from a mortar, how about you?"

"We only took small arms fire, how bad were you hit?"

"We've got a rip in the tail boom," Eric answered, praying his ship would hold together.

"Hang in there, Dog," his flight leader radioed. "The rest of you guys form up and let's get the hell out of here."

The men they had saved smelled like mud, sweat and fear, but they were the happiest troopers the crew had ever seen. They thanked everybody among war whoops and whistles. Eric looked back as two guys flipped a bird toward the ground.

"Too bad I don't feel as good," Eric told Paris. His co-pilot nodded his bandaged head. Both pilots knew how serious their situation had become. They had a gash in their tail boom, it was getting dark and they were low on fuel. There wasn't a radio beacon to home in on, and with nightfall there wouldn't be any terrain features to follow. The only means they had to find Ban Me Thout was a general heading. The troops in back settled down and began peering out at the growing darkness.

When they started flying in and out of fog, Eric turned to Paris and said, "It's getting close to pucker time. How are you doing?"

"My head feels like I've been hit with a baseball bat, but other than that I'm okay."

With the situation deteriorating, Captain Hutchins called the flight, "Let's get on top of this stuff." When they were above the fog they could only see the ground in patches and nobody knew exactly where they were. They flew on in silence.

I wish somebody would say something, Eric thought. He instinctively reached for a pack of cigarettes then realized he didn't have any. When he turned toward the back, he was startled by the face of his crew chief staring over his left shoulder. The red glare from the instrument panel accentuated the worried lines in his face.

Quintana slipped a pack onto Eric's left shoulder and said, "Help yourself." They both stared at the fuel gauge as Eric lit a cigarette.

Chalk Three broke the silence. "Hutch, we just got a twenty minute fuel warning light."

Hutchins acknowledged the call, and radioed Eric, "Chalk One, how's your fuel?"

Eric answered, "I'd say we're about two or three minutes to a light."

"How are you doing, Two?"

"A little more, seven or eight minutes."

"Mako, how about you?"

"Our light just came on, Hutch."

The pressure of the situation was reflected in the flight leader's voice as he said, "Okay, let's split up. Turn on your lights and let's try to find a place to land." Shortly after Hutchins turned on his search light, a stream of tracers came at it from the jungle. The light went off and the flight continued on in semi-darkness.

"I'm down to a hundred pounds of fuel," Chalk Three reported. That left them with ten minutes of flying time.

The situation was becoming dire. Running out of fuel over jungle would be bad anytime. If it happened at night, the pilots wouldn't be able to see when to pull in pitch to cushion their fall into the trees. A crash like that meant almost-certain death.

As if that wasn't bad enough, Eric wasn't sure if they had crossed the Cambodian border. He had been in other emergencies, but they had all been instantaneous with no time to think of the consequences. This was slow and excruciating. He wondered if they were going to wait until Chalk Three called that his engine had quit and he was going down. He decided not to wait for that. He found a dark hole in the fog and descended toward it. As he did, his door gunner screamed, "Look out right, there's a ship to our right."

Eric banked hard left and looked out the right window. The other ship had seen them and was veering away. It was Sharkey's gunship and they had almost collided as they both tried to enter the same opening. He called Sharkey, "That was close Mako. I'm closer--I'll go first." Sharkey clicked his mike twice.

Eric descended into the hole and broke out under the fog two hundred feet above the trees. He quickly radioed his flight leader, "Lead, Chalk One is under the fog with a two hundred foot ceiling."

"Good, we're coming down," Hutchins called back.

Eric peered into the growing darkness and spotted lights ahead.

"I've got lights at twelve o'clock, two miles. I'm going to have a look."

Hutchins called, "Turn on your strobe, Dog. I can't see you through the fog." Paris reached up and flicked the switch on and off.

"Okay we've got you."

Eric concentrated on the lights ahead. They aren't much, he thought, but at least somebody's out there. Quintana tapped his shoulder and asked, "Are we out of Indian Country?"

"We should have crossed the border a few minutes ago," Eric answered. "Those lights could be an enemy camp, so get back to your gun and tell those grunts to get ready. We're out of fuel, so we have to land no matter what."

They flew on in silence, with the clicks of weapons being checked the only sound in the ship. It could also be a small village with no place to land, Eric thought. What if there was just enough room for one or two ships Helicopters were going to start falling out of the sky in a few minutes.

When he neared the lights, Eric flipped on his search light and spotted an open area. "I've got a place to set down!" he radioed. "There is a clearing, and it has room for everybody. Watch out for a set of white rocks in the middle." He and Paris read what the rocks spelled and laughed in unison. They spelled, "No Choppers." It was English. They had found an American outpost. Eric landed straddling the N.

While the others landed, Eric shut down his engine and he and Paris took off their sweat-soaked helmets. They watched three soldiers approach in the flickering light of the other search lights. A captain yelled through Paris's blown-out window, "Can't you guys read English. This is a commo bunker for Christ's sake. We have sensitive antennas all over the goddamn place."

Eric fought back a smirk and said, "Sorry about that, Captain, but we didn't have a choice. Our flight leader is in the ship next to us and he'll explain everything."

The crews assembled in front of Eric's ship as Hutchins greeted the infantry captain and explained why they had landed in his commo field. The captain said, "Okay, I'm glad you're all safe. We've got room to put you up for the night, but bring your weapons and ammo, because your ships will be outside our perimeter."

The three infantrymen led the crews and soldiers up a small hill to their compound. The captain directed the enlisted men to an underground mess hall and then told the pilots to follow him down to an Operations bunker. When they were assembled, he walked to a map on the wall and pointed to an X near the Cambodian border. "Men, we are here, just inside Vietnam and about thirty miles from Ban Me Thout."

He turned and faced his audience. "I know you didn't have a choice, but you could have picked a better place for your emergency landing. We've been under attack for several days and I'm pretty sure when the enemy finds out we have five helicopters parked here they'll hit us with everything they've got. We haven't been resupplied in a week, so we're low on food and ammo, but we're supposed to get a shipment tomorrow."

Hutchins interrupted, "I wouldn't count on that until we get out of here."

The infantry captain looked at Hutchins and said, "I was afraid of that. By the way, how *are* you getting out of here?"

Hutchins answered in a tired voice, "Tomorrow morning we'll have a Chinook sling a fuel bladder in here and we'll leave as soon as we're fueled."

The briefing ended and the captain offered the men a pot of fresh-brewed coffee. Eric took a steaming mug and sat on a bench against a dirt wall. The knots in his stomach were starting to unwind, when Sharkey approached and stood over him. "You've got good eyes, Dog. That's twice you saved us and I just want to say thanks."

Eric looked up at the gunship pilot's pained expression and said, "I'm sorry about Barnes."

"Yeah," Sharkey said and then walked away without saying anything more.

After a meal of C rations and Kool Aid, a young soldier led Eric's crew to a dank bunker that was to serve as their sleeping quarters. Eric laid down on a moldy cot and thought of the day's activities. He knew it would be a long time before he would be able to sleep. Just that morning he had eaten breakfast with Barnes and his crew and now they were dead. He needed a drink and thought he was probably becoming an alcoholic, but it didn't matter. Drinking usually got him through another night.

The next morning he was awakened by a bad dream. It had started with him flying in his helicopter at night. The moon was so bright it illuminated the tall teak trees he was flying over. He checked the other seats and saw they were all empty with the machine guns in their stowed positions.

When he turned to peer out of the windshield he was shocked to see he was losing altitude. He quickly raised the collective and yanked back on the cyclic, but there was no response. He continued to hold both positions until the helicopter sank into the dark green carpet of trees.

The ship disintegrated and his body began falling through the branches. He was in a free fall and saw he was headed toward a section of the jungle floor that was illuminated by the moon. When his body hit the ground, a loud thud jarred him awake. The sound was still fresh in his mind as he sat up and heard his co-pilot ask, "What the hell was that?"

"Mortar," one of the local soldiers answered groggily.

Eric was drenched in sweat even though the bunker was cool and damp. He wiped his face with his T-shirt and looked toward one of the ground-level openings. The first faint rays of dawn filtered through the small opening. Charlie's up early, he thought.

He swung his legs off the cot and began putting on his flight shirt. Another loud explosion rocked the bunker and one of the locals said, "They do this every morning. I think they're trying to catch somebody outside taking a piss."

Eric checked on his crew. Quintana was lying on the cot next to him and said, "Nice neighborhood."

On the next bunk down, Pagliano still had his eyes closed.

126

Paris was on the cot behind Eric and said, "We've only been here one night and I already hate this goddamn place."

Eric turned toward his co-pilot and asked, "How's your face?"

"It's felt better, but I'll survive. Right now I'm just happy to *have* a face."

"Good point," Eric said.

The aircrew decided to go to the mess bunker for coffee. On the way, Quintana said he wanted to see if their ship had been damaged in the mortar attack. When Pagliano dutifully began to follow his fellow door gunner, Eric called to them, "You better take a couple of the troopers we picked up last night for protection."

Quintana stopped and said, "Good idea, there could be VC crawling all around this place."

Bader and Paris descended into the mess bunker where they were greeted by Hutchins. "Good morning guys. I just got word a Chinook will sling a fuel bladder here around noon."

Eric slapped hands with Paris and said, "That sounds good, Hutch. We're ready to get the hell out of there."

The two pilots finished a meager breakfast of peanut butter and jelly toast, and then decided to go to the commo field and check on their helicopter. The sun was still behind the horizon as they climbed out of the bunker. In the pre-dawn light they could make out the surrounding terrain. The hills around the compound were covered with dense jungle. Steam rising off the ground gave the place a serene, peaceful look.

Eric pointed at the hills. "It would have been a real bitch trying to find somewhere to land if this place hadn't been here."

Paris opened the gate and said, "And that commo field could have been full of mines instead of antennas."

They started down the hill and Eric said, "How would you like to do a tour in this hell hole?"

"Are you kidding?" Paris said. "I never thought our base at Ninh Hoa could look so good." He rubbed his sore chin and said, "It's hard to believe we've only been gone two days. It feels like two weeks."

When they reached their ship, the crew chief and door gunner were examining the tail section. Quintana saw the pilots approach and wiped his hands on a rag.

"How's it look, Nacho?" Eric asked.

"Not good Boss. That mortar put a nick in the tail rotor drive shaft." Quintana pointed at the notch. "I figure if it's got us this far, it should make the thirty miles to BMT."

Eric felt the nicked shaft with his right index finger. "Let's hope so," he said.

Dave Dawson and his co-pilot were checking on their ship while four infantry soldiers stood guard looking down the hillside. When they were assured their helicopters could fly, the pilots decided to walk back to the compound. They were halfway up the hill when they heard a whistle and thump in the distance. "That's a mortar," Eric yelled. "Run for it."

There was another whistle and a louder ka-THUMP, next to them, as the pilots dashed for the compound. They ran through the gate and jumped into a trench that ran the length of the compound. As they sat on the red dirt floor, catching their breath, small arms fire started around the perimeter of the compound. "We need to make a run for a bunker," Eric yelled.

They were about to climb out, when the other crewmen and soldiers jumped in with them. Quintana sat next to Eric with blood streaming down his face. "Son of a bitch that was close," he gasped. He rubbed his head and asked, "How bad does it look?"

Eric examined the wound and said, "It's not deep. You'll be okay. "

"That's good to hear," Quintana said, pressing the cut with his sleeve. "I'd hate to have my face messed up."

"We need to get out of here," Eric yelled. "Let's go."

The four soldiers and other crewmen ran for one bunker while Bader and his crew ran for another. They stumbled down the steps and sat on cots breathing hard. Four local soldiers were watching the action from two ground-level openings.

Eric found a first aid kit and began bandaging Quintana's forehead.

When he was finished, one of the men at the window yelled, "Somebody's been hit." Everyone went to look. A big sergeant was dragging a wounded Vietnamese soldier by the back of his collar. A helicopter circled overhead as the sergeant yelled into a radio.

"Who the hell is that?" Paris asked, as he stood on an ammo box and leaned out of the opening. "It's a medivac," he said, stepping off the box.

The sergeant hoisted the Vietnamese soldier over his shoulder and screamed into the radio. The sound of the firefight was hitting a crescendo when Eric said, "What is that guy doing? That Dustoff isn't going to come down in all this gun play."

A red cross was visible on the side of the helicopter as the bold sergeant popped a yellow smoke grenade. Moments later, a mortar round landed next to him. When the smoke cleared, he and the Vietnamese soldier lay in a lifeless pile. There was no longer a need for a medivac, so the Dustoff left .

While those at the window looked away, Eric surveyed the room. Most of them had a sick look on their faces. They're young guys growing up way too fast, he thought. He looked out the window as two soldiers ran up to the bodies and dragged them away. When they were out of sight, there was a shrill roar followed by three powerful explosions. A soldier standing next to Eric yelled, "Jets, F-4s." Everyone cheered as they ran to the window and watched three smoke trails maneuver for another run. The firing and mortars stopped and the only sounds were from the distant jet engines.

Soon there was another ear-piercing roar, followed by three more explosions. The men cheered again as they watched the explosions blossom into three orange and black napalm clusters. The helicopter crewmen had seen numerous air strikes, but never at close range. Eric was surprised by the ferocity of the explosions.

After they completed a third run, the F-4s departed, leaving the compound as quiet as a Vietnamese cemetery. Slowly the men in the bunkers began venturing out to check for damage. Bader told Paris to go to the command bunker and check on the fuel delivery and then added, "Tell maintenance about the damaged tail rotor shaft."

Eric, Quintana and Pagliano left for the antenna field with six Green Berets. When they approached the helicopters they were told by another crew chief that their ships appeared to have survived the attack unscathed. "That's amazing," Quintana said, as he walked up to his ship and began looking it over. "I wonder why they didn't hit these."

"They may have tried and missed," Eric said.

"I doubt it. They're sitting ducks," Quintana said.

"Then maybe they thought they could capture them."

"They don't have anybody that could fly one, do they?" Quintana asked.

Eric shrugged. "Maybe a couple of Russian advisers. I'm just glad they're flyable, so we can get out of this shit hole." He turned to the Green Berets and said, "No offense guys." The soldiers laughed.

Quintana walked around the helicopter and said, "I'm going to check for booby traps."

Paris walked down the hill and approached the helicopters. "How do they look?"

"Not too bad," Eric answered. "Remarkably the ships didn't get hit, so we should be able to get out of here. What did Ops say?"

"A Chinook will be here in an hour with a fuel bladder," Paris said. "As soon as we're fueled, we're supposed to fly to Ban Me Thout. Our two door gunners are supposed to fly out on one of the other Slicks. You and I take the two dead guys in our ship and nobody else."

Quintana heard the news and yelled, "Wait a minute, this is my ship. Where she goes, I go. I'm not riding with somebody else."

Paris shook his head and said, "The chief of maintenance said he doesn't want anybody riding in a helicopter with a nicked tail rotor drive shaft except the pilots."

Quintana turned to his AC and glared. Eric cut him off and said, "Sorry Nacho, if the man says you don't go, you don't go."

Quintana threw up his hands and said, "All right, but just this one time."

The Chinook arrived and set a large fuel bladder on the right side of the helicopters which meant it was farthest away from Eric's ship. There were six five gallon Jerry cans strapped to the bladder along with a hand pump. Two chew chiefs were soon pumping fuel into the cans and handing them to the other crew chiefs and door gunners who carried them to the helicopters.

While the helicopters were being fueled, Bader and Paris watched as four men struggled to load the body bag containing the sergeant into their ship. "What do you think he was trying to accomplish?" Eric asked.

Paris shook his head. "Who knows? What a waste."

When the fueling was complete Eric and Paris climbed into their seats as the small body bag of the Vietnamese soldier was loaded onto the deck next to the other body. Eric put on his seat belt and looked at the two dark green body bags lying in his helicopter. He turned to the front and waited for the other ships to start because he didn't want to put any more time on the tail rotor drive shaft than necessary. If it broke while they were in flight, it would be a helicopter pilot's worst nightmare. He didn't want to imagine what it would be like to be spinning out of control with no way to stop the spiral.

When he saw that the others were up and running he pulled the starter trigger. The igniters started ticking and the black rotors whirred to life. When they were up to speed, he called Hutchins, "Lead, Chalk One is up."

"Roger One," Hutchins answered.

"Chalk Two's ready."

"Three's also up."

"How about you Mako?"

"Let's do it, Hutch."

"Okay Dog, you're first in line," Hutchins said. "You lead the way and we'll keep an eye on you."

"Thanks Hutch," Eric radioed, while motioning for Paris to make the takeoff.

"I've got it," Paris said, before lifting the ship out of the small antennae field. He leveled off at four thousand feet and asked, "Do you feel a vibration?"

Eric smiled and said, "Of course I feel a vibration, this is a helicopter. It has a hundred parts all working in opposite directions."

"No, I'm serious," Paris said with a worried look. "I swear something feels different. Some kind of weird shimmy."

Eric took the controls for a minute and then motioned for Paris to take them back. "I think it's the rough engine over water syndrome."

"What's that?"

"If you fly a single-engine airplane over water, you'll swear it starts running rough as soon as you leave land. The farther out you get, the rougher the engine sounds. As you approach the other shore, it starts to sound better. When you're back over land it clears up."

"So you're saying it's all in my head."

"Let's see if it doesn't smooth out on our descent into BMT."

Both of the pilots remained silent for the rest of the trip. The town of Ban Me Thout came into view and Paris said, "Okay, you're right, everything feels normal now." When they were safely on the ground, the two pilots joined their fellow flight crews for lunch at the mess hall.

While they were eating, two local mechanics inspected the damaged helicopters. When the flight crews returned to the flight line, Sharkey was told his ship had sustained enough damage it would take at least a day for repairs. Eric was told his repairs would take longer because a new tail rotor shaft would have to come out of Saigon. The three flyable Slicks would be loaded for a mission back to the Green Beret compound.

With no flyable aircraft, Bader and Sharkey walked to Operations to see what was expected of them. They explained their situation to a heavily built staff sergeant who took a cigar from his mouth and said, "I know this is going to break your hearts girls, but you're going to have to take the rest of the day off."

The two pilots glanced at each other and the man said, "Let's see if you can stay out of trouble, okay? I caught a lot of shit the last time your unit was here."

Eric responded, "We weren't here that time Sarge and you don't have to worry about us."

The sergeant shot them a disbelieving look before going back to his paperwork.

Eric waited until they were out of earshot and asked, "Are you up for a trip into town? I'll understand if you're not."

Sharkey laughed. "That's a good one Bader. Two minutes after telling the Sarge he doesn't have to worry about us, you're asking if I want to go to a town that's off limits. I always thought you'd make a good Gunnie."

Eric stopped walking and turned toward Sharkey. "Hold on Mako. Just because I like drinking and chasing skirts, it doesn't mean I'm Gunnie material. This war has taken a considerable toll on my psyche, but I'm not that crazy."

Sharkey took his time before answering. "I definitely need to get my head fixed and an empty Officers Club doesn't sound like the place. Let's go into town. That's what Pete would have done if one of us had gotten killed."

Eric nodded. "You've got that right. Did you guys find a good place the other night?"

Sharkey shook his head. "We didn't get to town. You guessed what happened yesterday. The MPs nabbed us ten minutes outside the gate. They said we'd be spending the night in the stockade if they caught us again, so we bought a couple bottles of whiskey at the Class Six store and drank them on the back porch of the chow hall. The mess sergeant supplied us with glasses and ice."

Eric resumed walking and said, "I doubt if anyone will be looking for somebody sneaking into town at noon."

"Probably not—let's give it a try," Sharkey said.

The two of them rounded up their crew members and asked if they wanted to go along. The crews thought it would take their minds off what happened the day before, so they were up for it. Even the crew chiefs could join them, because they couldn't work on their ships until the parts arrived.

The group walked toward a back gate where Eric flagged down a supply convoy that agreed to give them a ride into town. Ten minutes later, the eight aviators unloaded onto the chaos of a Vietnamese road in the middle of the village of Ban Me Thout. The driver pointed up a cross street. "If you're looking for bars and girls, go up two blocks and then right."

The crews formed into two lines and began walking with Bader and Sharkey in the lead. The dusty street was crowded with mama-sans, young women and a few old papa-sans, all trying to avoid bicycles, motorbikes, three wheeled Lambrettas and an occasional cart pulled by a water buffalo. The only Vietnamese men in their twenties and thirties were those who had limbs missing.

When they reached the corner, Eric was approached by a scruffy-looking kid who asked, "Hey GI, you got cigarettes?" Eric shook his head and continued down the street. The boy walked alongside and said, "I know you got smokes, GI."

Eric looked at the boy and asked, "Why do you want cigarettes?"

"I trade for chop-chop, I no smoke."

The group continued down the road and the boy said, "Where you go now? You want girls? Boom-boom? I know good place, numba one girls." The boy extended his hand and said, "I show you."

Eric stopped and asked, "How much?"

"One dolla'."

Eric handed the boy a dollar, and the crews followed the boy toward a nearby building. As they approached the door, Eric asked, "You see many MPs here?"

With a concerned look, the boy said, "Beaucoup MPs in Ban Me Thout, GI."

The kid extended his left hand while pointing at his eyes with his right forefinger. "I look for you."

"For another dollar."

The boy nodded. "For one dollar, no problems for you, GI."

Eric handed the boy another dollar and walked toward the door. The boy pulled on Eric's shirt and asked, "You got cigarettes?"

Eric looked at Sharkey who took out a pack of Marlboros and handed the boy four cigarettes. The kid smiled at Sharkey and said, "You numba one, GI."

Sharkey said sternly, "You just watch for MPs, you little bandit."

The boy smiled up at the tall gunship pilot and said, "No problem, GI."

Bader was the first to enter the bar. As he walked from brilliant sunshine into the darkened room, the only thing he could make out was a neon beer sign. He was soon aware of someone pulling on his arm. He stumbled over a chair as he tried to focus on the long hair of a woman who was guiding him to a table. She stopped and said, "You stay with me--I show you numba one good time."

I'll bet, Eric thought as he realized how stupid they had been. There could have been a whole company of North Vietnamese regulars waiting inside and they wouldn't have known it. When he was seated, his eyes continued to adjust to the light. When they cleared he was able to make out the face of the girl seated next to him. She was pretty with clear skin. The girl began rubbing his crotch and said, "My name is Lan, would you like my company?"

Eric smiled and said, "Yes Lan, I would definitely like your company."

Eric and the girl were seated at the head of the table, with Sharkey to their left, and Paris to their right. When Eric turned to Sharkey, the gunship pilot looked over the top of his sunglasses and said, "You know, Dog, we've done smarter things than walking in here the way we did."

Eric stared at Sharkey. "The whole place could have been crawling with VC."

"We're lucky it wasn't," Sharkey said as he waved to the bartender. "Hey barkeep, we need some beers over here."

Eric looked around the table and decided he had the best-looking girl of the group. Sharkey and Paris had a couple of cute ones, but the rest were fairly homely.

The bartender approached with bottles of Tiger 33 beer, followed close behind by an old woman with a tray of ice-filled plastic glasses, the Vietnamese method of cooling beer.

Eric took a glass and inspected the ice for contaminants. It had a few black specks and he hoped the germs in the ice would be killed by the alcohol in the beer. He poured the beer as his girl continued to rub his crotch.

While Sharkey paid for the round, Eric leaned toward his co-pilot and said, "Look at Nacho down there. What language do you think he's speaking?"

With a French accent Paris answered, "Probably *zee* language of love, no?"

Eric laughed and said, "He's probably trying to get a freebie."

"Yeah, that man could get laid in a convent," Paris said respectfully.

Eric surveyed the others around the table. Although this was a more somber group than usual, he knew that out of the seven other guys, several would leave for the back rooms after a beer, while the others would need several more to work up their nerve. He stood and said, "Thanks for the beer, Mako. Lan and I are going to find a little more privacy."

The girl took Eric's arm and led him through a back door into a steamy courtyard filled with cement ponds and bamboo. Lan pointed at an old man seated on a concrete bench and said, "You pay Papa-san now. He keeps place clean for us."

When Eric approached, the old man stood and smiled a toothless grin. He had a wispy beard like Ho Chi Minh and Eric thought it could be his brother. He handed the Papa-san a dollar and he bowed gracefully. Eric nodded and followed the girl into a stifling little room with a bed and chair. The only ventilation was an narrow transom above the door.

Eric removed his holstered pistol and threw it on the bed against the wall. He sat on the chair and sipped his beer while the girl removed her clothes. She slipped off her *ao dai* dress and asked, "You have rubber?"

Eric was disgusted at leaving them in his go-go bag in the helicopter. He shook his head. "No, we'll have to chance it."

The girl removed her bra and Eric asked, "How much is this going to cost?"

"Ten dolla'," the girl said with a worried look.

"Ten dollars!" Eric blurted. "That's the most I've ever paid in Nam.

Are you telling me this place has been off limits for two weeks and you're still charging ten bucks?"

"Not all girls get ten dolla'," the girl said as she turned sideways. She arched her back, accenting her pointy breasts and asked, "I not ten dolla' girl?"

Eric choked on his beer and answered, "Okay, you ten dolla' girl." He threw a ten on the bed.

The girl picked it up and said, "You take off clothes now."

Eric untied his boots and asked, "Can you help with these? I've had a rough couple of days."

The girl pulled one boot off before there was a knock at the door and the old woman from the bar stuck her head in the room. The young girl took the ten dollars and walked to the door. While she was giving the woman the money, Eric said, "Tell Mama-san for ten dollars I get to stay for an hour."

Lan looked at him nervously, as he repeated, "Ten dollars, one hour."

The older woman peered over the girl's shoulder as she explained what Eric wanted. While they were talking, Eric took off his other boot, and muttered, "I haven't slept in two days--this is as good a place as any for a nap." He also didn't want to go back to the crappy bar until it was time to leave.

When the girl closed the door, Eric stood and took off his shirt. Lan slipped off her panties and said, "Mama-san say you stay one hour."

She walked to him and unfastened his pants. Eric pulled her to the bed and fell onto it. The girl took off his pants and climbed onto the bed. She straddled his crotch and lowered herself onto him. Moving her hips she rubbed his chest and asked, "You like, GI?"

"Oh yeah, I like that a lot," Eric sighed.

As Lan increased her movements, Eric was surprised to see she appeared to be enjoying it. She kept it up for five minutes, then rolled her eyes and moaned loudly. He came with her as she fell onto his sweaty body.

She slid to one side and put her head on his chest. As they lay entwined, several other people walked past the room. Eric grabbed his holstered pistol and placed it on his crotch. The cool leather felt good on his hot skin. A guy has to put it somewhere, he thought.

With the girl's head on his shoulder, he could smell her smoky hair and musty body odor. He fell asleep visualizing the dirt-floored bamboo hooch where she probably lived.

Forty minutes later, Eric was awakened by a loud knock on the door and his co-pilot yelling, "Hey Dog, you in there?"

"Yeah," Eric answered sleepily.

"What are you trying to do, enhance your reputation with the ladies?"

"Screw you, Frenchie."

"Hey man, we've had all we can take of the piss they call beer in this place."

"Okay, I'll be right out," Eric yelled as he reached for his shirt.

When he and Lan walked into the bar, the men were sitting on one side of the room while the women were on the other side combing each other's hair. Eric looked at the blank stares that greeted him and said, "I guess this means I don't have time for another one."

The group moaned and walked toward the door. Back in the sunshine, Eric put on his sunglasses and looked for the kid. When he saw he was gone he turned to Sharkey. "It looks like the little guy took our money and ran. He and his buddies are probably in a back alley smoking your cigarettes."

Sharkey laughed and said, "I never did trust the little bastard."

Back at the base, the group approached a check point. A burly Military Policeman stood in the door of the gate shack and asked, "Okay, where the hell have you guys been?"

Bader and Sharkey strode up to the man and Sharkey said, "We've been out on a recon patrol and we found a whole lot of fine booty."

The MP looked at the wings on the two pilots' flight suits, and said, "I'll bet you did." He waved them in saying, "I'll let you off this time, but don't try it again."

The officers walked to the O Club where Eric stepped up to the bar and ordered four Budweisers. He carried the chilled cans to a table and said, "Here you go guys, ice cold American beer."

Sharkey took a can and raised it in a toast. "Here's to Barnes and his crew."

The others joined him and then drank quietly. Eric thought of the gruesome task that awaited Sharkey when they returned to their home base. He would have to go through Barnes's belongings and pack them up for shipment back to the States.

Eric broke the silence by saying, "Pete Barnes was the kind of guy you would want next to you in a firefight."

Sharkey added, "That he was. It was good flying with him." He turned to Eric and said, "Barnes must have liked you Bader. You're the only Slickie he ever said anything good about. You know I'm going to be in a lead gunship now and I'm going to need a good wingman. I've been watching you and from what I've seen you'd make a good Gunnie. You're cool under pressure and you have good eyes."

Eric started to protest and Sharkey cut him off. "And besides that Bad Dog, you already have the name for it."

"That's a name I have never tried to live up to."

"Except the other day in the club," Sharkey said with a smile.

"That was one time and it was your damn monkey that made it look so bad."

Tom Paris interrupted and said, "What about the time you tried to blow the dress off the fat nurse at the Phan Rang hospital? That was a good one."

Eric was surprised and told his co-pilot, "So there's one other time."

Paris pushed the subject. "And then there's the time you careened off the cliff outside Dalat. You're one crazy pilot, Dog."

Eric waved him off and turned to Sharkey. "Okay, so there have been a few other times, but that doesn't make me Joker material."

Sharkey said in a flat voice, "I think you are."

Eric looked across the table at Sharkey and said, "I appreciate your confidence Mako, but I know what I'm doing in a Slick and I only have five more months of my tour. That makes me way too short to learn something new."

Sharkey extended his beer and said, "If you change your mind I'll talk to Captain Wilcox about a transfer."

They touched cans and Eric said, "Mako, if I do you'll be the first to know."

The next morning Bader and Sharkey checked in at Operations. Sharkey was told his gunship was ready, but it would be three more days before Eric's ship would be operational. His home unit had requested he and his crew be returned as soon as possible. They were scheduled to leave on an Air Force C-123 to Cam Rahn Bay that afternoon.

The C-123 was a high-winged propeller driven transport aircraft with two auxiliary jet pods on each wing, used for airlifting troops and cargo to and from short unimproved airfields. It could haul 60 fully equipped troops, 50 stretcher patients, or 24,000 pounds of cargo.

It had a rear ramp which was lowered and the passengers entered the aircraft. Eric and his crew sat on side-facing canvas seats as the ramp was raised. An Air Force co-pilot walked down a short flight of stairs from the cockpit to deliver a pre-takeoff briefing. He was wearing a flight helmet, and Eric thought the C-123 looked like a larger, faster version of a Huey.

When they landed at Cam Rahn Bay, they were told a Chinook would be leaving for Ninh Hoa in forty-five minutes. Eric led his crew into a Quonset hut terminal to wait for the flight. The waiting room had two rows of plastic chairs attached in rows of twenty. Eric was not in a mood to socialize, so he slumped into a chair away from the others. He was hung over, tired and feeling guilty about taking everyone to a cat house the day before.

He sat in silence until two female Army officers enter the terminal attired in dress greens. Eric recognized one of them as the nurse he had met in the hospital at Lai Khe. When they took seats across from him, he caught the lieutenant's eyes and smiled. She smiled back and he said, "We've met before. Can I join you?"

The nurse nodded. "You do look familiar. Where did we meet?"

Eric sat next to her and said, "At your hospital in Lai Khe. I'm Eric Bader."

The lieutenant extended her hand. "Cheryl Chapman."

Eric shook her hand. "I know. I remember your name and your face."

The lieutenant noticed the black wings on Eric's flight shirt and said, "Now I remember. You were looking for the downed helicopter crew."

"That was me. You helped find a friend I thought had been killed."

"Yes, is he okay?"

"He's doing well. I got him a non-flying job after that crash."

"That's great, how about you? Are you still flying?"

"Oh yeah, for another five months and then it's back to the World."

"That's not too long, is it? How often do you fly?"

"Almost every day."

"Oh, that is a long time." Lieutenant Chapman turned to her friend, and said, "This is Pam. We're returning from R & R in Hong Kong. We went shopping and shipped everything home."

Eric was about to ask where home was, when an Air Force sergeant entered the room and announced the Chinook for Ninh Hoa and Lai Khe was landing. After the Chinook shut down and the passengers had deplaned, Eric accompanied the two nurses to the helicopter amid stares from his crewmen. When they were seated, on side-facing troop seats, Lt. Chapman asked Eric, "Do you fly one of these?"

Eric shook his head and looked out the round window behind them. He pointed at a row of Hueys and said, "I fly one of those."

The lieutenant looked outside the window and said, "They look like our medivacs."

"Yeah, they're almost the same. I should be a medivac pilot then I would get to meet cute nurses everyday."

Lieutenant Chapman smiled at him and then looked back out the window. The sun coming through the window highlighted her face. Eric stared at it and marveled at how attractive she was. The engine started and she frowned at him. "These things are so noisy. How can you stand it?"

Eric shrugged. "You get used to it, and we wear helmets that help attenuate the noise."

After takeoff, the noise was too loud for conversation, but he kept sneaking looks at her. She caught him and smiled sadly. He wondered if she was thinking the same thing he was, if only it was another place and time.

They landed at Ninh Hoa and the ramp lowered. Lt. Chapman stood with Eric and gave him a hug. "Good luck during the rest of your tour. If you get to Lai Khe look me up."

Eric smiled and said, "I'll be sure to do that." He turned and walked down the ramp wondering if things could get any worse. A beautiful woman tells him to look her up and there isn't a damn thing he can do about it "Someday, things are going to be different," he muttered.

It was late in the day when Eric crossed the center court toward his room. Jungle Dog ran to greet him and Eric petted his dog before entering his room. Paul's helmet bag was on the floor, so he threw his bags next to it and left for the club. When he saw his roommate's face he knew something was wrong. Paul took him aside and said, "We need to talk, let's go to the room."

Outside the club, Paul said, "I heard your trip to Ban Me *Twat* got all fucked up."

"You could say that," Eric said.

They walked down the boardwalk and Paul said, "I've got good news and bad, which do you want first?"

"I always like to start with good news."

"In that case, I'm happy to report that the infamous Robert Reddick is gone. He just disappeared like he did from the 281st and nobody knows where he went."

Eric stopped and said, "You're kidding."

"Nope, I told you I'd get rid of that little prick."

"Did they ever have an investigation about what happened to him in the club?"

"No, Captain Hart said Reddick screeched like a mashed cat for a few days, but he wasn't able to talk the CO into taking action against us.

Speaking of Hart, he's been promoted to major and given a command in the Delta."

Eric opened the door to their room and said, "That's great news, he deserves it. Is anybody up for his position?"

"Rumor had it as either Captain Wilcox, or Captain Hutchins until Hutch got you guys lost the other night. What the hell happened out there, Dog? Five Hueys landing with less than a hundred pounds of fuel, *at night*!"

"There were extenuating circumstances," Eric said.

"I'm sure there were." Paul became serious and asked, "Did you guys hear what Hanoi Hanna said about Barnes and his crew?" Hanoi Hanna was a North Vietnamese radio propagandist much like Tokyo Rose in World War II.

Eric stared at his roommate. "No, what did she say?"

"She said the crew was captured and put into tiger cages. She read off every name."

"That lying *bitch*!" Eric said. "There's no way anybody could have survived that crash. The ship exploded over hundred-foot trees. When it blew it looked like a magnesium flare going off. If anyone did survive the explosion, the fall would have killed them. The VC must have gotten the names off their dog tags."

Eric slumped on his bunk. "How inhumane can you get? Now their families are going to think there's some hope they're alive and I'm telling you, there is *no fucking way*."

Paul sat across from him and said, "The bitch also singled out Pete's co-pilot, Metzger. She said his wife and kids are going to miss him. How the hell could she know that?"

Eric stared absently and said, "I don't know. He wore a wedding ring. She probably guessed about the kids."

"Do you know if he had any?"

"Yeah, two little girls."

After a moment of silence, Paul got up and went to his locker. He took down a bottle of whiskey and poured two drinks. He handed a cup to Eric and said, "You're going to need this. That's not all the bad news."

Eric took the drink and said, "You mean there's more?"

"I'm afraid so. When I landed this afternoon, I was told the major wants to talk with us tomorrow morning."

"The Old Man wants to talk with both of us. What for?"

"I don't know, but I don't think it's to let us know he's putting us in for our Air Medals."

Eric took a hefty swallow and said, "No shit, Dev, this is serious now that we don't have Captain Hart here as a buffer. There's no telling what he might be planning. Are you sure it isn't some kind of retaliation for what we did to Reddick?"

"It might be, but Captain Hart was sure there wasn't going to be any official action taken against us." Paul threw down his drink and said, "There's no sense worrying about it now. Let's go back to the club."

Eric lay down on his bunk and said, "You go ahead, I need some sleep. I haven't had a good night's rest since we left. I keep having bad dreams about Barnes and his crew. I was right above them when the ship exploded."

Paul walked toward the door and said, "I feel bad for you having to see that."

Eric put a towel over his head and slept until 0430. He got out of bed still dressed in his sweaty flight suit and boots. After a shower and shave he walked back to his room thinking the demons that had been plaguing him had finally been purged. He left the room dressed in a clean flight suit without waking Paul and wondered why the CO wanted to talk with them later that morning.

Jungle Dog was outside the room spinning in circles. Everyone in the company liked his dog, especially the cooks. They already had a heaping bowl of scraps waiting for him when they arrived at the mess hall. That morning it was ham, creamed carrots and rice.

Eric hadn't eaten for twenty-four hours and was famished. The mess hall was empty when he greeted the head cook. "Good morning Sarge, how are things with you?"

"Real good Mr. Bader. You're up early."

"I had a couple of rough days, so I went to bed early."

"It's good to have you back. I'll make you a breakfast of real eggs, fried ham and cottage potatoes."

"That sounds great," Eric said, as he poured himself a cup of coffee. "I haven't eaten since yesterday morning." There were several others in the mess hall, but he took his breakfast tray to a window table and looked out at the sunrise. The real food tasted great. A big improvement on the chipped beef on toast that he had been eating. The infamous meal that soldiers called "Shit on a Shingle."

At 0800 he and Paul walked into the office of their Commanding Officer. They saluted and Eric said, "Misters Bader and Eason reporting, Sir."

The major returned their salutes and said, "At ease." After several seconds of appraisal, he stood and said, "So you two are Bader and Eason." He walked around his desk and said, "You two don't look like trouble makers. That's what Captain Reddick called you. Fortunately for you, Captain Hart and all the flight leaders had a different opinion. They say you're two of the best pilots in the company. That's good, because I've always felt my best pilots should be in the guns. As of this morning, I'm transferring both of you to the Jokers."

The two pilots looked at each other in disbelief, then back at the CO. Before the major could continue, Eric cleared his throat and said, "With all due respect Sir, I've been a Slick pilot for over a year and I haven't been killed yet. I'd like to stay in them for the rest of my tour."

The major moved in front of Eric and said, "Mr. Bader, do you see this gold oak leaf on my collar?"

Eric stared at the collar and said, "Yes Sir."

The major raised his voice. "I'm not asking if you *want* to be a gunship pilot. I'm telling you that you *are* a gunship pilot. Is that understood?"

"Yes Sir."

The major turned to Paul and asked, "Mr. Eason, do you have a problem with becoming a Joker?"

Paul stared straight ahead and said, "No Sir!"

"Good, I want you to report to Captain Wilcox immediately.

Dismissed."

"Yes Sir," Paul said. They both saluted and left the room.

Outside the building Paul said, "I do not *believe* this shit. Can you imagine me as a fucking *Joker*? I knew that god damn monkey would come back to haunt us."

They walked to their new platoon leader's office in silence. When they knocked on the screen door, Captain Brett Wilcox said, "Come in."

Eason and Bader entered the room and Wilcox said, "Well what do we have here? If it isn't the Devil and the Dog." He motioned for them to sit. "Did the major figure as long as you were going to act like Gunnies you might as well be Gunnies?"

Both men shrugged and Wilcox continued, "I think it's rather humorous to have you two in the Jokers, especially you, Eason, after all your pranks. Whatever the reason, we can always use two more good sticks in the guns."

Wilcox turned to Eric and said, "Bader, I'm going to have you fly with Dan Sharkey until you get used to the new equipment. Eason, you'll do the same with Clay Boone."

Paul rolled his eyes and Wilcox said, "Do you have a problem with that Eason?"

Paul looked at his new platoon leader and said, "No Sir."

Wilcox walked around his desk and said, "That's good, because I know you've had a few adversarial confrontations with my men in the past and I want you to know that's just how I consider them, *in the past*! Is that understood?"

"Yes Sir."

"Good. You're one of us now and I don't want to hear about any more of that bullshit. I'll tell the other Jokers the same thing. Right now I want you to begin your transition into the Charlie model. Jim Cornelius is waiting for you down at the flight line to start your training."

Wilcox walked back behind his desk and said, "Good luck, men."

"Thanks Captain," Paul said, as they got up to leave.

On the way to their room, Paul said in disgust, "This keeps getting worse. Besides everything else, now I have to fly with Long John Silver."

Eric chuckled and Paul barked, "What are you laughing at? It's not like you're flying with Mister Sanity."

"Sharkey's not so bad when you get to know him," Eric said, as they neared their room.

Paul flung the screen door open and said, "Yeah, right."

They collected their flight gear and stormed out of the room. While they walked to the flight line, Eric asked, "Is there any upside to this situation?"

Paul thought for awhile and said, "The Gunnies are usually the first ones in the bar."

At the flight line, Jim "Slyde" Cornelius explained the differences between the "C" model Huey and the "D" model they were used to flying. "The biggest difference," Cornelius said, "will be backing out of the revetments and the initial takeoff. The takeoffs will be much heavier than what you're used to because of the heavy armaments. Once you begin burning fuel and firing the rockets, the load lightens considerably, so there usually isn't much of a difference on landing." Cornelius went on to explain how to fire the rockets and mini-gun. Eric and Paul traded off flying and firing the weaponry. When they were finished, they both declared it had been fun to shoot at things and blow them up.

It was still early afternoon when they left the flight line and walked toward the stairs that led to their compound. They were not used to being back that early and it was hot—almost too hot for life. As they climbed the three flights of stairs, Paul said, "I have to admit, shooting the rockets and mini-gun was easier than I thought."

"Yeah it was," Eric said. "I thought it would take longer to get used to flying and aiming at the same time, but it wasn't that hard. It was not only exciting, it gave me a feeling of power I've never felt before. It was like throwing sticks of dynamite. Maybe this job won't be as bad as we thought."

"It might be," Paul said, "if we didn't have to work with a bunch of misfits. Do you think we will ever be able to handle the macho gunship mentality? Not to mention we still have to face the harassment that Shooter and the other Gunnies are sure to stack on us. I don't know about you, but I feel like getting shit-faced."

Eric had wondered how his friend was going to face the razzing he was sure to get from the Jokers. Shit-faced drunk was probably as good a way as any. He continued climbing and said, "Sounds like a plan to me."

Sweat streamed down their faces at the top of the stairs. They set their helmet bags down and stopped to catch their breath. At that height they could feel an afternoon breeze coming off the South China Sea, but it didn't help. Eric was sure he could feel sweat running from his neck down to his boots. He looked toward the ocean and said, "I quit smoking and I still can't breathe. I've got to get back into shape."

Paul coughed and said, "I should quit too, but I'll start worrying about dying from smoking when I know a machine gun isn't going to blow a hole in my chest."

Their room had been turned into a little corner of hell by the sun shining on the tin roof. Jungle Dog was gone, probably hiding somewhere in the shade. They stayed in the room just long enough to deposit their gear and long-sleeved flight shirts. They left for the Officers' Club still dressed in their sweaty green T-shirts and flight pants. They opened the door and had to stand in the doorway to let their eyes adjust to the cool dark room. The Club had two air conditioners, a clean tile floor and a temperature of seventy-eight. When their eyes adjusted, they saw they had the place to themselves.

They slid onto their favorite bar stools, and Paul called to the two Vietnamese bar maids at the end of the bar. "Girls, we need two beers down here, pronto."

A new barmaid said something to Baby-San before slowly shuffling to the cooler, her sandals flapping on the tile floor. She warily eyed the two pilots as she placed two Budweisers in front of them.

Eric took a sip of beer and said, "This must be the equivalent of getting an afternoon off back in The World."

"Yeah, like I said, Gunnies are usually the first ones in here."

Baby-san approached with a bowl of popcorn and said, "Here is something new, American hors d' oeuvres."

Both pilots laughed and said, "Thanks Baby-san."

While they watched the shapely bartender walk back to her chair, the front door opened, flooding the bar with sunlight and the silhouette of their friend Jack Cates. Lieutenant Cates was tall and slim and was the company intellectual. He had let the war get to him and was fast becoming a troubled man in a disturbing place.

For the first six months of his Vietnam tour he had been one of the best Slick pilots in the company. During the second half, the war finally took its toll and he told the commanding officer he could no longer fly. Because of his heavy drinking the other Slick pilots thought it was a good idea.

The real live officers in the company thought the lieutenant didn't represent them because he lacked military bearing. Since most of the warrant officers also fit that description they adopted him and nicknamed him "Pounder Jack" for the speed at which he pounded down beers.

Cates took the stool next to Eric and said, "How's it going gents? I heard what happened this morning. Sounds grim."

"Yeah, real grim," Eric said, as he waved to the barmaid for another beer. As the young girl shuffled toward the cooler, Eric turned back to Cates and said, "So how are things with you, Jack? I see you're still off flight status."

Cates took the beer from the bar girl and said, "That will probably be a permanent situation. I've convinced the Old Man he doesn't want to trust one of his quarter-million-dollar helicopters to a nutcase. Last week he put me in charge of awards and decorations."

Paul laughed and said, "That's the first thing he's done that makes sense. Considering who's getting the awards and the bullshit they're getting them for, who better than you to write them up."

"I thought that was rather ironic myself," Cates said. "And speaking of ironic, how about you two guys as Jokers?"

Eric wiped foam from his lips and said, "Right now we're not going to worry about it, Jack. It's cool in here, we've got the afternoon off and Baby-san has a cooler full of beer. What else matters?"

Cates shook his head and said, "You guys are so fucking superficial."

Eric shot back, "We may be, Jack, but at least it keeps us sane. You ought to try it sometime."

Cates raised his voice and said, "Can't you guys see what's happening out there? Doesn't any of this senseless horseshit piss you off?"

"So what if it does?" Eric yelled back. "What good is that going to do? The fact is we're in the middle of a war we don't want to be in. We're trying to make the best of a bad situation and get out of here alive."

Eric lowered his voice. "Like I've told you before, Jack, you are expending entirely too much psychic energy worrying about the war and from what I've heard you're getting a little too close to the edge."

Cates spun his stool toward Eric and said, "If you think *I'm* nuts, this whole fucking war is nuts and you're nuts for fighting it. If the Vietnamese want to be Commies, let 'em. It's none of our God damned business. There are a lot of good people dying every day out there, so Dow Chemical can make a few more million bucks."

While Eric was deciding if he wanted to expend any more energy on his friend, the door opened and everyone turned toward the newcomer. A lieutenant colonel waited to let his eyes adjust before walking to the bar and sitting next to Cates. None of the three pilots had seen the colonel before, but they knew by the cross on his collar he had to be the new battalion chaplain.

Baby-San saw the silver oak leaves on his shoulders and quickly hid the Vietnamese comic she had been reading. She rushed to the center of the bar and the chaplain politely asked for an Orange Crush. The three pilots drank uneasily as the officer appraised his fellow bar mates. They rarely talked with a colonel, and the only time they saw a chaplain was at a memorial service. They had also been caught in a compromising position: mid afternoon and they were already drinking.

The colonel broke the silence. "Good afternoon men. It sure is hot out there."

When Cates didn't acknowledge him, Eric quickly looked around his friend and said, "Yeah, it sure is, Sir."

The chaplain looked around Cates and asked, "Are you boys pilots?"

"Yes Sir," Eric answered as Jack continued to stare straight ahead.

The chaplain smiled sympathetically and said, "I understand your unit lost some men the other day. Is that right?"

"Yes Sir, we did," Eric answered. He hoped the colonel would leave before Jack did something stupid. Sure enough, Cates set his beer on the bar and let out a loud belch. Eric turned to Paul for support, but his roommate shrugged and motioned for three more beers.

The chaplain frowned and said, "If you'd like to talk about that, or any other problems in your life, that's why I'm here."

Eric was out of yes Sirs, so he nodded and joined the other two as they reached for their fresh beers. With beer in hand, Cates turned to the chaplain and said, "I've got a problem Padre, and right now it's you sitting here next to me."

The colonel looked stunned, but composed himself quickly and asked, "Just what do you want out of life, son?"

Cates faced the bar and said, "You really want to know? I'll show you." He threw his head back and raised his beer to arm's length, pouring it into his mouth. For the last half of the can he clenched his teeth and the beer splashed onto the chaplain and Eric. The chaplain quickly moved away wiping beer off of his shirt. Eric rolled his eyes and let the beer splash onto his sweat-soaked T-shirt.

When the can was empty, Cates held it in position for several seconds then slammed it onto the bar. He smiled at the chaplain and said, "That's what I want out of life, Colonel." He spun around on his stool and strode for the door.

The chaplain was still brushing beer from his shirt as he said, "That man has problems!"

Eric looked at the colonel and said softly, "Yes Sir, he sure does."

The chaplain left the bar and Eric turned to Paul. "Do you ever get the feeling you and I are the only ones left in this fucking war who are still sane?"

Paul didn't answer. Instead he raised his beer to arm's length and began pouring it into his mouth. When the can was almost empty, he clenched his teeth so the beer splashed onto Eric's other shoulder. Eric watched the reflection of the scene in the mirror and said, "Okay, my mistake. *I'm* the only one who's still sane."

Twenty minutes later, the door opened and the silhouettes of the two Jokers, Zombie and Sphinx, waited while their eyes adjusted to the light. When Paul saw them, he said, "Oh great, here we go. I swear if those two start with their new meat crap I'm going to pop them."

Eric whispered to his friend, "Don't get too excited. Remember what Wilcox said."

Paul turned back to the bar. "Okay, I'll be good."

The two Gunnies ordered beers and then stood looking at Bader and Eason. Sphinx finally said, "We just heard you two are going to be gunship pilots."

When the roommates ignored him, he said, "You guys are both good and we can always use a couple more good pilots in the guns. Welcome to the Jokers."

Eric was surprised and turned to look at the young pilot. "Thanks Sphinx, we appreciate that."

Paul watched the Gunnies walk away and said, "Maybe this isn't going to be as bad as we thought."

Eric shook his head. "Don't count on it, we haven't seen Shooter yet."

Fifteen minutes later, Clay Boone and most of the other Jokers entered the bar hooting and laughing. They formed a half circle around Eric and Paul. The two roommates spun around on their bar stools and sat facing the crowd.

Boone moved in front of Paul and said, "Well, well, well, what comes around goes around, huh Eason?"

Paul shrugged and stared at Boone with a bored look. A half-dozen Slick pilots also entered the room and gathered around the bar. Boone turned to Eric and said, "My man Sharkey says you'll make a good gunship pilot, Bader." He looked at Paul and said, "You're pretty good too Eason--too bad you have such a big mouth."

Before Boone could continue, Paul scoffed and said, "I always thought a big mouth was a prerequisite to being a Gunnie, Shooter."

The crowd laughed and Boone looked around with a confident grin. He turned back to Paul and said, "You think you're real fuckin' cute don't you Eason? Well you belong to me now and we're going to see just how cute you are." Boone handed Paul a bag and said, "I always want my trainees to look good, so I got you a present. If you wear this for a couple of weeks you might get signed off to fly a gunship."

Eason opened the bag and removed a flight shirt with ten different Army patches sewn on it. Everyone jeered and laughed, as Paul put the shirt on and admired himself in the mirror. "It looks good, Shooter. I like it, but I'm not wearing it after tonight."

The crowd oohed as Paul sat down and lit a cigarette. He blew smoke at Boone and said, "You're forgetting something, aren't you Shooter? Chances are, someday I could be your trail gunner, and you wouldn't want to have a pissed off wingman would you? It might affect my aim."

The two men stared at each other until the laughter died down. Shooter extended his hand and said, "You'll make a good Gunnie, Eason. Welcome to the Jokers."

Eason shook his hand and yelled to the barmaid, "Baby-san, get my new friend here a beer. While you're at it, give everyone else one on me."

The party that followed was considered to be one of the best of all time. It was almost as good as the night of the Monkey Caper. It was so disgusting, Baby-san threatened to quit three times. When everyone had finally staggered to their rooms, Bader and Eason had been officially welcomed as new members of the Jokers.

The next morning the two new Jokers continued to familiarize themselves with the Charlie model gunship. Their trainer, Slyde Cornelius, weighted the ship down with a full load of fuel and rockets. Before they took their seats, he said, "Eason you take the first sortie when the ship is heaviest. I've heard that Bader already knows how to fly an overloaded Huey." The three pilots chuckled and Cornelius continued, "Like I said yesterday, the Delta and Charlie models are fairly similar except for the heavily loaded takeoffs. I'm sure you've seen the gunships flying down the runway with the front of the skids bouncing off the PSP with sparks flying. We probably won't do that today because we're one man short and there aren't any machine guns on board, but you'll get your chance later."

Paul made the takeoff without bouncing and Eric suggested they fly out to Free Fire Island and shoot at the abandoned buildings. Slyde Cornelius said, "Good idea," and then motioned for Paul to turn to the west. "We'll use the island for a graduation exercise."

When they reached the island, Cornelius told Eason to strafe the hootches along the beach. Paul fired the mini-gun at the abandoned houses, which caused large pieces of the thatched roofs to fly off. While he made a turn over the ocean, Cornelius set the rocket selector switch and said, "Okay Eason, I've set the selector for two pair. Make sure the ship is in trim and let's see if you can hit that mud building."

Paul fired a pair of rockets which missed to the right. He over corrected to the left and missed the building again. His trainer patted him on the shoulder and said, "That's good enough shooting for this stage of your training. Remember the rockets are like hand grenades, you just have to be close. "

Eric had been watching from between the seats and said, "I want to put a rocket in the window of that house I missed the last time I was here."

Cornelius turned to Eric and said, "Okay, we'll use that mud hut for your last target. Come up and trade seats. I saw a structure in the trees on the south side of the island that I want you to shoot at first. Assume it's an enemy bunker and hose it down with the mini-gun."

Eric circled to the south and began firing at the small shack. When he was finished, the hootch was half its size and Cornelius said, "That was pretty good shooting. Now let's see what you can do with the rockets."

Eric lined up on the building he had missed with his M-79 grenade launcher and fired off a pair of rockets that landed just in front of the hut. He raised the nose slightly and fired another pair, hitting it square in the middle.

Eric hooted and said, "It's about time I nailed that that damn hut."

When they were finished flying, the two roommates decided they had enough partying the night before and decided to spend the rest of the afternoon in their room.

Eric was reading a *Stars & Stripes* newspaper when he turned to Paul and said, "Another Slick crew was shot down around Pleiku. The pilot and crew chief were killed. The co-pilot and door gunner are missing in action. The ship went down in an area where they couldn't be rescued. By the time ground troops arrived, the two surviving crewmen were gone. Poor bastards, they're probably in tiger cages by now. Do you ever think what you'd do if that happened to you?"

Paul pointed at his poster of Raquel Welch and said, "Nah, all I can think about is getting back to my girl. She'd miss me if I didn't come home."

Eric continued, "I always thought if I got shot down I'd shoot as many bad guys as I could, then save the last bullet for myself. Now I think I'll take my chances on running away."

Eric went back to reading the paper. A minute later he held it up so Paul could see. "Look at this picture of Colson's wedding. Who the hell sent this in?"

Paul looked at the picture and said, "I can't believe he married that bar girl from Taiwan. He even moved her back to Nevada. What a goofball. When he gets home he'll be working in a tire store trying to keep her happy on ten grand a year."

Eric folded the paper and said, "Speaking of ten thousand dollars, my dad looked at my savings account and thinks I'll have that much by the time I get out of here."

"Then I'll have the same," Paul said.

"Yeah, that should be enough to get us through a winter in Austria." Eric paused and then said, "I wonder what Boone and Sharkey have in store for us tomorrow?"

Paul pointed at the screen door and said, "Funny you should ask. I see a shark out on the center court yard right now."

Eric handed the paper to Paul and asked, "Is he circling?"

"Nope, he's headed right at us."

Eric leaned toward Paul and said, "Listen, I have to fly with this guy, so can you hold the smart remarks until I get checked out?"

Paul feigned surprise and said, "I thought we smoked the peace pipe last night."

"We did--I just wanted to make sure you remembered."

Sharkey walked in without knocking and asked, "How are the Joker wannabes?"

Paul held up his hand and said, "Correction Mako, we are not Joker wannabes. We are Joker *told*-to-bes."

Sharkey ignored the remark and addressed Eric. "Dog, tomorrow is your lucky day. Not only do you get to fly with me, we may get into some action down by Ghia Nghia. We're going as a light fire team to support some ARVNs. Lambi will be our trail gunner."

Eric was surprised to hear about Lambi. "So Lambi's already an Aircraft Commander."

"Yeah, and he's a good one. Shooter knew what he was doing when he picked him. We need to be at a briefing in an hour."

Paul interrupted. "Have you heard what Boone and I are doing?"

"Yeah, you and Shooter are on gunship standby. That should give you guys more time to become buddies."

Paul rolled his eyes. "Oh goodie, I can't wait for that."

Sharkey walked toward the door and said, "See you at the briefing, Dog."

The next morning Eric met Sharkey on the flight line at 0630 hours. They both wore jackets because they would be crossing the mountains in the cool morning air. While Sharkey was introducing Eric to his crew, John Lambi walked up and welcomed Eric to the Jokers. Eric shook his hand and congratulated him on becoming an AC.

When Lambi was back at his gunship, Sharkey said, "Lambi's call sign is Buff."

"I know," Eric said. "I was in the club when Shooter gave it to him."

Sharkey motioned for Eric to follow and observe the difference in preflighting the Charlie model Huey with its gun pods and mini-gun. While they walked around the ship, Eric noticed the motto from a TV show printed on the side: "Have Gun Will Travel." Below the inscription were two rows of yellow conical hats.

The clouds were starting to clear as the two pilots buckled in. When Eric asked about the empty door gunner seats, Sharkey explained that because they were so heavy, the crew chief and door gunner would have to wait and board after they backed out of the revetments.

Sharkey started the engine and then skillfully backed the heavily loaded gunship out of the U- shaped parking space. He pointed it down the runway and then set the helicopter down, so the other two crew members could climb on board.

The crew chief buckled into his seat and reported that he and the door gunner were ready for takeoff. Then he chided Eric, "Do you think you can back her out like that Mr. Bader?"

Eric looked over his shoulder and said, "I've done it once or twice." Then to himself he mumbled, "Or maybe a couple hundred times."

Before they departed, Eric thought about how his career was regressing. He had been one of the most experienced Slick pilots in the company and now he was back in a trainee position. He knew it wouldn't be long before he was an Aircraft Commander again, but until then he would have to keep his mouth shut and gut it out.

Sharkey interrupted his thoughts when he radioed his trail gunner to ask if he was ready for takeoff. Lambi answered affirmative and Sharkey brought the ship up to take-off RPM. In the previous thirteen months, Eric had witnessed numerous takeoffs by heavily loaded gunships. From outside the helicopter, it looked scary; inside it was terrifying.

The pilot would pull in full power and leave the ground nose low and tail high. The goal was to gain airspeed as quickly as possible. For a few seconds the skids would be one or two feet above the ground. The pilots would be looking down at the rapidly moving runway just below their windshield. If the helicopter did not achieve airspeed quickly, the front of the skids bounced off of the perforated steel plate runway and sparks flew.

If the skids caught on anything, the helicopter might flip over and crash. With that in mind, Eric tightened his seat belt another notch. Because of the cool air, they only bounced once, which was still one too many.

When they were airborne and converting jet fuel into smoke and noise, Sharkey turned to Eric and asked, "Are we having fun yet?"

Eric looked Sharkey squarely in the eyes and said, "Loads."

When they reached the mountains, the clouds were so thick it was obvious they would not be able to fly a straight line to Ban Me Thout. Both pilots were familiar with the area and decided to press on following the highway. After an hour above the winding road, they finally saw the lowlands around BMT.

Eric played the dutiful co-pilot and said, "I'll call the tower."

Sharkey nodded his approval. "I hope the chow hall is still open. I need a coffee."

After a quick stop for coffee, the pilots attended a short briefing. Enemy troops were in the town of Ghia Nghia. The gunships were there to support a company of ARVNs who were attempting to drive the enemy from the village.

When the briefing was finished, the gunship pilots were introduced to a Forward Air Controller. The FAC explained that he would be flying in a small Cessna over the battle area and would coordinate the engagement with the ARVNs and the gunships. The young Air Force lieutenant emphasized he would be in charge and the helicopters would be taking orders from him.

The helicopter pilots walked out of the briefing, and Sharkey said, "I'm glad we don't have to work with that dip very often."

The gunships had been refueled, so they took off over the city. Eric watched as thatched roof hootches and concrete buildings slipped under the nose of the helicopter. They followed a road out of town that had a stream of people walking, or riding bicycles and motor bikes.

An Army bulldozer was widening the road and had scraped the

letters "F.T.A." in a clearing. The two pilots laughed and Sharkey said, "Fuck the Army, indeed."

The former French settlement of Ghia Nghia came into view. The small village was built in the style of French architecture and was surrounded by a tea plantation, so it reminded Eric of Dalat. They approached the area of operation and Eric pointed at the circling Cessna. Sharkey said, "I've got him and I'll give him a call. FAC-One the Jokers are here, armed and dangerous."

"Standby Jokers, I'm talking with the ARVNs."

"Jokers copy."

A minute later, the Forward Air Controller called back, "The ARVNs are in the town and are taking light fire, but they don't want you gunships to engage the enemy inside the city."

Sharkey reluctantly said, "Jokers copy." He turned to Eric and said, "Why the hell are we here if we can't shoot somebody? I'm going to do something to get them moving. We call it snoop and poop." Sharkey called his trail. "Cover me Buff. I'm going to see if I can find some bad guys."

"We copy," Lambi radioed back.

Sharkey prepared to make a run at the town and Eric adjusted his ceramic breast plate and made sure his sliding seat armor was in full extension. While they made a low-level run down a street they heard a burst of gunfire that sounded like a pack of firecrackers going off.

Sharkey quickly initiated a climbing left turn and called his crew, "Nothing hit up here. How are you guys?"

The crew chief quickly called, "All's good back here."

Sharkey called the FAC. "We heard some gunfire in the village."

"Yeah, the ARVN commander said they just took out an enemy hide-out."

"Roger that. I'm looking at some troops moving down by the river. Are they ours?"

"Let me check."

Sharkey turned to Eric and said, "That's your first lesson. If there isn't any action, you go looking for it. We're loaded with a bunch of rockets we do *not* want to haul back to the base."

"Joker Eight-One this is FAC-One. The ARVN colonel says the bad guys ran toward the river when they left the village. He says take them out."

"Joker Eight-One copies, here we go." Sharkey switched frequencies and asked his wingman, "Buff, did you copy?"

"I'm right behind you, Mako. Let's do it."

Sharkey made a turn to line up on the trees and pointed at an X on the windshield. "We've got a gun sight we can pull down, but most of us make a mark with a grease pencil on the windshield and use that to line up the target." He pointed at a dial on the pedestal and continued, "I'm sure you've been checked out on this selector switch. The co-pilot usually does it, but I'll put in two pair for this run." Sharkey radioed his trail, "Buff, I'm going to hit the left side of the tree line with two pair, you hit the right with two more."

"Copy, we're armed and hot."

They approached the mark and Sharkey said, "Okay, we're on line. Ready, ready . . . *now.*" He fired and two rockets from each side went screaming past the cockpit. As they hit, dirt flew and trees fell. When he was satisfied he had hit the target, Sharkey made a hard left turn, saying, "Now we'll get into position to cover Lambi's run."

They followed the other gunship and the two pilots watched as four more rockets slammed into the trees ahead. When Lambi made a left turn, Sharkey continued over the area to appraise their work. Sharkey called his trail and said, "Good work Buff. I don't see anything moving."

Sharkey called the controller and said, "FAC-One, it looks like we got 'em."

"FAC-One copies, good job. I'm going to make a quick recon of the village. I need you to climb above me."

"Jokers copy. We've got you in sight and we're climbing to three thousand feet."

Eric was thankful for the break. It had been thirty minutes of tight banking, climbing and diving at tree-top level.

While they loitered, Sharkey explained how the aircraft trim affected the flight of the rockets. "If you are out of trim just a little, the rockets will veer to the left or right of the target. They can also dive sooner than you want. That could be critical when you're working in close support of ground troops. If we have ammo left on the way home, we'll find a safe place and practice shooting."

The gray Cessna flew over the village and the Air Controller called, "Jokers, do you see the ornate building in the middle of the town square?"

"Yeah, what about it?" Sharkey asked.

"There's a flag flying from the roof. I think it's an enemy flag. I'm going to have a closer look."

"Roger, we're standing by."

Moments later the FAC called again, "Okay guys, just as I thought, it's a North Vietnamese flag. The ARVN commander says the building is a provincial capital, so he doesn't want it damaged. The enemy troops are gone, but he's sure the place is booby trapped. They don't want to go in it until a bomb squad checks it out."

The Controller was talking fast. "I say that flag has to come down before we leave. There can be no enemy flag flying over an allied city. It's a matter of principle!"

Eric and Sharkey laughed at the young officer's mini drama. With a smirk, Eric said, "This is like watching a crappy war movie. What does he want us to do, shoot the flag off the building?"

"That's what it sounds like," Sharkey said. "I'll call and ask. FAC-One, are you saying you want us to shoot the flag off that building?"

"That's exactly what I want. Do you think you can do it without hitting the building?"

Sharkey circled the square and said, "It's a pretty tight shot, but if I make the run toward the west I think I can do it."

"Good, I want that flag down."

Sharkey called his wingman and asked, "Buff, did you copy?"

"Yeah, do you want us to try and shoot it too?"

"No, we're going to have to get down real low to take the shot, so I want you to cover us."

When Sharkey made a practice run, he and Eric could see the flag was hung on a thin bamboo pole about fifteen feet above the roof. Sharkey turned to Eric and said, "This is going to be next to impossible. If we could blow the top off that building it would be a lot easier. Remember what I said about being in trim, or you may hit something you don't want. This is one of those times."

Sharkey made a hard turn to the west and said, "There's a soccer field past that side of the square, so I'm going to make my run that way. I'll try and be long if anything. If I'm short and hit the building, what can I say other than *Xin Loi*." Sorry.

The trees around the square stood higher than the building, so the gunship would have to wait until the last second before diving down to take a shot. There could still be enemy snipers in town waiting for an opportunity to down a helicopter.

Sharkey called his door gunners, "Okay guys, we're going down real low, so keep your eyes peeled."

As he lined up for the run, Sharkey said, "Dog, select me a pair." Eric set the switch and watched as Sharkey fired. The two rockets went on each side of the slim pole, missing by several feet and exploding in the soccer field. Sharkey fired another pair and they did the same thing, hitting farther down the dirt field. While they climbed out, Sharkey pointed and said, "It'll be a while before anybody scores a goal on that soccer field."

Eric looked at the two craters and said, "Maybe they can turn it into a community swimming pool." He tapped the fuel gauge and said, "We don't have the fuel to do this much longer."

Sharkey eyed the gauge and said, "Yeah, you're right. Luckily, I have a another plan. In this job you need to be creative"

Eric stared at Sharkey and said, "Define creative."

The tall gunship pilot smiled and said, "You'll see." He called his trail and said, "Cover us Buff. I'm going to make one more run. If I miss this time, we leave for fuel."

"Roger that, we're right behind you."

They banked hard for another run and Eric asked, "Are you going to do what I think?"

Sharkey lowered his helmet visor and grinned. "It's just a skinny little pole."

This is crazy, Eric thought. He couldn't believe what they were about to do. He lowered his own visor and moved his feet back. They approached the flag pole and Sharkey flared just before it whacked the front of the helicopter on Eric's side. The pole knocked out the Plexiglas window in front of his foot pedals causing air to rush into the cockpit.

Lambi radioed excitedly, "You got it that time Mako, no more flag."

Sharkey turned hard to the left and radioed the Controller. "There you go FAC-man. Mission accomplished. We need to go to BMT for fuel."

The Forward Air Controller radioed back, "Okay guys, good job. Maybe I'll see you there."

"You might," Sharkey said. "We've got a little unscheduled maintenance to take care of."

When Sharkey leveled off at their cruising altitude, he pointed at the broken chin bubble and said, "It looks like the rest of that Plexiglas is going to hold until we get on the ground."

Eric raised his visor and glared at Sharkey, who said defensively, "Hey, the guy said it was a matter of principle." There was no more talk for the remainder of the flight.

At the airfield, Sharkey landed on the concrete pad of the Petroleum, Oil & Lubrication fueling station. Before the rotors wound down Sharkey jumped out of the ship and walked to a trash barrel. He grabbed an empty oil can and threw it in front of the helicopter. When a maintenance sergeant walked out of a wood shack, Sharkey pointed at the can and said, "One of your idiots left that can where it could get sucked up into our rotor wash. It blew out a chin bubble window."

The sergeant poked at the broken Plexiglas and the vertical dent in the nose and said skeptically, "Nothing like this has ever happened before, but I'll tell my men to make sure they keep the area clean."

In a stern voice Sharkey said, "Make sure you do." Then he changed to a conciliatory tone and asked, "Can you fix the window?"

The sergeant frowned at the gunship pilot before pointing at a revetment. "As soon as you're fueled, move to that maintenance area. There's a couple of wrecked Hueys out back. We'll pop a window out of one of them and have you fixed in a couple of hours."

"That sounds good, "Sharkey said. "As soon as you're through we'll leave for Ninh Hoa."

The window was repaired and Sharkey asked Eric if he wanted to fly back to Ninh Hoa. Eric nodded and climbed into his seat. After start up, he confidently backed the ship out of the revetment. As he lined up for takeoff, Sharkey said, "Nice job, you must have studied my moves."

Eric glanced at Sharkey and said, "Yeah right. It was either that, or I've done it a hundred times before."

On the way home Sharkey jabbered about the mission. He laughed at the Forward Air Controller's mini drama, and then talked about his girlfriend in Queens, New York.

Eric didn't say a word. He was thinking of Paul's question about whether he thought he could fit into the macho Gunnie mentality. He also couldn't believe Sharkey had a girl friend.

After they shut down, the two pilots were walking up the stairs to the barracks when Sharkey slapped Eric on the shoulder and said, "Bader, you did okay today. I always knew you would make a good Gunnie. The only problem is you need to get tougher. You need some spunk. Try to be more like me. Next time I'll let you fly and maybe you can kill some bad guys."

In a flat voice Eric asked, "Are we going to shoot them, or run 'em over?"

Sharkey laughed and said, "That's a good one, Dog. Now you're getting the idea."

Ninh Hoa, South Vietnam – November 7, 1969

Two weeks after they had joined the gunship platoon, Eric and Paul were signed off as Aircraft Commanders. In the ensuing three months they had become accomplished gunship pilots and were fully assimilated into the Jokers.

The southern monsoon season had arrived and was in full force with its bugs, heat and unbearable humidity. The daily afternoon rainstorm was pelting down on the tin roof of their room as the two roommates sat on their beds reading. There was a knock on the screen door and they were surprised to see Captain Brett Wilcox enter the room. Their former platoon leader had been promoted to Executive Officer two months earlier. Both men said in unison, "Good afternoon Sir."

"Afternoon guys, how was today's flying?"

Eric answered, "Mostly uneventful. What brings you to this neighborhood, Captain?"

"I need to talk with you, Eric. I've got a special mission for you tomorrow. An infantry major at Song Mau has been training a number of ARVNs and needs to give them some helicopter assault experience. We had a ship down there for two days and they've been practicing loading and unloading. Now the major wants them to practice with real flights. I'm sending him three Slicks and a pair of gunships. The ARVNS will be flown to a clearing, several miles away, with your gunships providing cover to make it feel like the real thing. You'll be fire team leader, with Greg Houston as your trail. Greg hasn't had any combat experience since he was upgraded to AC. I think this exercise will be good training for him."

"Sounds good to me," Eric said.

"Good. Cliff Moore will be leading the Slicks. You'll get the details at a briefing tomorrow morning at 0600."

Wilcox stopped at the door and said, "You guys have worked out real well in the guns. I'm glad the major transferred you to the Jokers."

Both men said, "Thank you Sir."

Twenty minutes later there was another knock on the door. Eric yelled, "Come in," as he looked up from a magazine. The two roommates were surprised to see another real officer walk into their room. Their fellow warrants were always coming and going, but it was rare to have someone above the rank of warrant officer visit their hooch, much less two of them. The visitor was Lieutenant James Iverson. Neither of the roommates liked the lieutenant because of his arrogant attitude, so they didn't greet him.

Unfazed by their hostile stares, Iverson asked, "Do you guys want a cold one?" He reached into an aluminum dish pan, and held up a can of beer. Both men declined.

Eric watched water run over Iverson's aviator chronograph and asked, "Is that watch waterproof?"

"Down to fifty meters," the lieutenant answered proudly.

Eric nodded with appreciation and said, "If you get killed can I have it? That watch just screams 'pilot.' I'd probably get laid all the time if I had a watch like that."

The lieutenant stood with an awkward look. Although the phrase was often used, it was generally reserved for close friends. Eric realized his mistake and said, "Sorry Lieutenant, bad joke."

Eric wasn't concerned about the young officer's discomfort--he was more worried that now Iverson would think they were buddies. Annoyed at himself, he asked, "Why are you here, Lieutenant?"

"I just made Aircraft Commander and I think it would be good for me to participate in the Song Mau training exercise. I just talked with Captain Wilcox and he said it was okay with him. He wanted me to ask what you thought."

Eric shrugged and said, "I don't think it is going to be that big a deal, but I suppose it will be good practice. You need to talk with Cliff Moore, since he will be leading the Slicks."

"Okay, I'll see him next." Iverson paused and then asked, "Eric, do you think we will get into some action down there? I've heard there are Viet Cong running all over the place. I figure the more experience I get, the faster I'll get promoted."

166

With a sigh, Eric said, "Look Lieutenant, you fly a Slick. Slicks are always on the receiving end of any action. That may make for good stories in the club, but you want to *avoid* action, not go looking for it. And remember, never volunteer for anything. You've got a lot of time left in-country, so don't press your luck. It will probably run out soon enough."

The lieutenant smiled nervously and then walked toward the door saying, "I need to find Cliff Moore and get this worked out."

When the screen door closed, Paul looked toward Eric and said, "What a dip."

The following morning the sky was a tropical blue as twenty aviators joked and jostled their way to the flight line. Eric and Cliff Moore were walking together with Lt. Iverson close behind. Eric pointed at the sky and said, "Looks like we picked a good day for this show."

Lt. Iverson added, "I was pretty sure it would be. I could tell by looking at the moon last night."

Eric and Cliff looked back at Iverson, then at each other. When Iverson walked toward his helicopter, Eric asked Moore, "Is the lieutenant going to be Chalk Two or Three?"

"I'll put him at Chalk Two. Spence Knox will be Three. Knox is a good pilot. Between the two of us we'll keep an eye on Iverson."

"I know Knox," Eric said. "Do you know Greg Houston? He's my trail. This is his first mission as an AC. His call sign is Joker Nine-Eight."

Moore nodded. "Houston's a good officer. I wouldn't be surprised if he isn't XO someday. I'll see you out there."

When Eric reached his gunship, his crew chief Adam Belcher, had it ready for a preflight inspection. As he started to look it over, he was approached by his trail gunner, who asked nervously, "If we're leading the Slicks, how fast are we going to fly?"

Eric grinned at Houston and answered, "Fast enough to keep them from running over us. I'll set the airspeed, you just stay with me. If I'm going to make a major turn, I'll let you know."

Sensing the captain's nervousness, Eric added, "Listen Greg, there's an old saying about the three things the lead ship wants to hear from his wingman: Lead, trail's up, Lead, you're on fire, and okay I'll take the fat chick."

Houston laughed and said, "I'll remember that."

"Good, we might have more time to talk when we get to Song Mau."

Houston walked back to his ship and Eric finished his preflight. After start up, he finished his checklist and radioed the flight, "Lead's up."

Houston called, "Trail's up."

"Roger that. Chalk One how are you doing?"

"Chalk One's up."

"Chalk Two is up."

"Three's ready."

"Okay, let's get this show started," Eric said. "The initial heading will be one seven five."

Because they didn't have a full fuel load, the gunships took off without bouncing, with the three Slicks close behind. The weather was unusually stable for the rainy season and the air was smooth. Lush green mountains rose on their right, with the aqua blue ocean to the left. The war is still going on, Eric thought, but this day he wasn't going to be in the thick of it.

An hour later, the tropical green jungle gave way to the light brown grass surrounding Song Mau. Eric found the river that led to the Army compound. The five helicopters landed on a dusty airstrip next to the river.

Their rotors were still winding down, when a major approached the helicopters. Forty ARVN soldiers nervously milled around in the distance. Eric climbed down from his seat and shook hands with the major.

The major dispensed with small talk and led the pilots to a plywood board with maps pinned to it. He tapped his left palm with a pointer and said, "Gentlemen, we've spent three months training these troops and this is the grand finale. They've come a long way and I'm damn proud of them." The major turned toward the map and tapped it with the pointer. "We'll be inserting them six per ship into these grid coordinates. There will be three flights into the area with eighteen troops per flight."

While the other pilots leaned in to study the map, Eric looked over his right shoulder and realized the LZ was just past the river on top of a nearby hill. Eric raised his hand and asked, "Excuse me Sir, but isn't that open area over there the Landing Zone?"

Everyone turned to look where Eric was pointing. When they turned back, the major tightened his jaw and hissed, "Yes."

The pilots fought back smirks, as the major stepped forward and barked, "Who are the gunship pilots?" Bader and Houston raised their hands.

The major moved directly in front of them and said, "I want the gunships to start this insertion with rockets. I'll be in the first Slick of the second flight. After we're all on the ground, I want you to continue to fire around us, to give them the feel of real combat. I've ordered four tanks that will show up shortly after we start."

He tapped Eric on the shoulder. "As our friend here pointed out earlier, the area is only two miles away, so the whole insertion should take less than an hour. When we're all on the ground, you guys will come back here while we do some field work. A couple hours later I'll call for you to come pick us up.

"My sergeant is passing out the radio frequencies for the mission. Our colonel will be standing by at company headquarters in case you need a clearance for anything while I'm on the ground."

The major stepped back a few paces and asked, "Are there any questions?" When there weren't any, he added, "Okay men, let's get started. Good luck."

On the way back to the airstrip, Eric whispered to his wingman, "Too easy."

The Gunnies had to wait as the Slick crews went through the drill of showing the ARVNs how to approach and depart the aircraft. When they were finished, Cliff Moore signaled to Eric by circling his hand. Eric yelled to Houston and jumped into his ship. The two gunships took off first in a cloud of dust. The three Slicks waited for the air to clear and then lifted off for the LZ.

At the Area of Operation all five helicopters had to orbit while the major received a clearance from his colonel to start firing. It was only a few months after the My Lai massacre and there were new rules of engagement. The main one being to make sure to avoid killing civilians.

The major relayed the all-clear and Eric called his trail ship. "Okay Greg, let's give them a show. See that rock pile to the south of the LZ? Let's use that as a target for our mini-guns."

Eric lined up on the rocks and fired. Houston covered his turn by firing his mini-gun. Eric radioed, "Nice run Greg, you've got the right spacing."

Houston called back, "Thanks Eric, this is fun."

"Yeah, it's better when nobody is shooting at you. Let's make the next one a dry run."

He wanted to save their ammo in case they had a real mission. This was practice, but they were still in a war zone. When they finished the dry run, Eric radioed to Chalk One, "Cliff, you guys are cleared into the LZ. We'll do more firing after you drop off your troops."

"Roger, understand we're cleared in."

"Chalk Two copies," Lt. Iverson replied.

"Three's with you," Knox added.

The two gunships flew in close escort, as the flight of three Slicks sailed into the LZ in a single file. When the troops were safely on the ground, the Slicks returned to the airstrip to pick up the major and the next load of Vietnamese soldiers.

It was customary for the gunships to recon the area while the other ships were loading. Eric radioed his trail ship. "Let's head down to the river and look around. We might find something interesting."

While they flew down the river, Eric heard Iverson ask Cliff Moore if he could take over as the lead ship. It was a strange request. Being the lead helicopter was not a coveted position. It was not only more demanding, the lead ship was usually the first to take enemy fire.

Moore radioed back, "Go for it Lieutenant. I'll take Chalk Two."

"Roger that," the Lieutenant answered excitedly.

170

Eric was flying over the river when he saw a shadow pass over the ship. He looked around and saw it was dust from the airstrip. Lt. Iverson and the other Slicks had taken off and were almost at the LZ.

Eric radioed Houston. "We've got to get back to the LZ, fast." He called Iverson and said, "Hey Lieutenant, you're supposed to call the guns before you go into a Landing Zone."

Iverson radioed back, "Oh yeah, sorry Dog."

The Jokers caught up with the Slicks just as they were about to land. The troops from the first insertion had spread out and were covering the flight. As the gunships slid into position, Eric radioed the lead ship, "Okay, we've got you covered. You're cleared in."

Eric could hear popping sounds as he approached the LZ and saw the troops from the first insertion begin to run. He quickly called the flight, "Chalk One what's going on down there?"

With no answer, he tried again, "Lieutenant, do you hear me?"

Cliff Moore radioed excitedly, "Chalk Two's taking fire, we're hit. Chalk Three don't come down. Break off your run, there's something wrong here."

Knox made a hard right turn and said, "Roger, we're going back to the airstrip."

The lead ship was sitting in the LZ and Eric called again, "Chalk One, Chalk One, do you read me? What's going on?"

As he circled for a better look, his crew chief yelled, "Mr. Bader, the lead ship is on fire."

Eric banked toward the confusion on the ground. An all-out fire fight was in progress around the downed helicopter. Smoke poured out of the engine compartment as the rotor blades came to a stop.

Eric was appraising the situation when Cliff Moore called, "Joker Nine Three, Chalk Two and Three are back at the airstrip. My co-pilot's been shot and I almost took a round in the head. A medivac is on the way."

"Roger Cliff, call headquarters and tell them we need reinforcements." Eric radioed his trail ship. "Greg, can you see who's who down there? I've got uniformed troops everywhere and I can't tell who they are."

"I can't either. Where did all those guys come from?"

"I don't know, but if any of them start shooting at us, or the downed ship, we take them out."

"Roger that."

Eric knew he had to do something fast as he watched four men exit the downed helicopter. One of them pulled a body to the front of the ship. The body was dressed in a flight suit, so it was one of the crew.

Houston radioed Eric, "Do you see the crew in front of the ship?"

"Yeah, and I also see five guys sneaking up from the north. I'm going to make a run at them. If I draw fire, take them out with your mini-gun."

"Okay, I'm right behind you, but aren't we supposed to get a clearance before we start shooting at real enemy troops?"

Eric was disgusted and said, "Oh damn, that's right. I'll call the colonel. Come up on that frequency, so you can listen."

"Roger, going there now."

Eric quickly radioed the colonel, "Light Blue Head Quarters this is Joker Nine-Three, do you copy?"

When there was no reply, Eric wondered what he would do if he didn't get an answer. He could see three downed crewmen crawling toward a lone tree. Behind them was the major in his camouflage fatigues. The five figures to their north were closing in. He was going to have to do something fast.

Headquarters finally replied, "Joker-Nine Three, this is Light Blue."

"Light Blue, Joker Nine-Three is a helicopter gunship on a training mission near Song Mau. One of our ships has been shot down. We are requesting permission to return fire."

"Joker Nine-Three that is the training mission I approved three days ago. Major Smith assured me there were no enemy combatants in that area."

"Sir, I'm sure that is what he believed at the time, but we've got one helicopter down, one crew member possibly dead and the rest of them crawling for their lives. Major Smith is one of them and there are enemy troops closing in. We need to act now."

172

In a hesitant voice the colonel said, "Joker Nine-Three, if you think the situation is that critical, I will allow you to make the decision to fire. In view of the circumstances, I'm holding you directly responsible for any action taken. Furthermore, I will want a full report when this is over. Is that clear?"

"Yes Sir."

Eric quickly switched to the mission frequency and called Houston. "Do you believe that bullshit? Now I'm responsible for this screwed-up mess. Fuck it! Let's shoot those bastards."

It was the first time Eric had used the "F" word over the radio. Even in Vietnam, it was not approved radio protocol, but he was mad and getting more frustrated by the minute. Good people were going to get killed because a panty-waist colonel couldn't make a decision.

He put his gunship into a shallow dive and sized up the situation. He called his wingman. "I've got the crew in sight under that tree. The original group of bad guys is still there and now there are more sneaking up from the south."

Eric banked hard above the aircrew and saw one of them rise on one knee and begin shooting at the group to the south. A door gunner had carried his M-60 machine gun from the helicopter and was firing at the enemy with only grass as cover.

Eric called his partner. "Greg, look at that gunner. They must have taken some enemy fire. We need to give them a hand. The group to the south is further away. I'll take those guys out with rockets. You use your mini-gun on the group to the north."

"Copy that. I'm right behind you."

"Okay let's do it."

Eric started a dive and fired a pair of rockets which hit just to the right of the group. He turned a few degrees to the left and fired off another pair that slammed into the enemy as they tried to disperse.

He banked hard left as his trail ship rained bullets into the grass on the other side of the downed crew. Eric made a tight circle to follow Houston over the target area, but held his fire as he assessed the results of their first pass. Dust and smoke hung in the air, but there wasn't any movement from the two enemy groups. He flew over the downed crew who waved frantically.

Eric climbed for a better view and saw dust blowing off the hill to the east of the battle area. It was the tanks. He watched as four Army tanks sped along the crest and then stopped overlooking the chaos. He flew toward the tanks and told his co-pilot to put in their radio frequency. When he called the commander, there was no answer. They had been given the wrong frequency. "So what else is new," Eric said. The frequency they had for the ground troops didn't work either.

The tanks lowered their guns and began firing. Eric called Houston and said, "Look at those tanks. What the hell are they shooting at?"

Houston was circling the battle area, and quickly radioed back, "Now I see what's happening. There are enemy troops coming out of the ground like hornets. There must be a tunnel down there."

Eric banked hard to the left and said, "I'm coming back. Let's see if we can figure this out."

As he waited for his lead to return, Houston radioed, "I've got five guys running up a hill. I'm going to have a closer look." As he did, the men stopped running and quickly popped a yellow smoke grenade.

When he saw the smoke, Houston held his fire and turned before he flew over them. He called his lead and said, "I'm pretty sure they're bad guys, but I didn't shoot because they are dressed like ARVNs. I thought the enemy was supposed to wear black pajamas."

"Not all of them," Eric called back. "I think you're right, but I also don't want to shoot any friendlies. Somebody did their homework on this one, dressing the enemy in ARVN uniforms. They must have been tipped off about this exercise."

Eric turned toward the hillside and radioed his wingman, "Cover me, Greg. I'm going to have a look." As he approached the soldiers, they again popped a yellow smoke grenade and waved. Eric held his fire and broke hard before he reached the group. As he did, the troops picked up their rifles and began shooting at his helicopter. Eric heard the shots and the familiar whack, whack of bullets hitting metal.

"Shit!" Eric shouted and quickly radioed his wingman. "We just took a couple hits, Greg. If you've got a bead on the bastards, nail them."

"I'm lining up on them right now and going in hot with rockets." Houston fired two pair into the middle of the group and turned hard before over flying the target. "I think I got them. How are you doing, Eric?"

"My crew chief is checking right now. Nice shooting, Greg. You nailed them."

Eric looked back at his crew chief, Adam Belcher. He was hanging out of his door gunner position and said, "The bullets must have hit the belly. Did you feel anything weird when they hit?"

Eric answered, "No."

Belcher sat back down and yelled, "She's still flying--let's keep going."

"Okay," Eric said, as he turned back to reassess the situation on the ground.

He was forming a plan when Cliff Moore called, "Joker Nine-Three, this is Chalk Two."

"What's up Cliff?" Eric asked quickly.

"How's it going out there?"

"I've got troops all over the place. There are dead everywhere and I can't tell our guys from the enemy."

"That sounds normal." Moore said, "What about our downed crew?"

"Are you thinking about getting them out?"

"Yeah, if they're in a good spot I'd like to go get them."

"Good idea, but we have to move fast. We're getting low on fuel and ammo."

"Okay, Knox and I are coming back up in his ship."

"We'll cover you," Eric said and then called his trail. "Greg, did you copy?"

"Yeah, I'm right behind you."

The two gunships had been circling and began a shallow dive as they watched Moore take off from the airstrip. As the Slick neared the landing zone, Eric called, "You're cleared in."

The downed crew stayed low as Moore came in fast. The helicopter was barely on the ground when the aircrew and the major climbed in. When they were all on board, Cliff put the ship in a nose-low position and lifted off. "We're out of here," Moore called. The sound of cheering could be heard in the background.

"Good job, Cliff. We'll see you at the airstrip," Eric radioed, as he began a climb. He knew he couldn't stay out there much longer, so he called Houston and said, "Let's climb up to three thousand over the river. I'm going to guard frequency to see if we can get help." Houston clicked his mike twice.

As they climbed through fifteen hundred feet, Eric started his distress call: "Mayday, mayday, troops in peril, we need help."

He had never before made a mayday call, the most serious radio call a pilot could make. It was the second time that day he had used a phrase that he had never used in his sixteen months in combat.

As he climbed higher, he repeated again, "Mayday, mayday, mayday, this is Joker Nine-Three, we need assistance."

Eric was relieved to hear a familiar voice answer, "Joker Nine-Three this is Devilfish Four-One, heavy team of Snakes. What are your needs?"

Snakes were Huey Cobras, the newer Army helicopter gunships. If they were a heavy team, it meant there were at least three of them. The more the better, Eric thought. Before he answered, he remembered where he had heard the voice. It was a classmate from flight school. They had become good friends and had traveled together on the flight to Vietnam.

Eric smiled as he remembered his friend's call sign. He was a warrant officer, but at thirty-five he had been the oldest candidate in their class. His last name was Custer, so his classmates had nick named him "Colonel."

Eric called his friend and asked, "Devilfish Four-One, is that you Colonel?"

"That's me, is this Eric?"

"You've got it Colonel, and I'm damned glad to hear your voice."

"Same here. It sounds like we're in your neighborhood, what's your position?"

"We're three miles southeast of the village of Song Mau."

"We're headed that way. What can we do for you?"

"What we have is the remnants of a training exercise that turned into a major battle. You'll see it when you get closer because there's a downed helicopter in the middle of it. The ship was shot down with a pilot probably KIA. He's lying in front of the helicopter and we need to get him out. There are also twenty-three ARVNs that are still unaccounted for. They're all inexperienced in combat, so there's no telling how many are left. We rescued the crew from the downed ship along with a major who was supposed to be leading this exercise."

Eric saw the three Cobra gunships on the horizon and said, "I've got you in sight, Colonel. Do you have me circling above the burning ship?"

"Yeah, I've got you."

"Good. There are enemy troops coming out of a tunnel about fifty yards east of the downed ship. They are dressed like ARVNs, so the only way we can tell them from friendlies is when they shoot at us. I'm over the tunnel right now."

"Okay, I've got that."

Eric continued to fly toward the east. "There are also four of our tanks on a hill just below me now. They've been shooting at the gooks as they come out of the tunnel. I called for reinforcements, but haven't heard of an ETA. Hopefully they'll be here soon. One more thing, we were given a list of frequencies, but none of them has worked except one for a colonel that was no help at all. I'll have my co-pilot call yours with the freq list. Maybe you can raise somebody."

The gunship leader called back, "Okay, we got all that and we'll see what we can do."

"Thanks Colonel. I'm glad you were in the area. I was almost out of fuel, ammo and ideas, all at the same time. We've got to go."

"Okay Eric. See you."

When Eric turned toward the airstrip, two enemy soldiers jumped out of the grass and fired. One of the shots tore through the floor between the pilot seats. It was so loud it sounded like it was fired from inside the ship. Eric instinctively turned away from the enemy.

He quickly radioed Houston and yelled, "Greg we're hit again, did you see those two guys jump out of the grass?"

"Yeah, we saw them but we were too close to fire."

Eric turned back toward the enemy and said, "I've got them in sight and I'm going to take care of this before we leave, cover me."

"Okay, let's do it."

Eric zeroed in on the two soldiers who were running while looking over their shoulders. With only four rockets remaining, he knew he would have to make them count. He fired a pair and watched as they left his ship whistling past his cockpit window. The rockets missed to the right and the enemy soldiers dashed to the left. Eric banked hard left and fired off his last pair. Those rockets hit their mark leaving nothing but a smoking hole.

The Colonel called his friend and said, "Good shooting Eric. Any time you want to join a real gunship unit, give me a call."

Eric laughed and said, "At one time I might have done that Colonel, but right now I'm way too short. I only have two more months and I'll be on a Silver Dustoff out of here."

"I'll be there too," Custer said. "Maybe we'll be on the same flight."

"Let's hope so, but right now I have to leave. My low fuel light just came on."

"Okay, Adios Amigo."

The two gunships returned to the airstrip and landed next to the one flyable Slick. The other crew members were standing in front of Moore's helicopter. One of them was Iverson's co-pilot, which meant it was Iverson's body lying in front of the downed ship.

The gunship crews approached Moore's ship and noticed the bullet holes in the windshield. The one on the pilot's side had entered at such an angle it grazed the top of Cliff's helmet. The co-pilot's side had two bullet holes and blood on the seat and floor.

Cliff Moore saw the concern on their faces and said, "It looks worse than it was. My co-pilot was hit in the right arm and shoulder. The medic said his wounds shouldn't be life-threatening."

Eric pointed at the bullet hole on the pilot's side and said, "This was your lucky day, Cliff."

Moore held his helmet so the others could see the crease, and said, "I keep thinking what might have happened if I had been in the lead ship."

"It wasn't your fault, Cliff," Eric protested. "The lieutenant insisted on going first."

When Moore nodded solemnly, Eric turned to Iverson's co-pilot and asked, "How bad was it?"

The young pilot said, "It was bad. He took a bullet in the throat just as we started to flare. I had to take control to keep from crashing. Another round hit the nose of the ship and knocked out our radios. I tried calling you, but everything was dead. The engine was on fire, so I shut it down and got everybody out. I checked the lieutenant and there was no pulse, so I pulled him out of his seat and laid him on the ground. I didn't want him to burn up with the ship."

Eric was impressed by the young man's demeanor and extended his hand. "I don't think we've met, I'm Eric Bader."

The young pilot shook Eric's hand and said, "Everybody knows who you are, Eric. My name is Ken Alscott."

"Good to meet you Ken. Is this the first time you've been shot down?"

Alscott wiped the sweat from his face and said, "Yeah, I've only been here a month."

"You seem pretty cool for a new guy."

The co-pilot shrugged and said, "I was an ambulance driver in college. A funeral home owned the company and part of my pay was a free room over the parlor. Between bad accidents and the stiffs I had to pick up, I've seen a lot."

Eric asked, "Have you ever thought about becoming a gunship pilot?"

The young pilot's face brightened and he said, "I'd love to be a Gunnie."

Eric pointed at his co-pilot, and said, "I'm about to recommend

Coop here for AC. When I do, I'll try to get you assigned to the Jokers and I'll fly with you."

"That would be great," Alscott said with a grin. He pointed at the door gunners standing by Knox's helicopter. "Our door gunner would like to talk with you."

Eric looked toward the group and said, "Have him come over here."

Alscott waved to the man and Eric asked, "Is that the guy who took his machine gun with him?"

"Yes, he's the one." Alscott said and then did the introductions. "Eric, this is Pete Kolinsky. Pete this is Eric Bader."

Kolinsky shook Eric's hand and said, "Mr. Bader, I want to thank you for saving our lives. I have never seen anything that looked as good as you rolling in on us with that Joker emblem on the nose. I knew right then we had a chance. Your aim was right on. If you had hit any closer to us, we might have been killed and if you had missed the dinks would have killed us."

Kolinsky turned to Houston and said, "Captain, you did a great job with your mini gun."

The gunner paused and Eric said, "I have to commend you for having the foresight to take your machine gun with you."

"Thanks, I was trying to lay down some fire, but I was seriously outnumbered until you came along."

They were interrupted by Major Smith who yelled from a nearby Quonset. "That's enough chatting. I want to debrief immediately."

The pilots walked to the building and followed the major into his office. The major sat behind his desk and reached into a drawer for a bottle of Jack Daniel's. While he poured the whiskey the bottle clinked against the glass. He took a generous sip and offered the bottle to the pilots. They all declined because they couldn't drink until they were done flying.

The major replaced the bottle and stood. "Tell me again, who are the gunship pilots?"

Eric pointed at himself and Houston. The major walked around his desk and stood in front of the two Gunnies. "You two scared the hell out of me. Do you know how close those rockets came to us?"

Eric stared blankly at the major, not sure if they were being questioned, or scolded. The major took a quick drink and said, "And that mini-gun. Good Lord, the sound is terrifying. The ground was shaking as the bullets hit only fifty feet away."

The major changed his expression and said, "That was a very impressive display of airmanship, boys. I have never worked that close with a gunship and I hope I never do again. You guys were instrumental in saving our lives and you risked your necks to do it. You did a great job and I'm putting both of you in for the Distinguished Flying Cross."

Eric and Greg exchanged glances as the major continued, "Don't worry about the details. I've been in the Army long enough to know how to make these things happen. I want all of you pilots to write a narrative of what took place today. I'll need them in a couple of days when I send a report to the colonel. For now you're dismissed."

On the way back to the airstrip, Eric asked his wingman, "What do you think of the guns so far, Greg?"

Houston grinned and said, "This is good duty, Eric. I've only been on the job one day and I've already been put in for a DFC."

Eric laughed and said, "That's pretty good, I've been here sixteen months and it's my first."

Eric's crew chief had removed the belly panels of their gunship and determined the damage was minimal. He said the ship was flyable and could make it back to Ninh Hoa. As the gunship pilots buckled in, the Slick crews stoically climbed into their one flyable ship for the trip home.

The flight back was quiet with everyone thinking about Lieutenant Iverson. The only discussion inside Eric's ship was when his co-pilot asked, "How does it feel to only have two months left in-country?"

Eric answered softly, "On a day like today, it's still way too long."

At their home base, Eric entered his room where Paul and Tucker were sitting across from each other drinking beer. Tucker offered him a beer and asked, "How was your day?"

Eric declined the beer and said, "Not good. Iverson was killed and there was so much gun play we couldn't get him out. I need something stronger than beer. Do we have any whiskey?"

Paul pointed at his locker and said, "Purple sack, top shelf."

Eric opened the bottle and poured a hefty drink into a tin cup without once touching the edge. Still steady as a rock, he thought.

Several days later Jack Cates approached Bader as he left the Ops office. Cates was still awards and decorations officer and said, "Hey Eric, I just heard you and Captain Houston were put in for DFCs. What did you guys do at Song Mau?"

Eric shrugged and said, "I thought we were just doing our jobs, but a major down there thought otherwise."

Cates slapped Eric on the shoulder and said, "Well I'll do everything I can to make it happen."

"Thanks, Jack," Eric said as he turned toward his room.

The following week, Eric and his trail, Greg Houston, were covering a convoy of supply trucks climbing up the Duc Loc Pass. Eric kept his promise and had Ken Alscott transferred to the Jokers. This was Alscott's first time in a gunship. As they watched the trucks grinding up the steep grade, Eric said, "I pity those poor bastards. They're sitting ducks. I can't believe they haven't been hit." He turned to his new co-pilot and said, "You know Ken, there are harder ways to go through this war than what we do."

"I know," Alscott said. "Thanks for getting me transferred to the Jokers."

Eric looked out his side window just as the trucks reached the summit and started winding down the other side. The sun was close to setting when the trucks finally made it to their destination. Eric bid the lead driver goodbye and turned toward the east.

After they crossed a ridge, Eric noticed something in a jungle opening and radioed his trail gunner. "Greg, do you see that clearing off to our left? There's something moving through it. Let's go take a look."

Two elephants and four NVA soldiers were walking through the open area. The elephants had 122 mm rockets strapped to their sides.

Two soldiers were leading the animals, with the other two trailing behind. When they saw the helicopter they quickened their pace toward a thick stand of bamboo.

Eric told Alscott to call HQ and let them know what they had and to give them the coordinates. HQ called back that they wanted the gunships to take out the elephants and enemy soldiers, but to save the rockets for capture.

As part of an experiment, Eric's helicopter had been equipped with a .50 caliber machine gun instead of the standard .30 caliber M-60. The crew chief, Adam Belcher, was an avid hunter and when he heard the order from headquarters, he said, "Hey Boss, this is the perfect time to use the .50 cal. If you put me alongside those elephants, I'll nail them."

Eric told Belcher, "Okay, we'll give it a try." He called Houston, "Greg did you copy HQ?" Houston clicked his mike twice and Eric continued, "In order to save the rockets, we'll have to hit the elephants with our machine guns. We've got the .50 caliber on board, and my crew chief says he can take out the elephants with that. I need you to shoot the trialing NVA soldiers with your mini-gun. We'll take out the lead elephant and maybe the second one will stumble over it."

Houston radioed back, "We copy."

Eric lined up on the targets and called his crew chief. "Adam, I'm not going to go any lower than two hundred feet in case those gooks try to shoot at us. We'll be above and to the right. That should give you a good shot. Take out the lead elephant first."

The elephants and men were running hard as the helicopter came alongside. Belcher fired two rounds, missing high. He lowered his aim and hit the first elephant in the upper back. The animal's front knees buckled and it fell onto its belly. The second elephant veered to the left and dashed for a patch of bamboo. As it did, Houston nailed the trailing soldiers with his mini-gun.

The remaining elephant and two soldiers plowed into the vegetation and could barely be seen, making another shot with the .50 impossible.

Watching the parted bamboo move was the only way Eric could tell where the remaining elephant was located. He looked back at the clearing and saw there was no movement from the lead elephant and the two NVA soldiers.

He radioed Houston to cover him as he lined up on the moving vegetation. He was about to fire when tracers came at him from the bamboo. He lowered his sights and fired his mini gun at the tracers. The enemy fire stopped and he took aim at what he thought was the front of the elephant. After a short burst, the elephant stopped and Eric made a hard turn.

Houston followed at a close trail, but radioed that he didn't fire because he couldn't see the target. Eric banked hard to fly over the area. When he was above the elephant, he could see it lying on the ground moving its trunk. He prepared for another run and called Houston. "I saw the elephant. It's down, but still alive. I'm going to end this bullshit with a couple of rockets."

His co-pilot quickly turned the selector for two pair as Eric lined up on the downed elephant. When he fired, the rockets whistled into the bamboo causing a detonation that rocked the gunship. Eric made a sharp turn away from the target and called Houston. "By the looks of that secondary explosion I must have hit the rockets on the side of the elephant. That should have killed everything in the area, but the colonel lost some of his photo op. At least they have the ones on the other elephant."

The gunships turned toward their home base, and received a call that troopers were on the way to clean up the scene.

It was dark when they finally landed at Ninh Hoa. Paul was leaning against the operations building when Eric reached the top of the stairs. Paul handed him a beer and said, "I was getting worried. What kept you out so late?"

"I'll tell you at the mess hall if it's still open."

"It closed a half hour ago, so I brought a plate back to the room."

"Thanks man."

Eric relayed the elephant incident as he ate a plate of cold roast beef and potatoes. When he finished the story, Paul said, "That's a good one. Are you going to paint two elephants on the side of your gunship?"

Eric shook his head. "No, I felt bad about killing them. I wish I could have stopped them some other way."

Paul frowned and said, "You're not going soft on me are you? It wasn't your fault those elephants were in this fucking war."

"I know," Eric said. "My crew chief was excited about the shoot. He had me make a low pass, so he could get a picture of the downed elephant to send back to Kentucky. If we could have landed, he would have wanted a picture standing next to it."

Eric set his plate down. "When I was in high school, my friends and I hunted our share of deer and elk. It never bothered me unless I made a bad shot and the animal suffered. Eventually, I was able to make a clean kill with only one shot. Unfortunately, that didn't happen with the second elephant, so I went to rockets. I know it's not suffering now."

Paul said, "Would you have felt better if they had been hauling the rockets on two elk?"

Eric looked at his friend and said, "Okay, I see your point. I just need time to think this out."

The next afternoon, Eric and Paul had just entered their room when there was a knock on the door. Jack Cates walked in and announced, "We've got a problem."

Eric was standing next to his locker and asked, "What kind of problem?"

"Remember that statement you wrote about the engagement at Song Mau? We need to change a few things."

With an icy stare, Eric asked, "What exactly do we need to change?"

"Your narrative and the major's don't jibe. He's put himself in for a medal and he has his version of what happened and it's different from yours."

This is bullshit, Eric thought. Details were his specialty and someone questioning his report hit a nerve. "I don't give a damn what his story says, mine is exactly what happened."

Cates shook his head. "The stories are too far apart."

Eric walked toward Cates and asked, "Just how far apart are they,

Jack?"

"I can't say, but I can tell you what we need to change."

Eric got into his friend's face. "How the hell can we get the two reports together when I don't even know what his says?"

In a calm voice Cates said, "Listen, he's a major and he's leaving Vietnam in a month. He wants a Silver Star and you're impeding his efforts to go out a hero."

Paul opened his locker and said, "This sounds like it's going to take awhile. I'm going to have a drink. Anybody else want one?"

Cates turned to Paul and said, "Oh no, you don't. I know what you're doing and you're not going to bribe me with good booze."

Paul ignored him and poured Jack Daniel's into three cups. Cates reluctantly took one and said sullenly, "This is just between the three of us, right?"

Paul hoisted his drink and said, "It won't leave the room."

Cates took a long drink and then extended the clipboard. Eric grabbed it and sat on his bed. He leafed through the papers until he found the major's report. After reading it, he looked up at Cates with disgust. "This is total bullshit, Jack. The only thing that's true is he was shot down with Iverson. He says he led the inexperienced aircrew to a superior fighting position. How do you lead when you're the one trailing behind everyone else? The superior fighting position he writes about was a small tree and he was the last one there."

Eric got up and shoved the clipboard at Cates. "If there's a hero in this story, it's the door gunner who had the foresight to take his machine gun with him. Has he been put in for a medal?"

"Yes, that's Pete Kolinsky and we'll take care of him. What I need to know now, is what we're going to do about you. This isn't Sunday school, Eric. There are a lot of gray areas in war. Why can't you just change a few things?"

"What am I going to change?"

Cates paced back and forth in front of the door, and then stopped. "Look, all you have to do is massage a few paragraphs here and there and everyone will be happy."

Eric's anger was rising. "Since when does the truth need massaging, Jack? What's in my report is exactly what happened and I'm not changing a goddamn thing."

Cates pushed the door open and said over his shoulder, "The Joker Nine-Three martyr statue will be placed in front of the O Club."

As the screen door closed, Eric yelled, "I'm not going to lie in my report, so some asshole can get a medal."

Eric angrily turned toward his roommate who said, "Sorry Dog, but I think your Distinguished Flying Cross has wings on it."

The following evening, Eric and Paul were sitting in the club when they were approached by Jack Cates. "How'd the war go today, guys?"

Eric looked around and answered, "Not too bad, Jack. I think it was Patriots ten, Viet Cong zero. Are you and your buddy still working on that piece of fiction?"

Cates motioned for the two roommates to move to the end of the bar. When they were out of ear shot, he said, "Now that you ask, our offended major is even more pissed. He says you're the one who's the asshole and he's going to get his medal one way or the other. He also mentioned since you're not a team player all you'll get are leftovers."

Eric shook his head, as Paul piped up. "He can't do that, can he?"

Cates turned to Paul and said, "He can and he will. He's a major and he's got connections."

Paul looked at Eric. "We've got connections too, don't we, Dog?"

Eric shrugged and Cates said, "That's the point gentlemen. You should have changed your story."

Cates moved away and Eric said, "I'm getting real tired of this whole goddamn scene."

The two roommates drank in silence until they were approached by Greg Houston. "Hey Eric, Cates just told me there may be a problem with our DFCs."

Eric turned to his wingman and said, "There may be a problem with mine, but I don't think there is with yours. At least I hope not."

Houston sat next to Eric and said, "If you don't get one then I don't want one. We're in this together. How can I get a DFC and you don't?

You were leading the whole damn flight. That doesn't make sense."

"It doesn't have to make sense, Greg. Listen, you're a West Pointer and you've got a long career ahead of you. A Distinguished Flying Cross will definitely enhance your record. On the other hand, I only have forty-five days in this man's Army and then I'll be skiing in Austria and won't give a damn about any medals. I say we let the chips fall where they may. If I don't get one, that's the way it goes."

Three days later, Eric was reporting his flight time, when a company clerk approached him in the Ops office. "Mr. Bader, I need to inform you that you are to be present at an award ceremony at 1900 hours."

"Why do I need to be there?"

"Because you are receiving a medal."

"Do you know what it is?" Eric asked.

"No, and I couldn't tell you if I did."

"Okay, I'll be there."

Eric left the office and heard the familiar voice of Jack Cates say, "Hold up, Dog." He turned around and Cates handed him a pressed infantry uniform and steel helmet. "You're supposed to wear these to the award ceremony. The major says it will make you look more military."

Eric looked at the uniform and asked, "More military than what, Jack? You mean I don't look military in my flight suit?"

"Just put them on, okay? The CO thinks it looks good."

Eric took the gear and walked to his room. After changing into the uniform, he was viewing himself in the mirror when his roommate entered and said, "Don't you look strack. What's with the infantry uniform?"

Eric donned the camouflaged helmet and said, "Cute, huh? It's the Old Man's idea. He thinks it looks more military."

Paul laughed and said, "Oh yeah, I can see that."

Eric checked his watch and said, "I better get out there. You coming?"

Paul threw his flight bag on his bed, and said, "Are you kidding? I wouldn't miss this for anything."

By the time they reached the parade ground, a crowd had already gathered. Most of the men were seated in the bleachers. Jack Cates watched from the front row. The other men who were to receive medals milled around in front of the bleachers. Eric walked up to Cliff Moore and Greg Houston.

Before the ceremony started, a company clerk began arranging the men in a row. When he was finished, Eric was on the far left and would be last to receive an award.

Satisfied with the order, the clerk signaled the company's two senior officers who walked out from beside the bleachers. The Executive Officer called the formation to order and saluted the Commanding Officer.

Another clerk followed the CO carrying a box and the two stood in front of the first man to receive a medal: Pete Kolinsky, the door gunner of the downed helicopter at Song Mau. The clerk handed the CO a medal and began reading from the commendation. "For exceptional valor in the face of heavy enemy fire at the battle of Song Mau, Specialist Peter Kolinsky is awarded the Silver Star." The audience clapped and cheered. Most Silver Stars were given to the infantry and it was rare for a member of an air crew to received one.

The next five awards were Army Commendation Medals given to a combination of pilots and other crew members. The ACM was given to everyone who made it through six months of service in Vietnam.

The next two awards were presented to Cliff Moore and Spence Knox, who were awarded the Bronze Star with V Device, for exemplary valor at the battle of Song Mau in rescuing the downed aircrew under heavy enemy fire. The crowd cheered again.

Next in line was Greg Houston. The clerk handed the CO a medal and began reading, "For exceptional valor in the face of heavy enemy fire, during aerial combat at the battle of Song Mau, Captain Gregory Houston is hereby awarded the Distinguished Flying Cross."

The audience applauded as the Commanding Officer pinned the medal on him. Houston turned slightly to Eric and gave him a nod.

The CO moved in front of Eric, who glanced toward the bleachers where his roommate gave him thumbs up. The company clerk started reading again: "For heroism while engaged in aerial combat against a superior enemy force at the battle of Song Mau, Chief Warrant Officer Eric Bader is hereby awarded the Air Medal with V Device."

Eric and the audience were stunned. The crowd grumbled and booed. As the formation broke up, Eric looked at Paul who was shaking his head in disgust.

Those who had been at Song Mau gathered around Eric. He had been the fire team leader and was in command of the whole flight. The others had been awarded a Silver Star, two Bronze Stars and a Distinguished Flying Cross, while Eric had received an Air Medal. He probably already had ten—they were routinely awarded to anyone completing twenty-five air assaults.

Greg Houston removed his medal and said, "This is total bullshit. I don't even want this thing."

Eric put his hand on his wingman's shoulder and said, "Yes you do, Greg. We all know what happened. The Song Mau major screwed me. At least he did the right thing for you other guys."

Houston angrily said, "Well, I'm going to get to the bottom of this. I'll talk to the XO. There has to be something we can do."

Eric shook his head. "No there isn't. I told you we'd let the chips fall and we did--let it go."

The group slowly moved toward the club, while Bader and Eason returned to their room. Eric had just changed out of the infantry uniform, when the screen door opened and Jack Cates walked in. He looked at Eric and said, "I'm sorry, Dog. I did everything I could, but it was over my head. Major Smith was adamant you wouldn't get a Distinguished Flying Cross."

Cates held up a box and said, "But I intend to make things right."

Eric stared angrily at his friend, as Cates reached into the box and took out a DFC. After pinning it on Eric's shirt, the awards officer recited a commendation. "On behalf of the US Army I am honored to present the Distinguished Flying Cross to Chief Warrant Officer Eric Bader for valor above and beyond the call of duty against a superior enemy force

190

at the battle of Song Mau."

Eric looked at the DFC and thought it was an impressive-looking medal. It was bronze colored with a four bladed propeller on the face and a red, white and blue ribbon.

With some impairment, Cates pointed at the medal and said, "This DFC would usually cost ninety dollars, but under the circumstances I am going to give it to you for free." He pulled a Silver Star out of the box and dangled it in front of Eric. "If you would like one of these, it's fifty-five dollars, or two for ninety. Of course Bronze Stars are much more reasonably priced at thirty-five bucks."

Eric was sure Jack was joking about selling the medals, but he wondered where the weirdness was leading. At least he hadn't mentioned how cheap an Air Medal was.

Cates paused and then pointed at the DFC. "You don't want this do you?"

Eric answered crisply, "No."

Cates took the medal off Eric's shirt and staggered out of the room. When he was gone, Paul said, "Those were some classy looking medals. I wonder if those prices are good for me too."

Eric laughed and said, "You never quit, do you?"

"Would you want me to?"

Eric shook his head. "Let's go get a drink. I'm going to forget this damn thing ever happened."

As they walked down the boardwalk, a little voice in the back of Eric's head said, "No you won't."

A month later, Eric entered his room and flopped onto his bed. Paul was already there and gave his roommate a wide berth. The two of them knew when the other had been through a bad day. As Eric stared at the ceiling, Paul said, "I'm guessing there's a story here and it's not a good one."

Eric continued to look at the ceiling and said, "No it isn't. We lost another friend."

"Who was it this time?"

"Judd Lawrence."

"What happened to him?"

"It was really ugly and he wasn't even shot down. We were inserting some troops into a meadow north of Nha Trang, the one with the rock that looks like a Buddha."

"I've been there, what happened?"

"It was an easy mission, with no fire taken, four Slicks in a single file. Cliff Moore was in the lead with Lawrence second. Cliff had just touched down and Larry was about a hundred feet high. Greg and I were providing cover, when a puff of white smoke came out of Larry's exhaust pipe and he fell like a rock.

"He was too low to do a full auto rotation, so they hit real hard and the rotor blades flexed down and tore through the roof of the cockpit. I watched it like it was in slow-motion. The blade tore through the roof on Larry's side and took off the top of his head. I'm sure he didn't know what hit him. Then the blade flexed up enough to just hit the co-pilot with a glancing blow which knocked him out."

Eric wiped his face with a towel. "I radioed Cliff what happened, so he stayed on the ground to check things out. There was a medic in his ship, so he joined him. There wasn't anything they could do for Lawrence except put him in a body bag. They thought the co-pilot was dead too until the medic checked his pulse. While they were getting him out of his seat, he started to regain consciousness. He saw blood and brains all over the instrument panel and freaked out. I doubt if we'll see him in a cockpit again."

"Probably not. How are you doing?"

"I'll be okay, but I'm getting real tired of losing friends."

"Aren't we all? Do you feel like getting some chow?"

"No, I don't feel like doing anything. I'm just going to lay here."

Paul walked toward the door and said, "I'll bring you back a sandwich from the mess hall. By the way, Cates was looking for you."

"What did he want?"

"He didn't say."

Half an hour later, Paul returned with a sandwich and some scraps for their dog. Eric was lying on his bed with his eyes closed. Paul put the dog food in Jungle Dog's bowl and the sandwich on a shelf.

The next morning, Eric was awakened by a knock on the screen door. He opened his eyes and was alarmed to see the sun was shining and Paul's bunk was empty. He looked around the room and saw the Executive Officer standing at the foot of his bed. He bolted to a sitting position, thinking he must have slept through a mission.

Captain Wilcox saw the concern on his face and said, "Don't worry, you're not in trouble. I told Eason not to wake you. I'm giving everyone involved in yesterday's incident the day off."

Relieved, Eric said, "Thanks Captain, you had me worried. Is that why you're here?"

"No, I need to talk with you about Lt. Cates. I've been told you're the only friend he has left."

Eric rubbed his face and said, "I guess so, and maybe Eason."

The XO continued, "I know Cates has been bucking for a Section Eight, but the major and I have had all we can take of his insolence. Two days ago I called him in to talk about his slovenly appearance. The reason he gave for not shaving was because he doesn't want to die in a pool of piss in the latrine. When I asked what that meant, he said he was unstuck in time and could see into the future. He says he can see all the way to where he dies of a heart attack at ninety-six."

Eric nodded, knowing that Cates had gotten the "unstuck in time" line from a Kurt Vonnegut novel. Jack had correctly guessed that none of the senior officers would know that.

Wilcox continued in disgust, "Then Cates said when he looks into a mirror he sees himself as a ninety-six year old man. He says he's afraid the next time he sees the apparition he might suffer a heart attack and fall into a pool of piss. What do you think of that?"

Eric collected his thoughts and said, "It sounds like the ravings of a very disturbed man, Sir."

"That's what the major and I think, so we're going to have him evaluated by a psychiatrist in Saigon. A doctor there has agreed to examine him and he wants to talk with one of Jack's friends, so I'm sending you. You'll also be in charge of getting him to the appointment on time."

Eric was suddenly interested in the case and asked, "We're both going to Saigon, for how long?"

"Two days. We have a helicopter that needs heavy maintenance. Tucker Burdett and our maintenance officer are flying it down there tomorrow. You two will ride with them."

When Eric smiled, Wilcox said, "Listen Dog, I know your reputation and I don't want to hear about you two hustling women while you're there."

Eric held up his index finger and said, "It was only one lady and I got lucky."

"Well, I don't want you getting lucky on my watch. This is a business trip with no screwing around. Is that clear?"

"Yes Sir."

The XO turned to leave and Eric said, "Sir, in defense of Cates, he was once a good soldier. You didn't know him then, but he was one of our best Slick pilots. He flew as hard as any of us, right up to the day he crashed. It was almost identical to what happened to Lawrence yesterday. His engine quit just as he entered the dead-man zone. He tried to auto rotate, but he was too low. Cates came out of the crash with two cracked vertebrae. While he was recuperating he got hooked on pain killers. When the docs took him off them, he started drinking.

"To make matters worse, a board of review determined the damage to the helicopter was pilot error and that tipped him over the edge. I think he should be discharged with a medical instead of a Section Eight. Do you think that could happen?"

"Maybe, but right now let's see what the psych has to say."

"Okay, what time do we leave?"

"Oh eight hundred hours tomorrow. I'll want a verbal report when you get back."

"Yes Sir."

Wilcox walked out and Eric jumped out of bed ready for a day off. He wrapped a green towel around his waist and left for the latrine. Six

Vietnamese hootch maids were already in the shower squatting on the concrete floor, washing uniforms in aluminum pans. When they saw him they shook their heads in disgust. An older woman made a sound like the bray of a donkey, then stood and glared at Eric. She left the room with the other women following.

The day was already heating up, so a cold shower felt good. The thought of two days in Saigon was also starting to erase the pain of the previous day's events. He dressed in a clean flight suit and left for the mess hall. After he ate, a cook handed him a package of meatloaf. Jungle Dog would be a happy puppy that day.

Eric decided to drop in on Cates. He knocked on his door and his friend yelled, "Come in if you dare."

Cates was wearing a Hawaiian shirt, OD shorts and flip-flops. He stood in front of a table, stirring a pot on a hotplate. When he saw Eric, he said, "Good morning Dog, you're just in time for my electric stew."

"Thanks Jack, but I just had breakfast and I've got meatloaf for lunch."

Cates glanced at the package and said, "You won't like it. I had some of that shit last night. It's pretty bad."

"Okay, I lied, it's for my dog."

Cates looked at his friend and said, "Why would you do that to a nice pup like Jungle Dog?" He went back to stirring the pot, and said, "I was sorry to hear about Lawrence."

"Yeah, it was a bad break. He wasn't even shot down."

Cates scooped a spoonful of the stew onto a dirty plate and offered it to Eric. "You need to eat this for medicinal reasons. It will cure anything that's wrong with you."

Eric eyed the plate and said, "What if there isn't anything wrong with me."

Cates pushed the plate at him and said, "You drink too much."

"We all drink too much, Jack. It gets us through another day."

"Maybe so, but you still need to try this."

Eric took the plate and asked, "What's in it?"

"Dinty Moore beef stew and special herbs."

Eric took a bite of the concoction and said, "Captain Wilcox paid me a visit this morning. He said you and I are going to Saigon to see your shrink."

Cates tasted the stew and said, "Yeah, I was told to bring a friend and I picked you."

Eric placed the plate on the table. "Thanks, I appreciate that. We need to go over your game plan, but right now I don't have the time."

"Okay, I'll stop by your room later."

Eric was starting to get a tingling feeling and asked, "What kind of herbs are in that stuff, Jack? I'm starting to feel a little weird."

Cates smiled and said, "That's the cure."

"Where'd you get the herbs?"

"From a mama-san in town. I traded her a carton of Salems. You can get anything you want in Nam for a carton of menthols."

"Did the herbs come in a green sandbag?"

"Yeah, why?"

"Because that's how they sell dope, you dick. God damn it Jack, I haven't smoked weed since college and you better not have gotten me stoned now."

"Calm down, don't you think I know the difference between marijuana and herbs?"

"Okay, I'm sure you do," Eric said apologetically. He walked toward the door and said, "You know that stuff might be working. I don't think I'll need a drink until at least noon."

As the screen door closed, Cates yelled, "Thanks for going with me, Buddy."

Six hours later, Eric walked into his room with a sunburn. Paul looked at him and said, "Why do I get the feeling you had a better day than me?"

Eric threw a rusty sword on his bunk and said, "There's nothing like a day at the ocean to get your head fixed."

"So how long is this freeloading going to last?"

"Funny you should ask. Cates and I leave for Saigon in the morning."

"*Saigon*--how the hell did you pull that off?"

196

"Jack has to see a shrink and the doc wants to talk with one of his friends."

"And you're it."

"Yep."

"I'm his friend. How come I don't get to go?"

"Because he likes me better. Look, all I know is, he's got the major and the XO pissed off about his unstuck in time bullshit and they think he needs to be evaluated by a psychiatrist."

"I wouldn't doubt that. Either he's gone rogue, or it's a ploy to get out of the Army."

"I think it's the latter, but I wouldn't want to get out like that."

"Me neither," Paul said as he pointed at the door. "Speak of the devil, he's headed our way."

Cates peered through the screen and said, "How's it going gents?" He walked in and saw Eric's sunburn. "Look who went to the beach and didn't invite me."

"I needed some time alone, Jack." Eric grabbed the sword and waved it. "I found this while I was there. A bulldozer was excavating a new foundation and I decided to follow it to see if it turned up anything. Check the design of this sword. I think it looks more Spanish than Oriental."

Cates and Eason looked at the rusty blade, and Cates said, "The Spanish were in the Philippines, maybe they made if over here as well." He took the sword and said, "This is a nice find. I'll fashion a wood handle for it out of a piece of mahogany."

Eric took the sword back and asked, "So what's the plan for your shrink, Jack?"

"You mean my counselor? He's going to interview me and I'll tell him I'm crazy. Then he'll ask if you think I am and you will say yes."

"What if I don't think you are?"

"You tell him yes anyway."

Eric paused and said, "Okay, I'll play along. What about tomorrow night in Saigon. Do you know any good bars?"

"I've never been there."

Eric was surprised and asked, "Then what about the future? Can't you go there and find something?"

Paul laughed and said, "That's a good one, Dog."

Cates changed to a stern voice. "You guys think this is a big joke, but it's not. My whole life is at stake."

Eric scoffed and said, "Whatever you say, Jack. I think you're doing this all wrong, but that's just my opinion."

The next morning, Eric was seated in the back of a Huey headed south. A cool breeze was in his face and it felt good to have the another day off. Tucker Burdett was flying, with the maintenance officer in the co-pilot seat. Nha Trang came into view first, then Cam Rahn Bay and finally Saigon.

They landed at Tan Son Nhut Air Force Base, where a Jeep was waiting to take the three pilots to the Bachelor Officer's Quarters. As they left the flight line they passed a long line of C-130 aircraft. I should be flying one of those and living in an air-conditioned barracks, Eric thought.

At the BOQ, the desk clerk gave the two newcomers a pamphlet that read, "The Do's and Don'ts of Saigon." The clerk turned to Tucker and said, "Mr. Burdett, the Colonel has reserved his room for you."

"Good, put Mr. Bader in there with me. Lieutenant Cates is to have his own room."

"Very well Sir."

As they walked Cates to his hallway, Tucker said, "We'll come back for you in half an hour. That will give you time to get cleaned up. That means a shower and a shave, Jack. There isn't any piss on the floor in this place."

Cates sulked toward his room and Tucker and Eric walked toward the stairs. When they entered their room, Eric said, "This must be the general's room."

Burdett threw his bag on the bed and said, "No, this room is for colonels. The general stays down the hall. Our battalion commander reserves this for me when I'm here on his business."

The room had a queen bed, a stocked bar, a bathroom and an

adjoining bedroom with a twin bed. Tucker walked to the bar and asked, "Do you want a drink?"

Eric declined and said, "It's not even noon Tuck. I might be a drunk, but I'm not that bad. Besides, I need to pace myself." He held up the pamphlet on Saigon and asked, "Can you recommend a good place where Cates and I can go tonight?"

Burdett took the pamphlet and threw it in the waste basket. "Normally, I'd recommend what's on the do *not* do list, but in this case neither of you are going to have to worry about it."

"Why's that?"

"Because Cates isn't leaving the base and you're going into town with me."

"I am?"

"Yes you are. Tonight we're having dinner with a couple of construction contractors. I want you to entertain them with your gunship stories. They're fresh over here from Texas, and you know how rednecks love gun play."

Eric grinned and said, "I can do that."

"Tell them about knocking down the flag pole and the battle at Song Mau. Just don't tell them you didn't get the DFC. They'll start writing their congressmen and we don't need that kind of attention."

Burdett started to unpack and said, "By the way, I've been meaning to tell you I think the way you handled that medal situation was right on."

"Thanks Tuck, that means a lot. Greg Houston was the only other guy to agree with me. Everyone else thought I should have caved and gone for the medal."

Burdett scoffed. "Medals don't mean shit. What really matters is what you're going to do with the rest of your life. We need to talk about that later, but right now we need to get Cates and go to the O Club for lunch."

When the three pilots had finished eating, Burdett turned to Cates and said, "Jack, I need to explain the plan for tonight. Eric and I are going into Saigon to have dinner with two American contractors. You're going to spend the night here on the base."

"Wait a minute," Cates whined. "How come Eric gets to go and I don't?"

Burdett leaned across the table and whispered, "Because you're too fucking crazy that's why." He leaned back and said, "This is an important meeting and I don't want you screwing it up. In case you think about sneaking off base, I'm going to tell the MPs to be watching for you. If you're caught, you'll be spending the night in the stockade." Burdett stood and added, "We'll see you in the morning."

At the Officer's Quarters, Burdett called the the motor pool and secured a driver and Jeep to take them into the city. When it arrived, Tucker asked Eric if he had ever been to Saigon. Eric shook his head and Burdett said, "Get in front, this ride will assault your senses."

Along the route, they saw speeding motor bikes, Volkswagen bugs, a convoy of Army trucks, a French Citroen, two horse-drawn carts, an old green ambulance with a large red cross on the side, multiple three wheeled Lambrettas and a stake truck loaded with bananas.

In the center of town, the traffic slowed to a crawl when an Army bus with ARVN insignias made too wide a turn and blocked two lanes. As they waited next to a Shell station, Eric saw a 1960 Plymouth Savoy at the gas pumps. Not having seen an American automobile in more than a year, Eric said excitedly, "Tucker, check out the fins on that Plymouth. I forgot how big they are."

Burdett laughed and said, "You've been away from the World too long my friend."

Eric looked back and said, "You can say that again. How do you think that beauty got over here?"

"Probably some rich businessman."

They had just started moving again when they came to a red light and Eric said, "I haven't been stopped by one of these in a while."

While they waited, two shapely girls crossed the street dressed in black pants and white blouses with long tails flapping in the breeze. Crossing the other way was an old woman weighed down by two heavily laden fish baskets, suspended from a bamboo pole stretched across her shoulders. On the sidewalk, a young girl pushed a hand truck with a block of ice on the bottom and a case of bottled beer on top.

When the light changed, the driver sped down two blocks, turned a corner and parked in front of the Hotel Rex. Eric got out and stared up at the buildings. Burdett slapped his friend on the back and said, "Don't gawk. You're starting to look like a tourist. Come on, we need to check in."

Eric was confused and asked, "Why are we checking in here?"

Burdett grinned at his friend. "Because what I have planned for tonight, we won't be able to do at the BOQ." He saw Eric's worried face and added, "Relax, I'll have you back there by morning."

Inside the lobby, the desk clerk said, "Mr. Burdett, your usual room is not available, but I can give you one that is equally nice."

"Okay, give me that one and another one nearby for my friend Mr. Bader. Put both rooms on my bill."

"Yes Sir."

After they checked in, Burdett said, "This is where we're meeting the contractors for dinner. It has a great rooftop restaurant and bar. It's a bigger version of the Hotel Dalat, so you'll feel right at home. Right now I'm going to do some shopping. I need four more AK-47s for my shipment to Jakarta. You can kill time at the Ben Thanh Market. It's only a couple of blocks from here and has everything you would ever want. Go buy presents to take home." Burdett looked at his watch. "It's almost thirteen hundred now. Let's meet upstairs in three hours and we'll get the party started."

At four o'clock, Eric found Burdett sitting at the roof-top bar. They ordered whiskeys and walked toward a table overlooking the city. Tucker waved his arm and said, "I think the Rex has the best view of the city. This hotel used to be known for what was called the Five O'clock Follies. Every day at five, military brass would meet the press to brief them on the day's activities. Since the briefings seldom bore any resemblance to the facts, the press started calling them The Follies. They still do the briefings, but they've moved to a hotel down the street. The military is still bullshitting everybody about how well the war is going, but at least they're not doing it here in my favorite hotel."

Burdett pointed at the horizon. "When it gets dark, you can usually see explosions and tracers from here. Let's hope they light things up tonight. It will be a good backdrop for your gunship stories."

Eric raised his glass and said, "I'm just happy to be here."

Thirty minutes later, two Texans walked in with big hats and bigger egos. The two pilots stood to great them. Burdett made the introductions. "Eric, these are the men I've been telling you about. This is Jim Crenshaw and Avery Powell. Guys, this is my friend Eric Bader. He's one of our top gunship pilots."

The men shook hands and Crenshaw, asked, "Do they serve bourbon in this place?"

Tucker grinned and said, "I've already ordered a bottle."

After the drinks were served, Crenshaw said, "I'm glad to be able to talk with a couple of you helicopter fly boys. I've always wondered what all those controls and buttons do, but all the pilots I've flown with just sit up front and never say anything."

Tucker turned to Eric, who said, "Let's start with the control between our legs. It's called the cyclic and it works much like the stick in an airplane. We use it to make turns and small adjustments in altitude. The larger control to the pilot's left is called the collective, and is used to make the ship go up and down. If you pull up on the collective the houses get smaller, push down and they get bigger."

The two Texans chuckled and Eric continued. "The buttons you see are used to talk on the radio, trim the aircraft and to adjust the RPM of the rotors. In my gunship on top of the cyclic, I've got an extra red button that I use when somebody really pisses me off."

Avery Powell smiled and said, "There have been times when I'm driving around Dallas that I wish I had a button like that."

Eric smiled and said, "I'm sure I'll miss that button when I get back to the States."

The dinner that followed was a huge success. The fireworks on the horizon enhanced Eric's stories, and the contractors watched and listened with rapt attention. When he ended with the flag pole story,

Crenshaw slapped the table and said, "It was a matter of principle. That's a good one, Eric. You sure know how to tell a tale."

Eric thanked him and the man leaned toward Burdett. "Tucker, this has been a fun evening, but what I'm wondering now is where a guy can find some after-dinner entertainment?"

Burdett smiled and said, "I thought you might ask that." He signaled to a waiter, who ducked into the kitchen and walked out with two young Vietnamese women dressed in miniskirts. The waiter presented the girls like two desserts.

Burdett turned to the Texans and said, "Gentlemen, these two ladies tell me they would be more than happy to show you their beautiful city of Saigon."

The two men grinned and Powell said, "Tucker, I believe we're going to be doing a lot of business together."

The two contractors left with the girls and Burdett said, "You see that Eric, everybody's a winner. Those two got what they wanted, our colonel will get what he wants and we get what we want."

"What do we get, Tuck?"

"A night on the town and a little contribution to our helicopter venture in the islands. But let's forget about that for now. If you thought those lovelies were nice, wait until you see the two I saved for us."

Burdett signaled again and the waiter ducked into the kitchen and produced the most attractive Vietnamese women Eric had ever seen. They both had long black hair that fell onto their shoulders. The one on the left was dressed in a light yellow blouse, a gold sparkling mini skirt and sandals with white knee-high stockings. The girl on the right strutted toward Eric wearing a tight white blouse, a violet mini dress and high-heeled sandals. She sat next to him and said, "My name is Nhu. I am your date."

Eric looked into the girl's dark eyes and said, "Yes you are."

Burdett nudged Eric's shoulder and asked, "What do you think of Saigon so far, Eric?"

Without taking his eyes off the girl, Eric said, "I like the way you operate, Tucker."

As they left the bar, Eric said, "I'm pretty sure this is on the XO's don't do list."

Burdett laughed and said, "Your only responsibility is to get Cates to his appointment. Captain Wilcox will never know what happens between now and then."

The next morning, Eric was awakened by a knock on the door. He opened it and a young Army waiter said, "Your seven o'clock wake up, Sir. Would you like coffee or tea?"

Eric pointed at the bar and answered, "Coffee please--put it over there."

The waiter walked to the bar and said, "I brought you some croissants with strawberry jelly."

"Thank you," Eric said as he gave the kid a dollar.

Eric poured a cup and asked Tucker, ""Do you take anything in your coffee?"

Burdett swung his legs off the bed and said, "No, I prefer my coffee as black as my conscience."

Eric laughed and said, "Me too." He handed his friend a cup and said, "I have to hand it to you Tuck, we had the fun meter pegged last night. That was the best time I've had in Nam."

Burdett walked to the window and opened the blinds. "I've been telling you guys, you need to embrace the Oriental culture."

Eric poured himself a cup and said, "I'm sure we will, but Paul and I have other things to do after we leave here. We've already rented a ski chalet in Austria."

Tucker walked to the bar and grabbed a roll. "I know that, and I also know you two will be the only ones who will actually do what you say. A lot of other guys have big dreams, but how many of them do you think are going to follow through on their ideas?"

Eric answered, "Not many. Look, I'm not saying we don't want to go to Indonesia, we just have to make a few stops along the way."

"And those stops are going to cost you money. After eight months in Europe you'll be writing your old buddy Tucker for a job."

204

"I don't doubt that, and it's nice to know we have that possibility." Eric checked his watch. "Right now I better hit the shower and see if my charge is ready to see his shrink."

After a long hot shower, Eric changed into a new flight suit and left the room. Jack Cates opened his door and asked, "So what did you guys do last night?"

In a tired voice, Eric said, "We met with a couple of contractors. It was a lot of boring business talk. Are you ready?"

"Yeah, I found the building last night. It's not far from here."

Eric raised his eyebrows. "You're taking this seriously."

"Damn right I am. Getting out of the Army *is* serious business. Are you going to back up my story?"

Eric opened the door and said, "I'll do my best."

At the psychiatrist's office the two pilots were led into a waiting room. When the door to the examination rooms opened, a handsome white-haired doctor entered carrying medical charts. Both men jumped to their feet when they saw that the doctor was a full bird colonel. The doctor read Jack's name tag and extended his hand. "Lt. Cates, I'm Doctor Holloway."

Cates shook the doctor's hand and said, "Good to meet you, doctor. This is my friend Eric Bader."

The doctor shook Eric's hand and said, "Nice to meet you, Mr. Bader. I will want to talk with you later."

"That's why I'm here, Sir," Eric answered. He thought the doctor's eye contact and handshake lasted longer than normal.

Cates was led away and Eric was left in the waiting room to read magazines. When he had gone through the entire collection, the clock on the wall said twenty minutes had passed. He decided to stretch out in the chair and rest his eyes. Thirty minutes later he was awakened by someone shaking his shoulder. He sat up quickly, when he saw it was the doctor. "Sorry Colonel, I must have dozed off."

The doctor sat next to him and said in a fatherly manner, "No problem Eric. Do you mind if I call you Eric?"

"No, that's fine."

"Good. We can talk out here. I only have a few questions. Let's start with how long you've known Lt. Cates."

"About eight months."

The doctor wrote on a chart and asked, "Have you been friends during that time?"

"Yes, he was my co-pilot when he first got in-country and we've remained friends ever since."

"Was he a good pilot?"

"Yes, he's smart and learned quickly."

"But now he's off flight status—why's that?"

"He was in a crash and injured his back. I think he became addicted to pain killers and when his doctor took him off them he started to drink heavily."

"So you think it was the accident that caused the change in behavior?"

Eric shifted in his chair and said, "I do. He was like everyone else before that."

"So you don't think anything else could have caused his problems."

Eric shrugged. "I can't get inside his head, but I believe that was it."

"How long have you been in Vietnam?"

"Sixteen months."

"So you opted for the six-month extension."

"Yes Sir."

"You want out of the Army pretty bad."

Eric locked eyes with the doctor. "I bet my life on it, Doc."

The doctor adjusted his glasses. "Yes, I guess you did. You seem fairly well balanced after that much time in combat. To what do you attribute that?"

Eric took his time to answer. "That's a good question. I guess it's because I haven't let the war get to me and I take it one day at a time."

"That's a good approach. Obviously it's working." After a short pause the doctor continued, "Let's get back to Lt. Cates. He says he thinks he's crazy--what do you think?"

It was the question Eric had been waiting for and he paused before answering. "I think this place makes us all a little crazy, some more than others."

"But I just told you I think you seem more normal than most combat veterans."

Eric said, "That doesn't mean I don't have problems."

The doctor looked at his chart. "Okay, we aren't here to talk about you. I have one more question about Lt. Cates. Do you think he's using this as a ploy to get out of the Army?"

Eric squirmed in his chair and answered, "I think the Army would be better off without him. All he does now is awards and decorations and he's not very good at that."

The doctor looked up from his chart and said, "It sounds like you've had some personal experience with his job performance."

Eric thought for awhile and then said, "Not really."

The doctor stood and offered his hand. "Thank you for your time. You'll make sure Lieutenant Cates gets back to his unit?"

Eric jumped to his feet and shook the colonel's hand. "Yes Sir, I will."

While he waited for Cates, Eric thought he was glad he wasn't there for an evaluation. He had never met a psychiatrist before and he didn't want to meet another one. Cates finally walked out and the two of them left for the BOQ.

By the time the group returned to Ninh Hoa, it was almost dark. When Eric entered his room, Paul was napping with a towel over his head. He lifted the towel and looked at Eric. "Hey Slacker, how was Saigon?"

Eric dropped his bag and grinned. "Better than ether of us could have imagined."

"So you got laid."

"Only by the most beautiful woman in Vietnam."

Paul sat up and said, "Let's save that for later. What happened to Cates? Is he getting out of the Army?"

Eric sat on his bunk. "'He thinks so."

"Did the shrink talk to you?"

"Yeah, we had a little chat."

"Did he ask if you thought Cates was nuts?"

"Yeah, and I told him I wasn't sure. Then I told him the Army would be better off without him."

Paul nodded. "That's something you *didn't* have to lie about. Did he ask how you were doing?"

"He wanted to know how I've been able to stay sane after sixteen months in combat."

"Did you tell him a profuse amount of alcohol?"

Eric laughed and said, "No, but I should have. Speaking of that, I need some food and a drink." He petted Jungle Dog and said, "How about you, Buddy, are you ready for some chow?"

The next day, Eric and Paul were leaving the gunship standby shack when they were approached by a company clerk. "Mr. Eason, Captain Wilcox would like you to report to his office."

Paul looked at Eric and said, "Now what the hell?"

Fifteen minutes later, Paul opened the screen door to their room and angrily threw his helmet bag on the floor. "So much for us having an *in* with the XO because Wilcox got the job."

"Why, what happened?"

"You won't believe what a good deal he has for me. He wants me to give Milford a check ride for upgrade to AC in a Slick. Can you imagine me and Milford in the same helicopter? Hell, I didn't even know his real name."

"What is it?"

"It's Jerome Milton."

"Did you tell Wilcox it was a bad idea?"

"Of course I did. I told him I didn't think that goofball should be driving a honey wagon, much less a Slick, but he disagreed. He said he needed more Aircraft Commanders and he wanted Milford upgraded." Paul took off his sweaty flight shirt and stuffed it into a laundry bag. "How come he sent you to Song Mau and I get a shitty deal like this?"

Eric scoffed. "Oh yeah, like Song Mau really worked out for me."

"It was better than flying with a dickhead like Milford."

Eric frowned and said, "That does sound like bad juju. The XO can't make you do it, can he?"

"He probably can, but he didn't order me, he asked. He said he was in a bind because so many of his check airmen have DEROSed and he's short of Slick pilots."

"And Milford is the best candidate he's got?"

"Don't remind me."

"So I take it you're going to do it."

Paul went to his locker and made them each a drink. "Yeah, Wilcox is a good guy and an outstanding officer. He said if I do three check rides, he'll take me off flight status for the last two weeks of my tour. Apparently, they have plenty of gunship pilots."

Eric accepted the drink. "We didn't help the situation when we got Paris and Bookman moved to the Jokers. They were two of his best Slick pilots." He took a sip and asked, "Does Wilcox think this is going to be a fair evaluation?"

"I mentioned that and he said he considers me one of his best check airmen and he knows I'll give Milford a fair ride." Paul grabbed a towel. "I'm going to get cleaned up and then go to the club and get drunk, so I'll be real mean in the morning."

Eric yelled at the closing screen, "Sounds like a fair ride to me."

The next morning Paul was still in a surly mood when he asked Eric, "What's on your schedule for today?"

Eric yawned and said, "I'm afraid all I drew was gunship standby. It looks like another boring day in the ready shack."

Paul stood at the door and said, "If you want some excitement you can trade with me."

Eric shook his head. "I would, but I want to finish this novel I've been reading."

Paul kicked the screen door open and said, "I'll see you tonight."

That afternoon, Eric was reading in the gunship standby hut when a grim-faced Tucker Burdett entered the room. Eric saw the worried look on his friend's face and asked, "What's up Tucker?"

"I've got bad news. Eason was shot down an hour ago."

"What! How bad?"

"They say his injuries aren't life threatening, but they flew him to the hospital at Lai Khe. He probably won't be coming back here. He was the only one injured. The ship was hit on his side. Luckily, Paul was able to land in a clearing big enough for another ship to come to his rescue. The other crew members walked away."

With a quizzical look, Eric asked, "Did you say Paul made the landing? Why did he do that when he was the only one injured?"

Burdett shrugged. "Good question. We'll learn more when we talk with him tomorrow."

"We can't go tonight?"

"No, I have a maintenance flight in the morning and we'll use that to fly to Lai Khe for a quick visit. Let's plan for a 0830 departure. I'll get you off flight duty."

"Okay, see you then."

When Eric was done flying for the day he went to his room and held the door open for Jungle Dog. He was worried Paul's injuries might be worse than what Tucker had heard. He made himself a drink and looked around the room. There was Paul's picture of Raquel Welch. He raised his drink in a toast, and went to their tape player and turned on Jimi Hendrix.

It felt weird to think Paul wouldn't be coming back. Now he would have to pack up Paul's stuff and ship it to him. He thought how tough it must have been for other guys when their roommates had been killed. There were pictures of wives, girlfriends and kids to pack. Sometimes there were dog tags, wedding rings and watches to send home. It was an ugly job. At least his wouldn't be that bad.

Later that night he returned to his room and saw Jungle Dog with his head on Paul's bed. He petted his dog and said, "I miss him too, little buddy."

The next day he and Tucker flew to the hospital at Lai Khe. As they walked down the row of beds, Eric was the first to spot his roommate.

Paul had his left leg in a sling. When he saw his friends he said, "I knew you two would be here. Do I have to ask how you pulled it off?"

Eric pointed at Burdett and said, "It helps when you have a friend who runs the company." He placed a bag in Paul's lap and said, "Your shaving kit and the book you were reading are inside."

"Thanks man, it's good to see you guys."

"Same here, how are you feeling?"

"Not bad all things considered."

Eric pointed at the sling and asked, "Will you be able to ski in two months?"

"Oh yeah! Nothing is going to keep me from that."

Burdett looked up from a chart at the end of the bed and said, "We can talk about your injuries later. Right now we want to know what the hell happened."

Paul sat up as far as the sling would allow. "You'll find this hard to believe, but Milford was actually doing a good job. While we waited our turn into an opening, I offered to give him a break. We were at eight hundred feet, when the two ships below said they were taking fire.

"I was about to give the controls back to Milford, when I saw .50 cal tracers coming at us from the left. I made a hard bank to the right and the instant I did there was an explosion that blew out most of the door and window on my side of the ship. Air came rushing in and the left side of my body felt like it was on fire. I saw spots and thought I was about to pass out.

"The only thing that felt like it was still working was my right hand. I wasn't sure if the controls were jammed, so I asked Milford to check his side and take over. I couldn't hear any feedback, so I knew the blast had cut the cord to my helmet. I yelled to Milford to start flying. When I checked the instrument panel, we were losing altitude, so I glanced at Milford and his hands weren't on the controls. Instead he was staring at my bloody arm and leg. A gash on my forearm was spewing blood and the slipstream from the rushing air was blowing it over my chest and face. It was then I realized the spots I had been seeing were blood spots on my sunglasses.

"By then we were getting real low, so I screamed at Milford, God damn it, look at our altitude, pull up on the collective. He didn't respond, so I took my right hand and pulled my left leg against the cyclic and pinned it with my right leg. Then I reached for the collective on the other side and pulled up on it. That stopped our descent and started a shallow climb. I was really pissed at Milford, so when I let go of the collective I grabbed him by the collar. When I yelled at him to start flying, he rolled his eyes and fainted."

Eric shook his head. "Fucking Milford. I knew flying with him was bad juju."

Paul scoffed. "I did too, but I didn't know how bad. I yelled to the crew chief to come up and help. Luckily it was Tank Diehl. He got out of his seat and hit the seat release lever. It tipped back and he yanked Milford out of the seat and threw him on the floor. Can you imagine what the troopers in back were thinking when they saw that? Then he put the seat up and jumped in. I told him to call the others and tell them we were going to put down in a clearing just ahead. He said Chalk Four was at our six and had been trying to call us.

"I had Diehl move the pedals to see if they were still working and they were. We didn't have time for practice, so I told him to keep the nose pointed as straight as he could. Then we went to work on the collective. I took his hand and showed him how far I wanted him to lower it whenever I told him. We slowly started a descent into the clearing and Diehl did great. The closer we got, the better he did, but as we approached the trees, we both knew if he screwed up we were dead."

Paul grabbed his wounded leg and shifted his position on the bed. "When we were over the clearing, I told Diehl to slowly lower the collective all the way. I flared and he kept the nose straight, so it was a good landing. As soon as we were down, Diehl cut the engine."

Eric interrupted, "Jesus, if he hadn't kept the nose straight you could have rolled."

Paul nodded. "Yeah, luckily he did. When we were down, I remember somebody carrying me to another helicopter. It wasn't until then I realized how much pain I was in. One of the soldiers in Chalk Four was a medic, so he shot me up with morphine and bandaged my injuries. I vaguely remember them wheeling me into this place and then the lights went out. When I came around, I was in this bed."

Paul shifted again and Tucker said, "If you hadn't made that hard turn, it would have been curtains."

"Exactly. Diehl examined the damage and said the .50 cal round hit the ship and glanced to the outside. Without the turn, the round would have come through the door, and into my side."

Eric glanced at Tucker, and then back at Paul. "You always said you were going to quit smoking when you knew an enemy bullet wasn't going to blow a hole in your chest. Who knew one would come that close."

"I've been thinking about that and I'm quitting as of right now. Besides, I've got to get into shape for skiing."

Tucker pointed at Paul's bandages and asked, "How bad are your injuries?"

"Not as bad as they look. The doctor said there was shrapnel in my left leg, left arm and crotch. He was able to get the bigger pieces out of my arm and leg. The smaller ones will work their way out to my skin and I'll have to remove them later.

"As for my crotch, he said he had good news and bad. There were two pieces of metal in my prick that he was able to remove. He said the bad news was he had to leave several pieces in my scrotum. I told him that wasn't bad news because now I can tell the girls I have balls of steel."

Everyone laughed and Eric said, "I'm sure you'll get some mileage out of that." In a serious voice, Eric asked, "One question, where was your pistol?"

"In my lap, but when I made the hard turn, I ducked to the right and it must have shifted enough to let the shrapnel hit my crotch."

Eric winced and said, "That hurts just to think about. How long does your doctor think it will take to recover?"

"About a month, which will take me right up to the time I would have left Nam." Paul turned to Burdett. "Tucker, that reminds me. What happens if I get sent to a hospital in the States before I finish my eighteen-month commitment? Am I going to get credit for extending? If

I don't, I'll have to spend another two years in this fuckin' Army and there is no way I can take another two years in the Green Machine."

Burdett nodded. "I'll check on it as soon as I get back to the company. Speaking of that, we need to go. We'll be back in two days. What can we bring you?"

Paul thought for a moment and said, "The two uniforms in my foot locker, socks, underwear and something else to read."

As they were about to leave, Eric asked, "Have you met a nice-looking nurse named Cheryl Chapman?"

Paul shook his head. "No, but I'll ask around. How do you know her?"

"I've met her a few times." Eric turned to leave and said, "We'll see you in a couple days."

Bader and Burdett returned to the hospital three days later. As they entered the front door, Tucker asked Eric, "Are you going to tell him about Milford?"

"Yeah, I don't want him to hear it from somebody else."

"Okay, you tell him about that and I'll tell him about his medal and Captain Wilcox."

Paul saw them approach and said, "How's it going guys?"

Eric answered, "We're all right. More to the point, how are you?"

"I'm feeling a lot better than I was the other day. At least now my leg isn't in that damn sling and I can go to the bathroom on my own. Tucker, did you find out anything on my extension problem?"

"Yeah, it looks like you'll get credit for the five months you've already done, so you should be out of the Army when you finish your rehab. Knowing how the Army works, I took a precaution and had Captain Wilcox make a call. You'll be doing your rehab in Japan, so you'll have your eighteen months in before you get back to the States."

Paul grinned and said, "Japan sounds like the perfect place to end my Army time."

"Yeah, it will be," Tucker said. "I've got more good news. Captain Wilcox is putting you in for a Bronze Star for saving your helicopter under adverse conditions."

Paul grinned and said, "That's nice." He turned to his roommate. "Refresh my memory Dog, is a Bronze Star higher than an Air Medal?"

Eric laughed and said, "You dick, and to think I went to the trouble of bringing your favorite beverage." He reached into a laundry bag and produced a green plastic canteen. "This is full of purple sack. The other things you wanted are in the bag."

He placed the bag next to Paul's bed and asked, "Did you find out about Cheryl Chapman?"

"Yeah, she mustered out of the Army a month ago and is living in San Mateo."

"Just my luck," Eric said. "Oh well, I wouldn't have had time to do anything anyway."

Eric looked at Tucker, who said, "There's more good news. Captain Wilcox has been promoted to major and is going to be our new commanding officer. He says he's going back into a gunship and will be a flying CO."

Paul smiled and said, "That *is* good news. Tell him congratulations and thanks for getting me to Japan."

"Will do," Burdett said and then turned to Eric.

Eric paused before saying, "I guess we better get going. I have a flight this afternoon. It sounds like you'll be shipping out soon, so I probably won't see you until we're back in the States. You better start working out as soon as you can, or I'm going to smoke you on the ski hill."

Paul shook Eric's hand and said, "Don't worry Bro, I'll be ready. See you in a month."

Tucker shook Paul's hand and said, "Get well soon and I'll see you in Indonesia."

"Okay Tuck, thanks for the help. Tell the guys good bye for me."

When the two pilots were out of the hospital, Burdett said to Eric, "You chickened out. I thought you were going to tell him Milford got upgraded to Aircraft Commander."

Eric shook his head and said, "I decided it was better not to tell him. He was in a good mood and that would have really pissed him off. I'll tell him over a beer in Austria."

The pair continued toward their helicopter and Eric added, "Then again, maybe I never will."

December 31, 1969

It was New Year's Eve and Eric sat at the bar of the O Club. He was only two days and a wake-up from his DEROS date of January 3, 1970. He was off flight status and living the glorious life of a short timer.

To his right sat his old co-pilot Tom Paris. Eric was proud of his friend. He had signed Paris off as Aircraft Commander and three months later got him transferred to the gunship platoon. Tom sat laughing with the others sporting a shiny new Joker patch on his faded flight suit.

Paul's former co-pilot, Nick Bookman, sat next to Paris. He'd been transferred to the Jokers along with Tom. The two young pilots were the only close friends Eric had left in-country.

Armed Forces Radio blared through the bar's sound system with a disc jockey counting down the top forty songs of 1969. The number five song, "Bad Moon Rising," had just finished. The club was as raucous as Eric could remember. Sharkey's monkey was screeching and running up and down the bar.

"Honky Tonk Woman," began to play, and Eric swung around on his bar stool. How many good times had there been in this bar, he thought. In two days he would never see it again. He and Paul had held court there for so many nights and it was all coming to an end.

While he took in the scene, Eric noticed a company clerk enter the bar. The only reason a Spec 4 would be in an Officers Club was to summon somebody to company headquarters. It was going to be a bad night for someone. Good news waits until morning, bad news comes at night, he thought.

The clerk showed the two pilots closest to the door a piece of paper. Eric's heart skipped a beat when both men pointed at him. There has to be a mistake, he thought. Why would someone at HQ want to talk with a short-timer like him? There was only one reason, an emergency at home. If there was a Red Cross representative at the office it was going to be real bad news.

The clerk made his way through the crowded bar and asked, "Are you Eric Bader?"

"Yeah, that's me."

"Mr. Bader, the first sergeant would like to see you in his office."

"Any Red Cross people there?"

"No, this has nothing to do with anything outside the country."

"Then what is it?"

"I can't tell you, but it's about something that happened here today."

"How can that be?" Eric mumbled. All of his friends were either there with him, or had gone home. He nodded to the clerk and said, "Tell Top I'll be right there."

Eric slid off his stool and tapped Paris on the shoulder. "Hey Tom, save my seat. I have to go see the first sergeant."

Paris gave him a quizzical look and asked, "Why would Top want to talk with you now? It's almost midnight. They're about to play the number one song."

"I know, you'll have to tell me what it is when I get back. I've got to go."

"Okay, good luck."

The first sergeant's office was dimly lit by a bare light bulb hanging from the ceiling and a desk lamp. Eric peered through the screen door, and asked, "What's up Top?"

First Sergeant Harold Andrews waved him in. "Have a seat, Eric."

Andrews poured two fingers of whiskey into a glass and said, "I'm sure you've had a drink, but you're going to need another one."

Eric took the glass and waited for his top sergeant to tell him why he was there. Andrews poured himself a drink, and then leveled his eyes at Eric. "I've got bad news, Eric. Gary Jarvis is dead."

The words shocked Eric to his core. "Gary's dead? How the hell can that be? I thought he was off flight status. Are you sure there isn't a mistake?"

Andrews shook his head and solemnly answered, "There's no mistake. Remember when he took the job, I said he would have to fly on a recovery ship? We lost one this afternoon. All four on board were killed and Gary was one of them."

"Who are the others?"

"Copeland and Marsh were the pilots, and a mechanic named Law."

"Were they shot down?"

"No, it appears to be mechanical failure."

Eric looked at the glass in his hand and thought his friend's luck had finally run out. Now a dark green sedan really would pull up in front of his house. An officer in dress greens would knock on his wife's door and she would know why he was there.

Eric raised his head and said, "He only had a month to go."

Andrews paused and then said, "That's not all."

Eric felt a knot in his gut as he said softly, "What else could there be, Top?"

"I need to have you identify Gary's body tonight. His supervisor was the mechanic that got killed with him and the other enlisted men are too drunk to do it. Graves Registration has a flight out in the morning. They want him on it."

Eric waited before he said, "Top, I have more respect for you than anybody I've known in the Army, and so far, I've done everything that has been asked of me. But I'm not going to ID Gary's body."

Andrews glared at Eric as he continued, "I don't give a damn what GR wants. They'll have to wait until tomorrow when somebody else can do it. I want to remember Gary as he was in life, not some busted-up corpse."

Eric took a drink and returned his first sergeant's stare. He knew that Andrews was not used to someone telling him no, especially a good soldier and a friend. Andrews finally rubbed his white flat top and said, "Okay, it can wait until tomorrow."

Eric downed his drink and said, "Thanks Top."

He left knowing he was turning his back on his friendship with Andrews, but it didn't matter. There was no way he was going to identify Gary's body that night, or any other time.

He returned to an O Club that had gotten even more rowdy. As he approached his bar stool, a co-pilot jumped up and said, "I was just holding it for you, Dog."

Paris noticed Eric and spun around on his stool. "You missed the number one song. It wasn't what we thought. 'Proud Mary' came in second. Number one was 'Whole Lotta' Love' by Led Zeppelin."

"That's a better song anyway," Eric said as he sat down and waved to Baby-San for a drink. He turned to his friend and said, "Top had bad news, Tom. We lost another buddy. Gary Jarvis was killed today."

Paris looked like he had been hit in the face. "Jarvis--how the hell did that happen? I thought he had a non-flying job."

"He did for the most part, but it involved going out on a recovery ship and we lost one today. All on board were killed. The pilots were Copeland and Marsh. I don't remember the mechanic's name."

Paris whistled softly. "Copeland bought it too. Wasn't he flying on one of Gary's other crashes?"

"Yeah, apparently Gary's bad luck followed him."

"I'm glad nothing happened while we were in the air with him," Paris said.

"It almost did. Don't you remember the ricochet off the cliff outside Dalat?"

Paris held up his hand and said, "Speak for yourself Kimosabe, I wasn't with you on that one."

Eric thought for a second and said, "Oh yeah, I had that goofball lieutenant with me. He was the reason we almost got killed."

Paris stared at his mentor. "If I had been there none of that would have happened."

"I know that Tom," Eric said. "That's why you're a Joker and he's probably shuffling papers in an office somewhere."

Paris studied his beer. "It's such a bummer about Gary."

Eric downed his drink and said, "It definitely takes the fun out of celebrating the New Year. I'm going to my room. I'll see you tomorrow."

"Okay, I'll see you then."

Eric walked out of the raucous bar into a still night, illuminated by a bright moon. Instead of turning toward his room, he decided to go for a walk. The moon was framed by two palms next to the headquarters building. He stared at the scene and thought that he would soon be

220

looking at the moon shining on snow-covered trees around the house he and Paul had rented in Austria. A place more than halfway around the world. It was starting to sink in that he would soon be a free man.

He walked to the top of the stairs that overlooked the flight line and revetments. Dozens of helicopters were scattered around the field, illuminated by the moonlight. One of them was his old ship, but now it belonged to someone else. Maybe tomorrow he would go down and sit in it one last time.

It was a hot sticky night as he surveyed the eerie scene and thought of the controlled chaos that would be happening in just a few hours. A world he would never be a part of again. The thought of never flying again had never crossed his mind, but it could be a possibility. A lot of guys thought they would continue flying, but now they were back in their home towns selling insurance, or auto parts. Out of all the letters the company had received from former pilots, only two had found flying jobs. One was spraying wheat fields in Kansas and the other was fighting forest fires in the Northwest. He took one last look and walked toward his room. Jungle Dog came running his way and he knew saying goodbye to his dog would be the toughest part of leaving.

On the day he was to leave the company for good, he awoke early. His eighteen-month tour was over and he was headed home. He sat up in bed and petted his dog. There was a knock on the door and Tom Paris and Nick Bookman entered the room. Paris held up a thermos and said, "How about some coffee, Eric? We thought we'd say goodbye before going down to the flight line."

Eric smiled. "Thanks guys."

Paris poured a cup and said, "It's the least we can do after what you've done for us. Thanks again for getting us into the Jokers. We're having a blast." Paris pointed around the room and said, "We've decided to move in here. We figure if we're going to adopt Jungle Dog its best to leave him in his room. You know how much we like the little guy."

"It's good to know he's going to be in good hands," Eric said. "There's a half bottle of whiskey in my locker. You guys can have a hootch-warming party."

"Thanks man, we will. This is a better room anyway. It's closer to the club." Paris paused and said, "Speaking of the club, you didn't stay there very long last night."

Eric stood and smoothed out the sheet on his bed. "I'm not one for goodbyes. I decided to come back here and spend time with my dog."

Paris shook Eric's hand and said, "You know we'll take good care of him. Have a good trip back to the World."

Nick Bookman pointed at the poster of Raquel Welch and said, "You didn't send Paul his poster."

Eric looked at it hanging on the wall. "No I left Raquel because she's here to cheer up the troops. Where we're going we won't need cheering."

Bookman shook his hand and said, "Thanks, Dog. Send us some pictures of Austria."

Eric walked them to the door. "Will do. You guys fly safe."

Eric took a shower and then enjoyed a leisurely breakfast. For his last meal at the mess hall, the cooks broke out fresh eggs, ham and pancakes. When he finished, he carried a bowl of scraps to the door and fed his dog for the last time. As Jungle Dog lapped them up, Eric petted his back and told him goodbye.

He carried his duffel bag toward the flight line, stopping at the top of the stairs to look down at the revetments and runway. On the horizon was a C-123 transport aircraft that would take him to Cam Rahn Bay. It landed in a cloud of dust as he walked down the stairs for the last time.

The back ramp lowered and five replacements walked out: two enlisted men, two warrant officers, and a lieutenant. The officers wore wings on their new flight suits. Eric looked around at the surroundings as five enlisted men entered the aircraft. The heat and humidity were pushing ninety and everything looked bright green and tropical: a sight he knew he would always remember.

The load master broke his reverie. "Sir, if you're coming with us you'll have to get on board." Eric turned toward the airplane and walked up the ramp.

At the Cam Rahn Bay travel desk, he was told his flight to the States would leave at 1030 the next morning. His itinerary was Cam Rahn Bay to McChord Air Force Base, Washington, with a two-hour fuel stop in Japan.

After spending the night at the BOQ, he was up early. He couldn't wait to board the "Big Silver Dustoff" that would take him home. The plane was actually a red and white Northwest Orient 720B. He boarded and took a window seat on the right. When the plane lifted off the runway everyone cheered. They had made it out of Vietnam.

The initial climb toward the south afforded Eric one last view of the tropical panorama of Vietnam. He looked back to the right and saw the area around Dalat. Past that was Ghia Nghia and in the distance Bu Prang and the Cambodian border. All the memories of those places came rushing back. The plane banked to the left and his view of Vietnam was gone, perhaps forever.

Eric looked at the others around him. His seatmates were two infantry sergeants. The stewardess asked what they wanted to drink and all three ordered Cokes. When she was out of earshot, the trooper next to him said, "If you want something stronger, I smuggled a flask of whiskey on board."

Eric offered his glass. The man poured him a drink and said, "What are they going to do, cut off our hair and send us to Nam?" Eric raised his glass as his two seatmates laughed. He looked out at the shimmering ocean and hoped he had heard that joke for the last time.

Twenty-two hours later the airliner touched down on a rain-slicked runway at McChord Air Force Base, Washington. It was five thirty in the afternoon, overcast and an invigorating fifty-six degrees. Eric breathed in the cool evergreen-scented air as he walked down the stairs. It was a big relief from the stifling hot jungle he had left behind. While the passengers waited for their bags on the tarmac, Eric enjoyed the smell of fir trees and the sound of song birds. He was finally home. It would take awhile to get used to, but he was ready to put in the time.

He cleared customs, and exchanged his Military Payment

Certificates for real dollars and a pocket full of quarters. Outside the terminal, he boarded a blue Air Force bus that would take him to the Bachelor's Officers Quarters at Fort Lewis Army Base. Eric noticed the windows were not covered by chicken wire. He was in a place where you didn't have to worry about someone lobbing in a grenade.

At the BOQ, Eric took a long hot shower then decided he couldn't wait to get into civilian clothes. The only civies he had were a navy blue sweater, khaki pants and a yellow London Fog jacket. The evening had turned cool and misty as he left the barracks. The evergreen-scented rain reminded him of growing up in Flagstaff, Arizona. He needed to find a phone and call his parents, and then Paul.

It didn't take long to find a bank of pay phones outside an enlisted men's beer hall. He called collect to his parents and his father accepted the call. Both his parents were ecstatic to hear that he was finally home. His mother said she wouldn't be able to sleep that night. Then she said, "We really enjoyed the black and white photos you sent us. Your dad liked the one of you in your helicopter so much he hung it in his new den."

His father interrupted, "I put it alongside a picture of me sitting in a Corsair at Henderson Field, on Guadalcanal. We look real similar, except you had a plastic helmet and mine was canvas and leather."

Eric's father had been a Marine pilot in the Pacific during WWII. He was proud to think his dad had hung the two pictures together in his den.

"We are really looking forward to showing you our new house in Scottsdale," his mother said. "It's close to the airport, so it won't be a long drive to bring you home."

"Good, I can't wait to see it. I'll be home in two days and we can talk more then."

"Okay, good night honey."

"Good night Mom, Dad."

He hung up and poured four quarters into the phone and dialed the number for Paul's house. A recording said he would have five minutes to talk. It rang and a young female voice answered, "Hello."

Eric guessed it was Paul's sister. "Hi, is this Melanie?"

"Yes, who's this?"

"It's Eric Bader, Paul's friend from Vietnam."

"Oh, hi Eric, it's good to hear your voice. You must be back in the States."

"Yeah, I just landed in Washington. Is Paul there?"

"No he's out for the evening. He'll be disappointed he missed you. Can he call you back?"

"No, I'm staying in a barracks. I'll be in Arizona in two days and we can talk then."

"Okay, I'll tell him. It's so good to have you home safe."

"Thanks, it's been good talking with you."

"Same here, goodbye."

Eric left the booth remembering a picture he'd seen of Paul's sister. She sounded as sweet as she looks, he thought, but he wasn't going down that road.

He entered the small club next to the phones and ordered a beer. A Spec 4 bartender asked to see his military ID. When he saw that Eric was an officer, he said, "I'm sorry Sir, this is an enlisted men's club. If you want a drink you'll have to go to the O Club."

Eric was more weary than angry as he said, "Look Specialist, I just got off a twenty-two hour flight from Vietnam and I don't even know where the damn Club is. All I want is a beer, and you're telling me I can't buy one here?"

`The bartender moved to the beer taps and said, "That's exactly what I'm saying, because all the beers you want are on the house." The young man placed a beer on the bar and said, "Welcome home, Sir."

Eric raised the glass and said, "Thanks Specialist." He pointed at the jukebox and asked, "How much does it cost to play a tune these days?"

"It's still a dime a song, or three for a quarter."

Eric walked to the box and looked for "Rainy Night in Georgia" by Brook Benton. It had been popular when he was in boot camp at Ft. Ord, near Monterey. It seemed like it was always raining then and it was raining now. He took a seat as the song started to play. *Heavy rains a fallin', seems I hear your voice callin', it's all right. A rainy night in Georgia. A rainy night in Georgia. It seems like it's raining all over the world.*

Eric drank his beer and looked at the men sitting around him. They looked young and naive compared to the hardened soldiers he had flown with in Vietnam. They have no idea what they're in for, he thought. The way the war was going, half of them would probably be coming home in body bags. He finished his beer and left for his barracks room. He needed to get some sleep before his last day in the Army.

He was awakened the next morning by the sound of a drill sergeant marching his recruits. Outside there was a low, overcast sky, and it was still raining. The group directly in front of his window was singing their marching song with their sergeant.

Sergeant: Ain't no use in lookin' back, Jody's got your Cadillac,
Recruits: Ain't no use in lookin' back, Jody's got your Cadillac,
Sergeant: Ain't no use in goin' home, Jody's got your girl and gone,
Recruits: Ain't no use in goin' home, Jody's got your girl and gone,
Sergeant: Ain't no use in feeling sad, Jody's got the job you had,
Recruits: Ain't no use in feeling sad, Jody's got the job you had,
Sergeant: Sound off
Recruits: One, Two
Sergeant: Sound off
Recruits: Three, Four . . . One, Two, Three, Four . . . One, Two . . . *Three, Four.*

He watched them march off and thought of his own basic training. It had only been two and a half years, but it seemed like another lifetime. The war had changed him and he wondered if it was for the better, or the worse. Probably both—only time would tell.

His last day in the Army was spent standing in lines and sitting on hard chairs. The only highlight was when he reported to the finance section. A captain reviewing his file discovered he had been underpaid by $1,500. He happily watched as the captain counted out fifteen one hundred dollar bills and secured them with a rubber band. Eric stuffed the wad in his pocket and walked out of the office in a trance. He had several drinks and a steak dinner at the O Club, and then dragged his tired, jet-lagged body to bed. The next day he would finally be a free man.

The snow had returned and fell heavily as Eric and Paul bid Dr. Muller a good night. As the two walked toward their hotel, Paul said, "That was one hell of a proposal."

Eric pulled his collar up. "I had a feeling it was going to be something like that. Like you said, if everything goes as planned it should be relatively easy. If it doesn't we could be in for a world of hurt. I was getting real tired of the sound of bullets hitting metal when I left Nam."

They entered their hotel lobby and Paul said, "I think we should take a trip to the border to see what it looks like. We could even go up to Prague. It isn't that far from Vienna. If the operation looks too hairy we can back out."

"Good idea. Whether we do this job or not, we're going to Indonesia, so I think we still need to write Tucker."

"I agree. Let's get a letter out tomorrow."

Eric opened the door to their room and said, "I'll do it right now, but I don't think I'll mention this proposal in an international letter. We need to keep this a secret from everyone."

He removed his coat and sat at a desk and began to write.

Dear Tucker   April 2, 1970

It was good to get your letter and hear you have acquired your first helicopter. It sounds like things are on track there.

Paul and I still plan to travel to Indonesia later this year. We've been in Austria for almost three months. We started the trip in Munich, where we bought a 1958 Mercedes diesel. We love it, even though our European friends call it a land yacht. After the ski season we plan to drive it to Athens and sell it for part of the fare on either a plane, or tramp steamer to the Orient.

Austria turned out to be far better than we anticipated. The house we rented is fantastic. It costs way more than we wanted to pay, but it's well worth it. It is what is called a ski in-ski out chalet, located on a lower run of the St. Anton ski area. From our deck, we can ski down to a gondola that goes to the top of the mountain.

Three sides of the living room have glass windows and a wrap-around deck with incredible views. Most of the après ski parties are held at our place. When the weather is nice we're out on the decks. If it's snowing, we party in the living room with a wood fire going. Most of our friends are guys, but there are usually a number of ladies who attend our gatherings. The fact that we are the hosts hasn't done either of us any good with the Heidis. Somehow they always end up with someone else. The only action we've had has been with two SAS stews from Stockholm who were in St. Anton on a ski vacation. We talked them into staying at our place for their two week stay.

That covers most of what we have been doing. Right now we are in a hotel in Innsbruck and plan to ski this mountain tomorrow. We are moving to Vienna on May 1, so you will have to write us at the American Express office in Vienna: 2123 *Karntnerstrasse,* Vienna, Austria. We will keep you posted on when we will be heading your way.

Until then, Eric & Paul

The next morning, Eric was in a confident mood. New snow had fallen and there was a possibility of replenishing their dwindling bank account. Eric phoned the ski report and heard there were ten inches of fresh powder. Neither of them had skied Innsbruck, so they hired a local instructor to show them around. While they were dressing, their guide called and said he would meet their bus at eight-thirty and they would be skiing off *piste* snowfields.

The roommates quickly ate the hotel's continental breakfast, then gathered their gear and boarded a bus to the ski area. Their guide, Hans, was waiting for them as they unloaded: a short, stocky man with ruddy cheeks dressed in his red instructor's jacket. He introduced himself in a thick German accent, and then led them to a tram that would take them to the top of Axamer-Lizum, the largest of Innsbruck's ski satellites.

As they ascended the mountain, Hans pointed to the areas they would be skiing. He ended by saying, *"Ven ve* are finished, if you still have *zee* legs for it, *ve vill* ski *zee* nineteen sixty-four Winter Olympics men's downhill course."

Paul turned to their instructor and said, "Trust me, Hans, we'll ski the downhill."

The tram thumped to a stop and the three skiers unloaded into brilliant sunshine. On the platform, Hans said, "Follow me *unt ve vill* have much fun."

They clicked into their bindings and the two roommates looked around at the endless slopes of untracked powder. Their home mountain of St. Anton was good skiing, but this place was massive. As they watched their guide jump into the deep powder and explode into confident turns, Paul said, "I'm glad we had three months of skiing to prepare for this."

Paul pursued their instructor and yelled, "Follow me, my brother."

Eric jumped into the knee-deep snow and watched his companions glide down the hill like two leaves flowing down a mountain stream. The powder was so deep it occasionally sprayed into his mouth and over his head like cold smoke.

At the bottom of the run, Hans waited at a chairlift. Eric and Paul glided to a stop and he said, *"Ya goot,* you two almost ski like Austrians." It was lofty praise.

Paul leaned on his poles and said, "God that was fun, but I inhaled so much snow I'm going to need a snorkel for the next run."

The rest of the morning was filled with miles of unleashed skiing. At noon, Hans stopped halfway down the mountain and said, "You have one more hour of skiing with me. At one o'clock *ve vill* ski *zee* downhill, after that you *vill* be on your own. Your lift passes will be good for three more hours."

An hour later, Hans took his new friends to the starting point of the 1964 Olympic downhill run. As Eric and Paul peered over the edge at the near-vertical fall line, Hans said, "Gentlemen, I am happy to report that an Austrian named Egon Zimmermann won a gold medal on this run with a time of two minutes eighteen seconds. Let's see how fast *ve* can do it, but be careful, now there may be other skiers below."

Hans jumped off the ledge and pointed his skis straight down the slope. As his two charges watched their mentor speed down the hill, Eric said, "So that's how it's done."

Before he dived off the ledge, Paul said, "I think I'll make a few turns to see if my legs still work."

Eric followed his friend and yelled, "Good idea." He dug his ski edges into the icy slope knowing falling was not an option.

At the bottom of the hill, Hans was waiting with a grin. "You guys did *goot*. This has been much fun for me, but now I must leave. I need to attend a meeting."

The three skiers shook hands, and Eric tipped Hans a twenty dollar bill. The two friends watched their guide jauntily walk away carrying his skis. He had provided them with four hours of the most intense skiing of their lives. Eric stepped out of his bindings and said, "I've had enough. I say we go into town for lunch."

Paul was already out of his skis and said, "Sounds good to me. I'm glad it's a short walk to the bus. I don't mind saying, my ass is dragging."

While the bus driver loaded their ski gear into the baggage compartment, he said in German, "There is a cooler in the bus, help yourself to a beer."

They walked to the door and Paul said, "Even I understood that."

The cooler held bottles of regular and dark Austrian beers. They each grabbed a cold dark, and then walked down the aisle of the near-empty bus. They stopped in the middle, where Paul took a window seat on the left, Eric a window on the right. As Eric sat in the comfortable seat, he wondered if he would be able to get up when they reached the hotel.

He turned to Paul and said, "Here's to a great day of skiing."

Paul raised his bottle. "The best."

Eric took a sip and looked out the window. His seat was above the baggage compartment and he watched the driver load the gear of two lady skiers. He turned to Paul and said, "I think our luck is about to change."

Paul asked, "Oh yeah, why's that?"

"Because two lovelies are about to get on board. Their clothes look like they're American. Both are in their twenties. One has long blond hair, the other medium length brown. I like the brunette."

The driver led the two women up the stairs and offered them a beer. Eric yelled to the driver in German, "Can we have two more beers?"

The driver nodded and Eric asked in German, "Would you ladies please bring us the beers?"

The two women grabbed two more beers and started down the aisle. The brunette eyed Eric as she sauntered toward him. She stopped in front of the aisle seat and asked, *"Ist dieser platz frei?"* Is this seat free?

Eric smiled and answered, *"Ja, bitte setzen Sie sich."* Yes, please sit down.

The brunette sat and asked, "Do you speak English?"

When Eric nodded, she said, "Let me buy you a beer."

Eric took the beer and said, "Thank you. Are you ladies American?"

"Yes, do we look it?"

Eric smiled. "A little."

The brunette asked, "Do you live in Innsbruck?"

Eric shook his head and said, "No, St. Anton. We are here on holiday."

The blond heard Eric speaking English and asked, "Is this guy putting me on? The only words he says are yes and no."

Eric peered at her and asked, "Were you speaking German?"

"Yes."

"That's your problem. *Ja* and *nein* are the only two words he knows in German."

The girls laughed and the brunette said, "You guys are Americans. The way you skied we thought you were Austrian." She extended her hand and said, "My name is Beth Ward."

"Nice to meet you Beth, I'm Eric Bader and that guy over there is my friend Paul Eason."

Paul waved and the guys looked at the blond, who said, "I'm T.J. Weigel."

Beth turned back to Eric and asked, "Did you say you live in St. Anton?"

"Yes, we rented a ski chalet for the winter. Are you in Europe on vacation?"

"No, we're attending a German language school in Prien am Chemsee. It's between Munich and Saltsburg."

"Yes, we know Prien--we went there to see King Ludwig's castle. It's almost as impressive as the one at Neuschwanstein. "

"We think so too."

Two other couples boarded and the bus pulled out of the ski area. Eric and Beth looked out the window and Eric said, "How do you like Innsbruck?"

"The city is beautiful, but the ski hill wore us out."

He turned to face her and said, "Same for us. We hired a guide and the only time he stopped was at the bottom of the run. We're not complaining, it was one of our best days of skiing."

"We saw you with your guide," Beth said. "You both ski very well."

"Thank you. Are you ladies staying here tonight?"

"Yes, we'll drive back to Prien in the morning."

"Then why don't we have dinner? Unless you have other plans."

"No, dinner with you two sounds like fun."

"Good, why don't we start early?" Eric looked at his watch and asked, "Does five o'clock sound okay?"

"That will be great."

"Where are you staying?"

"We're at the Hotel Alpinpark."

Eric nodded. "We're just down the street. We'll be there at five."

Later that afternoon, the two couples left the Hotel Alpinpark as the city was starting to darken. The last rays of sunlight bathed the snow-covered peaks just beyond the city. While they walked up the street, a cold wind blew down from the mountains smelling of pine trees and glaciers.

Eric wore a sheepskin coat. He took Beth's hand and slid it into one of its fleece-lined pockets. Beth smiled and asked, "Where are we going?"

Eric pointed ahead and said, "A little place we found the other night."

Inside the bar, they pressed their way into a crowd of fit-looking patrons. Eric asked the girls what they wanted to drink. When they both answered white wine, he motioned to Paul and they moved to the bar.

When they returned, Eric asked the girls if they knew of the custom when a man and a woman become friends and want to start using the familiar version of the German language. The girls answered no and Eric entwined his right arm with Beth's. "First you do this with your arms, then you both take a drink and then you kiss. After that you're friends and can use the familiar '*Du*' form instead of the formal '*Sie*.'"

Eric and Beth took a drink and then kissed. They watched as Paul and T.J. did the same. Beth looked at Eric and said, "I like that ritual. Maybe we should do it again, just to be sure." Eric was happy to oblige.

After another round of drinks Eric suggested they find a place for dinner. They walked around the city until they decided on the Restaurant Kapeller. The ambiance was cozy Tyrolean. During dinner the girls told the guys their life stories. They had grown up in Alexandria, Virginia, and had known each other since the sixth grade. When they graduated from high school they attended different colleges, Beth to Duke and T.J. to Georgetown. After their graduations, they were both accepted at the University of Virginia's law school. They decided to take a year off from their studies to travel around Europe. To fund the trip, they spent the summer working as waitresses in the resort town of Myrtle Beach, S.C. Thinking it might be good to have another language during their travels they enrolled in the Goethe Institute in Prien, Germany, and had recently bought a Volkswagen camper to use on their trip.

When they finished, Paul said, "Weigel and Ward, that already sounds like a law firm." He turned to T.J. and asked, "What do your initials stand for?"

She frowned and answered, "Tiffany Jane. Does that sound like the name of an attorney? The first thing I'm going to do after I pass the bar is legally change my name to my initials."

Paul asked, "What will your mother think of that?"

"I'm not going to tell her."

Beth asked the guys why they weren't in the military. Eric glanced at Paul before he answered, "Because we have iron-clad deferments."

"Which are?"

"Four-A, the best there is."

"So you're not running from the draft."

Eric shook his head. "No, we've been deferred." He waved to the waiter and said, "I think we should move to the Café Control for coffee and schnapps."

At the Control, the ladies excused themselves to the restroom and Paul said, "I've got a new plan for tomorrow. I have T.J. talked into going back to St. Anton with me. Why don't you see if Beth will do the same."

"I doubt it, but I'll ask," Eric said.

As predicted, Beth didn't want to miss school, so Paul formulated a plan. He and T.J. would drive the Mercedes to St. Anton, while Eric and Beth would take the Volkswagen bus to Prien. In two days, Paul would drive T.J. to Prien and pick up Eric. Everyone agreed it sounded like a good plan.

The next morning it was snowing heavily as Eric drove Beth to Germany in the Volkswagen camper. The van's thin wiper blades were having a hard time keeping up with the wet snow and he had to pull over and wipe the windshield with a gloved hand.

He pulled back on to the highway and Beth asked, "Are you sorry you got the sensible one who doesn't want to skip school?"

Eric concentrated on the snowy road and answered, "No, I admire you for it. I would have done the same. We can go to St. Anton later."

Beth wiped fog off the windshield with a rag and said, "Thanks, I appreciate that. I want to get a graduation certificate, so I'll be eligible to attend a German or Austrian university. I doubt if I'll go, but it'll be nice to know I could. The final exam is in two weeks."

Eric glanced at her. "I think you need a boyfriend who can double as a tutor."

Beth laughed and said, "You think so? I've been meaning to ask where you learned to speak German so well."

"I grew up with it. I had to learn German to be able to talk with my fraternal grandmother. She and my grandfather emigrated with my father and his brother from Austria in 1939. My father, grandfather and uncle learned English, but my grandmother never did, so she taught me and my brother German."

"No wonder you speak like a native."

Without taking his eyes off the road Eric asked, "Do you want me to help you study?"

"That would be nice, but I forgot to mention, you aren't going to be able to stay with me in Prien. Tiff and I are renting a room from a very strict landlady, Frau Ziegler. Her house has a chain link fence around the yard and she has a husband with a huge German shepherd named Caesar. The husband and dog decide who are approved guests and you would not be one of them."

"I'm sure I wouldn't. In that case I'll have to get a hotel room. Do you want to stay with me? You already have your overnight bag."

"You move pretty fast Herr Bader."

"Yes I do. I've learned if I see something good I go for it."

Beth put her hand on Eric's arm and said, "And you think I'm something good."

"Most definitely."

When they arrived in Prien, it was late afternoon and they were both hungry. They went to Beth's favorite restaurant and dined on roast pork with gravy, mushroom dumplings and red cabbage. Afterward, they went to a bar where they each had a stein of German beer. At seven o'clock, Eric said, "I better find a room. Do you have any suggestions?"

"There's a little hotel that I've heard is fairly cheap because it's above a nightclub."

"That sounds like it will do. Have you decided to spend the night with me, or are you going back to the Ziegler compound?"

Beth frowned. "That does sound depressing, doesn't it? Okay, you've persuaded me."

While they climbed the stairs to the hotel, Beth asked, "Do you think we can get a room with two beds?"

Eric stopped and said, "We're checking in as a married couple. I don't think they'll buy it if we ask for separate beds."

Beth resumed climbing and said, "Okay, but you'll be a gentleman, right?"

Eric followed and answered, "I'll do my best."

The reception area was dark and gloomy. One light illuminated what looked like an old bank teller's counter. A sign next to a bell read, "Please ring for service." Eric rang it loudly.

A stout woman with white hair in a bun opened a swinging door from the kitchen wearing a gray dress and green apron. Both were covered with flour. She wiped her hands on a dish towel and welcomed them with the typical Bavarian greeting. "*Gruss Gott.*"

Eric returned the greeting and asked for a room with a double bed.

The woman walked behind the counter and turned on a desk lamp. She handed Eric a form and showed him where to fill in his and his wife's passport numbers. Eric wrote his in and then turned to Beth. "I hope you know your passport number, so you won't have to take it out."

"I do," she said as she took the form and filled it in.

Eric handed the form to the woman along with his passport. When she handed it back with a room key he was relieved that she hadn't ask to see his wife's passport with a different name. He felt like he was sneaking a girl into his grandmother's house, but it was kind of thrilling.

The woman led them to a door that opened into a living room with sofas, chairs and reading lamps. Six doors led off of the main room. She pointed at the one across from them and said, "Straight ahead is the shared bathroom. Your room is the third one on the right. Have a good night."

Their small room had a four-poster bed with a thick down

comforter, a sink and mirror was in one corner, a spinning wheel in another and a window in a third corner. Beth threw her coat on the bed and said, "Good Lord, it must be ninety degrees in here. Can you turn down the radiator?"

Beth unpacked while Eric tried to turn down the heat. After a minute, he admitted, "It's stuck open and won't budge." He went to the window and opened it just as a noisy group of revelers left the nightclub below. He closed the window and said, "I don't think we want to listen to that all night. I guess we'll have to sleep in our skivvies."

Beth laughed and said, "Don't you wish."

Eric stripped to his shorts and climbed onto the bed. "It's not like I haven't seen a girl in her underwear."

Beth locked eyes with him and said, "I'm sure you have, but you haven't seen me in mine."

Eric crossed his arms behind his head and leaned against the headboard. "I think if we're going to get off to a good start in this relationship, I should at least get to see the top half."

Beth paused for a moment and then removed her jeans and blouse. She unfastened her bra and let it fall to the floor. With her hands on her hips she asked, "Is this what you had in mind?"

Eric caught his breath as Beth jumped under the covers. He looked at her and said, "That's the nicest rack I've ever seen."

She snuggled next to him and said, "You tell that to all the girls."

Eric steadied his voice and said, "No, I would never kid about something like that."

Beth looked at him and said, "I can't believe I did that. Why am I so attracted to you, Eric Bader? Just because you're athletic and smart. You're probably good in bed too, aren't you?"

"I can hold my own."

She smiled and said, "I thought I was supposed to hold it."

Eric gave her a passionate kiss and said, "No problem there."

The next morning they awoke in a spoon position and immediately started making love again. When they finished and were lying in a sweaty heap, Eric kissed Beth and said, "I'm really starting to like you

Miss Ward."

She kissed him back and said, "I think I could get used to you too Mr. Bader."

It had been months since someone had called him Mr. Bader and it brought back a flood of memories. He couldn't believe he was finally in Europe after all the months of dreaming about it in Vietnam.

Beth interrupted his reverie. "I really didn't intend for things to move this fast."

Eric said, "I think we're moving along just right."

Beth rose onto an elbow. "I'm glad you think so."

Eric did the same and asked, "Are you ready for breakfast? I need a coffee."

Beth kissed his cheek and jumped out of bed. "Good idea, I'll get ready."

After they had eaten, Beth seemed preoccupied as she looked out the window of the restaurant. Eric put his hand on hers and said, "You look lost in thought--is it something I said?"

Beth shook her head. "No, it's not anything you've said, it's what you haven't said that bothers me. I've dated a few guys in my time and they all had a favorite subject: themselves. Then there's you. You never say anything about yourself, or your past. All I know is you grew up in Flagstaff and you went to Arizona State."

Eric took a sip of coffee and asked, "What would you like to know?"

"Let's start with those deferments you were so secretive about. What did you call them, 4-A? I thought about writing a friend to find out what that is, but then I thought, if I'm starting to fall for this guy he needs to tell me."

"I was going to tell you."

"When?"

"As soon as you asked."

"So what is a 4-A deferment?"

Eric poured more coffee. "Would you believe Paul and I are divinity students?"

Beth laughed and said, "Not after last night."

He held up his hands. "Okay, I'll come clean. It means we've had prior service."

"Prior service--you mean you've already been in the military?"

"Yeah, we were helicopter pilots in Vietnam."

Beth leaned across the table and said, "You guys were pilots in Vietnam. I never would have guessed that. For how long?"

"Eighteen months."

"That seems like a long time."

"It seemed longer if you were there."

"I can imagine. Were you wounded?"

"No, but Paul was. He has a good story I'm sure he'll be happy to tell you."

Beth met his eyes and asked, "So why the secrecy?"

Eric looked out the window. "Paul and I don't like to talk about our time in Nam. Most of us vets don't." He looked back at Beth and said, "The people who are against the war don't like those of us who were there, so we don't admit it. We think they should oppose the war, but not the warriors."

"Were you treated badly when you returned?"

"No, but others were. I'm sure you've heard the stories. It wasn't an issue for me because I was only in the Army for two days after I returned from Nam and those were spent on a military base. I did wear my uniform home, but I wasn't hassled.

"My parents met me at the Phoenix airport. They had recently moved to Scottsdale, so it wasn't a long ride to their house. My dad had been a Marine pilot in his war and he asked about mine. When we got home I took off my uniform and didn't mention Vietnam again. We didn't have much time to talk because I was only there for a week before I left for Austria."

Beth looked surprised. "You were only home for a week after being gone that long. Weren't your parents disappointed?"

"My mom was upset, but at least now she knows I'm out of harm's way, for the most part. Paul and I wanted to get to St. Anton because we had already rented a house. Besides, who wants to live in the States

240

now? It's much better over here."

"You said you're out of harm's way, for the most part. What does that mean?"

Eric laughed and said, "You don't miss much do you? You already sound like an attorney. I meant I don't have someone trying to kill me, but I still take risks."

Beth took a drink of water and said, "Okay, I see what you mean." After a pause she asked, "What kind of flying did you do?"

Eric sipped his coffee. "The first twelve months Paul and I flew Huey assault helicopters. They're the kind you see in the newsreels. We flew infantrymen into and out of battle and then resupplied them. After a year, we got crosswise with our commanding officer and he made us gunship pilots."

"gunships! You mean you shot at people?"

"Yeah, but only if they were shooting at us, or at those we were supposed to protect."

Beth ran a hand through her hair. "This is so overwhelming. Tiff and I thought you were just a couple of ski bums."

Eric smiled. "That's us. I hope this doesn't change things."

"It does. It makes you more interesting."

"I'm glad you're okay with it." After a pause, he asked, "Don't you have class today?"

"Yes, I better go. I'm late, so you'll have to drive me."

On the way they passed an onion-domed church in the middle of town and then drove down a street that went under the railroad tracks. They approached a compound with multiple flags and Eric said, "That must be the Goethe Institute."

Beth laughed and said, "A lot of people think that. It's actually in a little house around the corner. There are only six classrooms and a basement where they give us a continental breakfast every morning." Eric pulled in front of the house and Beth gave him a quick kiss. "I'll be done at five."

She opened the door and Eric said, "I'll be back then."

After dinner that evening, Eric asked Beth if she wanted to go to a bar. She shook her head and said, "Bars are too noisy. Let's get a bottle of wine and go back to the hotel."

"That sounds good," Eric said. "I found a wine shop nearby. I'll get a bottle of white."

They sat in the living room of the hotel and Eric opened the wine. Beth took a glass and asked, "Do you mind if we get back to questions and answers? I've thought of a few more."

Eric poured himself a glass. "No, I like talking with you. I might even become my own favorite subject."

Beth smiled. "That's doubtful." She took a sip of wine and asked, "You said you were in Vietnam for eighteen months. How often did you fly?"

"We had a few days off and two R & Rs, but for the most part it was every day."

"Was somebody always shooting at you?"

"It depended on what we were doing. Sometimes it was every day, other times once a week."

"That still sounds like a lot. Weren't you afraid to get out of bed in the morning?"

"I suppose I was when I first got there, but you get used to it. I had to believe it wasn't going to be my time." He held up his wine glass and said, "We also did a lot of drinking and that helped."

"Did you drink while you were flying?"

"No and we didn't smoke dope, but we drank every night unless we were in the field. It was usually with other pilots in the Officers' Club. We did it for relaxation, but there was also a lot of debriefing. A big benefit was to hear how other pilots dealt with all the crazy shit that came up. Some of the mechanical failures weren't covered in the flight manuals. There was also the camaraderie. You form a special bond with guys you spend time with in combat."

"I can imagine. Why do you think you weren't wounded?"

Eric shrugged. "PFM I guess."

"And that is?"

Eric hesitated before he said, "Pure fucking magic."

"So you think it was fate?"

"I'd like to think some skill was involved, but there were a couple of times I should have been killed, but wasn't. What would *you* call it?"

"I don't know. Did you ever pray?"

"A few times, when I was in a tight spot, but you usually didn't have time to think of anything except saving your ass."

Beth sipped her wine and asked, "Aren't you mad at the military for taking so much time out of your life?"

"No, I'm pissed at the politicians in Washington, but not the Army. We had a contract. They agreed to teach me how to fly and in exchange I agreed to give them four years of my life. As it turned out it was only two and a half years because I extended my tour in Vietnam to get out early."

"Wasn't that taking a big chance?"

"Probably, but it worked out. I'm here in Germany with a beautiful woman, instead of a crappy town in Texas with a bunch of ugly guys."

Beth laughed. "I'm glad you're here. Does talking about this bother you?"

"No, it's okay. Are we done with the questions?"

"Just one more. I've been wondering if you have any regrets about being a gunship pilot?"

"No, like I said, I only shot at those who were trying to kill me, or my fellow soldiers."

Eric poured more wine and said, "I guess I do have one regret. I had to kill a couple of elephants that were transporting enemy weapons. I hated doing it, but there wasn't any other way. They were with four North Vietnamese soldiers and were hauling rockets that were going to be used against our troops. If I hadn't stopped them, more of our guys would have been killed, so I took them out."

"It sounds like you didn't have a choice."

"And only seconds to decide. One of them almost got away."

"So you killed them all, including the soldiers?"

"Yeah, myself and my wingman. What's weird is, I was more bummed about killing the elephants than wasting the soldiers. The men were shooting at me, but the elephants weren't hurting anybody."

Beth looked at her wine glass and said, "Wow, you must have hundreds of stories like that." Eric didn't respond and she asked, "What did you think of Vietnam?"

"You mean the country?" When she nodded, Eric said, "Vietnam could be beautiful if it's cleaned up, especially the coast. I'd like to go back after the war. I wouldn't have minded it this time if there hadn't been so damn many people trying to kill me."

"Do you think Paul and Tiffany are talking about this?"

"Probably. Paul and I discussed telling you girls."

"What are you guys going to do at the end of ski season?"

Eric hesitated. He didn't want to start their relationship with a lie, but he had been sworn to secrecy by Dr. Muller. He finally answered, "Paul and I met with an Austrian doctor about starting a heli-ski operation. He's offered to pay for our Austrian pilot licenses."

Beth brightened and said, "So you will be staying in Austria."

"Yeah, we're moving to Vienna the first of May. That gives us about a month. If you girls are out of school on April fifteenth, why don't you come to St. Anton? We could ski for a few days and then do some traveling."

"That sounds like fun. Where would you like to go?"

"Paul and I have talked about going to Prague."

"Why Prague?"

"We'd like to see what life is like on the other side of the Iron Curtain."

Beth thought for a moment and said, "Okay, I'm in. I have to admit, you definitely aren't boring."

The next day Paul and Tiffany arrived in Prien. At lunch, the couples discussed the trip to Prague and both girls thought it would be an interesting trip. Afterward, Paul and Eric drove south toward St. Anton. Eric looked at a pocket calendar and said, "If the girls come to St. Anton on the sixteenth, we can ski for a week and then leave for Prague on the twenty-fourth. That will give us time to see Prague and survey the area around Veseli."

Paul said, "I'm looking forward to seeing the border."

Nine days later, Beth and Tiffany finished language school and arrived in St. Anton. After two days of skiing, the girls wanted to see some of the surrounding sites before traveling to Prague.

Tiffany wanted to see Salzburg, while Beth wanted to travel to Switzerland. Paul came up with a plan and said, "Eric, you and Beth take the Volkswagen to Switzerland. I want to spend a couple of extra days in Prague, so Tiffany and I will drive there in the Mercedes after Salzburg." He picked up a map. "It looks like Linz, Austria is about forty-five kilometers south of the Czech border. You can park the VW there and then take a train to meet us in Prague."

The next day was a big ski outing with their friends from St. Anton. Afterward, everyone was invited to a goodbye party at the chalet. Eric hired two local women to cook and serve traditional Austrian appetizers. Seven of their friends attended with some local ladies in tow. Beth and Tiffany were impressed with their European friends. They were from five different countries, all were good looking and spoke perfect English.

The following morning, Eric and Beth traveled north to Switzerland. When they arrived in Interlaken, they checked into the Hotel Splendid, and then walked to a nearby restaurant. After they ordered fondue and a bottle of wine, Beth said, "I've got one more question."

Eric poured the wine. "I thought you might."

"I've been wondering if you had a girl waiting at home while you were in Vietnam."

Eric shook his head. "No and neither did Paul. It was easier that way because it was one more thing you didn't have to worry about. Most of the guys that got a Dear John letter took it pretty hard. A couple even committed suicide."

"How about here in Europe?"

"Paul and I dated a couple of stewardesses from Stockholm."

"You dated them?"

"Okay, they spent two weeks with us at the chalet."

"That sounds more like it. I take it they're back in Sweden."

"Yes they are. How about you? Anybody waiting in Virginia?"

Beth shook her head. "Not any more. I lived with a guy the last semester of my senior year at Duke. He was in his third year of law school, and a teaching assistant in one of my pre-law classes. We broke up because his student deferment was going to run out after graduation. He figured he had three choices. He could go into the service, move to Canada, or go to jail. I told him I didn't want to be a part of any of them."

"How did he take that?"

"He understood because he didn't like any of the options either."

"Which one did he pick?"

"He didn't have to choose any. After graduation, he went back to his hometown in Michigan. He was drinking heavily before he got his pre-draft notice. A week before he was due to report for his physical, he started vomiting blood. He was diagnosed with a bleeding ulcer, so he took the X-rays to the screening and was declared ineligible for the draft."

"Lucky him. Are you going to get back together now that he's a free man?"

"Good Lord no. He wrote and asked if he could come here for a visit, but I told him no."

"I'm glad you did."

"So am I." She leaned toward him and gave him a kiss on the cheek. "I have a little confession about the day we met. Tiff and I followed you guys onto the bus. We had seen you on the ski hill, and wanted to meet you."

Eric smiled. "I'm glad you did. We would have done the same if we had seen you two." He poured more wine. "I've got a question. Why did you pick me?"

"I liked the way you looked in ski pants."

Eric laughed and said, "I have something to admit, too. When I was watching the driver load your skis, I described you girls to Paul and said I liked the brunette."

"That's nice to hear." They both smiled before Beth asked, "Have you ever been to Virginia?"

"No, I've never been east of the Mississippi."

"Would you like to visit sometime?"

"Sure, I'm a history buff and I've always wanted to see Monticello and Mt. Vernon, not to mention all the museums in D.C."

"I'll be happy to show you all of them. Do you think you could ever live there?"

Eric frowned and asked, "How could I know that when I haven't been there? Besides, what would I do? You're going to be a high priced attorney and the best I could hope for would be flying a news helicopter." He held his right hand to simulate talking into a microphone. "Good afternoon everybody, this is Eric Bader coming to you from Chopper Twelve."

Beth ignored the sarcasm and said, "That wouldn't be so bad would it? I'll bet you look great in a flight suit. The TV public would love you."

Eric chuckled. "I'm glad you think so, but even if there was a job opening there would be a thousand applicants. No, the best we can hope for is getting together for a vacation once in a while."

With a resigned sigh, Beth said, "I guess you're right, but I know I'm going to miss you."

"I'll miss you too, but right now I have too many things going on. I haven't even told you about Indonesia. Paul and I have jobs waiting for us there."

"What would you do?"

"Fly helicopters. Our best friend in Vietnam grew up there and has started a helicopter operation. He wants us to work for him, but we can talk about that later—for now, let's enjoy our time in this beautiful place."

Five days later, they drove the Volkswagen to Linz, Austria, where they put it in long term parking and boarded a train for Prague. Eric took a window seat on the right side of the train. Forty minutes later they stopped at the border and Eric watched nervously as armed guards led two German shepherds the length of the train. While he was watching the dogs, a Czech customs officer entered their car followed by a young Soviet soldier. Eric told Beth to change seats.

Eric studied the burly customs official and thought the guy was the kind of man you would not want to cross. In comparison, the soldier was skinny as a rail and looked like he was about twenty, with an AK-47 assault rifle slung over his left shoulder. When the pair stopped at their seat, Eric handed the two passports to the customs agent. He was relieved when the man asked if he spoke German. Eric answered yes and the man asked their destination. Eric answered, Prague and the agent asked, "Business or tourists?"

Eric almost answered business, but caught himself and said, "Tourists."

While the custom agent stamped their passports, Eric studied the soldier and his rifle. He hadn't been that close to an AK-47 in three months and it brought back bad memories. He realized it would be a young man like this who would come after him if he had to put down on the wrong side of the border. Soldiers who would shoot him without a second thought.

Fifteen minutes after the agent and soldier left the rail car, the train started on its trip toward the Czech capital. Eric asked to switch back to the window. The pickup zone would be southeast of the town of Veseli and he wanted to get a look at the topography.

After they switched seats, Beth said, "That customs agent gave me the creeps and so did the little weasel with the gun."

Eric nodded. "We better get used to it because there will probably be soldiers all over Prague."

Beth put her arm in his and said, "You sure know how to show a girl a good time."

Eric looked out the window at passing farm fields and said, "It's something to do."

Beth whispered in his ear, "Something tells me you like being on the edge."

Eric looked at her and nodded. He put the two passports into a black leather wallet along with his money. "I'm going to keep these in my front pocket. I did some research on Prague and it's the pickpocket capital of the world. The crooks may be able to cut something out of my back pocket, but there's no way anybody is getting anywhere near the front of my pants."

The first town they traveled through was Kaplice. Eric was surprised to see how dingy it looked compared to the picturesque villages they had left behind in Austria. He turned to Beth and said, "Look how grimy and run-down this town looks. It reminds me of when I was in college and we used to make trips to Mexico. The contrast between our side and theirs was like this."

Beth looked out the window and said, "I've heard Prague would be beautiful if it was cleaned up."

"Yeah, I've seen pictures. It's pretty drab."

Forty minutes later, Eric was relieved to see that the area around Veseli was hilly. If the mission was compromised and they had to make a run for the border, they might be able to hide in a ravine.

When they arrived at the Prague train station, Eric hailed a taxi to take them to the Inter-Continental Hotel. A pungent scent of soft coal smoke was in the air as Eric looked out the window. "You were right about this place needing to be cleaned up," he said. "The buildings are architecturally beautiful, but they haven't been painted in decades."

They approached the hotel and Beth said, "It has such an institutional façade compared to the other buildings in the city."

At the front door, Eric said, "I'm sure Paul picked this hotel because it's big and they speak English."

At check-in, Eric told the desk clerk they had friends staying at the hotel and requested their room number. The clerk said in a stern voice, "We cannot give out that information."

"Can you call and tell them we are in the lobby?"

The clerk shook his head and said, "No, you will have to wait until they come down."

Eric controlled his anger and turned to Beth. "Let's go to the bar. They're probably there, or soon will be."

At three-thirty in the afternoon the room was empty, except for one other couple. They walked to the bar and Eric asked Beth what she wanted to drink. Beth took a seat on a bar stool and said, "I've heard the beer in this country is excellent."

"Good idea," Eric said and then asked the bartender if he spoke English.

The man answered, "I try."

Eric said, "Two beers please."

The bartender shook his head. "No beers, today only champagne cocktails."

Eric pointed at the bottles behind the bar. "Okay, no beer, we'll have two whiskeys."

The man shook his head again. "No whiskey, no beers, only champagne cocktails."

Eric asked the barman for his name. When he answered, Eric said, "Look Johan, this is our first day in your country. We may not understand how things work here, but this is crazy. Are you saying we can't buy a beer, or a whiskey?"

"That is correct. Management says today we sell only champagne cocktails."

"What's in a champagne cocktail?"

The barman wiped a glass and answered, "Champagne, sugar, bitters and fruit if we have it."

Eric turned to Beth and whispered, "That sounds disgusting. I'm going to try something else. Let's hope this guy hates Commies as much as I do."

Eric motioned for the bartender to come closer and said softly, "Johan, I know this is not your fault, but we do not want a champagne cocktail. I have a bigger problem and need your advice. We have friends staying in this hotel and the desk clerk won't give us their room number. Should I try bribery?"

Johan turned on a faucet and leaned toward Eric. "No bribes, you need to beat the Communists at their own game. They are very suspicious of someone who is not in the right place. Tell a different clerk you rented a car with them and they are late. That should get them down here."

Eric thanked Johan and slipped him two dollars. At the reception area, the first clerk was at the far end of the desk. Eric approached another man and told him the story of the rental car. When the clerk angrily asked the person's name, Eric answered, "Last name Eason, first name Paul."

The clerk looked in a file and said, "He is in Room 301. A house phone is there by the elevators. Call Mr. Eason and tell him to come down immediately."

Eric thanked the clerk and moved toward the phone. When the clerk turned his back, he and Beth quickly entered an elevator. As they were going up, Beth said, "Good job."

Paul opened the door and said, "Hey guys, you're late. Any trouble finding us?"

Eric looked around the room and said, "Not really, how was your trip?"

"It was okay, except for some fun at the border."

Tiffany stepped toward them and interrupted. "The guards were so ugly and their dogs went over the whole damn car. If they had found something, I would have peed my pants right there."

Beth added, "The guys on the train were the same. The customs agent was huge and a Russian soldier followed him with a rifle. Can you imagine living like this?"

Paul turned to Eric and said, "There's a fairly large military presence in the city and it looks like the Soviets have a company of tanks stationed on the outskirts of town." He jingled the car keys. "But for now I say we go into town. We've found a couple of good bars and a restaurant with great food."

Eric looked at Beth. "Apparently we'll have better luck downtown than we had at this place."

The following day, the two couples were in the lobby when an amiable Czech gentleman offered to take them on a walking tour of the old city for five dollars. The sightseeing was interesting and the food and beer superb, but the group decided several days under Communism was long enough and planned to leave Prague the next day.

On the drive toward the Austrian border they stopped for lunch in Veseli. The girls went to freshen up and Eric said, "I wish we had gotten more information on where we will be making the pickup."

Paul looked toward the hills to the east and said, "Yeah, it would have been good to drive up there, but hard to explain to the girls. I think they're both ready to get out of this country."

At the border, the guards brought out sniffer dogs and began combing through the car. While the girls watched the guards, the guys studied the razor wire and wood fence that separated the two countries. Eric checked to see that the girls were out of earshot and said, "There is no way we would be able to get through that on foot. The clear area beyond the fence is called the death strip."

Paul stared at the narrow corridor and said, "I'm sure it's lived up to its name."

The guards finally signaled them to move on and they drove into Austria. Beth and Tiffany admitted they had been terrified the whole time they were in Czechoslovakia. They were not used to being around soldiers carrying weapons. They thanked the guys for taking them to Prague, but said they would never go back to a Communist country.

After spending the night in Linz, the couples ate breakfast and then separated to say their goodbyes. Eric walked Beth to the VW bus and said, "I don't do goodbyes very well. I even lied to my mother when I said goodbye to her. She wasn't happy about my leaving after such a short stay, so I told her I'd be back this summer even though I knew I wouldn't."

Beth looked into his eyes and asked, "Are you going to lie to me?"

"About what? That I'm going to miss you? You know I will. I wish the four of us could keep traveling. You girls didn't like Prague, but there are a lot of fun places to see like Italy and Greece." He paused and said, "Actually, I found Prague fascinating."

Beth frowned. "That's because you like an element of danger."

Eric ignored the comment and said, "Let's get together after Paul and I finish training. We'll be done in a month. Where are you going from here?"

"We're going to Italy and then the south of France. That's probably where we'll be in a month."

"Southern France sounds perfect. We could meet you there." He handed Beth a slip of paper. "This is our mailing address in Vienna. I'll write you at the American Express office in Rome when we get a phone number."

"Okay, let's stay in touch," Beth said. She gave him a kiss and said, "Good luck with your training."

The ladies traveled south to Venice and the guys drove east to Vienna.

It had been a month since Eric and Paul had met Dr. Muller in Innsbruck. He had given them his phone number, so Eric called him for directions. The doctor took the call. "Eric, it is good to hear from you. Are you in Vienna?"

"Yes Sir we are, and we need directions to your house."

"I will have my butler give those to you when we finish. I just want to say how happy I am that you boys have decided to come and talk about my proposal. I have had the guest house cleaned and stocked. It is a modest little place, but I think it will do. I'll see you this evening."

The doctor's house was in an upscale, wooded neighborhood north of Vienna. When Paul saw it he said, "Christ, we should have asked for forty thousand."

Eric surveyed the grounds and said, "Yeah, it looks like the doctor is doing all right for himself."

At the front door, they were greeted by the butler who instructed them to park in back near the guest house. When they drove to the other house, the butler appeared out of nowhere and opened the door.

The guest house was small but elegant, the living room was furnished with an ornate couch and love seat. An antique coffee table was placed between the couches. Opposite the door stood a sideboard cabinet topped with a silver tray and three crystal liquor decanters. To the right, a short hallway led to two bedrooms separated by a bathroom. On the left, an archway led to the kitchen.

After showing them the house, the butler announced, "Dr. Muller has invited you gentlemen for drinks in his study at seven o'clock."

The butler left, and Paul said, "I think this will do."

Eric chuckled and said, "Yeah, when I called the doctor he said his guest house was small but comfortable. That was an understatement. He also said his wife speaks very little English, so I'll have to translate."

The two pilots ate a quick dinner, and then walked to the front door. They were again greeted by the butler who led them to the living room where he introduced them to the doctor's wife. Mrs. Muller was a strikingly handsome woman in her forties, tall and slim with black hair.

She greeted them and then led them down a hallway toward the study. She stopped in front of three wedding pictures and said in German, "The doctor and I are in the middle picture. On each side are pictures of our two daughters. Both of them used my wedding dress. I call it three weddings, one dress."

Eric translated as Mrs. Muller walked away and Paul said, "I'd call it three weddings, three babes."

Mrs. Muller stopped and said in English, "I heard that."

Paul whispered to Eric, "I thought you said she didn't speak English."

Eric shrugged. "That's what I was told."

Mrs. Muller opened the door to the study. The doctor rose from behind his desk and welcomed them into the room. The study's hardwood floor was nearly covered by an Afghan rug. A bookcase took up most of the wall behind the desk. A fire burned in a fireplace adjacent to the book case, with two plush leather chairs nearby. Two wooden chairs with leather pads were placed in front of the desk. A wooden plant stand held a humidor, matches and a cigar cutter.

They shook hands and the doctor led them to a bar opposite his desk. "Gentlemen, what would you prefer? I have Scotch whiskey, English gin, or Russian vodka."

The guys ordered Scotch and the doctor poured three whiskeys saying, "Good choice. I think this single malt is the best the Highlands have to offer. A Scottish friend of mine told me the only way to drink their whiskey is as the good Lord intended, straight from the bottle. He said if you dare, you can add a little water, but anything more is pollution."

Eric agreed with the Scot and said, "Then I'll have mine neat."

"I'll have the same," Paul said, and then added, "We're used to drinking our whiskey without ice Doc, but back then it was out of a tin cup."

The doctor chuckled and handed them their drinks in crystal glasses. He opened the humidor and said, "I always like a good Cuban with my whiskey. Would either of you care for one?"

The two friends exchanged glances before Eric said, "We quit smoking Doc, but in this case I think we can make an exception."

"Good. If one of you will move another chair to the fireplace, I'll get some ashtrays."

After they were seated and the cigars lit, the doctor said, "Thank you for coming to Vienna. I trust your accommodations are acceptable."

Eric puffed on his cigar and said, "Very nice, thank you."

The doctor smiled. "I appreciate you giving me the chance to explain my idea on how to get my family out of East Germany. I checked with a helicopter aviation company about what it will take to obtain your Austrian pilot's licenses. There shouldn't be a problem with you getting a license Eric, because you will be able to read the Austrian regulations. Paul, you will just get checked out in the helicopter."

Paul laughed and said, "That's all right. I've been flying for two years without a license."

The doctor continued, "Your instructor speaks English and since the international language of aviation is English, you will be able to talk to air traffic control. Eric will be certified to fly in Austria and will rent the helicopter. I met with your instructor and I would guess you two have considerably more experience than he has. I have been reading about the Vietnam War and the role you helicopter pilots played. I am quite impressed."

Eric waved his cigar. "I don't think it's any more impressive than flying a fighter in World War II. Did you say you flew an ME-109? That sounds exciting. How were you shot down?"

"I got too close to a B-17. Your Army called it a Flying Fortress. I found that to be true. I was a night fighter, sent up to intercept bombers coming out of England. Our airbase was west of Hanover, on a direct line between London and Berlin."

The doctor had to relight his cigar before he continued. "Our airfield was one of the best-kept secrets of the war. Just before daylight a series of pumps flooded the airport with a foot of water that made it look like a lake. We would run out a couple of row boats on wheels and sometimes to add to the illusion, we put men in the boats with fishing poles. Next to the airfield were barns that we used as hangers. One of the barns hid an elevator that would run our airplanes down to underground hangers much like those on an aircraft carrier.

"At sundown the pumps emptied the water back into the river, exposing the runway. It drove the Allied Forces mad because they couldn't figure out where we were coming from. They wanted to bomb the airfield, but their reconnaissance flights couldn't find it. They never did until after the war and by then the hangars were empty."

The doctor paused and Eric said, "So you bailed out at night."

"Yes, we took on a squadron of bombers around midnight. Each night we would hit them in a different locale. That night we were on the border of Holland and Germany."

The doctor drew on his cigar and waved the smoke away. "That night I was shooting at a B-17. I had just knocked out their number three engine when the tail gunner hit mine. The airplane was flyable, but there were flames in front of the cockpit. I turned toward Germany and hoped I was past enemy lines when I bailed out--unfortunately I wasn't. I hit a tree which collapsed my chute and I fell about twenty feet. My right leg was broken, so I lay there until daylight when a farmer in a hay wagon picked me up and took me to his house. His wife administered to my leg while he sent for the authorities. I spent the rest of the war as a guest of your American Army."

Eric said, "That's worse than anything that happened to us, except maybe when Paul got shot down. He will have to tell you about that at a later time." Eric shifted in his chair and said, "Let's get back to the mission. What was the reason you gave the aviation company for renting a helicopter?"

"I told them what you suggested, that we are thinking of starting a heli-ski operation and we want to look for sites."

"That's good," Eric said. "The helicopter training should be the easy part. What we need to know is what to expect once we are on the other side of that fence. On our way here, we took a trip to Prague and crossed the Czech border. It looked formidable, with stone guard towers, rolled razor wire and a wood pole fence. There's bound to be radar coverage along the perimeter. We need to know if there are holes in it."

The doctor flicked some ashes and said, "I expected those questions, so I hired a former West German Army officer to brief you. His name is Helmut Hessing and he was a Lieutenant Colonel in the Special Forces. He has experience on both the East German and Czech borders. He will tell you what to expect. Since I plan on going along I also want to know all available information."

"What the hell, Doc, you never said *you* were going along," Paul said. "If you go along, there won't be enough room for both of us."

"I know, so that means Eric will fly the mission."

Paul stood and paced in front of the fireplace. "Then why am I wasting time getting checked out in the Alouette?"

"Because I want a backup in case something happens to Eric right before we leave. Let me explain my plan. I learned a lesson the last time I was behind enemy lines and if something goes wrong this time, I will be prepared. I will be dressed in an East German suit and have an East German passport. That is why Eric has to fly the mission. We will be disguised as East German doctors."

Paul sulked back to his chair and Eric said, "You mean I'll have a fake passport too? Doesn't that mean we could be charged as spies if we're caught?"

"We won't have diplomatic protection, so they can do anything they want. The passports are just a precaution. The chances of using them are remote. Colonel Hessing will be here next week to explain everything. You should feel better after you talk with him."

Eric leaned toward the doctor and said, "I hope so Doc, because right now I'm not too hot on your plan. Where will you get the passports?"

"In my line of work one comes in contact with a number of unsavory characters. One of them was a forger who needed a new identity. He still owes me a favor."

Eric blew smoke toward the ceiling and said, "I'm not sure if I agree with the passports, but I'll reserve judgment until we talk with the colonel."

The doctor exhaled a stream of smoke and said, "Good. If you decide to take the offer I will transfer ten thousand dollars into a Swiss bank account here in Vienna. After we return, I will deposit another ten thousand. You will be able to draw from it anywhere in the world."

Eric looked toward Paul and said, "I like the sound of that."

The doctor stood. "Good. Let me refresh our drinks."

While the doctor poured more whiskey, Eric said, "Doctor, you have a beautiful wife, but she doesn't look German. Do you mind if I ask her nationality?"

The doctor handed them their drinks and said, "No I don't mind and you are right, she's not German. She is half Egyptian and half Russian. Her father was a sea captain who met her mother in Alexandria, Egypt. My wife spent her youth living in the two countries, so she speaks Arabic and Russian. She attended university in Zurich, where she learned German. We met while she was in school."

"Does she speak English?"

The doctor shook his head. "Very little."

Eric glanced at Paul and shrugged.

Twenty minutes later the doctor led his new friends to the back door and thanked them. While the two pilots walked to the guest house, Eric said, "I'm still not too sure about the passports."

Paul opened the door to their house and said, "Look, the whole mission will probably take about sixty minutes. That's twenty thousand dollars an hour. Where else are we going to make that kind of money? "

Eric followed him and said, "Okay, you're right. Even counting the training, that's a lot of money for that amount of work. It's also going to get us back into flying."

Paul moved to the sidebar to make drinks. "It will definitely feel good to get back into a helicopter." He handed Eric a glass and said, "While we were talking with the doctor, I thought of a question for you. Do you have any reservations about working with him? After all, he was a Nazi during the war, and didn't your family leave Austria to get away from Hitler and his Third Reich?"

"Yes, they probably wouldn't be too keen on working with the doctor, but all that happened years before I was born. I don't have a problem with him. Do you?"

Paul shook his head. "Nope."

"Good," Eric said. "Besides, don't you get the feeling he isn't that different from us? Just a regular guy who got swept up into a crazy military force that was out of his control."

Paul nodded. "That's exactly what I think."

The two pilots were five days into their training when they received a message that Colonel Helmut Hessing would meet with them the following morning at nine o'clock. They arrived at the house and were met at the door by the doctor. He led them to the study where Colonel Hessing was waiting. The colonel was fit, with a chiseled face and short white hair, dressed in a black T-shirt and tan cargo pants bloused inside hunting boots.

The doctor performed the introductions: "Colonel Hessing, this is Eric Bader and Paul Eason."

The colonel shook their hands and greeted them in English. "Good to meet you gentlemen. Dr. Muller tells me you were both helicopter pilots in Vietnam. Did you fly Slicks or gunships?"

Eric was impressed by the colonel's knowledge of Army aviation and answered, "We flew both, twelve months in Slicks and six in the guns."

The colonel nodded. "Eighteen months is a lot of time in combat." He turned toward Eric and said, "I understand you speak German and you will be flying the mission."

"That's correct."

"With that much time in a war zone, I'm sure you realize the risks you will be facing. Those are not Boy Scouts guarding the fence."

"I know."

"My next question is more practical: why are you doing this?"

Eric glanced at Paul before he said, "We need the money."

The colonel walked to a map on an easel and said, "I guessed as much." He pointed at three chairs and said, "Have a seat gentlemen,

260

and we'll have a look at what we've got. I'm sure Dr. Muller has told you I have extensive experience with both the East German and Czech frontiers." He tapped the map with a pointer. "The family is going to be here on a hill southeast of Veseli. I would like to get them closer to the border, but the doctor thinks that is as close as they can get without raising suspicion.

"The location for both the entry point and exit is here, between the towns of Schrems and Horn. I usually like the penetration point to be different from the exit, but I checked with the Austrian Army and they told me this is the weakest point in the Czech surveillance. The only road in this area is a small trail along the death strip, so we shouldn't be detected by ground forces. It will be eighty kilometers from the border to the pickup zone, or forty-three nautical miles. What will that take in an Alouette III?"

Eric was quick to answer, "About twenty-five minutes. The cruise speed is a hundred knots per hour."

"How long will it take to load the passengers?"

"Ten minutes, fifteen max." After a short pause, Eric asked, "You said *we*, Colonel. Are you going along?"

"No, I was just speaking for the group. I did try to talk Dr. Muller into letting me go instead of him. I think it would be more useful to have me along with my Uzi."

"That sounds better to me too," Eric said, as both men turned toward the doctor.

In an authoritative voice, Dr. Muller said, "I'm going because I am the only one who knows my family, and I can't ask someone to do something I'm not willing to do myself."

Colonel Hessing turned back to Eric. "The doctor is also paying the bills, so that settles that. If it takes twenty-five minutes to the pickup zone, another fifteen to load the passengers, you will be forty minutes into the mission when you start back. This is the route I want you to fly. The penetration point is between these two guard towers which are far enough apart they won't be able to see you. They may hear you, but our side is always testing their security, so they will probably think it is only another test."

Eric interrupted, "Could you have the Austrian Army do some maneuvers to create a diversion?"

Colonel Hessing shook his head. "I used to have that authority, but not anymore. If you think you've been compromised you can always abort the mission."

The colonel turned to the map and continued, "After you cross the border here, I want you to fly a heading of straight north for seventeen nautical miles. That will get you away from the border and the radar coverage. When you see this highway, turn to a heading of three hundred and ten degrees which will take you two miles to the south of the small village of Hradec. Continue on that heading for another five miles. That should put you right at the pickup zone. If everything goes as planned, you should not be on the other side for more than seventy minutes. I wouldn't want you over there any longer. You will take this map with you. Are there any questions so far?"

Eric raised his hand. "If we're discovered and they send aircraft to intercept us, what will they be and where are their bases?"

Colonel Hessing pointed again. "The closest base to the pickup zone is here in Bechyne, a Soviet helicopter gunship base. The next closest is this Mig-21 base west of Ceske Budejovice. There is another Mig base here at Bruno near the entry and exit point."

When the colonel paused, Eric asked, "So the closest base to the pickup zone is a helicopter gunship base?"

"That is correct. It is here fifty kilometers to the north."

Eric pointed at the map and said, "Colonel, you probably think the Migs are the bigger threat, but they aren't. We did an exercise in Vietnam where we had F-4 Phantoms and our helicopter gunships trying to shoot us down. The helicopters turned out to be more of a threat. If we stayed low, the jets had a hard time finding us. When they did, they would over-fly us before they could get off a shot, which gave us time to out-maneuver them. The helicopter gunships could match our maneuverability and could have shot us down. Lucky for us the North Vietnamese didn't have helicopter gunships."

The colonel leveled his eyes at Eric and said, "Unfortunately, the Ivans do." When Eric frowned, the colonel added, "As long as you stay low and avoid villages you should get in and out undetected."

Colonel Hessing moved in front of Eric. "One more thing, the doctor tells me you are not convinced that having an East German passport is a good idea. As someone who has made several extractions from the Czech countryside, I can tell you we always had Czech passports and money. We were also dressed in local clothing, so we could blend into the local populous."

Eric nodded and the colonel continued, "If you are forced down on the other side, your forged documents and Czech money will give you the possibility of getting to a train station where you can buy a ticket to Prague. The doctor speaks Czech and has friends in Prague who can get you to a safe house. From there his people can get you to your respective embassies and they should be able to get you out of the country."

Eric was surprised. "You think they can?"

The colonel looked at the doctor and then at Eric. "Yes, the Czechs aren't as worried about defectors as the Soviets and you two aren't Czech citizens."

Colonel Hessing moved back to the map and said, "The day before the mission, I want you to move to the city of Linz, just south of the penetration point. The doctor will accompany Eric in the helicopter."

He turned to Paul. "I've reserved a rental van that you will drive to the Linz airport to pick them up. You will also use it to transport the family back to Vienna. I've included a map of the city in this packet. You will see that the airport is northwest of Linz on Flughafenstrasse, Airport Road in English. You will all stay at the Hotel Drei Mohren in downtown Linz. I've booked a room for each of you."

The colonel handed the packet to Paul and the map to Eric. "Gentlemen, that concludes the briefing. Are there any questions?" When there weren't any, Colonel Hessing said, "Good luck men. If you will excuse me, I have to catch a plane to Frankfurt."

The two pilots accompanied the colonel to his rental car. When they reached the car, Colonel Hessing handed Eric his card and said, "If you two are interested, I can get you more jobs like this for more money. Give me a call and we'll talk."

Eric looked at the card and said, "Thanks Colonel. You might be hearing from us."

Two days later, Doctor Muller and Eric went to meet the forger. As they approached the door of the photography shop, a window next to the door displayed a black and white poster of Bob Dylan dressed in a black suit wearing sunglasses. At the bottom, a script read, *London 1966.*

The forger greeted them in German and Eric asked if he had taken the Dylan photo. The forger answered that he wished he had, and then led them to the back of the studio through a cloth curtain. The forger turned on a bright light and said, "So you two want East German passports. You will also need fake driver's licenses. Fill in these cards with the names you wish to use, your weights, heights, and eye color. I will also need dates and cities of birth. Are you going to use doctor as your occupations?"

Dr. Muller answered, "Yes."

"I have suits and ties that were made in East Germany. We will use them for the passport photos. You can borrow them for your trip. I will have shirts and pants when you return for the papers."

The forger read Eric's information and said, "Herr Strobel, we need to make you look older. You don't look like a twenty-nine year old doctor. Have you ever grown a beard?"

Eric answered, "Yes, once in college."

"Was it fine or coarse?"

"I guess I would say fine."

The forger turned and said, "I'll get my make-up kit."

He fitted Eric with a beard and asked if it looked similar to his real beard. Eric examined himself in the mirror and said, "It's very close."

The forger handed Eric a jar of hair cream and a pair of wire-rimmed glasses. "Slick your hair back and put these on."

When the disguise was complete, Eric checked a mirror and thought it did make him look older. It also made him look like a Wall Street stockbroker.

The man took Eric's picture in the suit and then had him take off the coat and tie for the driver's license picture. When he was done, the forger told Eric to start growing a beard to look like the photos. He took pictures of the doctor and told him he would have the documents ready in six days.

Later that week, the butler appeared at the door with an oversized envelope. Eric opened it and looked at the passport. When he handed it to Paul, his friend laughed and said, "I guess you could pass for a doctor, but I think you look more like a bus driver in a suit."

Eric grabbed the passport and said, "Thanks for the encouragement. If you'll remember, we used to *be* bus drivers." He opened his briefcase and put the passport in his black ID wallet along with his American passport. "I should hide that somewhere," he said, before moving to the sidebar to make a drink.

Paul followed him to the bar and said, "I should be finished with my training tomorrow and I've heard the skiing is still good in St. Anton. I think I'll take the train there when I'm finished and catch a few more days on the slopes."

Eric sipped his drink and said, "I'd do the same if I could, but studying alone will be good for me. I'm still having trouble with the Austrian regulations. When I pass my check ride, I'll meet you there."

The following day, Eric drove Paul to the station and returned to the guest house. He had just walked in when the phone rang. He answered it and heard a familiar voice. "Hi Eric, it's Beth."

He was surprised and said, "Hey Babe, where are you?"

"I'm in Vienna."

"What are you doing here?"

"Missing you."

"I miss you too, but aren't you supposed to be on a trip through *alles Europa?*"

"I was, but Tiffany lost her grandmother and had to fly home for the funeral. When she left, I asked myself what should I do while I wait for her to return? Visiting you was the first thing that came to mind. Am I interrupting anything?"

"No, this is perfect timing because I'm here alone."

"Where's Paul?"

"He just left for St. Anton."

"Are you still training?"

"Yes, but I'm almost done. All I have to do is struggle through some boring regulations and then take my check ride. Why don't you stay here until I finish?"

"I was hoping you'd say that."

The next morning, Eric and Beth were seated in a crowded coffee house. Eric leaned toward Beth and pointed at a woman with a stern face and severe hair. "Check out the woman reading the newspaper. How many spies do you think she's running?"

In a conspiratorial voice, Beth whispered, "This whole city is full of intrigue. Are you going to show it to me?"

"Absolutely. I thought today we would visit a few of the main attractions, then have dinner and attend a Beethoven concert. The symphony is performing his Piano Concerto Number Five."

Beth laughed and said, "Aren't you full of surprises? A pilot who likes classical music."

"You're forgetting my family is Austrian. I grew up listening to Mozart and Beethoven."

"That all sounds like fun, but aren't you supposed to be studying?"

"I can take a day off. It's nice to have you here."

Beth smiled. "It's good to be here."

While they waited for the concert to begin that evening, Beth noticed Julie Christie seated in the row in front of them. "Look who's there," Beth whispered. "She's even more beautiful in person."

Eric looked at the actress and said, "She is stunning. I loved her in *Dr. Zhivago.*"

The next morning they sat in the Café Sacher drinking espresso. Eric was reading a local newspaper and said, "The Lipizzaner Stallions are performing tonight, would you like to see them?"

Beth looked up from a *Herald Tribune* and said, "Yes, I'd love to."

"Good, I'll get tickets on the way to the airport. I should be back around four."

Beth folded the paper and said, "I'll take the tram into the city and spend the day sight-seeing and shopping."

At five o'clock Eric returned to the guest house. A Viennese sunset flooded the room with a soft glow. Beth was lying on the couch reading a book. She looked up and asked, "How did it go today?"

Eric walked across the room and set his briefcase on the sideboard. "It went well. I did okay on the oral and I know I'm going to ace the flying." He poured a drink and said, "I bought the tickets this morning, so we can go to dinner as soon as I get cleaned up. I'm having a whiskey, would you like one?"

"Yes thanks. What time does the performance start?"

"I think at eight, let me check." He opened his brief case and looked at the tickets. "Yeah, it starts at eight, so we have plenty of time." He picked up his drink and walked toward the bathroom. "I'm going to take a shower."

In the bathroom, he threw his clothes on the floor and stepped into the shower. With the hot water cascading over his body, he thought he would never take a hot shower for granted again. He was confident about his check flight the next day and he had a pretty lady waiting for him in the living room. Life is good, he thought. He dried off and walked out of the bathroom with a towel wrapped around his waist.

In the living room he was taken aback by the expression on Beth's face. "What the hell happened, Babe? You look like you just heard somebody died."

Beth glared at him and said, "Now that you mention it, somebody did. His name was Eric Bader."

Eric frowned and asked, "What the hell are you talk--?" He stopped in mid-syllable when he noticed that she was holding the two passports.

She flipped them at him. "Which one of these is the real one Eric, or should I ask Herr Strobel?"

Eric picked up the passports and threw them into his briefcase. Why didn't I hide that *goddamn* passport when I had the chance, he thought.

He turned to face her and said, "You know it's the American one, or you wouldn't be here. I know how this must look, but it's not what you think."

Beth paced in front of the window. "Oh I'll just bet it isn't." She stopped and pointed at his briefcase. "I was reminiscing about our trips and picked up your passport wallet. When I felt there were two passports in it I thought you must be traveling with another woman. You can imagine my surprise when I saw the other one was issued to a Heinrich Strobel with *your* picture in it. As if that isn't bad enough, it's a goddamn *East German passport,* Eric."

She paused to collect herself. "I finally realized you must be CIA, aren't you? And you had the audacity to tell me you've never been to Virginia. Hell, you probably work out of Langley. Do you have a wife and kids there too?"

Eric shook his head and said softly, "No, I was telling the truth when I said I've never been there."

"Oh sure, and where do I fit in here, Eric? Was I part of your cover? No wonder you guys wanted to go to Prague. Did you deliver something to an agent?" Tears welled as she said, "I fell for you and you used me." She crossed her arms and stared out at the growing darkness.

In a calm voice, Eric said, "Think about it Beth. If I *was* a spy, would I leave a fake passport lying around where someone could find it? Of course not, I forgot about it because I'm *not* a spy. All I am is a damn helicopter pilot."

Beth looked over her shoulder and said, "Who just happens to have an East German passport."

"Yes, but there is a reason. I haven't told you everything about our association with Dr. Muller. Paul and I were sworn to secrecy, but here's the truth: the heli-ski operation is just a cover to rent a helicopter. What we're really going to do is fly the doctor's family out of Czechoslovakia."

Beth turned around and stared in disbelief as Eric continued, "The fake passport was the doctor's idea. He had them made in case we go down on the other side. If we do, we're going to pose as East German

268

doctors."

With an incredulous look, Beth said, "In case you go *down* on the other side. My God Eric, what the hell are you talking about? Why would you want to do something that foolish? You saw all those soldiers over there."

Eric turned back to the sideboard and began to make a drink. When he didn't respond, Beth shouted, "Well?"

Over his shoulder he said, "Because we need the money. The doctor is paying us twenty grand to do it."

Beth continued to shout as she said, "You mean you're going to risk your freedom and maybe your life for twenty thousand dollars?"

Eric turned to face her and said, "I used to risk it for a lot less."

"But then you had to."

"I still do."

"Why?"

"Because I told the doctor I would, and there are four people on the other side of that fence who are counting on me to get them over it."

"And you're the only one who can."

"No, but I'm the one who's going to try." He took his drink and walked to his bedroom.

At dinner they barely talked. During the Lipizzaner performance they only discussed the magnificent horses. When they returned to the guest house Beth said, "I need time to think this out. I'd like to sleep in Paul's bedroom tonight."

"I understand," Eric said, and turned toward his room. "I'll see you in the morning."

He awoke in a bad mood. He was still angry at himself for the passport mess and he had to face an inspector from the Austrian Aviation Administration. He rubbed his face and thought, I've had worse mornings. He got out of bed and made a pot of coffee.

Beth walked in as the coffee finished brewing. He poured her a cup and said, "I'm sorry about yesterday. I hope you're not going to let this come between us. You said you liked me because I'm not boring. This isn't boring."

She took the cup and said, "But it *is* crazy. I still can't believe you're going to do this, Eric. You saw all those goons with guns over there."

Eric poured himself a cup. "You have to understand," he said. "I'm not planning on meeting any of them. I'm going to be in a helicopter. If everything goes as planned, I'll never be on the ground except to pick up the people."

Beth didn't respond and Eric continued, "Listen, Dr. Muller hired a German Army colonel to brief us on the border. He showed us the weak spots in their radar coverage and planned the whole mission. We'll only be on the other side for a little more than an hour."

"Is Paul going with you?"

"No, there isn't enough room because Dr. Muller's going."

Beth crossed her arms. "I just wish you had told me about this before I found out the way I did."

"I wanted to tell you, but we made a promise to the doctor not to tell anyone. And I didn't expect to see you until this was over."

Beth relaxed and said, "Okay, I understand, but I'm not going to wait until you get back. I'll worry about you, but I'm not staying. When Tiff returns, we're driving to Paris. I would appreciate you writing me there as soon as this is over."

"I'll write as soon as I'm back."

"Thank you. I have to pack," Beth said and turned to leave.

Eric asked, "Where are you going from here?"

Beth stopped and said, "I need to meet Tiffany at the Munich airport in four days."

Eric turned her around and said, "I don't want you to leave. Why don't you stay with me until then? I'll be finished with my training today. Tomorrow I'm driving to St. Anton. We can stay there until you leave for Munich. It's only a three-hour drive from St. Anton."

Beth thought for a moment and said, "I guess that would be better than spending four days alone."

"Of course it will," Eric said. He checked his watch. "I have to go, but I should be back around two o'clock."

Beth held back for awhile, and then kissed his cheek. "Good luck on your check ride."

Eric finished early and returned to the guest house beaming. "I'm happy to report I am now certified to fly helicopters in Austria and anywhere else in Europe, legally or otherwise."

"Congratulations," Beth said. "You seem pretty cavalier about all this craziness."

"I'd call it confidence," Eric said. "I know I've done everything possible to prepare and those goons on the other side don't even know I'm coming. In Nam, it seemed like the bad guys knew where we were going before we did. That's a big difference."

"I'm glad you feel that way because I don't. I still think it's a bad idea."

Eric took her in his arms. "Look, I'm not going to change your mind and you're not going to change mine, so let's do something to take our minds off it."

She gave him a sexy smile. "And what would that be, Mr. Bader?"

"I reserved the helicopter for this afternoon. Let's go for a flight."

Beth stepped back. "You mean right now? I've never been close to a helicopter, let alone inside one."

"Then it's time you were." He took her hand and said, "Come on. I want to show you what I do."

On the drive to the airport, Beth said, "Listen Eric, I'm a little nervous about this. You won't do something crazy to scare me, will you?"

He shot her a reassuring smile. "My dear, all I want to do is take you on a helicopter ride. You don't mind jet travel. This will be much more fun. It's a fabulous day, and we'll be flying over historic Austrian countryside."

Beth began to relax and smiled at him.

At the helicopter company, Eric introduced Beth as a friend from the States. They walked out on the ramp and she squeezed his hand. They approached three helicopters and Eric pointed at the one with a blunt nose and said, "That's ours."

Beth suppressed a giggle. "It looks like a big white whale."

271

Eric chuckled. "I guess it does. It was built in France and is called an Alouette, which is lark in French."

"Well it doesn't look like a lark," Beth said as she pointed at the two sleek helicopters next to it. "Why can't we take one of those? This one looks so . . . so ungainly."

Eric opened the left cockpit door, and said, "This is the one I'm certified to fly. Besides, look at all those windows. You'll be able to see everything. This one also serves a purpose. If you were in Czechoslovakia and saw this fly over, would you think it looked dangerous?"

"Okay, I see the point," Beth said.

The Alouette sat on three wheels instead of skids and could carry six people, two in front and four on a bench seat in the back. The aft section had two sliding side doors for easy loading and unloading, which would be essential at the pickup zone.

Eric reached into the helicopter and grabbed an orange flight suit. He handed it to Beth and said, "This is the smallest one I could find."

Beth put it on. "Do I *have* to wear this? she asked. "It's not very flattering."

Eric said, "I think you look cute as hell. As for your question, no, we don't have to wear them, but I thought they'd look good in the pictures. My instructor will be here to take some."

He donned a green flight suit and Beth said, "I knew you'd look good in one of those. I wish I would have known you in the Army."

Eric shook his head. "I don't think so." He flashed back to thoughts of Lieutenant Chapman and how difficult it had been to spend time with her. Now he could take a pretty girl on a helicopter ride any time he wanted. He pointed toward the office and said, "My instructor is coming this way."

After the introductions, Beth pointed at Eric and asked, "Is it safe to fly with this guy?"

The instructor answered, "He's better than safe. He handled everything we threw at him with ease. I'd let my grandmother fly with him."

Beth smiled at Eric. "I figured as much."

The instructor took photos of them inside and out of the helicopter. When he was finished he handed Eric the camera. "You two have a nice flight," he said.

Eric helped Beth buckle into her harness. He handed her a headset and showed her how to use the "press to talk" button. Before he closed the door, he said, "Relax, you're going to enjoy this."

When he was situated in his own seat, he ran through a preflight checklist and then flipped the starter switch. The rhythmic vibrations of the three blades quickly smoothed out as they reached operating RPM. He gave Beth a reassuring smile and asked, "Ready?"

She nodded and clutched both sides of her seat. Eric pulled pitch into the blades with the collective and the nose wheel slowly lifted off the ground, followed by the two rear wheels. He held the helicopter at a hover a few feet above the ground while he checked on his passenger. She was looking straight ahead with her jaw clenched. She's an adventurous chick, he thought. She'll love it once she gets used to it.

Eric lifted the helicopter several feet higher and then slowly rotated while hovering over the same spot on the ramp. As they turned, first the tower came into view, then hangers, the runway, trees and finally the office all moved as if they were images projected around them in a theater.

When he stopped the rotation, Beth's face had changed from apprehension to wonder. She pushed the intercom button and said, "That was incredible. How can you do that?"

Eric smiled and said, "You do it enough times it becomes easy. This machine can do a lot of neat tricks. Let's go do a few."

He received a takeoff clearance and departed to the north toward the Danube River. While they flew over the river Beth looked down in awe. Past the city Eric turned west over the Vienna Woods and then climbed toward the foothills, where he skimmed the top of a hill covered with grass and wildflowers. Beth watched as the ground zipped under the chin bubble and said, "Wow, I'm beginning to understand why you love this so much, even if it does make you do stupid things."

Eric chuckled and said, "It's not flying a helicopter that makes me do stupid things. It's rich people with money."

Beth furrowed her brow and looked over the top of her sunglasses. She was no longer clutching the sides of her seat. Eric lowered the collective and descended into a valley filled with cattle, horses and old farms. After twenty minutes of flying around pastoral villages and buildings, he swooped to the top of a nearby hill and said, "I think we should put down and take a break."

Beth looked worried and said, "You're going to land out here?"

"Sure, why not?" Eric said. "I'm used to landing on top of hills and this one should be a lot friendlier." He lined up for the landing and said, "Besides that, it has shorter grass."

When they were on the ground, they climbed out of the helicopter and walked toward the west. Beth pointed at the snow-capped mountains and said, "Eric, this is like a scene from *The Sound of Music*." She looked into his eyes and said, "You were right, I love this."

When he started to speak, she put her index finger on his lips and said, "And I love you."

Eric didn't respond and Beth said, "I know that probably caught you off guard, but I just want to let you to know how I feel."

Eric took her into his arms. "Don't you think you're just caught up in the moment?"

Beth shook her head. "No, it's more than that. I started falling for you when we were in that funky little hotel in Prien."

Eric was pleased to hear it, but was out of replies. He looked toward the city and said, "Why don't we get this helicopter back to the airport and go to dinner?"

He led her back to the ship and helped her in. After starting the turbine engine, he said, "Here's what we're going to do. After we lift off, I'm going to move us to edge of this hill and then fly straight down. It will feel like we're on the biggest roller coaster in the world."

Beth nodded and reached for the sides of her seat. Eric patted her shoulder and said, "It's not going to be that scary."

He lifted the Alouette several feet high and flew it to where the hill dropped off. He pointed the ship down the slope and they flew faster and faster until they reached the bottom of the valley and he raised the nose to stop their descent. When they were straight and level he checked on Beth and saw she was smiling. He smiled back and thought this time was a lot more fun than when he bounced off the cliff by Dalat.

Eric got a clearance to traverse the city on their way back to the airport. The first attraction they came to was the city hall, and he said, "That impressive-looking building is the Rathaus which you probably know is City Hall. To our left is the University of Vienna. Maybe you'll be attending there someday." He pointed ahead and said, "That long white structure is the Austrian Parliament Building. We probably shouldn't fly over that."

He turned to the northeast and flew to Prater Park and its giant Ferris wheel. Next was the massive Schonbrun Palace. They had toured it the day before and Eric had saved it for the last, so Beth could see the sculpted gardens from the air. She looked down at them and said, "Look how beautiful they are from up here. This whole flight has been fantastic. Can we do it again, someday?"

Eric made a turn toward the airport and said, "Sure." And then thought, provided I don't get my ass shot down in Czechoslovakia.

That evening at dinner Beth said, "I want to thank you for one of the most memorable days of my life."

Eric smiled. "I'm glad you enjoyed it. Does that mean I'm forgiven?"

In a sultry voice, Beth said, "Let me put it this way. I'm not sleeping in Paul's bedroom tonight."

The weather was beautiful during Eric and Beth's three days of skiing in St. Anton. When it was time for Beth to leave for Munich, Eric walked her to the camper van and asked, "Why don't you girls meet us in Greece?"

Beth shook her head. "No, that would mean driving through Yugoslavia and we are *not* going into another Communist country."

"Okay, then we could send you the train fare? You wouldn't have to get off until you reach Athens."

Beth opened the driver's side door and said, "Why don't we talk after you get back from your little jaunt over the fence?" She looked him in the eyes and said, "You know I'm going to miss you the moment I leave here. I'll also really be pissed if you get killed, so don't screw up, okay?"

Eric kissed her and said, "I'll give it my best shot."

The night before they were to leave for Linz, Eric and Paul went to dinner at a popular Viennese Gasthous. Eric poured the last of a bottle of wine and said, "You know Dev, we've come a long way in the four months since we left the Army. We blew through most of our twenty thousand dollars, and now we have a Swiss bank account with a new ten grand. We're both qualified to fly helicopters in Austria, and I have an East German passport that says I'm a twenty-nine year old doctor."

Paul cracked a smile. "It has been an interesting four months. My favorite part is you as a doctor."

"Yeah that's a good one," Eric said as he waved for the check. "Right now I better get some sleep. I doubt if I'll get much between now and Sunday."

Paul frowned and said, "I wish I was going with you."

Eric took the check. "I wish you were too."

The next morning they were invited to breakfast with Doctor and Mrs. Muller. The doctor was in a jovial mood as he greeted his two new friends at the door. While they walked down the hallway, the doctor said, "I have good news. My family is in Veseli. Everything is going according to plan."

In the dining room, Mrs. Muller was already seated. Eric and Paul wished her a good morning, as they took their places. The table was set with a typical Austrian breakfast of cold cuts, slices of cheese, soft boiled eggs in egg cups, various types of hard rolls, dark breads, butter, jams and a large pot of coffee. During the meal, the doctor was talkative, switching from English to German to translate for his wife. Mrs. Muller sat stoically without saying a word. Eric looked at her and thought, I don't think she likes the idea of this trip either.

When they were finished, Paul drove Eric and the doctor to the Vienna airport. He wished them a good trip before leaving for Linz in the rental van. In the helicopter, Eric helped the doctor with his seat belt, and showed him how to work the press to talk button on the headset. He did a preflight check and then took off toward the west. After he signed off with air traffic control he turned to the doctor and said, "Doc, once you get a helicopter into the air, it flies much like an airplane. It even has a stick like the fighters you flew in the war. Why don't you fly us to Linz?"

The doctor eyed him with apprehension and shook his head. Eric pointed at the cyclic in front of the doctor and said, "Go ahead, you will enjoy it."

The doctor grabbed the stick and said, "*Warum nicht?*" Why not?

Eric said, "Make a few turns, but keep that highway off to our left. It will lead us to St. Polten. Just west of there we will see the Danube River and follow it to the Linz airport. It should be a beautiful trip."

Dr. Muller started a turn to the left, then back to the right. "This feels good Eric. We need to do it again when we have more time."

"I'd like that," Eric said, hoping they would both be around long enough to do it. He pointed at the horizon. "That town ahead is St. Polten. Continue to fly toward that."

Several miles past St. Polten, the Danube flowed down from the north and turned west before them. On each side of the river was rolling farmland, occasionally broken by patches of trees and hedgerows. The Danube is brown, not blue Eric thought. Kind of like the "Silver Dustoff" wasn't silver.

The ruins of an old castle came into view and the doctor turned to fly over it. Past the castle he veered toward a small village. As an onion-domed church passed under the nose, Doctor Muller exclaimed, "*Wunderbar!*"

They approached the outskirts of Linz and Eric said, "I see the airport, Doc. I'll take it from here."

"Thank you Eric. I enjoyed that more than I can say."

Eric took the controls and said, "I thought you would." He got a clearance to land and softly set the Alouette down on the ramp, the rear wheels first and then the nose wheel. Paul arrived an hour later and drove them into the city.

Later that night, the doctor was still in a good mood as they sat down to dinner. He turned to Eric and said, "I want to thank you for letting me fly today. I haven't felt this good in a long time. Are you sure you two won't stay in Austria? We could actually start a heli-ski operation."

"That's a good offer, Doc, but we have other commitments," Eric said. " I'm glad you enjoyed the flight. We'll do it again before we leave Vienna."

After dinner the three of them retired to their rooms. Eric looked at the fine furnishings in his room and thought the place probably looked a lot better than a Czech jail. He quickly brushed the thought from his mind. It was like the time he imagined himself in a body bag outside the hospital at Lai Khe. He had made it through Nam and he would make it through this.

A few minutes later there were two loud knocks on the door and he knew who it was. Eric opened the door and asked, "How are you doing?"

Paul rushed in and answered, "Not good. I think I should go with you. Why don't we leave Doc here and do this without him? What is he going to do when we get back, other than thank us?"

Eric closed the door and said, "That's if everything goes as planned. What if the family isn't where they're supposed to be and we have to go looking for them?"

"So what are we looking for, two women and two boys in a little yellow car? How hard can that be?"

"Probably not very, but as Colonel Hessing said, the doctor is paying the bills. This is his show. If we go over there and don't bring them back, we won't get the rest of the twenty grand. Hell, he might even take back the original ten thousand. *Then* what do we do? I say we have a plan and we need to fly it."

Paul paused before sulking toward the door. "Okay, I'll see you in the morning."

Eric slept fitfully until five o'clock when he was awakened by a nightmare. He was back in Vietnam and heard the sound of bullets hitting sheet metal. He collected his thoughts and realized the radiator was ticking loudly. He was soaked in sweat and told himself it was because he'd been sleeping under a down comforter. He got out of bed and mumbled, "Yeah right."

In the bathroom, he threw cold water on his face and then took a glass of water to a window in the bedroom. A bright moon was shining through scattered clouds. It would be a good fly day. He remembered a novel he had read about an American bomber pilot who was about to embark on a massive offensive against Nazi Germany. The pilot was in a hotel room in England and had gotten up to look at the sky. The difference between that pilot and him was the bomber pilot had other crewmen he could rely on. If he was shot down, there may even be friendlies around to rescue him. The bomber pilot also had a woman sleeping in his bed. Eric had none of those things.

He walked back to the bathroom. Sleep would be futile, so he changed into pants and a sweater and slipped down to the lobby. When he got off the elevator, he saw Paul reading a newspaper and drinking coffee. "I see you couldn't sleep either," he said.

Paul folded the paper and said, "No, how many hours did you get?"

"Not enough," Eric answered yawning. "I was awakened by a Nam-mare. I dreamed I was back in the jungle and bullets were ripping my helicopter. What worries me is I was flying an Alouette, not a Huey."

Paul whistled and said, "That's not good."

Eric nodded. "Now I know why we drank so much in Nam. You don't have nightmares when you're passed out."

Paul laughed. "I knew there was a reason."

Eric pointed toward the restaurant. "I'm going to take a coffee up to my room and get ready. I'll see you at seven."

After a shower, Eric put on his East German suit pants and white shirt. It took him three tries to get his tie right. After slicking back his hair, he donned the wire-rimmed glasses and compared the image in the mirror with the fake passport picture. Close enough, he thought. With his bag in hand, he left the room.

Paul and the doctor were huddled in the lobby when he entered. The doctor greeted him, "Good morning Eric, how are you? Or should I ask Dr. Strobel."

Eric smiled and said, "I'm okay, Doc. How are you?"

"I'm fine," the doctor said as he stood. "I think we should go to a café down the street for a real breakfast. All they have here is a continental."

The restaurant smelled of fresh-baked pastries and was crowded with Sunday morning patrons. Eric watched as a young man placed trays of bread into a large oven, his long hair tucked into a hair net. As he watched him work, Eric thought the kid didn't have a care in the world. He would spend the whole day in the restaurant placing tray after tray of bread and rolls into the oven. He would also probably never leave Austria, or know what it was like to live on the edge. For just that one day Eric wished he could trade places with the baker and spend time in a nice, warm kitchen.

Before they left for the airport, Eric told the doctor, "Let's take our suit coats off and put on flight suits, so we'll fit in on the ramp."

At the airport, Paul helped preflight the helicopter, and then wished them a good flight. Eric helped the doctor with his harness and reminded him on how to use the push to talk button. He climbed into his seat and thought the weather was perfect and the flight should be a piece of cake--if the family would only be in the right place.

He finished his checklist and took off toward the town of Zwettl. When he flew past the town of Horn, he turned to the north, took a deep breath and looked at the doctor. "It's go time, Doc," he said. The doctor nodded, never taking his eyes off the border.

They would cross into Czech territory at tree-top level. Eric's heartbeat quickened as he saw the fence and death strip. He glanced to the left and right: no guard towers. Over the death strip, he again looked both ways. No one was on the road. They had made a clean entry. In a whispered voice, he said, "Thank you Colonel Hessing."

Ten minutes later Highway E84 came into view and Eric turned to a heading of 320 degrees. This would take them to the south of Hradec and straight at the town of Veseli. The pickup zone was southeast of the village, so they wouldn't have to fly over it.

Dr. Muller looked up from his map and pointed to the right. "That is Hradec. I recognize the town square."

Eric looked toward the town. "We're right on course. That should be Veseli just ahead. See anything familiar?"

"Yes, fly down this road coming off the main highway. The hill is just ahead to the left, past that stone fence."

Eric started a circle around the hill and said, "There's nobody here, Doc. Are you sure this is the place?"

"Yes, this is it."

Eric looked toward the west and saw a small yellow car, with suitcases strapped to the top, turn off the highway onto a secondary road. Doctor Muller saw the car and exclaimed, "That is my aunt's Skoda. That is them for certain. We need to land."

"Not yet Doc, we have to make a positive identification. Your people weren't where they were supposed to be. Our plan may have been exposed and that car could be full of Czech STB. I'm going to make a low pass to see who's in the car."

Eric's heart was racing as he made a turn to line up on the car that had stalled about fifty feet from the top of the hill. When a teenage boy jumped out to push, Dr. Muller said, "That is my nephew."

Eric slowed abruptly and said, "Okay, I'm going to set down with them on your side, so you can help them load."

He made a turn to the west to see if they had been followed, and saw what he feared most: a black Tatra sedan speeding down the secondary road. Eric pointed at the sedan and said, "Bad guys."

Doctor Muller looked startled. "*Scheisse*, it is STB. We need to hurry."

Eric continued his descent toward the hill. The yellow Skoda had stopped and two women and two boys stood outside. One woman reached into the car and pulled out a third woman. When he saw who it was, the doctor said, *"Gott im Himmel, die ist meine Tante.* My aunt is not supposed to be here. She has a big mouth and probably told somebody she was going to Austria. That is why the STB are following."

Eric landed and yelled, "It doesn't matter now. You need to help them up the hill and get them in here, fast. Put the women in the back with the small boy and bring the other boy up here with us. Be sure to keep their heads below the rotors."

The doctor jumped out, slid the back door open and then limped toward his family. When he reached his mother, he gave her a hug and then led her up the hill. His sister and nephew helped the aunt struggle toward the idling helicopter. The black Tatra climbed toward them and Eric said, "I knew I should have brought the colonel and his Uzi."

The family reached the helicopter and the doctor quickly helped the three women and younger boy into the back seat. He closed the door and helped the other boy into the front. He was climbing in when there was a popping sound and bullets hit the helicopter.

"God damn," Eric said, as he pulled the oldest boy into the ship. More shots rang out and Dr. Muller moaned and fell to the ground.

Eric yelled to the boy, "Help him, hurry."

The boy stared in panic and Eric realized the kid didn't speak English. He switched to German. *"Helf ihm. Schnell, schnell."*

The boy moved to get out, but the doctor waved him off. *"Nein! Nein! Gehen Sie! Schnell!"* No! No! Go! Hurry!

When the boy hesitated, Eric pulled him back by his shirt and told him to close the door. The doctor was right, if the boy got out he would get hit too. He made a hasty take-off as the doctor's mother sobbed, *"Nein, nein, nein."*

They were just above the ground when two more bullets hit the ship up high. Eric hoped they hadn't hit the transmission. He had lost one in Vietnam and it was not good. The first thing he'd noticed was the smell of hot metal as the transmission started to disintegrate. That was followed by the rotor wash picking up the leaking transmission fluid and spraying it all over the windshield. If that were to happen now he would have to land immediately—he'd know either way, in a few seconds.

282

He made a turn to the west to get a look at what was happening on the ground. He also wanted it to appear they were headed for West Germany. He needed to confuse the enemy aircraft that would soon be on their way.

He rolled out and looked toward the ground. The black sedan was parked at the top of the hill and two men in suits walked toward the doctor with pistols drawn. The doctor's mother and sister were crying in the back seat.

"Sorry Doc," Eric said, as he took one last look and then checked the instrument panel for vital signs. All readings were normal and the fuel gauge read three quarters.

When he was out of sight of the STB, he made a turn to the south. He wanted to keep going straight toward Austria, but the map said that would take him directly toward a road checkpoint and a heavily armed guard tower. It was better to risk going back to the exit point than to get shot down by ground fire. It was only fifteen minutes away, an eternity when outrunning Czech Migs and Soviet helicopter gunships. He visualized the two Migs taking off, their landing gears coming up, the pilots with their helmet visors down, oxygen masks covering their faces, young men on their way to kill him.

It was another twenty miles before he could safely turn south toward the border. Instinctively he checked his instrument panel—everything was still normal except the fuel gauge. He was shaken when he saw it hovered just above one quarter. He had lost half a tank of fuel in ten minutes. One of the rounds must have hit the tank.

He had to turn south immediately. Luckily there was a shallow ravine he could duck into. He lowered the collective and dived toward the cover of the valley. If he could get low enough the enemy aircraft might not see him.

The crying in back continued as he checked his map and saw he was headed straight toward a guard tower. He was leaking fuel so fast it didn't matter. He wanted to take a look behind, but didn't have the time.

With the fuel gauge just above an eighth of a tank, his worries about the Migs and gunships had become secondary. He still had six miles to the border with a leaking fuel supply. Which would come first, he thought, the safety of Austria, or an empty fuel tank? He flashed back to Dalat when he was plowing through elephant grass toward the cliff's edge. He shook his head and wondered what the hell he was thinking when he agreed to take on this mission?

The ravine closed in and he knew it was decision time. He popped up and saw the tower about a hundred yards ahead and to the right. He saw three muzzle flashes and banked hard left. A round hit the right front door, knocking out his side window. The women in back screamed and he glanced to see if they had been hit by the broken Plexiglas. They were all praying, but appeared to be okay.

The ship was now broadside to the tower, but the tracers were falling just behind him. He knew that wouldn't last, so he found another gully and dived toward its cover. As he descended, a Jeep with a mounted machine gun raced out of a tree line. As if I don't have enough problems, he thought.

Inside the ravine, he checked the fuel gauge and saw it had stabilized at one eighth, enough fuel to make it over the fence if he could evade the ground and aircraft fire. He knew the tower had radioed his position, so the Migs and gunships would be on top of him in minutes.

He made a quick pedal turn to the west and scanned the horizon. The silhouettes of two fast-movers were headed straight at him. He hoped the Migs couldn't see him and would blow right by, giving him a small window to make a dash for the border.

The jets shot by and he started a climb. The Jeep had stopped and began shooting. The guard tower also resumed firing, so a line of bullets came at him from both directions. The shooters were still not leading him, so the tracers fell short. He pulled back on the cyclic and initiated a climbing left turn away from the guard tower. When he leveled off, two rounds hit the tail section and he swore if he got out of this mess he would never do anything this stupid again.

At the higher altitude, he could see the death strip a hundred feet away. A scout car roared down the road with the passenger firing a machine pistol. Two more bullets hit the tail as the fence slid under the nose. He had made it, but he figured the Migs would still fire at them even though they were in Austrian airspace. He had to hide quickly. A bridge was just ahead, but it wasn't high enough to land under. He found a hayfield with a line of tall trees on the north side. Past the trees, he made a pedal turn to look back to the north. Two Soviet gunships hovered on the border. Eric flipped them the bird before settling behind the trees. One gunship fired in frustration, knocking the tops out of two trees. Through his filtered view Eric could see that the helicopters were staying on their side of the border.

After he landed, Eric checked the instruments. They were still normal and the fuel gauge read just below one eighth, about fifteen gallons. He shut down the engine and turned to his passengers. The older women had their heads in their hands. The doctor's sister comforted her youngest son. The older boy stared at him with a frightened look. Eric unbuckled and told them they were safely in Austria.

He checked his map and figured he was about six miles from the village of Schrems. The town of Horn was twice as far, but it was on the main highway between Vienna and Prague and would likely have a filling station. He decided he could make the twelve miles to Horn, but first he had to inspect the helicopter.

It didn't take long to find the hole in the fuel tank. It was the circumference of a pencil, but it had dumped most of his precious fuel. He was sure he could fashion a wood plug to fill it, but first he had to find fuel.

The tail boom had four holes poked in it. The top side looked good except for two holes above the right door. He knew an aircraft mechanic should inspect the ship before it flew again, but he didn't have that luxury. He wanted to get the family to Vienna before nightfall, so he decided to press on. He remembered what his crew chiefs used to say in Vietnam: "She's still flying, let's go."

He climbed back into the helicopter, buckled in and flicked the start switch. When all of the instruments read normal, he lifted the ship to a hover and checked the horizon for aircraft. There weren't any and he climbed out toward Horn.

The village soon came into view and he found a gas station on the west side of town. He landed as close as he could to the pumps. As the rotors slowed to a stop, a heavy-set man in greasy coveralls came out of the shop. Eric jumped from the ship and greeted him in German, "Guten Morgan." Good morning.

The man returned his greeting and then looked over the helicopter. He pointed toward the southwest and said, "The Linz airport is only eighty kilometers. Why didn't you land there?"

Eric answered that he was out of fuel, and then led him to the rear of the helicopter. He pointed at the hole and said, "This is the fuel tank. I need to plug it."

The man probed the hole with an oily finger and asked, "How did this happen?"

Eric admitted, "It's from a bullet."

The man looked in at the refugees dressed in their drab gray clothing and asked, "Czechoslovakia?"

Eric said, "Yes."

The man turned toward him and said, "I will fix it. I have family over there."

Eric followed him into the station. "I also need to make a telephone call to Linz. Do you have a phone?"

The mechanic pointed toward the village. "They have one in town."

For Christ's sake, Eric thought, how the hell can I get there? He calmed down and said, "If you have a phone, I will pay you."

The man motioned toward a messy office. Eric followed and handed him a piece of paper with the Linz Aviation Company's number. The mechanic dialed the number and handed the receiver to Eric before leaving the office.

A receptionist answered and Eric asked for Paul. When he reached the phone Paul yelled, "Where the hell are you?"

"I'm in the village of Horn. Things got all fucked up and I lost the

Doc."

"Is he dead?"

"No, but he probably wishes he was. He has a bullet in is leg and the Czech STB have him."

"Shit. How did that happen?"

"He got shot when he was getting back into the ship. I had to leave him, or we all would have been captured."

"Did you get the family out?" Paul asked.

"Yeah, they're all here with me. I'll explain everything later. Right now we've got to get together. Do you have your map on you?"

"No, it's in the van."

"Then remember this. I'm in Horn because we took a round in the fuel tank and lost so much fuel I didn't have enough to get back to Linz. It would take you a couple of hours to drive here, so I'm going to plug the hole and put on enough fuel to get to St. Polten. It's on the highway between Vienna and Linz and looks like it's about seventy-five klicks from where you are."

"I remember going through it."

"Good, then drive back to the St. Polten airport and I'll meet you there. I've got to fix the bullet hole and get fuel, so we should get there about the same time. St. Polten is only sixty kilometers from Vienna, so I plan to leave the ship there tonight. I have to do something with these people and I don't want to take the time to explain why I'm returning a shot-up helicopter."

"What are you going to do with the family?" Paul asked.

"I'll have to give them to Mrs. Muller. What else can I do?"

Paul said, "Okay, I better get going. I'll see you there."

Eric hung up as the mechanic walked in with a small branch. He took a knife and whittled it down to three inches. After scoring a ring around the middle, he picked up a hammer and walked to the helicopter. Eric watched him gently tap the plug into place. When he was satisfied with the fix, the man asked, "How many liters do you want?"

Eric made the calculation from gallons to liters and said, "Two hundred twenty-five liters of diesel fuel. This is a jet engine, so it shouldn't burn auto gas."

The mechanic walked into his shop for a fuel can and funnel.

While he waited to be fueled, Eric opened the doors to the helicopter and asked the family if they wanted to use the restroom. When they nodded yes, he helped them out and introduced himself. The doctor's mother hugged him and began to cry. His sister introduced herself and then led the others toward the station. When they returned Eric helped them back into the helicopter. After they were loaded, he told them they would be in Vienna that night.

The mechanic finished fueling and went to see if the plug was leaking. He and Eric saw that it wasn't and the man said, "*Es ist gut.*" It's good.

Eric took a wad of Austrian bills from under his seat to pay for the fuel. The mechanic took the money and said, "Don't worry about the phone call. I will pay for that."

Eric thanked him and climbed into the helicopter hoping the plug would hold until they reached St. Polten and then Vienna.

Paul arrived shortly after Eric landed and they loaded the family into the van. Eric closed the door and thought they looked like refugees from a German prison camp. Paul rolled his eyes and climbed into the driver's seat.

On the road to Vienna, Eric told Paul about the botched pick-up, the Doc waving them off, and how much he hated the sound of bullets hitting metal. When he finished, Paul said, "That was way too close."

Eric nodded. "The doctor said the fat woman in back is his aunt and probably told somebody she was going to sneak onto a flight going to Austria. That's probably how the STB got tipped off."

As they approached Dr. Muller's house, Paul asked, "Do you want me to go in with you?"

"No, you unload our bags and make me a drink. I'm going to need one."

Thirty minutes later, Eric entered the guest house. Paul handed him a glass of whiskey and asked, "How did that go?"

Eric took the drink and slumped onto the couch. "About like you'd expect. Mrs. Muller started to cry when she saw me without her husband. She's a strong woman and felt much better when I told her the doctor was still alive."

Paul sat across from Eric. "What did she think of the family Von Trapp?"

Eric smiled. "She welcomed them and offered them something to eat and drink. She's going to take them to Immigration in the morning. Hopefully, I won't have to get involved with that."

"Yeah, we're going to have enough trouble getting rid of a shot-up helicopter. How much do you think it will cost to repair?"

Eric sipped his drink. "I've been thinking about that," he said. "Replacing the fuel tank will probably be the biggest expense unless they can patch it. That will be about a grand. The right door will have to be replaced. Two other rounds hit above the door. The skin hits shouldn't be too much, but I'm sure they will tack on another grand because they will be so pissed off. I'm guessing the whole thing will come to about six thousand dollars."

Paul jumped up. "God damn it, that will eat up most of our ten grand and I doubt we'll get the other ten."

Eric rose and walked to the sideboard. "I'm sure of that, which means we did all this crazy shit for next to nothing."

Paul followed him and said, "I *knew* I should have gone with you. I would have had the family in the ship and out of there before they could have gotten off a shot."

The next morning the Eric and Paul were about to leave for the airport when the phone rang. Eric listened to the caller and said, "*Ja, danka.*" He hung up and said, "Mrs. Muller has invited us for breakfast. She says the family wants to thank us for getting them out of East Germany. She says they know we did our best."

Paul shot him an angry look. "Oh great, we'll get a long way on their thanks. Do you think they smuggled out a few gold goblets to pay for our troubles?"

Eric opened the door. "Look, we're here because of Mrs. Muller's hospitality. Let's tell them they're welcome and not make a scene."

Paul followed Eric out the door. "Okay, I'll be good."

The family greeted them in the dining room. Mrs. Muller explained there was some hope of getting the doctor out of Czechoslovakia. She and the doctor had influential friends in the Austrian Parliament and she was going to call one of them that afternoon.

After breakfast, Eric handed Mrs. Muller a letter addressed to Paris, France and asked her to mail it for him. Then he turned to the family and told them he and Paul would return to say goodbye before they left Vienna.

At the St. Polten airport, Eric was inspecting the ship, when Paul yelled, "Hey Dog, your suit coats are hanging in the back."

Eric called back, "My fake documents should be in the breast pocket. Check to see if the doctor's are in his suit coat."

"Yeah, they're all here. I think we should burn them."

"Good idea, take them with you. At least the STB won't be able to accuse the doctor of spying." Eric climbed into the helicopter and said, "I'd feel better if you were with me for the ass-chewing."

Paul looked in the door. "It'll be in German, so I wouldn't appreciate it anyway."

Before he closed the door, Eric said, "Let's hope I'm waiting for you at the airport and not in a Viennese jail."

Paul laughed and said, "That would be good."

An hour later, Paul pulled up to the helicopter company in the van. Eric climbed in and said, "That was fun."

Paul pulled away from the curb and said, "I can imagine the manager was not too pleased with what you had to tell him."

They turned onto a highway and Eric said, "You could say that again. I went right to his office and confessed that we didn't get licensed to start a heli-ski operation. He glared at me when I told him we actually flew into Czechoslovakia to rescue Dr. Muller's family. He asked where the doctor was and I told him the Czech STB had him. Then he asked if his helicopter was okay. When I told him it was out on the ramp with a half a dozen bullet holes in it, he blew up. He began yelling German obscenities that I didn't even understand. He calmed down when I told him we would pay for the repairs."

Paul pounded the steering wheel and yelled, "Damn it all. That's our money you're talking about." He stared out the windshield and said, "Let's go to a bar. I feel like drinking lunch."

Eric looked out his side window and said, "Gee, we've never done that before."

The next day the two friends spent the morning packing the Mercedes for their trip to Athens. Their plan was to drive to Greece, sell the car and hopefully have enough money to catch a plane to Jakarta, Indonesia.

They ate lunch and then drove to the helicopter company to get the estimate for the repairs. A receptionist called the head mechanic, who came out of the shop with the bill in hand. After he gave it to Eric, he said in German, "For your convenience I have changed it from shillings to dollars. The bill for the flight time is also included."

Eric glanced at Paul and said, "We forgot about the flight time." He winced as he read the figure of $8,370. Eric passed it to Paul and said, "The total is in dollars on the bottom."

Paul read the amount and said, "God damn, after we pay this we won't have any money left."

Paul began to pace in front of the front door, as the mechanic handed Eric a bag with five spent bullets. Eric took the bag and said, "If I had kept my slugs from Vietnam I'd have enough for a necklace."

The mechanic stared with a blank look and Eric added, "We have to go to the bank. We'll be back tomorrow with the money."

Eric turned toward the door and said, "I can't believe we forgot about the flight time."

Paul pushed his way out the door. "What I can't believe is we only have sixteen hundred dollars to get to fucking Indonesia. Do you know how much fun we could have had on the way? Now we'll be lucky to *get* there."

Eric opened the car door and said, "We may have to become bartenders, or something. I hear they're looking for help at the Army R

& R center in Berchtesgaden, Germany."

Paul sat in the car and said, "Yeah, I heard they need ski instructors too. Spring is always a good time to be looking for a winter job." He paused and then said, "Wait a minute, we don't have to do that. Let's call Colonel Hessing and see what he has to offer. I'll take the next mission."

"No way," Eric said. "We've pressed our luck far enough. Trust me, you do *not* want to hear the sound of bullets hitting metal and I don't want to go to Indonesia alone. Let's hope we get enough money for this car to get to Hong Kong. From there we can wire Tucker for the rest of the fare."

Paul started the car and said, "I think we should still write the colonel, but we'll go with your plan for now."

At the guest house, a note from Mrs. Muller asked for a meeting. Eric called the butler. After he hung up, he turned to Paul. "Mrs. Muller wants to see us."

Paul pointed at the door. "You go. I'm in a bad mood, and it will be easier for you to tell me what happened than have to translate for me."

"You keep using that for an excuse, but this time you're right." Eric stopped at the door and said, "I wonder why she wants to talk with us now? Maybe she has some news on the doctor."

Forty minutes later, Eric returned beaming. "That definitely went better than I thought."

Paul walked in from the kitchen wiping his hands with a towel. "You were gone so long I was beginning to think you were doing more than consoling the merry widow."

Eric grinned and then turned serious. "She's not a widow yet, but it may not be that long."

Paul walked to the sidebar. "Why's that?"

"The doctor's limp wasn't because of his war wound. He has inoperable bone cancer. It started five months ago in his right leg and spread to his lymph nodes. His doctor had just given him six months to live. That's why Frau Muller is trying so hard to get him back."

Paul handed Eric a drink. "So she still thinks she can do that?"

"Yeah, she talked to their friends in the Austrian Parliament and was told a prisoner exchange is already in the works. The Austrians have requested the Czech government add the doctor. They think the Czechs will give him up because of his medical issues."

Paul stood in front of the bar and said, "Let's hope he has some time left when he gets out."

"Yeah, Mrs. Muller said the Doc really enjoyed our company. He thought of us as the sons he never had. He called her from Linz and said how much he enjoyed our flight, and he was looking forward to flying again."

Paul frowned. "Too bad that won't happen." He paused and said, "You looked like you had good news when you came back."

"I do. Mrs. Muller asked about the helicopter expenses. When I showed her the bill, she said she would pay for everything."

Paul pumped his right arm. "That means we get to keep the whole damn ten grand. Oh man, we are back in business. Jakarta here we come. We need to stop in Bangkok on the way. "

Eric held up a bank receipt and said, "There's more."

Paul grabbed the paper. "More good news?"

"Yeah, the night before we left, the doctor gave Mrs. Muller a check for ten thousand dollars. He said if he didn't make it back, she was supposed to deposit the check into our bank account. She did this morning. That's the receipt."

Paul read the amount and said, "Twenty thousand dollars! I don't believe it. Now we can really live it up. I think we should sail around the Greek Isles for a couple of months. We can write the girls and pay for their trip down."

With a quizzical look, Eric said, "That sounds good, but I don't remember you mentioning you know how to sail."

"I've done a little."

"How little is little?"

"Twice, but how hard can it be? We fly helicopters for Christ's sake. We should be able to sail a damn boat." Paul took Eric's glass and moved toward the sidebar. "We need to celebrate." He poured them each a Scotch and handed one to Eric. He raised his glass and said, "Here's to the Doc."

Eric raised his glass. "To the Doc."

Paul chuckled and said, "I still can't believe we got the whole damn twenty grand. You know what's been troubling me for the last two days."

"What's that?"

"That you almost risked your life for a lousy sixteen hundred bucks."

Eric smiled. "That was bothering me too, until I remembered we used to risk it for a lot less."

Paul clinked Eric's glass and said, "That we did, Dog, that we did."

Island of Symi, Aegean Sea, Greece

The sailboat heeled to port as the southeast wind increased, filling the two brilliant white sails. The only sound was the rush of sparkling blue water under the hull. Paul was on the port side with his right hand on the helm, his face into the wind wearing his aviator sunglasses. During the month since they had attended a Greek sailing course, Paul and Eric had become accomplished sail trimmers.

They were off the Greek Island of Symi. Its sheer rock cliffs had been filmed in the movie "The Guns of Navarrone" starring Gregory Peck. The boat felt like it was gliding as Eric watched the white cliffs slip by and then give way to a rocky hillside with goat herds grazing on steep slopes.

Beth and Tiffany sat on the bow on lounging cushions. As the boat entered the strait between the islands of Symi and Nimos, Beth went to the rail. When they turned toward the capital city of Gialos, she walked skillfully to the aft, holding on to rails and cables.

Eric watched her approach and wondered how he had gotten so lucky. She would soon be returning to Virginia to attend law school, and where was he headed? Nowhere.

When she reached him, she asked, "Are we going to eat lunch on the boat, or in town?"

Eric answered, "I think we should have lunch on the quay."

Accommodations and boat slips had been in short supply in the capital city, so Eric and Paul had opted to anchor to a buoy in the harbor and live on the boat. They were used to cramped quarters and sweltering heat at night, but the girls weren't. Although they hadn't complained, the guys knew they needed to move to a more comfortable living space. The previous day the four of them had gone on a resupply trip to the village. While Eric took Beth and Tiffany shopping for groceries, Paul rented two studio apartments that overlooked the seaport.

Paul steered around the peninsula that made up the right side of a natural waterfront amphitheater. When they were inside the bay they lowered the sails and powered into the harbor on a gas outboard motor. Eric secured the boat to their buoy, and the two couples took a dingy to the marina.

Their quaint apartments had kitchenettes and balconies that overlooked the water. They were tastefully decorated with a bed and couch in the main room. A bar was between that room and the kitchen.

Eric walked onto the terrace and looked down at the bay. All of the boats were pointed into a southerly breeze. When Beth joined him, Eric pointed at their sailboat and said, "I've always wanted to have a house where I could see my boat moored in a bay. I've finally made it, but unfortunately I don't own a tile in this place, or teak board on that boat." He paused and then said, "I guess it's a start."

Beth put her arm in his and said, "I think it's a damn good start."

The confined quarters of the sailboat hadn't allowed for much intimacy, so in a lascivious voice Beth whispered, "I wish we had told them we were going to take a nap before lunch."

Eric walked to the left of the balcony and said, "That's not a problem." He leaned toward the room next door and yelled, "Hey guys, we'll see you in an hour. We're going to take a nap."

"Good idea," Paul replied from the next apartment.

After the naps, the two couples walked to the marina and found a small seaside restaurant. They dined on grilled octopus and stuffed grape leaves for appetizers, and a whole fried fish for the main course. When a roving minstrel band played a tune for them, Paul tried to trade his Army watch for the song. The band leader shook him off with a confused look. He was either not sure what Paul meant, or didn't know how to split a watch four ways. Paul finally gave him a wad of Greek money and requested they play away from their table.

Two hours into the lunch they had consumed two bottles of white wine and a half bottle of Ouzo. The men had been entertaining the ladies with their exploits from Vietnam. When Paul paused to pour more wine, Beth said, "Those are some great stories. You two need to write a book."

Paul lit up and turned to Eric. "That's a good idea. Why don't we give it a try."

Eric smirked and said, "If we did, it would probably take us more than twenty years to get it done."

Beth continued, "Well, I think you should at least put your stories down on paper."

She stood and said, "I'm going to the ladies room." Tiffany joined her and when they returned, Beth said, "It feels like the earth is still moving under our feet. We're going to the rooms and take real naps on real beds. After that we want to go dancing, so you guys better pace yourselves."

Eric smiled at his lady and said, "We'll be ready."

As they left, Paul said, "They're a couple of good chicks. They just don't have their sea legs."

Eric watched the girls walk down the dock. "This week has been a lot of fun. I'm glad they were able to come down, but I'm worried about what's going to happen when it's time for them to leave. I have to admit I've fallen for Beth, but I can't move to Virginia."

Paul nodded. "Yeah, I've always bragged I haven't met a woman I couldn't forget in a month, but I don't want to forget this one. Tiff is definitely the best woman I've met, but as you said, moving to Virginia isn't in the plan. Speaking of a plan, I'm glad we have a little time alone. I've wanted to discuss a new idea I've come up with."

Eric set his drink on the table. "Why do I always get nervous when you have a new plan?"

Paul grinned and said, "I'm sure this one won't be any different, but hear me out." He pointed at an array of tiered, multicolored houses around the harbor. "Look at this place, it's beautiful. I'm really getting used to this lifestyle and I've become addicted to sailing, not to mention the great food and drinks." He looked back at Eric and said, "I think we need to keep this going, so here's what I've decided. We need to write Colonel Hessing and see what kind of jobs he was talking about. It sounded like one mission would pay enough to keep this up for at least two months, maybe more. I've already said I'll take the next one."

Eric shook his head. "I thought we decided we weren't going to do that. Besides, I'm the one with the helicopter license."

Paul leaned across the table and said, "That isn't going to matter. The kinds of jobs the Colonel will have are going to be in places where they don't check for certification. Hell, some probably won't even be in Europe. There are a lot of nefarious activities going on in Africa right now. Even Portugal is bogged down in its own Vietnam type war in Angola. Sure there will be an element of danger, but the Colonel's missions have to be a hell of a lot more secure than the one you went on. Who knew you'd be ratted out by the Doc's fat aunt?"

Eric thought for a moment and said, "Yeah, that job would have been a milk run if the two STB agents hadn't shown up."

"That's what I mean," Paul said, leaning back in his chair. "Listen, here's how it will work. We airline to wherever the jobs are, work a couple of weeks and then take two months off. We need to visit more places like this. I'm thinking Italy's Amalfi Coast, and the south of France would be good places to sail to next. We might even want to sail the Chesapeake, but how can we do that if we're working full time jobs? Let's face it, I'm not sure if we will ever be able to work nine to five."

Paul paused and then said, "We're also a couple of adrenaline junkies. I was really pissed when I didn't get to go on the last mission. Do you know how frustrating it was to get checked out in the Alouette and not get to go along?"

Eric nodded. "Okay, your idea is starting to get traction, but I thought we promised Tucker we would help him start his company. What are we going to tell him?"

"We'll tell him we found something better. We never did ask him what kind of schedule we'd be working, or how much it was going to pay. Hell, we probably won't even get any time off to start with. The only reason we said we'd work for Tucker was because we thought those would be the only flying jobs available. The Colonel is offering something that pays more, so I say we take it."

"But it does involve being shot at," Eric said. "Where have I heard that before?"

"Okay, so it does, but how dangerous is island hopping in a single-engine helicopter? And do we really want to go back to the Orient? We've already vetoed flying for Air America in Laos and Cambodia. We could have jobs there tomorrow if we wanted to go back and fly for the CIA, but there's no way I'm flying out of some shit hole in either of those two countries."

Eric looked out to sea and said, "Yeah, the last time I was in Cambodia was the worst day of my life." He looked back at Paul and said, "I also just dodged spending time in a Czech jail and I'm not looking forward to chancing another one in some shitty place in Africa. At least the Czech jail would have had electricity and running water."

Paul waved him off. "Like I said before, I'm sure the Colonel does everything he can to mitigate the risks. As far as us stiffing Tucker, I don't feel that bad because there are all kinds of guys who want to fly for him. Hell, Sharkey even wrote you to get Tucker's address."

Eric smiled and said, "Yeah that was good. He's probably already tired of life on Long Island with his 'Olive Oil' girl friend."

Paul chuckled. "Pretty bad?"

"Yeah, I saw a picture. She's tall and skinny with thick glasses."

Paul nodded. "That sounds about right, but it was good to hear from Mako, and get caught up on a couple of our friends. It's cool that he got to see Slyde Cornelius playing flute in a Greenwich Village band, and how about Little Eli working in a Fresno mobile home factory until he gets on with a company that flies helicopters on forest fires?"

Eric smiled and said, "And it sounds like Shooter is finally ready to quit gunships, and wants to fly for Tucker."

Paul threw his arms out. "That's what I'm saying. There are plenty of guys that want to work for him because those dog faces don't know any better, but we do." He grinned and said, "I have to laugh every time I think of the recommendation you gave Tucker about Sharkey and Shooter: hire them, but don't arm them. That was good, Dog."

They both laughed and Paul asked, "So are we going to write Colonel Hessing, or not?"

Eric looked around the harbor and said, "I guess it wouldn't hurt to hear what he has to offer. I'm also getting real used to this lifestyle."

"That's more like it, Dog," Paul said excitedly and then turned serious. "You know we're not just doing this for ourselves. We're doing it for all the guys that didn't make it back. Every time we go out to a bar we need to raise a glass to them."

Eric toasted Paul's glass and said, "You're getting a little maudlin on me, Dev."

Paul stared at his friend. "Damn right I am and I've also had too much to drink, but that doesn't mean I'm not making sense. I had a lot of time to think about those guys when I was lying in that hospital at Lai Khe. That's when I realized I wasn't going to die young after all. How we both made it through all that craziness is beyond me."

Eric nodded. "What that means is we're playing with house money."

"Exactly," Paul exclaimed. "So let's take advantage of it. It's time to dust off a new script and get the show on the road." He pointed toward the ocean and said, "There's a big-ass world waiting out there and we're *just getting started*."

Eric looked at their sailboat rocking in the bay and said, "Okay, let's do it."

Glossary

AC	Aircraft Commander
AHC	Assault Helicopter Company
AK-47	A Russian made 7.62mm automatic rifle used primarily by the enemy
AO	Area of Operation
Ao dai	Vietnamese dress slit up the side
ARVN	Army of the Republic of South Vietnam. Also, a soldier in the South Vietnamese Army
Ash & Trash	Term used for carrying supplies in a helicopter
AWOL	Absent without leave
Baby-san	Term for a young Vietnamese woman
Battalion	A unit of three or more companies
Beaucoup	Vietnamese word for much or many, borrowed from the French
Boom-Boom	Vietnamese slang for sexual intercourse, a boom-boom girl was a prostitute
Boonies	The bush or jungle
Brigade	A unit of battalions
C&C	Command and control
C-model	gunship version of the UH-1 Huey, also known as the "Charlie Model"

Chalk	Position of an aircraft in a formation. "One" being in first position behind Lead
Charlie	General term for Vietnamese enemy, short for Victor Charlie, Viet Cong, and Charlie Cong
Cherry	A new guy
Chicken plate	Armored chest plate worn by aerial crew members
Chinook	CH-47, a twin-rotored helicopter, also called a Hook or Shithook
Chop-chop	Vietnamese slang for food and eating
Claymore	Remotely detonated antipersonnel mine used on defensive perimeters
CO	Commanding Officer, usually a Company commander, nicknamed the "Old Man"
Cobra	AH-1G helicopter gunship, nicknamed the "Snake"
Collective	Control held in a helicopter pilot's left hand for adjustments in throttle and angle of attack of main rotor blades
Company	A military unit consisting of two or more platoons
Cordite	An explosive powder
Crew Chief	Left door gunner on a Huey, responsible for the mechanical operation of the aircraft
Cyclic	The stick held in the helicopter pilot's right hand that controls the tilt of the main rotor
DEROS	Date eligible to return from overseas, used as a verb to leave Vietnam
Dink	Slang word for the enemy

Dien cai dau	Vietnamese phrase for crazy, pronounced by GI's as dinky-dow
Dustoff	Medical evacuation helicopter
F-4	Fighter bomber, nicknamed "Phantom"
FAC	Forward Air Controller, a tactical air director
Fast mover	Jet aircraft
First sergeant	Senior NCO, grade of E-8, nicknamed "Top"
FNG	Fucking new guy
Fragged	Killing someone with a fragmentation grenade
Freedom Bird	G.I. term for the airplane that would take them back to the States
FTA	Fuck the Army
Go Hot	Instruction from pilot to the door gunners to fire their weapons
Gook	Slang name for the enemy, also known as gooners or dinks
Green Maggot	A pilot or soldier dressed in a green flight suit or fatigues
Huey	UH-1 helicopter, the main helicopter used in the Vietnam War, crewed by two pilots and two door gunners
Hootch	Vietnamese thatched roof house or hut, also a term GI's called their rooms and sleeping areas
Jody	A person who stayed home and did not go into the military

Jokers	Call sign or nickname for gunship pilots in the 48th Assault Helicopter Company
KIA	Killed in action, a dead soldier of either side
Klick	Military slang for a kilometer .62 of a mile
LOH	A Hughes OH-6A light observation helicopter, nicknamed the "Loach" manned with one pilot and one door gunner-crew chief
LRRP	Long range reconnaissance patrol
LZ	Landing Zone
Mattie Mattel	Nickname for the M-16 automatic rifle because it was made out of plastic
MIA	Missing in action
M-16	A Colt 5.56mm automatic rifle used by the U.S. infantry. Nicknamed the Mattie Mattel
M-60	A 7.62mm machine gun used by the U.S. infantry and door gunners on Hueys
Medivac	Medical evacuation helicopter, nicknamed "Dustoff"
Mini-gun	Electrically driven 7.62mm machine gun on helicopter gunships capable of 2000 to 4000 rounds per minute
Nam-mare	A nightmare about the Vietnam War
NCO	Noncommissioned officer or sergeant
NVA	North Vietnamese Army
Nomex	Flame retardant material used in flight suits and flight gloves

Number one	Vietnamese slang for good or best, Number ten was bad, Number sixty-nine was very bad or worst
OD	Olive drab, green color, also Officer of the Day
Old Man	Military slang for Commanding Officer
Ops	Operations office
Pathfinder	Trained infantrymen who were inserted in the field to assist in air operations
Platoon	Formed by two or more squads, two or more platoons form a company
PFC	Private First Class
PFM	Pure fucking magic
RLO	Real Live Officer, a term used by warrant officers to describe commissioned officers
POL	Petroleum, oil, lubricants; generally used to refer to the refueling area for aircraft
PSP	Perforated steel plate; sectional, interlocking steel panels used to make a hard surfaced runway or tarmac
Piss Can	Urination station for male personnel, usually a 55 gallon drum embedded in the ground and covered with a screen
Poncho liner	Lightweight, camouflaged quilt, commonly used for bedding
PX	Post Exchange, a retail facility on a military base
PZ	Pickup zone
R & R	Rest and Relaxation

REMF	Rear Echelon Mother Fucker
Rotor wash	The wind produced by a helicopter's rotor blades
RPG	Rocket propelled grenade
RPM	Revolutions per minute
SAC	Senior Aircraft Commander
Section Eight	U.S. Army discharge for being psychologically unfit for military service
Shit can	Half of a 55 gallon drum used in latrines, the contents were burned periodically with diesel fuel which was known as a shit burning detail
Shit burning	The odious task of burning the waste from the latrine by lighting diesel fuel poured on it
Silver Dustoff	Soldiers term for the airplane that would take them back to the States, usually called the "Big Silver Dustoff" or "Freedom Bird"
Spec 4	Specialist forth class, grade E-4
Slick	A Huey helicopter mainly used to transport troops and supplies. The term was due to the absence of weapons pods on the sides.
Stars & Stripes	An armed forces newspaper produced in Vietnam
Stick	A slang word for pilot, as in he's a good stick
STB	Czech secret service police much like the Soviet KGB
Top	Army slang for First Sergeant E-8

UH-1	A utility helicopter, nicknamed "Huey," built by Bell Helicopters
Uncle Ho	North Vietnamese President Ho Chi Minh
VC	Viet Cong, translated as Vietnamese communist, also an American soldier's word for the enemy, also described as Charlie, Charlie Cong and Victor Charlie
Warrant Officer	A rank above enlisted men and below commissioned officers
World	GI term used in Vietnam for the United States, usually described as "The World"
WIA	Wounded in action, wounded soldier on either side
WO	Warrant Officer, also known as a warrant
Xin Loi	Vietnamese word for sorry
XO	Executive Officer, second in command under Commanding Officer

40389563R00178

Made in the USA
Lexington, KY
06 April 2015